A Smoking Dot in the Distance

by
Ivor Gould

BLACK SWAN

A SMOKING DOT IN THE DISTANCE
A BLACK SWAN BOOK 0 552 99466 9

Originally published in Great Britain by
Sinclair-Stevenson Limited

PRINTING HISTORY
Sinclair Stevenson edition published 1991
Black Swan edition published 1992

Black Swan Books are published by
Transworld Publishers Ltd, 61–63 Uxbridge
Road, London W5 5SA, in Australia by
Transworld Publishers (Australia) Pty Ltd,
15–23 Helles Avenue, Moorebank, NSW 2170,
and in New Zealand by Transworld
Publishers (NZ) Ltd, Cnr Moselle and
Waipareira Avenues, Henderson, Auckland.

Made and printed in Great Britain by
Cox & Wyman Ltd, Reading, Berks.

'My grandfather, who lived most of his life in one room – behind a second hand clothes shop, with "Grandma" Lizzie, a relation of James Connolly – claimed to be descended from Copernicus. He once presented to me a customer buying a pair of working boots as: "The gentleman who hit Sir Oswald Mosley with a brick on the steps of Leeds Town Hall."

'Born in Vilnus, he knew Keir Hardy and Bernard Shaw, but was not on speaking terms with my father, who had sold patent trouser presses door to door; or with my father's father, who had traded beads and top hats along the coast of West Africa. Though I understand he got on reasonably with my grandmother's French lover, who hid in their attic throughout the First World War.

'My father, who played "When I Grow Too Old To Dream" on the trombone, brought home a small violin when I was eight. "Stop making that bloody noise!" he said, an hour later, and took it back to the shop; exchanging it for a trumpet, which I blew until my eyes bulged without producing a sound. "The boy has no talent" he said, more in anger than in sorrow, and replaced it – my last chance – with a kit of drums. This was in chrome and black, with silver stars; with a gong, a high hat and scarlet skulls; and my senses swam. In the front room, while my father ate his tea in the kitchen, and after a little brush work – fast, the cymbals hissing to "Bye Bye Blues" – I spun the sticks in my fingers and, with a series of rim shots, doing Bob Haggard's double bass with my mouth, went into "Big Noise From Winetka".

'The serving hatch slid open, and I saw his mouth moving below the black moustache. "If all you can do," it said, "is make a noise, it goes back in the morning".

'My son, Millfield and Kings College, London, plays the gramophone in something called "The Irresistible Force".'

Ivor Gould divides his time between a Greek island and a riverside house in London, a stone's throw from where Ivy Benson once lived.

Author photograph by Laurel Wade

The author is grateful to William Collins Sons & Co Ltd, for permission to quote from *The Nicolson Diaries*; and to Penguin Books, and Odysseus Elytis, for the two lines from his poem 'Beauty and the Illiterate'.

For Netia, Morris, and the man who
washed out Pomfrets' churns

Introduction

Shortly after 11 pm on June 15th 1989, the management of the Skegness Hilton telephoned the police, worried that a guest, a Mr Jeffrey Cork, had not yet come in. After a day on the beach, apparently in his right mind, he had left his seaweed in the foyer, saying that he was going to have a look at the floral clock before dinner. No one had seen him since. A fellow guest claimed to have heard him mention going to Cleethorpes, but no one took this seriously. The Lincolnshire Constabulary, while alerting beat officers on their walkie-talkies, had counselled waiting for dawn before bringing in frogmen and specially equipped pedaloes.

The following morning his room was entered and found to contain only a suitcase and a parcel of rock in the shape of ladies' legs. In the case, beside some woollies and an amusing hat bought locally, was a booklet in the 'Little Lenin' series entitled *Left Wing Communism; An Infantile Disorder*, bound in brown paper, and a copy of *The Friendship Book of Francis Day*. Wrapped in a length of soft white cotton material was the manuscript of this book. No trace of Jeffrey Cork was ever found.

Some months later the publishers were approached by a Mr Desmond Cork, who asked if we were interested in publishing his father's memoirs.

The first reader's report, while commenting favourably on the typing, pointed out that few people under the age of fifty would know what a bagwash was, or be particularly interested in discovering Geraldo's real name.

The board, most of whom mourned the passing of the bagwash, and were intrigued to learn about Mr Gerald Bright, then called in a test panel, drawn from all walks of life, who were given the MS to read, with refreshments.

They were of the opinion that the book as a whole was 'A good read', and excellent value for money. All said they had laughed, some of them several times; and one man, brought in from the string room to make up the number, admitted that he had cried at the end.

On the basis of all this, and on the casting vote of The Founder, the company decided to go ahead and publish.

Now read on.

. . . Mussolini had been caught and murdered, and we had really dreadful photographs of his corpse and that of his mistress hanging upside down and side by side. They looked like turkeys outside a poulterer's: the slim legs of the mistress and the huge stomach of Mussolini could both be detected. It was a most unpleasant picture and caused a grave reaction in his favour. It was terribly ignominious – *Sejanus ducitur unco* – but Mrs Groves said that he deserved it thoroughly, 'a married man like that driving about in a car with his mistress'.

Harold Nicolson,

Diaries and Letters 1939–45

Part One

Chapter One

It was difficult to believe that in only four years' time the country would come off the Gold Standard. At Number 10 Downing Street, Mr Ramsay MacDonald (Prime Minister), a moustached, Scottish and illegitimate crofter's son, was riding high. Up there with him was Mr J. H. Thomas (Engine Driver) and Mr Philip Snowden, who has I believe a statue in Bradford. All of them members of the Labour Party, they had donned court dress (black velvet breeches gartered above nice black stockings, and a hat) and had kissed hands to become the Government.

As De Kuyper pointed out to me in fairness while telling the story, the black stockings worn by the Labour cabinet came only to the gartered knee. There was none of that exposed skin above stocking tops, that rosebud-trimmed suspenders nonsense which Snowden, if not Thomas, would have deplored.

There was also Mr George Lansbury, from Bow (like Burlington Bertie) and Sir Oswald Mosley, from Manchester, with his eyes and his hypnotic oratory, then engaged in forming his New Party.

He, Sir Oswald, known to family and friends for obvious reasons as 'Tom', had an eventful life; though he never actually got anywhere. Briefly, he wanted to be the leader, but people would not let him. After 'The Battle of Cable Street' (see Chapter Three) he toured the country, making speeches (with drums) and being hit by stones. Most historians now agree, had he played his cards right, he could have been whatever he wanted; and the merest glance at the talent available at the time shows this to be true.

King George the Fifth, 'The Sailor King', bearded and newly returned from simple Bognor as it then was, can still be seen on old tins and tea caddies. By his side you will invariably see Queen Mary, who wore hats like cake frills (called 'toques') and is remembered as a ship. Very much like her relatives the Battenbergs, who live on as four-coloured cake. His last words, 'Bugger Bognor', are now thought to be apocryphal: ie not true.

While all this had been going on, Her Majesty Queen Elizabeth the Second had just been born, in a modest town house near Hyde Park, though of course she did not yet know who she was. Her mother (who knew perfectly well who she was) was destined to become none other than Queen Mum. Gracious ladies, they are said not to be able to answer back.

In the clubs and 'dens' of Mayfair, run by ladies like Kate Meyrick, you could find people in silver stockings and spats, with hair like Enid Blyton, and with skirts so short you could, as De Kuyper said, see all they'd got. They sat on gilt chairs and drank cocktails, or 'jazzed' to the music of Jack Payne ('Say It with Music') and Geraldo ('Hello again, we're on the radio again') who conducted their 'boys', in evening dress, with vigorous movements of their batons.

These clubs did not have snooker tables or green baize notice boards, though they did have a man outside with epaulettes and a flat hat. Nor were they members of the Clubs & Institutes Union, allowing in as they did both black people and women, though not of course together.

They were in the main well-run establishments; the black people being restricted to singing and dancing and playing the trumpet, and the ladies not allowed to pay for themselves. One sat at a small round table, with a flower in a glass, and ate haute cuisine late at night. They were licensed for singing and dancing and the sale of tobacco, and you were entertained by people like Hutch and 'Snake Hips' Johnson, and Arthur Tracey ('The Street Singer'), who I understand carried around with him his own lamppost. In their own way they were very fussy whom they let in; full evening dress and a car with a leather strap around the engine being the least of their requirements.

Geraldo (Gerald Bright) can be forgiven for his name. It was difficult to know what to call oneself in those days, there being people around and making a living under the name of No Smoking. Starting as he did as a Gypsy Fiddler, with a real silk bolero jacket, he had no choice. ('Brighto' I suppose, but then he would have had trouble with the makers of Duraglit.)

Outside in the foggy streets of London town were lamplighters and shouting newsboys and Oxo in electric lights. The River Police patrolled Old Father Thames, chugging beneath the bascules of Tower Bridge, waving at the dockers and fishing out bodies. Flower ladies in men's boots hawked their primulas under the colonnade of St Paul's (the actors' church;) and east, beyond the blazing lights of the Opera House, where ladies and gentlemen sang along to the music of Wagner – east beyond Old Aldgate Pump, in the beating heart of Cockaigne – costermongers, with the wife's knickers on the donkeys' front legs, trotted through the new effete suburbs to the Derby.

The East End of London, once a rural village, with no doubt a duck pond and a bearded cricket team, was by the time the Huguenots arrived to set up their looms in Spitalfields already part of 'The Great Wen'. These industrious people, weaving silk in their front rooms and

5

no trouble to anyone, seem to have become extinct. Then of course the Jews arrived, most of them under the impression that they were in New York, where they had paid to be taken. They were a stable and respected community, life revolving for them as it did around the family. However, soon, doctors and opticians and people like Arnold Wesker began to flood out over London. But for some time yet, before moving on to make way for Pakistanis, they formed a vibrant and colourful part of London. With their own food and customs, easily spotted in their black overcoats, they and their religion (which puts less emphasis on Jesus Christ) came to be completely accepted. They could go almost anywhere.

There were of course many Gentiles living in the area, mainly boxers or well-known people like Jack the Ripper and Dr Barnardo. They were employed in lighting fires for Jews on Saturdays. (Sometimes, in a reciprocal gesture, Jews would collect the *Empire News* for them on a Sunday morning.)

Where England ended, beyond the frontier post of Ramsgate, with its beautiful floral clock, beyond the cold grey English Channel swum by Captain Webb, lay the dark mass of Europe. It was there that Lord North had observed, some time before, that 'The lights are going out'; though by now they had come on again.

It was the end of The Roaring Twenties. The year was nineteen twenty-nine.

The site was only just being prepared, in Portland Place, of Broadcasting House. Here, behind the Epstein carvings, and under the legend 'Nation Shall Speak Peace Unto Nation', Lord John Reith would lay down the foundations for 'Life with the Lyons'.

In the basements of Grosvenor Square and Eaton Place, (called Downstairs), plump cooks put pies to cool on area window ledges, whence they were stolen by rubicund policemen in buttoned-up collars, putting down their bull's-eye lanterns, looking both ways before sinking their teeth into the delicious pastry. While in drawing rooms on the first floor, (called Upstairs), people sat around in spats and silver stockings, waiting for Kate Meyrick's to open.

You could have a bagwash if you wanted, up to eight or nine o'clock at night; and it was still possible to buy a Flit gun or a mangle at shops like Harrods and Debenhams. Or you could go up to 'Appy 'Ampstead, as it was called, and ride on the gilded roundabouts; marvel at The Pig Faced Lady.

For a night out you could take a rattling tram, the driver's frozen hand in a sock, to the Holborn Empire. Alighting, you could gaze for a moment at the whoopee cushions in Ellisdons' window, before you went in through the white Doric columns, into the red-plush warmth and smell of orange peel and the toilets.

As the orchestra struck up with an overture, you could buy a programme informing you that cigarettes were by Abdullah, and look up at the great chandelier and the ornate ceiling, pitted (as the wags said) with the marks of fly buttons.

Here, under the direction of Prince Littler (not of course a real one), you might have seen Wilson, Keppel and Betty; or Dante the fat magician, who cried 'Bim Sala Bim!' when he did his stuff. Wilson and Keppel, though wearing a fez, were English. They danced on sand to an Egyptian tune and went, it was said, through a lot of Bettys in their time.

Then, just before the interval, there would be the Star. G. H. Elliot perhaps, ('The Chocolate Coloured Coon'), who would imitate a black man in white gym shoes. Or someone called 'The White Eyed Kaffir' who, I think, (although I never saw him), was a black man who imitated a white one.

After the show you could have pie and mash or jellied eels, or fish and chips with a cucumber or a pickled egg. Most of these bright and steamy emporia were Jewish, with jolly fat 'Mamas' in white coats, and perhaps a Talmudic scholar glimpsed in the back room.

Then, if you were that way inclined, you could go on to buy five Wild Woodbines and a box of matches, (England's Glory and a joke), and perhaps a copy of Arthur Mee's *Children's Newspaper* from the ragamuffin at the corner . . . and still have change left out of a shilling! Or 'bob' as it was called.

In Charles Dickens's phrase (and he could turn a pretty one), 'It was the best of times, it was the worst of times', for in parts of the land people were hungry and children went barefoot to school. In a clever move to maintain prices, (essential in a free market), bananas were brought here from the West Indies, turning nicely yellow on the way, and then dropped into the Irish Sea off Liverpool. De Kuyper told me of Socialists, (who were against that kind of thing), going round the Wirral taking down the names of children who had been deprived of the exotic fruit.

But in general people did not worry. They might say, if in a queue at the Home and Colonial, 'I hear we might be going off the Gold Standard, Albert.'

'Oh, Gawd help us!' might be the reply of the aproned man patting the butter. Or 'Strewth!' Or even 'Fucking roll on!' Though the latter would be more likely to be heard in the Co-op than Liptons. But they were resilient. They were after all what was left of those 'Lions led by donkeys' who had advanced so cheerily at Ypres and the Somme. Dribbling footballs into the mouth of hell, to the wailing of the pipes; while officers made notes with little pencils, later to be written up into poetry.

They swung their mufflers, in the crocheted colours perhaps of Accrington Stanley, adjusted their cloth caps at a jaunty angle, and played with their whippets. Some of them put their heads in the gas oven, but most did not.

Resilient, and resourceful. The working-class housewife, the 'Mum' as she was called, in her flowered pinny and with her bobbed hair, was now allowed to wear make-up and smoke cigarettes, if she had any. To sustain her 'bairns'

8

throughout the day she would make quantities of 'cinder tea'. You could surprise your friends with this.

Simply take a slice of well-done toast, lay it across the mouth of a cup or beaker – or indeed mug if you have one – and pour freshly boiling water through. Do not add either milk or lemon. The soggy toast can be given to your racing pigeons. Waste not, want not.

Speaking of children, those in the north often wore little clogs, in pretty colours and delightfully patterned with brass studs. You could in fact dance in these, and I once saw a couple doing it professionally outside the Alhambra Theatre, Bradford, on the flagstones in front of the black lady dressed as Queen Victoria.

What else was going on in nineteen twenty-nine? Quite a lot really. From time to time they hung people. Some other people, playing a mouth organ, walked all the way down from Jarrow, ('The town that was murdered'), where the Venerable Bede once lived.

What else? Well, there was 'Our Gracie', 'The English Piaf' as she was called. She was a working-class girl from Lancashire who sang the songs of the mill workers. She wore a handkerchief around her head and married, finally, a Yugoslav wireless mechanic on the Italian island of Capri. Truth, as they say, is stranger than fiction.

But what of the provinces? What was going on there? You will be surprised to learn that nothing at all happened in Ireland, and very little in Scotland or North Wales. But in South Wales, along the valleys that had once been green, miners sang in the chapels (a kind of working-class church), praying with Deacons to be allowed to go under-ground and play with the blind ponies. Or to save each other when the roof fell in. 'Dada!' they would cry as they tore at the rubble with their bare hands. 'Blood On The Coal' the newspapers called it then, but my mother said they were their own worst enemy.

When they were working, and the roof not falling in, they all got in the bath together, like footballers, with the

9

water just high enough. Or, if they were that way inclined, they would sit feeling for the soap in front of a blazing fire, the grate black-leaded with Zebo, while their wives fried seaweed in the kitchen.

The miners were represented by men like Mr Arthur Horner and Mr A. J. Cook, who were inclined to castigate the mine owners, as they themselves were castigated by the *South Wales Echo*. A newspaper which I remember De Kuyper saying on more than one occasion was unlikely, for two reasons, ever to win the Pulitzer Prize. Horner and Cook were 'checkweighmen', elected by their workmates to ensure that the mine owners did not pinch the big bits of coal while they were singing in the chapel. It was said that both men on arriving home would lift a trapdoor to reveal an Aladdin's cave of heaped roubles and exotic mistresses, though this was never proved.

And what of the mine owners? I happened to meet one once, in his grey-stone castellated folly overlooking the Vale of Glamorgan (or Clwyd as it is now called). We had tea on the polished black terrace, next to the ornamental Gatling gun. Earl Grey if my memory serves me right, with coconut creams on a doily; and he had a neat gadget I recall, in hallmarked silver and in the form of a pithead winding frame, for lifting the sugar from the bone china sucrier. A good-looking man, very proud of his stamp collection, some of which he pointed out to me, his fingers tightening on my arm, were printed upside down.

We strolled afterwards in the garden, and I could not help noticing the spiked helmets of the Glamorgan Constabulary (known now I suppose as the Clwyd Constabulary) behind the privet hedge. 'Over there,' said my host, tossing a biscuit to the voracious Dobermans, pointing in the direction of Abergavenny. There was the slightest tremor in his hand, his voice dropped an octave so as not to alarm the policemen. 'Over there,' he went on, 'lies the Comintern.' I took his point.

So that then was the state of the nation, on Friday,

(Amami Night), March 29th, 1929. Ramsay MacDonald riding high; the cabinet in black stockings; The Sailor King safely back from Bognor; donkeys in Winceyette drawers trotting through the streets of Lower Norwood; Lord John Reith chivying the building workers in Portland Place; policemen stealing pies; children dancing in clogs; people walking their whippets, putting their heads in gas ovens; the Comintern not that far away from Abergavenny . . . and in Jasmine Villa, a solid red-brick Victorian house on the outskirts of a sleepy market town on the Lincolnshire border, at ten fifteen in the evening, a not unimportant event.

For it was there and then that I was born; to Mr Alfred Simeon Cork and his wife Gloria.

Chapter Two

The house was set on a small lawned hill overlooking the main road to London; indeed it is still called London Road. It has been compared (by the Rev Eli Wannamaker) to I Tatti, the antique dealer Bernard Berenson's place. His was larger I believe, with more trees and pictures, and of course in Italy.

The black-painted iron gate, on the spear points of which my friend Bernard impaled his scrotum, swings open at the foot of six stone steps. Around you is the rockery, where alpine plants were supposed to grow; and dark and dusty rhododendrons, in which we played 'Doctors and Nurses'. (This is a traditional game for two, or more, surprisingly not covered by the Opies. Choose one of you to be the doctor before you start. You can take turns.)

The tiled path to the green front door, with its polished brass letterbox, knocker and knob, was a masterpiece of Art Nouveau, depicting a woman in a sheet carrying a casserole. Edged by a kind of gadrooning in terra cotta, if you know what I mean, the grass to either side was neatly tended and shaded by a privet hedge.

It was here, at tea one summer afternoon, with crocheted cloths and Robinsons Lemon Barley Water, looking out across the valley to the blueish hills, that I heard my grandmother say: 'I don't believe in God, but I do believe in keeping clean.'

I was seven, a thoughtful child already active in the Rechabites. When asked what I was going to grow up to be, by adults as they ruffled my golden curls, I replied, 'A Christian scholar, sir.' Sometimes I got half a crown. Sometimes not. I wore a plum-covered velvet suit with a collar of broderie anglaise, and a visiting adult once kicked me between the legs as he was leaving.

My father being what he was, I had to be a scholar of some kind, and I had read somewhere, possibly in one of Arthur Mee's editorials, that you could be either a Christian or a Muscular scholar. On reflection this could have read Muscular Christian, which I had no wish to be. It is all a long time ago.

Anyway, my father had given me, as the eldest son, the choice. I had taken, I am afraid, the easy way out. So he had sent away for a book of instructions, from an advertisement illustrated by a pointing hand, and I worshipped God in the mornings, asking Him to look after The Sailor King. In the afternoons I traced maps of Africa, (the red parts), having no truck with the Belgian Congo. For a time I wore my collar back to front; until my father found me one evening, a Halloween mask of Rudolph Valentino on the back of my head, walking backwards down the London Road. Giving me a barley sugar he took me home, the incident not being mentioned again.

My first hero was General 'Chinese' Gordon, whom the Mad Mahdi got halfway up the stairs at Khartoum.

Sometimes, on Thursday, I was helped by the Rev Eli Wannamaker, who called to convert De Kuyper in the kitchen and to stir the lemon cheese. For a time my grandmother assisted on the secular side, but this came to an end because of a school essay.

'Jeffrey,' said my grandmother, 'you can't say "Blueish hills". They are green.'

'But they look blueish,' I replied, politely I'm sure, but with all the insouciance of a child.

'That may well be,' she said, 'but they are covered with grass, which is *green*!'

'But grandmama,' I insisted, 'they look blueish from here!'

She took in long deep breaths, then: 'But . . . (she spoke slowly) 'we–know–they–are–not. Don't we?' Something like a smile cracked her powdered face, probably because my mother was Hoovering round us. As she left the room, my grandmother held me in what I learned later was called the whore's grip. 'What colour is grass, Jeffrey?' she hissed.

'Green,' I muttered, sullenly.

'Then–write–down–the–sodding–*greenish*–hills!' she snarled, jabbing me with her crochet needle.

I remember I lay on my back, my knees pale in the light from the window, looking up my grandmother's nose. I knew then that there were easier ways to fame and fortune than the path of creative writing.

I am afraid that our relationship was never the same again. On all future visits, even before the Silver Ghost had come to a halt, Jurgens the chauffeur grey-liveried and goggled, she would shout from the window: 'What's the colour of grass, you little sod?' It was no surprise to anyone when Jurgens inherited the money and married Mrs Gorman the cook. We cut him (and her) dead when they came to the Bring and Buy sale.

But all this was yet to come. Let us now, cleaning our shoes on the period scraper, cross the threshold of Jasmine Villa, stepping lightly on the gleaming linoleum.

Facing the door hung a portrait of my grandfather, who was of course a Cork. Beside it was an early daguerrotype of his dog Bimbo, by all accounts a talented animal. Beneath these pictures (not perhaps what Berenson was used to, and which I later gave to the Museum of Lincolnshire Life) was an umbrella stand made from an elephant's foot, which the Rev Eli Wannamaker assured me had been painlessly removed. In this were kept canes and camp stools, and the stick with the hook at the end that my father carried when he went out at night.

Turn to the right now, past the oak hall table on which stood the telephone and a brass bell, in the shape of a Dutch girl. Uncle Frank used to finger her clapper while he made a coarse joke, until my mother insisted that he use the back door.

Now we enter The Front Room, where I used to make a train out of the Queen Anne style chairs, with the pouffe as The Mallard, the fastest train in the world. It was on one of those chairs, (the one with the loose bottom so that he could drop through), that I posed Bernard as a Christmas Tableau, sheeted as a client of Sweeney Todd. With tomato sauce on his neck and me beside him holding the bread knife. There was a short silence when the blanket was pulled aside, as when the last notes of a great symphony die away, and then Bernard's parents said they would have to be getting home. Uncle Frank, who clapped and shouted 'More!', said he thought I would go far.

That front room is full of memories. It was in there that they laid out my Uncle Frank and, later, when he had been taken away, that I hurt my hand on a pin in Agatha Jennings's knickers. Once a sunny room, it changed character when a lean-to garage was built against the window to house the bull-nosed Morris Oxford. I never quite got used to pulling back the cretonne curtains, printed in a green and orange Vorticist design, expecting to be refreshed by sunlight, the sky and the countryside . . . only to find dark creosote gloom, the maid in the driving seat rubbing the gear lever with a duster and staring in at me.

The maid we had was from Mexborough, ('It's near Wombwell,' she used to explain), a miner's daughter whose only domestic experience until she came to us was clipping the hairs out of her father's nostrils. He liked to have it done after dinner. My mother, always a believer in

'Start as you mean to go on', told her that it was not something that would be required of her at Jasmine Villa. Her name was Molly, and she did well for herself, eventually marrying a pork butcher from Wakefield. But I remember finding out, with an odd thrill just after the war, that Henry Moore (the OM) had been born only three streets away from her! To think that if he had been a girl he could have been our maid! He would have lain up in the attic in his lisle stockings, imagining the stain on the ceiling in stone. That is if Uncle Frank had left her alone. There would have been no chance of dragging a block of marble upstairs, to work on on Wednesday afternoons, but I would certainly have loaned her some of my plasticine if I had known.

That then was the front room. With a pot plant on a bamboo table, a gadrooned silver tray on which callers were supposed to leave their cards, and what I think was a genuine Pre-Raphaelite picture in black and white (monochrome I think is the term) of a lady in a sheet floating up the beam of a searchlight. I often wonder what became of it.

Turn right now; two strides down the coconut matting, and we come to my father's study. A real man's room this, in brown, with a gun and half an elk. His bookcase, glass fronted and curtained, was kept locked; but once I found the tiny key and spent a rainy afternoon curled in his leather armchair, browsing through *The Story of a Tree* and eating his mints.

My father was in fact *the* Alfred Simeon Cork, inventor and patentee of the New Improved Liberty Bodice. A reticent man of medium height, with problems which I will not go into here, he was known in the factory as 'The Mutterer'. 'Here comes The Mutterer,' I have heard them say, in their brown overalls and caps. 'Good morning, sir.'

(The Liberty Bodice seems for some reason to have gone out of favour, though it is difficult to find evidence for this. The family firm, of which, for a short time, I was both proprietor and sales director, was taken over in the mid-Fifties. I put my money into National Savings, in response to an appeal by Lord Mackintosh of Halifax, whose toffees I had always enjoyed.)

My father would spend hours in his den, and was always sucking something. Often he was accompanied by Miss Parkinson from the office, who I once observed through the window (I was in the apple tree with Sooty) putting on a record of David Rose's 'Musical Typewriter', and doing something with my father that I believe can only have added to his problems.

I can see him now coming up through the rhododendrons with his bag of samples, waving to the half an elk through the window. He it was who told me the difference between right and wrong, but I am afraid I have forgotten what it was. I was very fond of him.

As you leave my father's study you turn right once again, and through the bead curtain ('Like a Japanese knocking shop,' my Uncle Frank always used to say, until my mother screamed) was the parlour, or living room. This is where we were all photographed for the *News of the World*. Older readers will probably remember this. More cretonne curtains, with the pattern carried on in the wallpaper, and fumed oak wall lights which were popular at the time. An oak-framed oval mirror, positioned so that my mother could see what Uncle Frank was doing, and a clock in brown wood that was presented to my father when he became, for a short time, a non-political councillor.

If I may digress for a moment. This emergence into public life led to a lot of trouble. It started one morning when Uncle Frank decided that he wanted to be the High Sheriff of Lincoln. He had written out an 'application' as he called it, and wanted my father to post it for him, and to put a word in if needed.

'It'll keep me out from under your feet,' he said, buttering his toast and becoming quite animated. 'There'll be banquets and things, and days out, and that'll save you on the housekeeping; and' – he pointed with the jam spoon – 'I shall wear robes, so that'll save on clothes. And it'll be an interest.'

'You've got egg on the cloth again,' said my mother.

'You can't be the High Sheriff of Lincoln,' said my father, patiently, from behind the *Lincolnshire Standard*. 'You haven't got any "O" Levels, and you're not a ratepayer.' Which just about summed it up.

Anyway, Uncle Frank had apologised for the egg and gone straight up to his room to write a letter to the King. This led to correspondence with a Gentleman in Waiting. The impressive letters were left on the hall table for us all to see. Then we heard (you can keep nothing quiet in a village) that he was seeing Mrs Gorman (this is before she became Mrs Jurgens) and she was making him a Sheriff's outfit. Having been promised that I could be a Page or a Herald, (depending on whether I could learn to play the trumpet), and watch him come out on top of Lincoln Cathedral, I was bitterly disappointed when my mother took his trousers away and called in the doctor.

Now back to the evocative description of the parlour at Jasmine Villa.

To the right of the fireplace, gleaming with Zebo (I can hear you saying, 'Did they have a trivet and a hob?' Yes, indeed we did) was my father's mahogany-framed gentleman's chair. My mother sat facing him, on a fawn pouffe with a silken cord and tassel. To her left, beside the tooled leather cover of the *Radio Times*, she kept a jar of Scott's Emulsion. This was a more or less edible Brylcreem that we swallowed from a tablespoon to the chimes of Big Ben. 'Bong!' 'Yaaagh.' 'Bong!' 'Yaaagh' and so on. We were, I suppose, the kind of average English middle-class family that J. B. ('Jack') Priestley based his plays on; though no mill girl, so far as I know, ever drank disinfectant because of us.

Yasmin and I, with her Enid Blyton hair and a ribbon around her waist, sat on the rug in front of the chrome-plated fender, close to my father's brogues, listening to the veneered Ekco radiogram. This had glowing valves and a little cup to hold blunt needles. On its dial, as well as places like Daventry, was Radio Luxembourg, the Ovaltinies' radio station. It was on this machine, as I later discovered, while we were out, that De Kuyper used to play 'The Laughing Policeman' by Charles Penrose. For some reason she had all his records, ('The Laughing Milkman', 'The Laughing Newsagent', etc) and the man with the tic from MI5 took them away, wrapped in brown paper, giving my father a receipt.

On Mondays, if my father was out, we were allowed to stay up for 'Monday Night at Eight'. With Ronnie Waldman's 'Puzzle Corner'; and The Old Nightwatchman; and The Old Junk Dealer. 'Day after day, I'm on me way, any rags bo'els or bones . . . ' I can hear him singing now, before I had to go to bed to let Yasmin do her exercises.

But our favourite of course was 'Children's Hour'; and in particular 'Toytown', by none other than S. J. Hume Beaman. With Larry the Lamb, Mr Growser, and Ernest the Policeman. It was probably this larger-than-life portrait of an English bobby, with his excessive fondness for Mrs Goose's cream buns, and his 'Now you h'animals, mind what you're a doing of . . . ' that led Lord Trenchard to set up the Hendon Police College.

We also liked Romany, a well-spoken itinerant who took Aunty Doris into the woods to have a look at his vardo. And of course there was Uncle Mac, reputed to have a bad leg, who was always saying 'Are you there, Northern Ireland?' Little did we know that the piano was being played by none other than Ena Sharples.

But I digress again. Let us go now, still on the coconut matting, through the green-baize door and into the kitchen.

We had pine long before it was fashionable, and we painted it brown. But in the main the kitchen was tiled, like the Home and Colonial or a toilet. On the wall was a calendar from the makers of Biro flour, featuring a sallow girl, in sepia and a chef's hat, about to do something with a wooden spoon.

In the corner, mottled grey with a white door and brass taps, the New Improved Gas Cooker stood on little cabriolet legs. With, more often than not, a slowly bubbling pan of lemon cheese, of which my father was inordinately fond. How many children today have tasted hot lemon cheese? Very few.

De Kuyper (and believe me, I am not, with hindsight, being sarcastic) could turn her hand to anything. But it was in the bad winter of '38, when we had some Jewish people to stay the night, that she showed what she was really made of.

We had heard from Old Pomfret, in a cry torn from his lips by the wind, that the bridges were down. Alvar Liddell had been on the wireless, warning people to get well wrapped up before they went out. It was late afternoon and I had been posted at the hall window, to take in the evening paper before it got wet, when suddenly I saw the old-fashioned steam waggon. Piled high with ladies' frocks and lengths of material it had come to a hissing halt, its coal wet, outside our front gate. Through the driving rain we could clearly see the strange device on the side of the vehicle.

'Schmutter,' muttered my father to himself, and we looked at each other in consternation.

My father telephoned the Council for Christians and Jews and spoke to the Duty Officer, but they could offer no advice in such a situation. Outside the thunder rumbled, great flashes of lightning lit up the blueish hills. The rain thudded into the sodden lawn, ran in torrents over the lady with the casserole. Though we had of course switched off all the lights, we knew it was possible to see the half of an elk through my father's study window and imagine that the house was occupied.

The water was rising rapidly around the solid tyres

of the steam waggon. No smoke now from its stubby blackened chimney, and pathetic white faces stared up at the dark Gentile mansion. We heard Sooty enter through his flap and pad down the coconut matting, his plaid coat sopping wet. From the kitchen, lit only by the glow of the boiling lemon cheese, we heard De Kuyper reciting: 'Saw a poodle in a jacket, fastened with a pin; saw a door opened and a cat let in . . . '

Surprisingly, it was my mother who cracked first. She turned her white face from the window. The rain beat in flurries against the glass, shadows of rivulets running down her cheeks. 'For God's sake, Alfred!' she cried. 'Even if they did kill Our Saviour! Can we leave them . . . ?'

'THE ROMANS KILLED JESUS!' The Huddersfield accent roared down the passage, where the green-baize door stood open. Candle in hand, her pinny askew, De Kuyper's eyes were blazing. I crept into a corner, having been through all this before. Though not a Jew herself, De Kuyper had no time for the Romans.

'That's enough,' muttered my father, checking his fly buttons and opening the front door. 'They're in the trade, aren't they?' And fastening a mezuzah he happened to have in his pocket to the lintel of the door, he snapped open his umbrella and went out, head down, to receive the Hebrews.

NOTE: A mezuzah is a rolled-up Jewish prayer in a small tin box, like a Chinese fortune cookie, which is fastened over portals or lintels; the kind of thing which Sir Oswald Mosley was so firmly against. The nearest English equivalent is probably 'Bless This House' ('Oh Lord we pray . . . ') which my friend Dr Edith sings so movingly.

Well, as I was saying, De Kuyper turned up trumps. The Jews were dried and given cocoa, which they seemed to like, and were put into Uncle Frank's room (he of course was no longer with us), and in the morning she unlocked their door and took them along to the bathroom. My mother had drawn the line at ritual bathing, but they seemed to accept this.

Then, with a barely concealed look of triumph, De Kuyper served up a tureen of matzo balls with her customary full English breakfast; placing with a blush and a flourish a lemon next to the teapot. I thought she looked quite beautiful. My father, who had been out to enquire about a Yiddish edition of the *Daily Express* (it had stopped raining) had the grace to put his hat over the saucer which my mother had placed in the hall.

They were given a shovelful of hot coals to start their vehicle, and they chugged away towards the south, where my mother said they would be happier. Waving and blowing kisses, the lady of the family even went so far as to take off and wave her wig.

'Always remember this,' said my father to his assembled family on the front step, as the steam waggon became a smoking dot in the distance. 'There is good and bad in everyone.'

I thought about that, remembering the man with the combs who had never come back with the change, as my mother said, softly to herself, 'Like Mr Swan.' My father glanced at her and frowned. 'He wasn't Jewish,' he muttered. 'I always felt he was,' murmured my mother, keeping a straight face.

'And Spinoza,' said De Kuyper loudly from behind us in the hall.

'Yes, and Montague Burton,' said my father, ending the catalogue of Great Jews before Yasmin and I could think of anybody. We all waved, to a world washed clean, and went inside to finish off the matzo balls.

So that was De Kuyper. Though as events were to prove we did not know her at all. But it was from her that I learnt how to spin a top with a rawhide whip, chalking the top (if you understand what I mean by the top of a top) in strange cabalistic patterns, which merged at high speed into dazzling display. She it was who encouraged me to take ever more responsible posts in the Junior Rechabites, and would often go through the minutes with me, making notes on her starched cuffs.

NOTE: People often ask, 'What were – or are – the Rechabites?' I tell them that in my time it was a temperance organisation, verging on the militant. Our headquarters were where the chip shop is now. A genuine bottle of Guinness, handed down unopened through several generations, would be carefully unpacked by the eldest son of the Rev Eli Wannamaker and passed amongst us. He would point to the sediment in the bottom and tell us stories of cats and dogs, and even drunken Irish people, who fell into the enormous vats in Dublin and were never seen again.

Regarding as she did my sister Yasmin as little better than a Roman, it was into my ear that De Kuyper whispered the secret recipes for lemon cheese. These, with much else, were kept under lock and key in her tin trunk, which was stuck all over with photographs of the Duke of Windsor. (He was, she maintained, 'out of his depth'.) It was in her pantry, under serried ranks of yellow jars, that Agatha Jennings – who claimed to have lost her maidenhead on a tricycle – demonstrated what people did when they were married.

But again; all this was yet to come. Stay with me, because now we are going upstairs.

Real red 'Turkey' carpet of course, and brown bannisters and gleaming brass stair rods. At the bend in the stairs, where Uncle Frank fell over his trousers, on the ledge below the window of red, white and blue stained glass, a stone statue of a naked lady. I often saw my father touch it ('For luck' he would say if he saw me watching) as he climbed up to bed with his Instant Postum. (An indescribable American drink.)

The door on the right at the top of the stairs was the bathroom, my mother's pride and joy. It was not the practice then to 'box in' the bath and at the head of ours, with its rubber pillow and plunger mechanism, fitted by Uncle Frank in happier days, was the geyser. Made in Wolverhampton, this was something I respected but never came to terms with. The reader will forgive me not being more precise, but I was never a physics scholar.

The rubber ducks (Daddy, Mummy and a baby, yellow with red lips and a hole in their bottoms) were kept with my father's cruiser squadron and the Pears soap (made from coal tar and through which you could see), along with the loofah, in a recess in the tiled surround. As I say, we were in some things ahead of our time.

Across the landing was my parents' bedroom, with mottoes on the wall and my father's apparatus screwed behind the door. From their window, as I was to learn in that fateful hot summer of 1940 (when as you probably know we stood alone), they could see right into the rhododendron bushes.

Ahead of you as you reached the top of the stairs, across the mat where Sooty used to sleep, until Uncle Frank had his accident, was the locked door to Yasmin's sanctum. 'Virgin territory' as my father called it, rather wistfully. I only went in there once, when De Kuyper had filled the house with acrid smoke. Shoulder against my sister's door, while my father muttered persuasively on the telephone to his insurance broker, I called out loudly in a calming voice, 'Fire! Fire! Those that are sober shall be saved!' as I had been taught to do by the Rechabites.

We all had a good laugh about it later of course but my father, stern and just as always, forbade De Kuyper her ration for the following fortnight.

To the right of Yasmin's room, next to the framed cutting from *John Bull* showing Aunty Mamie with Diaghilef, right next to my room (which you will notice I am keeping to last), the carpet ended. Green-painted stairs twisted up to the maid's and the spare room, unused since Uncle Frank had been taken away. (That was where the Jews had slept.)

I once asked De Kuyper, 'Are you a maid?' as children

will, and she had grinned and answered, 'No, I'm not. But don't tell your mother.'

I must say she had made her room into a proper home from home. It even had its own smell. On one wall, to the left as you came in, was a full-length portrait of Jean de Reszke. (A tenor I think, and a Pole; also a cigarette of the time like Du Maurier, who was an actor.) On her pillow, trimmed with broderie anglaise, (my father being what he was we had a lot of this in the house) sat Sunny Jim. Her books completely filled the opposite wall (my mother used to bring up incredulous friends on Wednesday afternoons), covering the damage where Uncle Frank had attempted to break through, and I recall some of the titles still.

There was a fat red volume about a Queen Edna (long overdue at the library) who had ruled part of the Balkans at one time. De Kuyper admired her greatly. 'She used to go out with Vlad the Impaler,' she once explained, but I was no wiser. (Though looking back now, Bernard would have been interested.) She also had a complete set, in the yellow jackets of Victor Gollancz, of the writings of The False Rabbi of Pomerania. When I went to bed early on some winter evenings, there being Henry Hall on the wireless, she would read me passages from *The Yoks of Upper Silesia*, or humorous bits from the *Shikser's Vade Mecum*.

There were many detective stories and thrillers, all about aristocrats coming to a sticky end, as well as the ingenious works of Dennis Wheatley: like *Murder in Miami* with its cellophane envelope of 'poison' pills (dolly mixtures really, she let me eat one), and clues like burnt matches and cigarette ends. She also had one by an imitator, in which on turning the title page a boxing glove on a strong spring hit you in the face. You had to guess who done it.

Below the dormer window she kept her conjuring set, in a black box from Hamleys, with which she entertained those of our friends who had threepence. 'For a good cause,' she would say, dropping the warm coins down the front of her vest. Almost a professional, she could do a nail through a finger, a rubber fried egg or the floating sugar, that had us round-eyed with wonder. Just before it all came to a head, she had sent away for a Seebackroscope in order to look round corners.

A downright unbeliever in Joan the Wad, which I think was the main cause of the rift between her and my mother, the rest of us were very fond of her. Too old for an Ovaltinie, we none the less thought of her as one of us. (When of course she was one of them!)

And now, at last, to my room.

When I was very young of course my mother was responsible for the decor, and it was brown because I was a boy. But on the day I was promoted to a responsible position in the Junior Rechabites (purely honorary) I was allowed more or less carte blanche.

That was an important day for me. After the initiation ceremony, the band of the 1st Detachment had marched along the London Road, playing what sounds like 'Let's Have Another One' but is really an old temperance tune. The drum major hurling his mace high, hand on hip, as they came abreast of the gate, and Bernard emerging from the rhododendrons to wave. I caught a glimpse of Agatha Jennings's white socks and perforated sandals, and my mother's proud face beside that of the elk in the study window.

But back to my room, and the carte blanche I was given.

I at once put up lots of shelves. On these I arranged my trophies; smallest to the front, tallest to the rear, as they say. My mice (every boy had mice in those days) lived in a wired enclosure below the window. I had made them a cardboard replica of the Rechabites' Drill Hall, with a little flag, and though eating much the same as the rest of the household they had never of course tasted strong liquor. White with brown spots, they were adept at working a system of treadwheels and pulleys that drew Agatha Jennings up the front of the house in a crate stencilled 'Fyffes Bananas'.

NOTE: Perhaps the reader, reared on *Look and Learn* and the proud possessor – and rightly so – of an 'O' Level in physics, has a nagging doubt about the ability of mice to draw Agatha Jennings up the front of Jasmine Villa, even with the advantage of their never having touched strong liquor and with a system of treadwheels and pulleys. I can only say that I got the plans for this from *101 Things a Boy Can Do*, which a well-spoken man gave De Kuyper at the door in exchange for a subscription to the *Daily Express* (Lord Beaverbrook's organ). And after all, who was it who said 'Give me a fulcrum and I will move the world?' Agatha Jennings was hardly that.

To the right of the mice was the cocoa tin I spoke into to reach, via a taut string, my friend Bernard who lived next door. It was through this, late on evenings of low humidity, that he fed me the relevant chapters of Havelock Ellis; and I told him what I saw his mother do with the milkman, twice, behind the washing. As a matter of interest, some years later, she was the first person to have yoghurt round our way.

Just inside the door of my room I had hung a picture of the above-mentioned Lord Beaverbrook (known then I believe as Aitken), all lips and bristly hair. During the war he was, for a short time, Minister of Aircraft Production, playing a vital role in collecting railings and aluminium saucepans. (Which he was later found to have buried in a large hole in the ground; but no action was taken.) He was also responsible for the cardboard thermometer outside the wool shop, and by 1943 we had raised enough money for half a Spitfire. For £5,000 you could buy a whole one, though you were not allowed to fly it yourself.

The picture, which I had cut out of *Tit Bits*, served to give any intruder (I was not allowed to lock the door in case hair grew on the palms of my hands) a completely false idea of my personality; and to distract them should Agatha Jennings be on the way up.

That was my room then. You could call it a real boy's den. With flagons of Tizer ('The appetizer') and dandelion and burdock. On the bedside cabinet was an electric warning machine that had been my father's, and his father's before him.

And that was the house. Jasmine Villa. Home of the Corks.

I have left out the lavatory (pale green acanthus leaves on white porcelain, mahogany seat and a brass chain) out of delicacy. There was nothing of great interest in there, except for Uncle Frank's last message.

Outside the kitchen door, beyond De Kuyper's washhouse, was the shed in which my father indulged in his favourite pastime.

Chapter Three

*The boy with the purple head – King George V has a Jubilee
– King George VI sings – King Edward VIII is undone –
The Three Stooges – Keyhole Kate and Gustave Doré – The
City of Jam – Was William Brown Jewish? – The Munich
Crisis – My father speaks – Chamberlain declares war – The
masses are politically motivated – I go away to school*

Between 1934 and 1939, while war clouds gathered over
Europe, I was of course a Mixed Infant, in Mrs Dooley's
class, where I sat next to a boy with a purple head.

Bernard would wait for me every morning at the gate
(this was before he impaled his scrotum), and I recall that
he was very interested in the Riff Wars, which were on at
the time. But I had got no higher up than the Cameroons
with my tracing, and had gone off the idea of becoming a
Christian Scholar.

Looking back now, how uninformed and naive I was.
Though we took both the *Daily* and the *Sunday Express* (my
father going so far, for a short time, as to wear his trousers
in the style of Adam the Gardener), I was uncertain as to
the rights and wrongs of the Spanish Civil War; confusing
Franco with Vimto and covering myself with embarrassment in front of Mrs Dooley.

My Aunty Florence, whom I have never seen, took one
of the first mobile chip shops over the goat tracks of
the Pyrenees and into Spain. There she served in the
commissariat of the International Brigade; an organisation,
according to my mother, of 'Busybodies in the service of

the Anti-Christ'; whose 'officers' wore razor blades in the peaks of their caps.

These often crude Glaswegians were headed – indeed named after – a renegade Englishman called Clement Attlee. Known to the men as 'The Major', or simply (bearing in mind what kind of men they were) 'Clem'. He seemed to us a ferocious brigand-like figure as he scowled from the front page of the *Children's Newspaper*, hung about with bandoliers and hand grenades, bitten fingernails never far from the pearl-handled revolvers he wore, in the style of his contemporary, 'Two Gun' Cohen.

Some years later I remember commenting to a deaf woman next to me, while watching him on Movietone News declare open a new Labour Exchange in Balham, what a transformation had taken place. How taking office had changed the man. Prime Minister now and clean shaven but for a slight moustache, bespectacled and dark suited, wearing a tie and smoking a pipe, he was a member of the Labour Party and had an interest in a club in the East End of London. (Though not, one should say, the kind in which you would find Arthur Tracey or 'Snake Hips' Johnson.)

Milk Monitor and reserve for the rounders team, always quick with a bean bag, I served Mrs Dooley well, as those sunlit years went past in the ante-room to the groves of academe. Bluebells in jam jars, newts and tadpoles in the sink, tall windows opened by a rope and pulley mechanism, very like that invented by the *Daily Express*.

Soon I was of an age to be able to reach through a hole in my trouser pocket and finger my pencil, half red and half blue, with a rubber at the end, which I kept tucked into my stocking. I would practise whipping it out quickly, like Tom Mix or a Scotsman. (Tom Mix, for younger readers, was a cowboy hero of the silver screen with a big white hat, white horse and tight white trousers. His adventures were often in mines. Unlike those beneath the Vale of Clwyd you walked straight into these, rather than having your Woodbines confiscated and going down in a lift. They were more like ghost trains, with little trucks rattling around corners. Good fun really, but very often they blew up.)

I also painted my first picture (something like a Hockney I suppose, only stronger if you know what I mean) titled 'Daddy, Mummy, De Kuyper and Sooty, in front of the washhouse'. Mrs Dooley helped with the lettering. Many years later, when the man with the tic from MI5 asked for a photograph, it was all we could come up with.

I began to fill out above my grey, gartered stockings, my knees scarred from the broken glass on Agatha Jennings's window sill, and to rove out into the wide world. In the evenings and on Saturday mornings Bernard and I would wander round the town, nodding to people and poking wet fingers, in turn, into a bag of lemonade crystals. On occasion we would buy Fry's Motoring Chocolate (though of course we did not have a car) from the corner shop run by Mrs Moss and her fat son, who went to the open-air school. It was said that all she could remember of the fat son's father was that he wore striped trousers and spoke with a London accent. My mother, who said that the Londoner was unlikely to have said much more than 'Fanks very much', could never bring herself to set foot in the shop.

We used to eat the chocolate by the horse trough, the Eros as it were, the centre of our town; washing it down with spring water which ran from the nostrils of the stone horse's head. This useful centrepiece had been presented to the town to mark an outlying hamlet being named, by the *Daily Telegraph*, as having the highest percentage of its population killed in the Great War (ie almost all of them). A quiet place now, the hamlet had an obelisk and a spiked chain to keep people off the grass. Really, of course, they should have had the horse trough as well; but at the time it had been felt that they couldn't expect to have both it *and* an obelisk.

The trough was in the shape of an open sarcophagus, with stone seats for the horse drivers to sit on. It was all pinnacles, wedges of marble and polished stone, animals' nostrils and ears streaming water, bird baths and a dog's basin. You could buy glossy postcards of it at the news-agents. There was also a drinking fountain, which didn't work, and an iron mug on a chain. This, according to my mother, held all the diseases known to man. At the very top, facing the Railway Hotel, was a bust of the man who had paid for it. He wore a crown of poppies on Armistice Day and Sep Pomfret, in his beret and white gauntlets, always threw him a crashing salute.

Mossies was also the toy shop: a celluloid doll in a knitted dress, with moulded ginger hair, sitting on crepe paper in the window with its legs apart.

We read a good deal, mainly *The Hotspur* and *The Wizard*; in which Wilson, who was hundreds of years old, had the knack of being able to run a mile in under a minute by slowing down his heart. There was also another person, somewhat younger, who battered in Pathans' heads ('like eggshells') with what he called his 'clicky ba'. He was of course blackish, but despite his speech impediment very firmly on our side.

When I was seven there was quite a lot going on. King George V and Queen Mary had a Jubilee, and I received a lovely beaker, which I will let a colleague of Bernard Berenson have one of these days. Then The Sailor King died and was replaced, for a short time, by King Edward VIII; who also gave away beakers and was a friend of Mrs Simpson. A lady, according to my mother, who was on a par with Mrs Moss. He was supported to some extent by De Kuyper, but was undone by the Bishop of Bradford, a Dr Blunt, who probably knew the statue of the black lady dressed as Queen Victoria, if not that of the Right Hon Philip Snowden.

After that came King George VI, whom we have already met living in his modest town house close to Hyde Park.

(The 'Queen Dad' as it were.) He sang a little number called 'Under The Spreading Chestnut Tree' at a jamboree, (though a grown man he was allowed to be a Boy Scout), touching his *chest*, his head ('nut') and then holding out his arms in time to the music. Chest – nut – tree.

Sliced bread now arrived. Lady hikers appeared on the empty Sunday streets in shorts and rolled-down stockings, taking snaps of the horse trough, and we had The Battle of Cable Street.

This is of course in the East End of London, and introduces once again our old friend Sir Oswald Mosley. It took place while I was wearing my plum-coloured velvet suit and struggling with my grandmother for my artistic integrity. I heard the full story from Mr Davies, the postman, friend of De Kuyper and a great reader, who people said was only in the job (like the telegram boys) because of the bicycle.

As I have explained earlier there were a lot of Jews living in that area (the East End). With an unknown number of Gentiles, and those who put knickers on donkeys, and, quite possibly, (who knows?), even the odd Huguenot or so. Well, what happened was this. Sir Oswald just wanted to walk through. He was not actually going anywhere; like, say, Romford in Essex, or Billericay. He just wanted to walk down Cable Street with a few friends, being quite prepared to walk in the middle of the road if the pavements were crowded. He was very keen, not to say obsessive, about walking down certain streets; going nowhere in particular, just nodding to the odd Jew or Huguenot as they waved from their windows.

Perfectly proper, you might say. But as the Jews put it to the Chief Commissioner at Scotland Yard, you did not find Montague Burton, or indeed the Chief Rabbi, with all their friends, plus flags and sidedrums, walking through Bury St Edmunds or Putney; nodding to the odd Anglican and possibly embarrassing him. And of course they had a point.

Well, the Commissioner said that it was Sir Oswald's right as an Englishman, (which he was), to walk through Cable Street, even if he was not actually going anywhere; and that really put the cat among the pigeons. So on the day of the walk, all those bobbies not hanging around basement windows were asked to form a 'human screen' around Sir Oswald, in order to see fair play, which is after all what the police are for.

I should point out that most of the bobbies were Gentiles of various persuasions. (Jews not as a rule becoming bobbies, possibly because of the canteen food.) Though they were certainly not biased, this being not allowed, the bobbies did consider that if Sir Oswald, (who was after all one of them), wished to walk down anyone's street, even if going nowhere in particular, he should be allowed – indeed assisted – to do so.

So that was the scene on that fateful day in 1936. A man who could have been Prime Minister of England, Labour or Conservative, with his friends (and drums), at one end of Cable Street; and barring the way to Romford, Essex, a lot of what can only be described as not very well-dressed people.

The drummer started to play. Picture the scene. Probably, like Geraldo's drummer, he would have his name painted on the skin; but he would not of course have had with him a 'high hat' or a row of imitation scarlet skulls. The flags would be lifted high, their varnished poles in the little leather cups between the legs that were my mother's only objection to me joining the Rechabites. Policemen tightened their chinstraps. There would be shouted words of command from Sir Oswald in his Lancashire accent; and then, adjusting his armband, possibly looking around to see if Fruity Metcalfe had turned up, he set off towards Billericay.

But at once, without the slightest provocation, people started to throw things.

The Commissioner of Police, who was there in person,

(looking very smart in his uniform and carrying a stick), asked them to stop at once. But they did not. Possibly not being able to hear him because of the drummer and the shuffling feet of the bobbies. They were really very annoyed, and began to throw things. Some quite rude remarks were passed and some of the missiles, by mistake, hit the helmets of the bobbies. Now it was their turn to get annoyed, and some of them slid their truncheons out from their trousers. (The British bobby does not carry a gun.)

After a few moments of what can only be described as a riot, the Chief Commissioner, saluting correctly, said to Sir Oswald: 'I'm very sorry, sir; but I'm afraid you cannot go to Romford, Essex, today.' A far cry indeed from Ernest the Policeman, and a complete vindication of Lord Trenchard and all he stood for. And Sir Oswald, quite clearly disappointed, agreed. He was after all on the side of law and order. He then went home in a motor car.

Now that is what I call a vignette. There will be more of these sketches of stirring events from our past. A doctor's wife from Tiverton to whom I showed these pages said that I was 'a dab hand' at painting with words. I said that it was just style; though she could well be right.

You will notice that I have left out details like old Jews being thrown through plate glass windows. This was on the advice of my solicitor, Mr Rim.

'Were you there?' he asked in his forthright manner. I muttered something about being seven years old at the time, and how as a rule street demonstrations were not reported by the *Children's Newspaper*. He took what he laughingly called the liberty of presenting me with his account. 'Leave Sir Oswald alone,' he said, laying his index finger on the side of his nose. 'There are those in high places . . . ' He said no more and I left his hut, closing the door as he requested. Mr Rim, like most of his kind, is a man whose advice is not to be ignored.

But enough of England for the moment. What of the New World?

George and Ira Gershwin, that talented couple, had their names in lights on The Great White Way. Albert Jolson, possibly the first black Jew, was the toast of New York. 'Toot toot tootsie, don't cry . . . ' It must have seemed like a nightmare to you-know-who. A box of Milk Tray in the back row of the Odeon, Leicester Square, with the lovely fur-swathed Miss Guinness, his smart black-shirted arm daringly along the back of the seat . . . *and there he is . . . on the screen . . . huge, in monochrome . . . the white-gloved hands jiggling . . . the thick lips and the nose!*

Those people in shawls lucky enough to have gone all the way; those who had not been dropped off at the Albert Dock; the 'huddled masses yearning to be free'; were now exploding like 'wheat shot from guns' out of The Bronx and The Bowery. These colourful areas were similar to the East End of London, with not only Jews but Italians as well, and fire escapes, and infant prodigies keeping you awake at night. But at least the people living there were spared the sight of donkeys in knickers racing through the streets, or massed Anglicans marching down the middle of the road. The policemen and the priests were Irish, ('Good morning, Father'), and swung their truncheons in their right hand; taking the odd apple from a 'pushcart' with the other. An act which I suppose could be traced back to those cooling pies in Belgravia.

It was called 'The Great Melting Pot'. Looking back now, they seemed to be in a frenzy of activity, at least in comparison to Swinehurst; though this could be partly explained by the Rechabites being in control of the White House at the time.

Nowhere was this frenzy more evident than on the literary scene. For example, Dorothy Parker, a poetess who didn't clear up after her dogs. Once, on entering the Algonquin Hotel, she was told that a group of socialites giggling around a tub in the foyer were 'ducking for apples'. 'That,' she said, 'but for a typographical error, is the story of my life!' I think that gives the flavour of the

American literary scene, as well as saying something about the Algonquin Hotel.

This was a hostelry that actually encouraged Dorothy Parker and people with names like Heywood Broun and Ambrose Bierce to sit around, always at the same table, quaffing the American equivalent of Vimto and throwing bread rolls about. The kind of thing which, if done in England, gives a pub the reputation of being 'cliquey'.

In the streets of 'The Big Apple', you could see black people, or Red Indians, or Bums. (A word perfectly acceptable over there; they used to travel about underneath trains.) Gene Krupa, a better drummer than either Geraldo's or Sir Oswald's, took drugs; (like the man offered Elspeth as she was leaving the clock golf in Skegness, hidden in a sherbet lemon), which sent him mad I was told; like one of the Three Stooges. One of the others had died, and the third had got married; or so we were told at the time.

Krupa played with Benny Goodman, born a poor boy with glasses, one of those who kept people awake at night; who ended up, in full evening dress, playing Mozart at Carnegie Hall. All the best people were there.

This place, like our Albert, was named after Andrew Carnegie, a Scotsman who gave away libraries. He tried to give one to Bradford, but they spurned him, not liking the way he had made his money. Possibly they considered him yet another parvenu, like the sauce-brewing father of Violet Elizabeth Bott. Or they may already have had a library. They were certainly not without a cultural infrastructure, having as I have already told you the statue of a black lady dressed as Queen Victoria.

On the subject of drummers: Appleby, at my prep school, had a cousin who played in a naval dance band, (something you never think about); and he served, for a short time, on a Free French destroyer. He said that the toilets were awful.

But it was Hollywood rather than New York that called to my generation, and in particular Charlie Chaplin, whom everyone loved. He was born near the Oval, and had gone to America with Fred Karno's Army. Deciding to go into films, he put on a short black jacket, baggy trousers, a toothbrush moustache, and twirled his never-to-be-forgotten cane with a hook at the end; very like the one my father took with him when he went out at night.

Charlie, as he was called, became a much-loved figure everywhere. 'Charlo' the French called him, and one wonders how the state of their cinema toilets compared to those of the French navy. He married the lovely Paulette Goddard, who wore a torn dress, like Yasmin did when she returned from the 'Holidays at Home' dance in the tent.

Charlie went on to make films like 'The Great Dictator' in which he took the part of Adolf Hitler, bouncing a balloon globe of the world to Jack Oakie from a barber's chair.

Talk about Jack Oakie! Before he was Mussolini he made many films with Alice Faye, who was lovely. She had fair hair and cried as she was singing, usually with her hands behind her back on a veranda, with a full moon over the water.

But what we really liked were the cowboys. Sobering to think that if it had not been for the great masters of the cinema, like David Wark Griffith, not to speak of our own Danziger brothers, we would not have known about these. Though I cannot speak for other parts of Britain, certainly in my own county of Lincolnshire, men who looked after cows carried a stick and had their dinner in a handkerchief.

These 'horse operas' were usually set in The Saloon, which was like a big pub. Sometimes there was a stage with, hopefully, Alice Faye crying and singing. The Licensee was not to be trusted, unless he was woman. He could normally be found standing sideways at the bar, dressed somewhat better than the average cowboy, watching the beer slide past or playing cards for money. (If you were found cheating, just like if you went mad on the beach at Dunkirk, you were shot out of hand.) There were rooms to let upstairs, but one had to be careful as the bannisters broke away very easily. There were also slot machines, and a cowardly man at the piano with garters on his arms.

The action would move then to The Sheriff's Office, which had antique office chairs on the veranda, the Sheriff often setting a bad example by tipping these dangerously backwards. There was no lavatory in the office, not even a pot in the cell, which had a little barred window which a horse could pull out of the wall with a clothesline. The rear entrance to the building was used by an Indian woman, with a tray of dinner and a gun concealed under a doily.

There was also The Office of the Local Newspaper. This had a gate in a little fence just inside the door, and was owned by a small middle-aged man wearing a tennis umpire's eyeshade. He had an attractive and spirited daughter who was quite capable, after he had been shot, of bringing out the next edition by herself. A single parent, he was found lying just inside the little swing gate, with the boxes of type upturned all over the room. This is, incidentally, called Printers' Pie.

There was The Livery Stable, a kind of garage for horses, usually run by a man with a bad leg, which often burnt down; and The Church, painted white and on the edge of town. One could not be sure of the denomination, but I took it to have been C of A. Everybody went there, except for the Licensee and Alice Faye (who only caused a lot of whispering if she came in). The congregation, wearing poke bonnets and string ties, sang 'Bringing in the Sheaves'; and the Vicar would know by the presence of the camera behind the pulpit that before they had finished, the door at the far end would crash open and the Sheriff come down the aisle, shot in the shoulder, to ask them to clean up the town.

Other characters included a Dentist with a shocking cough, and The Doctor, who also had a handsome daughter and drove around in a horse and cart. Like the Newspaper Proprietor, his wife was no more than a sepia photograph on a crocheted cloth, and he too was very often shot at night. A cowardly man, like the Pianist with garters on his arms, he normally repented after an emotional scene with his daughter.

The Schoolteacher was a vigorous young woman with an uneasy relationship with the parents. Inclined to the religious, she was none the less attracted to lone strangers who drifted into town, moody and secretive, whom most people wanted to hang from a tree.

The Banker was not someone the big five clearing banks would wish to have been associated with. Fat, cigar smoking, usually Edward Arnold, he was a close friend of the Licensee and very often fancied Alice Faye. He was normally shot before the Editor, usually by his erstwhile friend the Licensee, though you did not see him do it. The moody and secretive friend of the Schoolteacher invariably got the blame.

Besides a Telegraph Office Clerk, who wore an eyeshade like the crusading newspaperman and worked part-time as an informant for the Licensee there was, as required, a Blacksmith, a small boy who heard or saw things, and about a dozen outraged townsfolk. These were decent people who gathered in front of the saloon to demand a clean-up of the town, or outside the Sheriff's office to insist on hanging one of his inmates. This he would not allow. To give them all some form of light relief, once a year a horse-drawn caravan would arrive, like Romany's vardo. This was full of youngish women in liberty bodices, under the supervision of an older lady with a heart of gold. Their precise calling was never explained, but one got the impression that it was no job for Alice Faye.

What these towns could look forward to (if they got the railroad) was large herds of cows being brought through on their way to market. These would be escorted by mounted cowboys, waving their hats and shouting 'Yippeee!' They had come a long way, playing mouthorgans and eating bacon and beans with a fork, and were ready when they hit town for some fun. This consisted of riding through the main street firing your gun into the air, before going in to hear Alice Faye sing.

Now we come to the Red Indians, the Sheep Herders, and the Dirt Farmers. The Red Indians attacked the white man at every opportunity, and the white woman too. They shot them with arrows, or rifles bought from rene-gade whites like J. Carrol Naish; poked them with pen-nanted spears, as carried by leading cadres of the Junior Rechabites; and/or went at them with tomahawks. Or, and this was the worst, gave them to the squaws. Then, finally, when they were dead, they scalped them. It was hardly the attitude, you will agree, of people seeking peaceful co-existence. To claim, as they did, that because they were there first it all belonged to them, was just not good enough. Partial to a glass of 'firewater', though unable like aboriginals and Scotsmen to hold their drink, they lay about hiccuping and giggling.

The only good Injun, said the cowboys, was a dead 'un; though a purse made out of part of a squaw was a prized possession. But even lower than the Indians were the Sheep Herders; and their sheep. They were, if I may use the phrase, a different breed of men; not wearing the same hats and floppy trouser legs, and probably not even enjoying good old bacon and beans. Mutton pie or crown of lamb was more their style. They also did not, as a rule, wear guns in their belts. Altogether, though it was never said in so many words, there was undeniably something of the raving poof about them.

The cowboys maintained that the sheep ate the grass, which was true. But in fairness, sheep being what they are, there was not a lot that the sheep herders could do –

other than put up wire fences, thereby further annoying the cowboys, who were accustomed to taking short cuts across country with their cows. There was also some trouble I believe about sheep droppings, but we have all been upset by these in our time. And cows really have nothing to talk about.

Finally, the Dirt Farmers. They were somewhere between the dead Indians and the Sheep Herders, with a toothless granny in a rocking chair. Even their best friends would hardly have called them 'snappy' dressers, and they drank water from a cake tin on a stick. They planted runner beans and cabbages, possibly a few homely hollyhocks, and did not ride horses, or even go into town very often to see Alice Faye; and of course they put up fences as well, to keep the cows and sheep off the veg. In other words they were just asking for trouble.

All this, and Eldorado ice cream, under the corrugated roof of the Pavilion De Luxe; Prop, Captain Drew, who dressed up every night like B. Goodman at Carnegie Hall. It was there that I was first introduced to The Clutching Hand.

There was always a Full Supporting Programme; and we thrilled to The March of Time (I am actually singing the theme music as I write), with a long queue of people going right round the world. I was always put in mind of Mrs Dooley's observation that if every Chinaman ordered an extra half inch to the tail of his shirt, it would keep the mills of Lancashire in work for a long time. A hundred years I think she said.

No organ came up in the Pavilion De Luxe, the music swelling as the coloured lights changed, as in the Dominion, Tottenham Court Road, where Ena Baga held sway. Though Captain Drew did have a sing song, while Pomfret's sister changed the reels, with a bouncing ball and a gramophone. I must say that when the curtains closed on The King, in full colour, with the wind waving the flag – and Agatha Jennings had adjusted her dress as the notice requested, before the wall lights came on – we knew we had had value for money.

Before leaving the cinema, we should surely mention the great comedians of the screen. Our Charlie we have mentioned, but what about Ben Turpin, with his bad eyes? And Harold Lloyd, whose eyes were not much better? Buster Keaton ('Old Stoneface') was a genius who never spoke. In fact *none* of them spoke, until Al Jolson so upset Sir Oswald and Diana.

I remember Fatty Arbuckle, a comedian whose career was destroyed because of what he did to a girl. They all did things to girls of course, but Fatty went a bit too far. He was the reason for the setting up of the Hays Office, which ruled that you could say 'bum' but not 'arse'; the former, as I have said, riding about under trains.

Mack Sennet. The great Mack Sennet and his bathing beauties: girls who had managed to evade Fatty Arbuckle by wearing Dr Scholl's shoes and baggy swimming costumes. He it was who came up with the idea of amusing policemen.

In this country we had gone as far as a Laughing Policeman, and the French of course had their 'Beau gendarme'. But no one had thought of Floyd Sterling as a whiskery inspector gabbling into the telephone; then the whole police station turning out, running behind and falling over as the vintage police car sped away. This went sideways, like Floyd Sterling wore his hat, crossing railroad tracks seconds before a wood-burning locomotive clanked past. Its engineer, shaking his fist at the Keystone Kops, was a member of The Brotherhood of Railroad Engineers, who were all white.

But people did not mind; they thought it only a quid pro quo of The Brotherhood of Railroad Porters, who were all black. They were thrilled and amused to see these cops in their ill-fitting uniforms, running about with truncheons rampant in their hands. In this country, as you know, they have always been kept circumspectly inside the trousers.

I don't think that an English version, with Scotland Yard turning out into Whitehall, ill-dressed bobbies falling from their bicycles, spilling their pies onto the pavements of the Home Office, would have been approved by Lord Trenchard.

When it came to careers, Bernard and I often thought about becoming a film director, in jodhpurs without flies and with your name on a chair. Not to mince words, we dreamt of stepping lightly along the secret passages to the stars' dressing rooms. Sliding back the concealed panel with the tip of a Corona Corona, with a suave 'Hi there, babe!', taking a grateful Ginger Rogers or Janet Gaynor unawares. In the case of Alice Faye, of course, we would have knocked, and taken with us an orchid in a glass box.

When they sing on my video, as they do, 'That's Entertainment', I murmur to myself 'It was indeed!' And I have not mentioned the wonderful Busby Berkeley, looking down on his girls as they all opened their legs in perfect unison. Or my own favourite, hairy little Cheetah, almost human, gibbering in Maureen O'Sullivan's knickers. And of course the great Ed McGarrity and Dorothy Turnowitz. He with the hump – audiences used to fall about when he shrugged his shoulders – and she, 'Otty as he called her, because he had no roof to his mouth, pulled about on a little cart because she had no legs. We shall not look upon their like again.

People often attempt to reject the modern age, closing their eyes, hearing the music of the tingalary and wishing themselves back in a street hung with washing, with a jaunty but respectful newsboy to steer one across the road between the horse manure. But I say: where would we be without the video? Wherever I am, whatever else I should be doing, every Sunday afternoon Jolson Sings Again, and again. I relish the moment, ever fresh, when Evelyn Keyes is overcome with stagefright at the top of a staircase. You know it of course. The orchestra strikes up but she is paralysed, in a spangled leotard, in an awful state.

Then the young Larry Parks rises in the orchestra stalls. Obviously Un-American, but dressed in the style of Captain Drew, he sings with Al Jolson's voice: 'Liza, Liza, don't be late . . .'; and with a lovely smile of gratitude, with confidence now, Evelyn Keyes dances down to the stage to tumultuous applause. What incredible legs!

But do not get the idea that we were obsessed by films. We went to the pictures no more than once or twice a week, not counting Saturday mornings; though if it was good we sometimes stayed round to see it again. On other evenings, after tea, if it was not the night for the Rechabites, we read comics. I have already mentioned *The Hotspur* and *The Wizard*; but to supplement these, and the *Children's Newspaper*, we had *The Beano* and *The Dandy*. These we exchanged on a Tuesday, and later in the week we swopped *The Champion* and *The Rover*, or even *Film Fun*, which came out I think on a Friday. Yasmin had *Sunny Stories*, mostly about pixies; which, if stuck, I sometimes took to the lavatory. She later moved on to *The Red Letter* and *The People's Friend*, being advised in this by De Kuyper, who later admitted that they were not quite what she thought they would be.

We liked Keyhole Kate, who wore a gymslip like Agatha Jennings, and Korky The Cat (Kat?). He was always being chased along river banks by irate farmers in hairy brown tweed suits. But the story we turned to first, after feeling for the free gift, was Lord Snooty and His Pals. Unlike Keyhole Kate and Korky, Lord Snooty was not in colour, but more in the style of Gustave Doré. He and his friends lined up at the head of the page outside Lord Snooty's house, which was grey and castellated like the mine owner's place in the Vale of Clwyd.

Lord Snooty was on the left. I don't of course mean politically; these journals were published in Dundee (The City of Jam), where you were not allowed to have politics or trade unions. No, Lord Snooty, who was about ten, was on the left-hand side of his gang. A thin boy with prominent ears, his face the colour of newsprint, in a big collar, a top hat and tight striped trousers. We were mildly surprised that he was allowed to play out, dressed like that. All the other scamps – the 'Pals' – quite obviously working class, were ranged across in declining size. At the end was a walking baby in combinations, with a buttoned flap at the back, and a small mongrel dog. Being poor they looked much happier than Lord Snooty, or for that matter the two aristocratic aunts, both resembling Lady Violet Bonham-Carter, who waved to him from the battlements when he went out.

We were also very keen on 'William' books, by Richmal Crompton, who was a woman. The illustrations, by Thomas Henry, a disciple of Gustave Doré, showed a likeable boy, a little older than Lord Snooty, with baggy stockings and a smudge on his cheek. His cap, which he wore at all times (he could of course have been Jewish) had concentric rings, and his sister's name was Ethel. She looked like the kind of girl who 'jazzed' in between the haute cuisine with 'Snake Hips' Johnson. His elder brother, Robert, had a thing about silver-backed hair brushes. Not one for Kate Meyrick's perhaps, or for Sunday morning rambles with the ladies in their rolled-down stockings, he was what my Uncle Frank called 'a prick'.

William's gang was called The Outlaws, and were all the same class. They met in The Old Barn, where they sat on packing cases, thoughtfully provided by the owner. There was Ginger and Henry, and Douglas, and, sometimes, the daughter of a nouveau riche who was always threatening to scream until she was sick. Once William (never referred to as 'Bill') blacked out the 'O' in Theobald Barber, making the shop sign read The Bald Barber. I thought that was very good.

On another occasion The Outlaws learned of Adolf Hitler extorting money from Jews. William was deeply impressed. Seated on his packing case he asked his friends for more information. (His ignorance was his most endearing attraction; that and his ambition to be a tramp.)

'He puts the wind up the Jews,' explained Douglas, who was obviously destined for a grammar school, and who I seem to remember wearing what can only be described as a three-piece suit. 'So that they give him things.'

'How much do they give him?' demanded William, his black-leaded eyes shining.

'I dunno,' said Douglas, who hadn't really gone into it. 'Half a crown I suppose. Whatever he wants.'

William thought this was just about the most terrific idea he had ever come across. He couldn't wait to get down to the local Jewish shop, where he acted 'sinister' and asked for money. If I remember rightly, the man with the big nose told him to clear off.

I had twenty-three of these books, up to *William and the Evacuees*, not counting the one that fell into the chamber. I had my name down at Hodgson's Rooms at one time, in case any first editions of the later stories came up for sale, but I never heard anything.

'William' books cost three and sixpence (17½p) in hardback, bound in red cloth. The one that fell into the chamber dried to a hunting pink, but was readable and smelled only slightly. Towards the end of the war there was rumoured to be a transatlantic edition, starting off with *William Gets Laid*; illustrated, but not by Thomas Henry. I was never able to find this, although I asked at Boots. On their minimal sex lives: William himself had a thing going with a dark-haired piece called Joan, like me and Agatha Jennings. But Ginger, Henry, and certainly Douglas, were pre-pubertal.

And then, suddenly, there was a war.

This was not entirely unexpected, (except by the *Daily Express*), and was caused, primarily, by Adolf Hitler, at that time head of the Germans. You will remember that we had already had Bernard's Riff Wars in the Atlas

47

Mountains, and Aunty Flo's adventures in Spain; not to speak of the Italians invading the ancient land of The Lion of Judah, which I had traced.

There had been a crisis in 1938, when Bernard had been issued with a Mickey Mouse gas mask (because of his scrotum), at a time when everyone was singing 'The Sun Has Got Its Hat On' and looking out for Lobby Ludd.

NOTE: He (Lobby) was employed by the *News Chronicle*, a newspaper that was admired so much that it later had to close down. His job was to stroll along promenades and sunken gardens at seaside watering places; to loiter in front of floral clocks. People would approach him in the correct manner, holding a copy of the much admired newspaper, and saying out loud: 'You are Mr Lobby Ludd of the *News Chronicle*, and I claim my five pounds.' Which he would give them if he was, or call for a constable to take them away if he was not. I suppose some check was made to prevent relations following him around and making an easy living.

But back to the crisis. There was now a general awareness in the country. Newspapers were full of current affairs, prizes being given by the popular press to readers who could spell Czechoslovakia, with a special prize for anyone who knew where it was. We happened to be bound by a treaty to Poland, which until recently had been run by a pianist. When German soldiers attacked that country, on motorbikes with sidecars and in itchy-looking overcoats, wearing what looked like tins of Bournvita slung on their backs, Mr Chamberlain told them to stop it at once. Or else. As you probably know, they did not. So Mr Chamberlain went on the wireless, at a time normally reserved for Troise and his Mandoliers, to announce that 'A state of war' existed as from eleven o'clock that morning.

My father was waiting for me in his study, under the elk. Through the window I could see a small plane writing 'Bile

Beans' in smoke across the immense Lincolnshire sky. A little lower down, under a pussy willow, sat Sooty, looking sad. He knew.

'Nobody knows,' said my father, 'when this war will end.' I shifted in my white plimsolls, so called after Samuel Plimsoll, who had put a line around ships and saved many mariners' lives. I did not know why I had been summoned, why De Kuyper was at that moment packing my trunk; why my mother was being consoled in the front room by the Rev Eli Wannamaker.

Things had been a little fraught the evening before in the rhododendrons, with Bernard breaking cover, evading the chilly fingers of Agatha Jennings and leaping the fence to safety. (This was just after he had had the stitches out, and he made a small sound as he went through the air.) As I brushed down De Kuyper's cast-off pinny, which took the place of a white coat in my role as a Consultant, I had glanced up at my parents' bedroom window. I thought I had seen someone – the elk perhaps, or the smooth-shaven face of my father – but he made no reference to this now.

'You now have all the groundwork,' he went on, 'of a Christian Scholar.' He passed me a barley sugar and I relaxed a little, letting my thumbs hang away from the seams of my grey flannel shorts. 'Now it is time to put you into the hands of others,' he said. Our eyes met, for a short time, and I knew it had not been the elk at the window the evening before.

He turned back to his desk, and I saw a touch of silver in his auburn hair. 'I have here,' he said, picking up a sheet of embossed notepaper, 'a letter from the headmaster of Traggets, accepting you as a boarder for the autumn term, with special attention to woodwork and the Church of England.'

A bee buzzed. Bile Beans was spreading and fading in the pale blue sky. My eyes filled with tears. My father's old school! Where they all sat out in a field in long rows, the back rank standing and matron sitting in front with the dog.

'Who knows what will happen to us.' My father was speaking again, a barley sugar rattling against his teeth. He pointed through the window, across the privet hedge, towards the blueish hills. 'Maybe the Hun will overrun us. Maybe not. But I know this . . . ' and he turned his small eyes to me, reaching up to finger my ear before changing his mind. For a moment he seemed choked for words, the barley sugar appearing between his lips, sucked translucent like a tiny cake of Pears soap. Then he turned aside to lower the needle onto a record, already on the purple velvet of the turntable. Releasing the brake he raised a finger, and we stood, singing from the first word, father and son together. 'There'll Always Be An England!'

'Red, *white* and blue!' we sang, enunciating clearly, the barley sugar shooting from my father's mouth. 'What does it mean to you? Shout it out loud, you can be proud!' I marked time in my plimsolls, knees rising as my father's brogues tramped on the coconut matting. 'The Empire too, we can depend on you . . . !'

And so we sang, making one circuit of the room then marching down the hall. My mother slid the bolt on the door of the downstairs lavatory, but we caught De Kuyper in the kitchen and stood together, my knees still rising and falling, De Kuyper's contralto soaring above our bass and treble as we came to the last line . . . 'If England means as much to you, as England [pause, two, three, four, chanted my father] means to me!'

So I went away to school; and war came to England.

But it soon became obvious that this was not going to be quite so easy as the last one, when, as Uncle Frank used to sing, 'We Put The Kybosh On The Kaiser'. We knew now that it took about four years; that we were better than they were, especially when it came to a taste for cold steel; and of course many people went about saying that we had right on our side. But in many ways this war was going to be different. Technology, not least the motor car and the aeroplane, meant things would never be the same. (Though the only way to get a message, for example, to the station master at Welwyn Garden City, should you know him, from the footplate of The Flying Scotsman, was (is!) to wrap it round a lump of coal and hurl it through his window as you thundered past.)

The Government hurriedly started political education, for this was to be a 'People's War'. Everybody had to understand exactly who and what they were fighting against. And, just as importantly, what they were fighting *for*. No more oafish cannon fodder; no more blind obedience to calls to Duty, for King and Country; no more Jingoist 'My Country Right or Wrong'. *They had to be convinced politically!* The campaign therefore began, with songs like 'Heil Hitler, Yah, Yah, Yah, Oh What a Funny Little Man You Are'.

De Kuyper, singing the sequel to this ('I Heil' – rude noise – 'Heil' – rude noise – 'Right in the Führer's Face'), stuck brown paper over the windows of Jasmine Villa. My mother was of the opinion that it should have been in strips rather than sheets, but did not wish to argue at such a time.

My father formed a local unit of the LDV, forerunner of the Home Guard. ('Look, Duck and Vanish' the wags called it.) They wore armbands and leather spats and turned signposts the wrong way round.

Captain Drew offered the Pavilion De Luxe, during the daytime, as what the Americans would call a 'comfort station', and what today we would call a Leisure Centre. (Though of course such things, complete with wave machines and work simulators, were undreamed of in 1939.) The gold-sprayed basket of paper flowers was removed from the stage, and a placard set up informing people that walls had ears.

As I steamed away from the junction on that bright crisp morning, the elderberries trembled as the earth shook with the marching hordes in the east. Pomfret's brother threw over polished levers in his flower-bedecked signal box. The wooden letters that spelt out the name of our station had been removed by my father's men; but, as when people said, 'There are no flies on him,' you could see where they had been.

I looked, for what I thought could be the last time, at the scarlet Nestlé's chocolate machine; heard the roaring waters of the Adamsez urinals. De Kuyper waved from a porter's iron-wheeled trolley, her face pale in the shadow of the platform canopy.

There was (were?) no Bile Beans in the high blue sky, which further to the south was already filling with the high white traces, the lines of warfare, of The Battle of Britain, as I rattled away over the points, beneath a water-colour of Corfe Castle.

It was, we were later told, Our Finest Hour.

Chapter Four

My father's school – A surprise in the night – 'The Magician'
– The Phoney War – Enter Rufus Real – We meet a tramp
– The fall of France – The North African campaign – The
Yanks are coming – We salute the Russian bear – Home for
the holidays

Traggets, my father's school, was on the Isle of Avalon, once the site of Camelot, now called Glastonbury. It is where a sword called Excalibur was pulled from a stone by King Arthur, whose death was written about, in French, by a man called White. You probably know the story.

The school was divided into five houses: Lancelot's, Gawain's, and Merlin's, which were three bare-floored storeys of a concrete wing, and Arthur's, which was of course the main house and had a flag. Behind a hedge and thick chicken wire was Guinevere's, the girls' house, originally the house next door.

Boys at Traggets wore grey, with a badge of a red-silk embroidered table top. Girls also wore grey, without trousers, with a blue table top so that you could tell them apart. Every Sunday, headed and separated by Dr and Mrs Hazlit, he carrying the *Sunday Dispatch* with its Gothic title and distinctive splash of purple, we walked to the village church, feeling the acorns and filthy handkerchiefs in our pockets.

I was in Gawain's, my father's old house, in a corner bed beneath a barred window. Next to Tonto, who wore a custom-made ('bespoke' he called it) homburg hat. His real name was Broomhead, and the hat was tolerated because of the high standing and frequent visits of his father, who was, so everyone said, a big button maker. For many years he made rubber ones for my father's liberty bodices and, so I was told, brass fly buttons for The Brigade of Guards.

The two Broomheads wore their homburgs even on Open Day, when they took part in the Fathers' and Sons' Wheelbarrow Race. In my first year Tonto's mother and sister, ending months of quiet speculation, appeared in crimson felt with a pearl-buttoned band, a style recognisably descended from the homburg. This was the first occasion on which I heard the proverb 'Red hat, no drawers'.

Facing me in the dormitory was Wheelan, from just outside Bury St Edmunds. We rarely spoke. He had found a dried elephant's penis in his attic at home, and had brought it to school in his cricket bag. He never said where it came from or, to me at least, what his parents used it for. (Though we accepted at the time, as boys do, that like the elephant's foot it had been painlessly removed.) It was slung by wire underneath his bed, so the maids could not play with it; and on my first lonely night I held the stiff sheet below my eyes and watched the enormous shadow rise on the cream distempered wall.

Wheelan manipulated the elephant's organ by means of a string and a system of pulleys, very much like my own arrangement for raising Agatha Jennings in the banana crate. He could swing it out across the cold brown linoleum, like the barrel of a naval gun, tapping the grizzled foreskin on the end of your bed. (Which, as Bernard pointed out, was more than I could do at that time for Agatha Jennings.) It could have been a frightening thing for a boy of my age, but De Kuyper had prepared me for worse. As I have already said, Wheelan and I rarely spoke to each other; though looking back now, I suppose, the great swinging thing on a string, thumping on the black enamel, was an attempt at communication; possibly a cry for help.

I took Broomhead's advice and treated it with the contempt it deserved; though I noticed him watching through narrowed eyes from beneath the brim of his hat. There had been, I believe, in the term before I arrived, an attempt to organise parties from other dormitories at sixpence a head. Wheelan had offered to rig up a sheet and move the thing about in silhouette, wearing a hat. (The thing would wear the hat, that is, not Wheelan.) Chamfering, the Greek classical scholar, said it would be like Kariaghozi the shadow puppet, but Wheelan said it wouldn't, it would be like a prick with a hat on. As a kind of trailer, Wheelan had strapped the thing around his waist, in the manner of the lady in Sussex Gardens, and set off to tour the other dorms after prep. He intended just to poke it inside the door and shout 'What about that then?', but unfortunately, while wagging it, he overbalanced on the stairs and hurt his nose. It was cut off (his thing that is) just in time, before Matron arrived with the Germolene.

In charge of us at Traggets we had people called house masters. They wore cloaks made out of blackout material but not, at least in my time, tasselled mortar boards. While not really expecting Greyfriars or Red Circle School, I had expected a Quadrangle and a Remove, and a rich brownish boy in a jewelled turban. I have read 'George Orwell' (like Geraldo, a pseudonym) on this, and can only say that if he had visited Traggets he would have found plenty of lavatories.

Another absentee was Billy Bunter, which was probably just as well. I have had a lifelong horror of waking up one morning next to his sister, pink lips flecked with pastry, steel-rimmed spectacles smeared with confectioner's cream. It is often said that fat girls are more feminine, but I have never wished to find out.

Mr Beeston, 'The Magician', housemaster of course of

Merlin's, a sandy-haired man with a short tie, who lectured on alternate Mondays on 'Social Responsibility', used to say things like 'Never disregard the old or the ugly. They might not smell nice, but they will be grateful.' We had to write that down. He it was who cried out 'Red hat, no drawers!' when he saw Mrs Broomhead and her daughter. He had a fund of aphorisms, like Richelieu or Voltaire: such as 'They're all the same size lying down,' and 'Leave it in for five minutes after you've finished and they will be your slave for ever.' That one is almost certainly true, though women do tend to forget the things that you do for them.

Mr Croxton, who stared at you, and who sailed alone on summer evenings on the lake below the cricket pitch, until it dried up, was in charge of Lancelot's. I was once in the reeds, for a project on Moses, and heard him talking to himself. He was alone, a dark shape against the setting sun, wearing a cloak and a hat like Gladys Cooper. The small sail of the boat was furled as he floated on the trickle of sunlight across the water, and I was invisible, being up to my private parts in the bog, the basket having sunk. I have forgotten now what he said, but it was probably in Latin. Mr Croxton (Ralph, I discovered) joined the RAF, the 'Brylcreem Boys' as we called them, and when he got leave would return to the school to stare at us.

Mention of the fighting services brings me to the war, which you will remember was going on at the time. As I have told you it had started in the September of 1939, at eleven o'clock in the morning, against Germany.

At first nothing happened. Dr Hazlit had strengthened the outer perimeter and gave us speeches about filling up the walls with our English dead. There was much discussion about the propriety of dropping bombs on German factories; people pointing out that these were private property. Equally valid was the view of the French Government, which warned that if we hurt any Germans they were likely to retaliate.

Letters from home told me that Lincolnshire was ready. Yellowbellies, though slow to anger, manned the ramparts of Mablethorpe and Chapel St Leonards; Cleethorpes was an armed camp. Trucks rumbled through the night, moving floral clocks to a place of safety. A cryptic postscript from De Kuyper stressed that if London fell I was to make my way, travelling at night and speaking to no one, to a certain boarding house in Weston Super Mare; and to wait. I had my gas mask, my goggles, and a recognition chart of German aeroplanes in silhouette. I was ready; and in sober mood went home for a quiet Christmas.

I got a ventriloquist's doll called Charlie, in black-cotton evening dress and a monocle. His hair style was similar to the doll in Mossies' window and his hat was glued on, which was a disappointment. I sat him on my knee and put my hand up, but it didn't seem to work; like the Jews' harp which I had got the year before, and which had given me a swollen face. However, I persevered, and at one time could speak without moving my lips, though nobody could understand what I was saying. We saw in the New Year en famille: 'Farewell to the Thirties!' we cried as we lifted our glasses. Shortly after this Yasmin started advanced classes – and then the Germans cheated.

Everyone had expected that with the Siegfried and Maginot Lines facing each other, their great guns poking out of the concrete like Wheelan's thing, that the stage was set for an updated replay of the last war. This would have made sense, needing only the stringing of barbed wire, the digging of additional trenches, with spaces left in 'No Man's Land' on which to play impromptu games of football on Christmas day. But, with true Boche mentality, the Germans invaded *through Belgium* (my italics), neatly turning the flank of the poilu in their seamed helmets, riding about in little trains below ground. The war was on with a vengeance!

We brought back, at once, Winston Spencer Churchill, very probably the world's greatest man, who wore a hat like the Broomheads'. Here was a man who had ridden with the cavalry at Omdurman against the Mad Mahdi. (The same Mad Mahdi who had got General 'Chinese' Gordon halfway up the stairs at Khartoum.) He had been responsible for Gallipoli, where Aussies and New Zealanders, in turned-up hats, had battled with Johnny Turk between the sun-baked rocks. A Tory, and then a Liberal, and then a Tory again, (but never Labour), he had masterminded the attack on Tonypandy; and the assault on Peter the Painter in Sydney Street.

NOTE: He (Peter the Painter) was an anarchist, believing like the tramp Rufus and I met in the churchyard in 'Fuck all', if you will forgive the colloquialism. Winston Spencer Churchill was very much against this, which is why he led the Scots Guards, in their overcoats and sans busbies, into the East End of London. Wearing himself a top hat, he pointed around a corner at Peter the Painter's house and, after considerately telling the soldiers to lie down on *Evening Standard* placards, ordered them to open fire. I am pleased to be able to tell you that we won.

Painter in oils, writer and amateur bricklayer, cigar smoker, hat collector and populariser of the Siren Suit, (based on the combinations worn by the smallest of Lord Snooty's Pals), Winston Spencer Churchill was clearly the man for the job.

But at first things went badly. In fact we were rocked back on our heels. France fell; but by what people said was a miracle, an armada of small boats brought most of our lads back home. Though if you went mad on the beach at Dunkirk, while waiting for a boat, you were shot out of hand. Belgium, Holland, Norway, Lichtenstein, even little Andorra, all had gone the way of Poland and Czechoslavakia. We stood alone. The stage was set for The Battle of Britain.

As this is well known I shall not go on about it, but on the day that 158 black-painted warplanes thudded into the rich earth of The Garden of England, I met a man who was to play a not unimportant role in my life.

He was twelve at the time, and his name was Rufus Real. It was pronounced in the French way and they came over with the Normans. (Like the Huguenots, they are of course completely assimilated now.) They had a house in London (the Reals that is) and one in the country, not far from the Nabisco factory, where Shredded Wheat is made. Rufus's school near Canterbury had been bombed and he moved into the bed next to the awful Wheelan, and severed the string with nail clippers on his first night. The elephant's thing lay on the lino, though it did not shrink, and we heard Wheelan sobbing in the darkness.

Rufus dressed like Lord Snooty; but Dr Hazlit, whilst appreciative of the cachet that Rufus gave to the school, drew the line at the top hat. One homburg, I suppose, was enough. So Rufus wore a cap with puce and yellow rings, like William Brown and the rest of us, which went well with his swallow-tailed coat but gave him a faintly Jewish appearance.

Hampers came for him regularly, in a car like my grandmother's, along with (pace Billy Bunter) postal orders for vast amounts. We held dorm feasts, with Peabody serving canapés and jellies, and rabbit-shaped blancmange. For Rufus had been sternly told by his father, a Colonel and classical scholar (sic!) who had an important job steaming open other people's letters, that this (as I have told you) was to be a People's War.

NOTE: Peabody, Rufus's manservant, who was not allowed to sleep with us, was, like most of his kind, faithful unto death; or at least until he was taken, tears in his eyes, into the Royal Army Pay Corps. This was a crack regiment, Rufus told him, that included among its officers – mess jacketed and suave as they swung their ladies to the lilting music of Strauss, the regimental silver glittering under the chandelier – none other than the man who, in a black beret with two cap badges, and from a distance, looked like Bernard Montgomery.

Rufus had quite clear-cut ideas as to what he wanted to do in later life. On his sixteenth birthday (assuming the Germans had left Paris) he was to be taken to the French capital and deflowered by a friend of his father's on the Rue Mazarin. Then, if he was good, he was to have his first bicycle. At seventeen he was to enter either his father's old regiment or college, depending on whether the war was over. At twenty-one, along with a big cardboard key (and if his father had fallen in battle, which seemed unlikely in view of his job), he would enter into his inheritance. Become as they say 'monarch of all he surveyed'. In fact he showed me his notebook in which his plans were carefully laid.

Rufus and I were fast friends, roaming the West Country together, sometimes going as far afield as Shepton Mallet. But perhaps we were happiest in some small country churchyard, in the long grass by weatherbeaten tombstones, masturbating or urinating on fireflies. This was a practice unknown to us (I speak of masturbation, not urinating on fireflies) until Mr Beeston introduced it one Monday morning. He had promised us something new, and had a coloured chart and a working model. He told us all about going blind and having to sell matches, and about hair growing in the palms of our hands. At playtime he watched us scatter, heedless of the milk or the hairy handshakes, to the four corners of the campus to find out.

It was in one particular churchyard that we met a tramp. Just as William did every day, and Pip in Charles Dickens – though ours did not frighten us. (Incidentally, Finlay Currie was by far the best Magwitch; and as for Jean Simmons as the young Estelle . . . !! I sigh as I write, but remember Mr Beeston's warning.)

We looked with awe at the tramp, keeping a respectful distance as The Outlaws would have done, as he sat on the wing of a sleeping angel chewing a straw.

'You're absolutely free!' exclaimed Rufus, his eyes shining. 'No work, no school, no home, no responsibilities!'

'Fuck all,' said the tramp, like Peter the Painter might have done.

We exchanged glances. It was a word we knew, but had never heard out loud, in the open air, from the wing of a sleeping angel. 'Say some more,' said Rufus.

'Bugger,' said the tramp, tentatively, but we had heard that one.

'You just lay out and sleep on the ground, do you?' asked Rufus. 'No baths every morning and washing behind your ears?'

'Or cleaning your teeth,' I put in, 'or having your hair cut.'

'And for a bog you just go behind a tree?' Rufus's voice was on the point of breaking and threatened to do so right now.

The tramp smirked with pride, the straw drooping.

'Dirty bastard!' we both shouted together, and went off to fetch a policeman; though Rufus was in favour of kicking him and seeing what he'd got in his handkerchief. As he said to me later, quoting from that year's school play, it reminded one of the worst excesses of the French Revolution.

It was in yet another churchyard, where we had gone to see who could piss the highest up against the tomb of the Watchett family, that we met Lilian Heath, a Somerset Agatha Jennings. We had just put them away when she stood up from behind the grass cuttings and asked if we wanted to play. I said I would be very pleased to, and Rufus said he would watch. She was big for her age (which was more than you could say for Rufus) but I must say, to use one of my mother's expressions, as common as muck.

All this was idyllic in a way, but we were aware of the war still going on.

The Germans now had almost the whole of Europe, except Great Britain of course. The Nazi flag flew from the

Eiffel tower, and Adolf Hitler, in person, came to Paris for a victory parade. One can only speculate as to the fate of the lady on the Rue Mazarin.

Perhaps at this point we should say a few words about the Germans, and what the war was all about.

I think it is generally accepted now that it was the Germans' fault. As I have already mentioned they had done it before, in 1914, and before that in 1870 against the French, when all the animals in the Paris zoo were fricasseed and done in sauce.

They are an odd race, singing loudly and drinking beer with hinged lids on. God knows what they are afraid of getting in it. A kind of Hansel and Gretel country of forests and old-fashioned houses, they have produced well-known people like Beethoven, the deaf composer whose white head can be found on many pianos. There was also Martin Luther, after whom the black man in America was named, who nailed up his 'credo' or message, something to do with religion, on a church door.

They wore spiked helmets, 'pickelhaubes', and waxed moustaches. Not the women and children of course, but certainly the Prussians and the Junkers. It was often said that British troops led by German officers would be an unbeatable combination; though nobody as far as I know ever tried it. They had at one time bits of Africa (see 'The African Queen' with H. Bogart), but really were after any country they could get: maintaining that they needed the extra room.

In the early Nineteen Twenties – when you needed a wheelbarrow full of German money to buy a newspaper, in order to read all about inflation – Adolf Hitler, a house-painter who was said to chew carpets, had written a book called *Mein Kampf*. I have not actually read this, but its theme was that most problems were the fault of the Jews.

The Germans read the book, and they agreed with most of A. Hitler's ideas. On the question of Jews they divided, in the main, into three groups. Those that went about, like

William Brown, 'leaning' on Jews; those that didn't know any Jews; and German Jews, who were predictably against the whole thing. There had been a fourth group, but these were locked up or dead. Most people liked the new uniforms A. Hitler designed, and the flags he put everywhere. He introduced a new salute and drove around giving it, in a car that would not have looked out of place outside Kate Meyrick's. His friends included Herman Goering, a fat man with medals who had his own car; and Goebbels, a little man with a bad foot, who was generally acknowledged to be a good family man, until he shot them.

The people who followed A. Hitler were called, by Mr Churchill, 'Narzis'. Benito Mussolini in Italy, who was also fat, with medals, but with a bigger chin, was one; and so was General Franco in Spain. (Remember when I was very young and confused him with Vimto?)

So there were Rufus and I, sporting with Lilian Heath in the green and rolling countryside around Shepton Mallet, while Europe lay in darkness; ('The lights are going out' . . . remember?) and the war moved to the sunny wastes of North Africa.

Mr Pelham, who played the ukelele, the first person I ever saw in leatherette elbow patches, pulled down the map, the colour of eggy porridge, and tapped the Atlas Mountains with his stick. 'Here,' he said, 'the fate of our civilisation will be decided.' He found Mersa Matrūh. 'The forces of the German beast, the Anti-Christ, the baby killer and violator of decent women, are locked in combat with the ordinary British Tommy.' He let the words sink in.

'The battle for North Africa is vital,' exclaimed Mr Pelham, now prodding the island of Malta and raising his voice, so that Rufus and I (and Outhwaite, who had to sit by himself) could hear at the back of the room. Mr Pelham had a moustache like Ronald Coleman, if not the wardrobe, and it was said that he cleaned his teeth after his morning milk, and if anyone gave him a sweet.

'This is Cairo, the capital of the wogs,' he cried, poking

the map with unerring aim. 'If Rommel gets the Sphinx and the Pyramids, where are we?'

We all realised that it was rhetoric, except for Rufus, carried away by the inspired teaching. 'In the shit, sir!' he cried, standing up and sitting down.

'Exactly!' said Mr Pelham, with several slow and heavy nods. The tip of the stick began to move south east, as those of us who were taking map reading realised. 'First Cairo, and then Alexandria. The Suez Canal is cut! The Hun is down the Red Sea and amok in the Indian Ocean . . . the very lifeline to India is threatened!' It was playtime then, and he had to stop, but we could see how serious it was.

Actually Rommel (the man in charge in North Africa, a decent German who was later allowed to shoot himself) was not permitted to run amok in the Indian Ocean. Montgomery, or someone who looked very much like him, halted his advance at El Alamein. He attacked in the early morning, before breakfast; the kind of thing, one has to say, that the Mad Mahdi would have done. British Tommies in khaki shorts, bayonets fixed, advanced across the sands under the pitiless sun; accompanied again by Aussies and New Zealanders in turned-up hats. Sons of those who had fought Johnny Turk, they had with them units of the (English-officered) Indian army, playing bagpipes and riding horses, who of course didn't mind the sand.

Mrs Hazlit celebrated our first major victory with a special cake; sand coloured, topped by marzipan barbed wire strung with blotting-paper German corpses. A good effort, like the ruins of Cologne in royal icing, but certainly not up to De Kuyper's standard.

But where were the French when all this was going on? You might well ask. What about the French navy – irrespective of the state of their toilets? Sunk, I'm afraid, and some of them by us. But many Frenchmen fought back, organising 'the underground'. This was, predictably, run from restaurants, off-duty German officers eating sauce-drenched food, perhaps listening to a French Alice Faye, while upstairs Le Resistance listened to the World Service of the BBC.

Then – and this was a welcome surprise – the Americans joined in; and on our side.

This came about because the Japanese bombed the American naval base at Pearl Harbour. (In Honolulu, where they wear grass skirts and play guitars flat across their knees.)

It was a total disaster. (For the Americans that is.) The Japanese came out of the rising sun, early in the morning; in the style of the Mad Mahdi and Bernard Montgomery. The grey battleships lay at anchor, totally unprotected, their crews still ashore in pork-pie hats and bell bottoms, tap dancing on the bollards like Gene Kelly and Dan Dailey. But at least it gave us an ally.

We then got another ally when A. Hitler attacked Russia. (Otherwise known as the Soviet Union.) This is where, since 1917, they have had a system called Communism, as advocated by the man who washed out Pomfrets' churns. Very good in theory, (something like Christianity really), it is rather different in practice.

When I boarded the train at Castle Carey, going home for the long holidays of 1941, we were no longer alone. 'Up we go, into the wild blue yonder . . . ' sang the American Army Air Corps. 'From the halls of Montezumah, to the shores of Tripolee . . . ' thundered the American marines. While a thousand miles east of Ramsgate, Russians set fire to towns and villages in the path of the advancing German army. Which they could well afford to do, seeing that there was no such thing as private property.

Chapter Five

Home for the hols – Agatha Jennings again – I lose my mother – A military gentleman – An emotional scene with my father – Out to get Pickersgill – Vignette at the sewage farm – The fall of Singapore – The Home Front – Earth-shattering news

I was growing up. I realised that as I walked home from the station that hot July day in 1941. Kitbag on my shoulder, I wore my cadet uniform, with highly polished boots, and what was called a 'forage' cap; a hat in the shape of an upturned boat that was held on my brilliantined head by my right ear. I had discovered on the train, having nothing to read, that it was possible to open out the many folds of the hat and fasten it with a press stud below my chin. It was warm and comforting, though the world around was muted.

I was thirteen, but felt that I was an educated, sophisticated 'man of the world'. In comparison with those I saw as I rounded the corner of the Railway Hotel, I was a veritable Jack Buchanan. They were lounging, (as to be fair I had once lounged), against Mossies' window, which was masked by brown paper to protect the celluloid doll from bomb blast.

Thinking a whiff of the military would do them good I marched across the square, as if ordered forward as 'right marker'; hoping that the whitened stripe (awarded because of my Rechabite background) could be clearly seen. As I reached the pavement, stamping to a halt and standing at ease, I saw with a quick glance that nothing in Mossies' window had changed. The doll lay on her back with the dead flies, on the sun-bleached paper, showing her green hand-knitted knickers. The revolving iron spikes which the far-seeing Victorians had built into the window sill had been removed, by an agent of Lord Beaverbrook, and my contemporaries sat in a row; sandals, plimsolls and scabby knees. Among them was Agatha Jennings, who had gone red in the face. There was Bernard, with a bag of sherbet, and two boys we had not spoken to in my time. Sitting close to Agatha Jennings was Pickersgill, whom many mothers had complained about, and who had been sent home early the year before from the Sunshine Holiday Home near Clacton.

Their eyes were upon me and their mouths moved, and for an unpleasant moment I thought they were mocking me, until I unfastened the earflaps of the hat. 'Hello,' I said, hearing the Co-op van go past, wishing I had been allowed to bring home my gun.

'You're in the army!' said Agatha, impressed.

'No,' I said with a deprecating smile, stamping my boots so that the lead weights in my trousers hung nicely over my gaiters, and nodding to them all, even Pickersgill. 'Not exactly. We are certainly up against it, but the old country is not in such a bad way that they have started to call up boys of my age; albeit fit and ready to do their duty for King and Country.' Or something like that. I know I then gave a light laugh.

' 'E's in a reformatry,' said Pickersgill. 'That's 'is yewniform. 'E's bin sent away!'

'No, he's not,' said Agatha, wriggling away from him and showing the same kind of knickers as the doll. 'He's at a school.'

'A *special* school,' said Bernard, who hadn't yet bothered to say hello. He sucked a yellowed finger, which drew his eyes together as he stared at me.

'That's wot I ment,' explained Pickersgill. 'Sent away to a special school!'

'He's got patent boots,' said one of the two I didn't talk to.

'A prep school,' I said, ignoring him and keeping remarkably calm, 'in the west country.'

Pickersgill leered into Agatha's face and then tittered to the others. 'Wot country's that?' he said.

'Where d'you get the patent boots?' asked the unspeakable. 'I never seen 'em in the shoe shop.'

'What's prep?' asked Agatha.

'It's what most people do every evening,' I said. 'Instead of looking into Mossies' window.' I thought that was rather good. I then refolded my hat and picked up my kitbag, wishing I knew what had happened to Bernard, and walked away.

Having nothing better to do I suppose, they followed me, past the horse trough and into the London Road. Pickersgill close behind kicking a stone, then Bernard and Agatha in silence. I ignored them of course, saying 'Good evening' to several people, some of whom answered. I moved the kitbag, full of woodwork and laundry, to the other shoulder.

'What have you got in your sack, Jeffrey?' called Agatha.

'Prep,' I heard Pickersgill say. 'It's full of fucking prep, innit?'

'How are you, sir?' I called across the road to the Rev Eli Wannamaker. I waved to people in their gardens 'Digging for Victory', and determined to have it out with Agatha Jennings as soon as I could. As I reached Jasmine Villa, closing the gate, which was mercifully still there, a tepid cow pat wrapped itself around the back of my neck. In some cultures (though I did not know this at the time) this is considered to be a folk medicine. Telling myself that it must have been thrown by Pickersgill, and of course wiping it off, I climbed the steps through the rhododendrons.

At the doorway I turned and looked out at the blueish hills. The hobbledehoys who had followed me home were out of sight in the road below. There was the scent of cut grass and the more pungent smell of lemon cheese from the kitchen; then De Kuyper came around the corner of the house, and told me my father was in his study with Miss Parkinson. She made a face that said it all.

Tea was over and everyone had admired the stool, saying how useful it would be when it was finished. My school report had been read and put on one side for framing; and my father, having mopped up the last of the salad cream, had taken his stick from the elephant's foot and gone out. I was coming downstairs, having changed out of my uniform, when a thought struck me. As the green-baize door was open (and that was significant in itself) I called down the passage. 'I say . . . De Kuyper . . . where's my mother?'

She appeared in the doorway (De Kuyper that is), sucking a wooden spoon. (You will know what I mean when I say that she had a generous mouth.) 'I thought you'd ask,' she said.

Following her into the kitchen I declined, for the moment, to lick out the basin. De Kuyper stood at the New Improved gas stove, her back towards me. There was obviously something going on. Something had happened, and I had a feeling that it concerned my mother. But what foolishness! I tried to laugh away my fears and De Kuyper turned round to see what I was doing.

'Tell me,' I said. 'Please. I want to know.' There was, possibly, a hint of panic in my voice.

De Kuyper smoothed down her pinny, choosing her words carefully. 'Saturday,' she said, 'soon as she'd finished her tea.' I nodded. I understood, and felt in my pocket for a handkerchief.

'Did she . . . did she say anything? Before she went?' My conkers fell to the floor as I drew forth the handkerchief.

'Not to me she didn't.' De Kuyper's eyes held mine. She was with me, as she had always been; now willing me on and over the first big hurdle in my life.

I held back my tears, swallowing my disappointment at there not being a note left for me, a few words on her scented paper; or some money. 'Where is she?' I asked. 'I'd like to go and visit her.'

De Kuyper had turned back to the stove; opening the oven door she stared inside, like they used to do in Accrington. 'She didn't go far,' she said, her voice resonant. 'Number 17.' In the silence that followed a bubble rose to the surface of the lemon cheese and burst with an audible 'plop!'

The next morning I rested, playing with my things; so that it was after lunch before I walked down the road, past Bernard's house – which I tried not to look at – to Number 17.

My mother was sitting in the garden between two gnomes. Another gnome, wearing spectacles, was fishing behind her. A black prayer book lay in her lap, the place marked by a bus ticket; and she was fast asleep with her mouth open. Though you could see where they had been, there was no gate or railing to the house. Silent in my plimsolls, I walked up the path and stood for a moment, looking at the woman through whom I had entered the world. She appeared quite content and relaxed, and I noticed a bag of jelly babies on the grass below her chair. A fly moved across her cheek to the first hairs of her moustache. As it touched the painted rim of her mouth her lips pursed and twitched and the fly flew away.

Thoughts and emotions tumbled through my head. William Brown would have known what to do. He would have sold her to the Bon Marché, as the latest thing in breathing and scented dummies; or hung a placard reading 'Peny for the Guy' from her pearls and stood beside her holding out his cap. I tiptoed away through the roses and onto the road.

I found De Kuyper in her part of the garden, shelling peas. They rolled into the starched white hollow of her lap, the green reminding me of Agatha Jennings's new knickers. I had only just entered into them, but I knew that the teenage years were going to prove difficult.

'See her?' asked the rock to which I now clung, slipping a pea into her mouth, knowing I would say nothing. I nodded, sitting down on the grass beside her. 'With the gnomes,' I said. 'And a prayer book.'

'Always remember her that way,' said De Kuyper.

The sun was warm and I lay back and joined her in a pea, watching small wisps of cloud drift across towards Nottinghamshire. Henry Hall was playing softly inside the house. 'De Kuyper,' I said, 'I'd like to know all about it.'

She glanced at me quickly. '*All?*' she asked, with heavy emphasis.

I got up and walked away through the garden, afraid to hear her voice behind me, out of the back gate and down to the rubbish tip. Bernard was not there. I threw stones at a rat and tried to come to terms with the fact that my mother had left me, without leaving so much as a note; not even a pound note. Then a stone hit me on the side of the head, and for a moment I thought that the rats were throwing them back; but then saw one of Pickersgill's minions scramble up the far side of the quarry. It was silent again and I was alone with my thoughts, and the smell.

I knew of course about broken homes. It would be no great novelty at school, but would it be held against me in the Common Entrance Exam? My mind, as you can imagine, reeled. What would be the effect on my father? And Yasmin; how would she take it? Problems tumbled through my mind. Had someone had the presence of mind to cancel *Women's Realm*? I walked slowly back home, bending low beneath the privet as I passed the back gate of Number 17 and catching, for a moment, a fragment of tango music.

De Kuyper stood up as I entered the garden, the peas cascading from her pinny into the colander. In silence we put the pods into Sooty's dish and went into the kitchen. I sat on the draining board swinging my legs, watching her prepare a rhubarb pie, a favourite of my father's, deftly pressing pastry into the long narrow baking dish.

'When you want to know something,' she said, without looking at me, 'you'll ask.'

'Please!' I said, in a low voice, after a long moment's silence.

De Kuyper cleared her throat; she had obviously given it some thought. 'Men and women,' she began, 'cannot be understood by children. Do you understand?' I nodded. 'Your mother's gone to live with Colonel Trewin at Number 17, and I shouldn't think she's coming back. All right?'

I shook my head dumbly, starting to redden where the cow pat had landed. *'Live with'?* It was the rudest thing De Kuyper had ever said; worse than the little book with the diagrams that the Rev Eli Wannamaker had left for me in a sealed brown envelope.

Wiping her hands De Kuyper sat down on her commode, one of a matching pair that my mother had bought for her and Uncle Frank in happier days. She had spread some thick slices of Hovis with the crust of the day's lemon cheese (what she called the 'premier cru') and now passed one across to me. 'Now,' she said, 'listen to me.' I stared miserably out of the window, watching Bernard dressed as a Riff pass in a crouching walk behind the privet, as she told me the facts of life.

'Your father is a petit bourgeois,' she began. I stared at her defiantly, tight lipped, but then had to open my mouth to take a bite of the bread. I had not known that.

'He is what we call "One of them",' she went on. 'And you'll probably turn out to be one as well. Okay?' I nodded. She started to rock the commode, something that the makers specifically warn against on a label on the bottom. 'Your sister, not to put too fine a point on it, is no better than she should be.' She bit into the lemon cheese and brown bread with enjoyment, chewing for a moment. 'Your Uncle Frank's dead, and your Aunty Florence is in New Zealand.' There was a pause while she considered the rest of the family. 'And you know I've never been all that keen on the animal.' We looked out together through the open door, to where Sooty was nosing the pea pods.

'And that sums up my family,' she said in a flat voice. There seemed nothing I could usefully add so I waited for her to go on.

'I can't stand that Queen Mary,' she said suddenly, the commode creaking as she rocked even faster. 'Those hats! And I despise bourgeois democracy! Despise it! Do you understand?'

To slow down the galloping commode and prevent a nasty accident, and because I was alarmed at her vehemence, I agreed. I nodded vigorously, saying that bourgeois democracy was something I just couldn't stand, never could, as she well knew. The commode slowed, but she was silent now as if regretting the outburst, staring straight ahead at the Biro calendar, at the girl with the wooden spoon.

I wandered through the empty house and out into the front garden, through pools of sunlight and the shadows of flowers, standing in the rhododenrons and thinking back to so many childhood games. I would have given a lot just then to be holding Mrs Dooley's bean bags. Walking sadly down the steps I swung to and fro on the gate, thinking of Lord Beaverbrook's carts piled high with wrought iron.

We didn't notice each other until Bernard was almost upon me, and then it was too late for him to avoid the encounter, though I saw his eyes move shiftily from side to side. Maintaining the proud hauteur of a Riff chieftain he bent over, pretending he had to suddenly roll down his wellingtons. I swung slowly on the gate, feeling the tip of the central spike with my finger.

'How's your scrotum?' I asked.

'All right,' said Bernard, straightening up. 'How's yours?'

We walked up the road, cutting into the fields by

unspoken agreement to avoid passing Number 17. 'Who threw the cow shit?' I asked. 'Wasn't you, was it?'

'No,' said Bernard, and I believed him. 'Her.'

We were silent until we came to The Drain, a Lincolnshire river, across which in those days the local constabulary pushed the suicides with a long pole, so that they would be found and processed in the Soke of Peterborough. We had a den there, in which we had once acted out Rider Haggard. Sitting in the long grass we finished off Bernard's bag of sherbet and he, who had once been *She*, wanted to know about Traggets.

'It's a school,' I said, 'an ordinary public school, only we sleep there because it's too far to come home at night.'

Why didn't we have a charabanc, he enquired, like the open-air school?; and did we dress up like Lord Snooty? No, I told him, we did not. Most of us didn't anyway. And no, there were no infant Maharajahs or boys with X-ray eyes in my class; no teachers like Rockfist Rogan in a tight vest, or boys like Billy Bunter. Certainly no girls like his sister.

How far was it, he wanted to know, to the west country? Was there an east country? What did I mean that it had been my father's school? Was I now stuck up? Did I now think I was better than he was?

I told him straight. Yes, I did. I always had done. In fact everyone thought they were better than anyone else, though it wasn't true. Some were, and some weren't. Then, finally, did I think that I had been sent away to school so that I wouldn't find out about you-know-what?

'What do you mean, you-know-what?'

'Your mum and the Colonel.' And he moved his yellow fingers in a suggestive fashion.

I had him down in the mud, doing unarmed combat on him, when I felt the sting of a malacca cane on the seat of my herringbone trousers, a hand on my collar and heard a sharp military voice in my ear. 'Stop it, you two! D'you hear me?'

I was pulled away, still kicking and gouging in the approved fashion. Bernard, tucking in his shirt, scrambled up the bank of The Drain and ran towards the flat horizon. At a safe distance he halted for breath, silhouetted against the immense sky. The mud that I had been so furiously stuffing in dribbled from his open flies.

'What's it all about then, eh? You young ruffians. Both working class, are you?'

I rolled over and looked up the broad purple nose of Colonel Trewin, DSO with bar. His moustache, ginger and more pronounced than my mother's, wafted in his heavy breathing. His beetling brows blotted out the sun and there was the smell of curry, made the English way with apples and sultanas, on his breath. He was dressed in the fashion of the gentlemen farmers who chased Korky the Cat.

'No, sir,' I said, 'I'm a prep-school boy.'

He released me at once, planted his shooting stick into the ground and sat down. 'Then I'm surprised to see you brawling on the ground,' he said. 'Boys of your class ought to have the gloves on. Or épées or sabres, with your hand on your hip. Eh? Always assuming your opponent is from a decent family.'

'He made accusations against my mother, sir,' I said.

'Did he, by God! You should have kicked him straight in his Mahatma Gandhis!'

'Yes, sir.' I stood up. Mr Beeston had told us about the Mahatma Gandhis. The Colonel looked me over with an appraising eye.

'Your mater's been having a bit of an extra feed on the side, has she? And that young bounder blew the whistle on her, eh?' He felt in his tweed pocket for a mint, which he looked at for a moment then fed to a horse, which had come to the edge of the next field to watch the excitement. 'What . . . er . . . what kind of a woman is your mother. Eh?'

'She's a lady, sir.'

'Eh? Yes, of course. I meant . . . is she a looker? You

75

know . . . what's her hair like, and her gams? Blonde is she? Tall?' His china-blue eyes came out towards me as if on wires, like those of Yasmin's old doll. He held large clawed hands in front of his chest. 'Big in the titty line, is she?' The Colonel's tongue, veined with blue worms, licked right around his lips.

'I once heard my father say that her and . . . ' I corrected myself, '*she* and Miss Parkinson were the only people who should never wear a liberty bodice. He said it was a crime.' I felt that it was incumbent upon me to defend my family.

'Did he?' said the Colonel, smiling at me. 'He said that did he? And who's Miss Parkinson, eh?'

'She's a friend of my father's,' I said. 'She . . . ' I remembered Sooty's tongue lolling further and further out of his mouth that day in the apple tree. 'She plays with him,' I said, feeling a bit of a fool. That was not quite the right word.

'Does she, begod,' said the Colonel, and I noted a trace of the Protestant ascendancy. 'Live around here, do you?'

'Yes, sir,' I said, nodding across the fields. 'Just over there.'

'And where's your father now then, eh? Eighth Army is he? With old Monty? Indian Army, eh? Or prisoner of war? Or dead?' he finished hopefully.

'No, sir,' I said. 'He's reserved. He's a leading manufacturer.'

'Manufacturer, eh?' And I didn't care for the way he said it. 'Of what?'

'Ladies clothes, sir.' The Colonel cupped a hand to his ear and leaned forward. 'LADIES CLOTHES!' I shouted, startling the horse which rolled its eyes. Then, as always, I had to swallow before I could utter the six syllables. 'Liberty bodices.'

The Colonel's face froze in a half smile, his cupped hand sliding slowly down his florid cheek. A little bit of the mint dropped from the horse's mouth.

'What do you call your mother?'

'Mum, sometimes,' I said, not looking at him.

He stood up, folding the shooting stick. 'Gloria,' he said. 'That your mother's name?'

'Mrs Cork!' I said, defiantly, starting to redden round the neck. There was a pause while we faced each other. So this was him. The one who had what she had left my father for. Would he now drop to his knees in the mud . . . arms open, head on one side, 'When there are grey skies, I don't mind the grey skies, I'll make them blue, Sonny Boy . . . ' that would be my cue to climb onto his knee, look up his nose . . .

'Away at school are you?' He walked away, helping the horse to find the bit of mint in the long grass.

'Yes,' I said, something in his manner making me drop the 'sir'. He started back along the path; his stout brogues, glowing with bull's blood, leaving an indented address in Jermyn Street in the soft ground. He seemed to know that I was following.

'Do English at school, do you?' he called over his shoulder.

'Yes.'

'Old English? Anglo Saxon? Chaucer and that stuff?'

'Yes,' I said. 'We go right up to Dickens.'

We had reached the road now and I caught him up as he waited for the dustcart to pass. The horse turned to look at him from between its leather blinkers, brasses clinking and glittering in the sun, great feathered feet following in Lucille's footsteps. 'Then you'll understand what I mean,' the Colonel said, quite civilly, 'when I say fuck off! I'll put my boot up your arse if I ever see you down this end of the road again.' He strode away, lifting his cap to the postwoman, and I saw through the window of Number 17 my mother, in a blue and white polka-dot dress, dancing with a long-stemmed glass in her hand.

I walked back home, that much older and wiser, with from then on a revised attitude towards the military man. Not to speak of tango music.

So, as the shadows lengthened on the first full day of my holidays, I sat in my room and watched Bernard go in and out of his pathetic attempt at a Beduin tent; noting sardonically the washing his mother had hung out, and making a mental note to tell him again about the milkman. Indeed, I called him up on the cocoa tin, but was unable to get through; there being of course no extension in the tent.

I was still at the window, the chief Riff having gone in for his tea, when my father arrived home from work. Unobserved, I watched him close the gate, and then his hat move through the rhododendrons, his shoes reflecting the last rays of the sun as he climbed the path. Gas mask on his hip, in pale brown Rexine edged with blue, tightly-rolled newspaper in his hand – which he had been taught how to use if confronted by a German paratrooper – I suddenly felt how alone he was. When all was said and done, what had he got to come home to?

In a flash I was off the window seat and out of the door. Sliding down the bannisters, zipping round the bend by the nude lady, leaping off nimbly backwards at the fourth stair so that the pineapple finial only brushed my scrotum, I was running across the hall, my arms open, as my father reached the doorway. The sun, in a last blaze of glory before dipping behind the blueish hills, irradiated his head in a halo of golden light. Reaching for him, I launched myself forward from the lino, aching to feel his arms hold me, the bristle of his cheek, the smell of his breath, and the witch hazel he bathed his eyes in to stay awake in the afternoons.

'Daddy!' I cried; then, louder, 'DADDY!'

Quickness of thought and speed of reflex have, we are told, saved nations; and my father proved his mettle now. In a flash his stick, which now had a luminous stripe and a mustard-gas detector fixed to the handle, was raised to the horizontal and I was trapped. Pinned like a butterfly against the ferrule, flailing my puny limbs, still sobbing and calling out but at a safe distance.

So we stood until I had quietened down, and De Kuyper had hurried from the kitchen to splash cold water in my face. My father pushing me steadily backwards with the stick, closing the front door behind him and reaching with his free hand to pull across the curtain on the hall window, until I was sitting on the little monk's carved seat.

'That was a close thing,' De Kuyper said, her face white in the shadows. 'Whatever came over you?'

'I wanted to see my daddy,' I said, trying to ease the stick away from my chest so that it could heave convulsively. 'I wanted to say hello.'

De Kuyper and I watched my father as he breathed through his nose. A small muscle twitched in his cheek. The house was silent, the only sound that of Sooty drinking from the commode.

'Hello,' muttered my father, his eyes on his shoes, which were now dark, and went to wash his hands.

The next morning I bought a bag of sherbet and took it into Bernard's tent. He was seated cross-legged, eating the nearest he could get to typical Riff food, and waved me to a cushion beside him. He said I had just missed his mother (who indulged him) doing a dance and playing the finger cymbals. Nothing was said, then or later, of the events of the previous day.

'What about Agatha?' he asked, after some discussion about the war, and how the Riffs were doing at the moment. I was silent, having as you will understand mixed feelings.

'She is . . . she was . . . my fiancée,' I said at last, watching the shadow of a black and rampant bull on the sunlit canvas of the tent. This turned out to be Sooty, attracted by the Riff food.

'She threw the cow shit at you,' Bernard reminded me.

I nodded. 'So what about Pickersgill?' he went on. 'You going to get him?'

I thought about it. Pickersgill was thin and wiry and almost as tall as I was. But I knew that he smoked string, and ate apples late at night; already the tell-tale marks of debauchery were beginning to appear on his face. Whereas I was well built and hard muscled for my age. Relatively clean living and the spartan regime of Traggets – and the fact that I had never set foot inside a public house – meant that I was at the time a first-class specimen of English boyhood. I was, and I say this in no boastful fashion, expert at single stick and the lightweight pike; being able to steer a bicycle with my knees, while firing a catapult or whirling a gaucho's bolas. I had also done PT. In short, I could take care of myself; and my enemy was not only lumpen, and unhealthy, but also two years younger than me.

We set off after lunch, carrying haversack rations, and our first hunch led us directly to them. From the long grass of the sewage farm, keeping out of sight of the soldiers guarding it, we looked down into the hollow behind the pumping station in which the lovers had set up home. Bernard nudged me as Agatha Jennings came into view, pegging out a vest on a string tied to an elderberry bush. She had her hair in toy curlers, covered by a handkerchief tied beneath her chin, and the pockets of her pinny were knobbly with clothes pegs.

I borrowed Bernard's telescope, given to him by his mother in order to see the Atlas Mountains, and brought my late love's face into full focus. She stared at me, unseeing, close enough to touch, as she pretended to shake the dust from a doormat. Her full lips were reddened with cachous from Mossies, and a Mickey Mouse cigarette hung from the corner of her mouth. On her feet were carpet slippers, a circlet of pink fur around her lisle ankles.

She retired within the elderberry bush, having looked

up and down the street to see if the milkman was coming, and at once Pickersgill appeared, like a weatherman at the opposite end of the pivot. He had taken off his pullover and wore garters on his arms, like the pianist in a western saloon. He stood, poor thin face turned up to the sun, pulling his braces forward with his thumbs and making his trousers rise above the tops of his boots. No doubt the two unspeakables would be arriving at any moment, to play the parts of Rent Man and Tally Man, or the sons coming home for Sunday dinner. Or indeed the bailiffs in bowler hats, come to put them into the street.

Lowering the telescope I turned to look into Bernard's face. Without a word we lay down on our backs and stared at the sky. Bernard sucked a blade of grass, but seeing where we were I decided not to.

'What'll you be when you grow up?' asked Bernard, the sun on our faces.

'I don't know.' I wanted to say that I wished to be exactly like Rufus Real. But his was a name I had not yet mentioned at home. 'What are you going to do?'

'Either explore,' he said, 'or be a telegram boy.'

I remember the stab of jealousy I felt at him wearing the uniform, the leather purse on a belt and the red bicycle.

If this were a film script, I would instruct the director at this point to pull the camera back, high into the air, leaving two innocents far below us, on the green grass of an England of yesteryear. As the music swells – The Squad-ronaires, leader Paul Fenoulet (pronounced like Real in the French way) – to what I believe they call 'counterpoint,' I would indicate a long shot of the wide, empty sky. Two small dots on the horizon, approaching at speed – to roar into full shot as Spitfires, wingtip to wingtip, targets painted on their sides, their Merlin engines competing with the music. The helmeted, young and handsome pilots, silk scarves at their throats, would raise gloved hands to us in salute as they fly into the sun, towards glory; and the music finishes with cymbals.

Now to bring you up to date with the war.

On the European land mass nothing was happening. The lights had gone out, and that – for the moment – was that. But in the Far East the Japanese, not content with attacking Pearl Harbour, now made what was to prove the fatal mistake of grappling with the British Empire. The Japanese Emperor, a small moustached man who lived in a chalet with sliding doors, was playing for high stakes.

It was a sad and savage story. As the *Daily Express* kept telling us, we should never forget what they did to our nurses. But what hurt most of all was what happened in Singapore. We had been there since the days of Raffles, the gentleman burglar, and to defend the Singaporeans we had installed, at great expense, enormous guns. (The size of which recall the shadow on the dorm wall on my first night at Traggets.)

These guns meant that enemy warships sailing into the harbour without permission could be blasted out of the water on the word of command. They were manned by men of The Royal Artillery, trained to a hair's breadth; but once again history repeated itself. Like the Mad Mahdi at Omdurman, and the Germans in their motor-bikes and sidecars, the Japanese chose not to fight fair. Moving down through the Malayan bush on bicycles, like slit-eyed telegram boys, they attacked Singapore *from the rear*!

This, as you can imagine, caused havoc. Everyone had to turn round. Rubber planters and their wives, having long cool drinks on the veranda with gunner subalterns, avid for the latest news of Kate Meyrick's, were thrown into confusion.

'Can you turn your guns round?' demanded the Governor, a fine sight in his cockaded hat.

'Good morning, sir,' said the Commanding Officer.

'Sorry. Good morning. Well, can you?'

'No, sir,' said the Commanding Officer, standing smartly at the salute. Born in the reign of Queen Victoria, it must have been difficult for him to remember whether his guns fired shells or balls.

'Right,' said the Governor, or something similar, and the band played in the shade of the banyan tree as they went off to work on the railway.

The Empire crumbled. We had been warned often enough about The Yellow Peril, and now there was an uneasy feeling that they would want, when their junks and battleships sailed into the mouth of the Thames, much more than an extra inch on the tails of their shirts.

The fear was – what would they do to our women? Well, we knew what they would do to them; the worry was how long would they keep on doing it. Though some people pointed out that the two nations had a common bond in their attitude to tea, although they did not take milk.

Let me now briefly review what was happening on the other war fronts. There was skirmishing in North Africa. In the north Atlantic, German U boats were sinking British ships. If you went down in a convoy you were left, literally, to sink or swim. Even though frigates cut through the water with klaxons sounding; their young officers, only yesterday habitues of Kate Meyrick's, tight lipped at the wheel. Behind them, in the shadows of the bridge, would be Noël Coward, in his overcoat, with a mug of cocoa.

Here at home we waited. Jerry had not yet turned up to fight. But we knew by now the deceitful ways in which he could arrive; and we were ready. As the searchlights played across the skies, barrage balloons floated on their cables, grim-faced men in khaki stared out across the North Sea; entertained each night, it must be said, by Elsie and Doris Waters.

But what was happening to me? You might well ask. My father was about to impart to me, in the last week of the holiday, the most earth-shattering news.

Chapter Six

A cataclysmic event – My father revealed – Miss Parkinson moves in – A Frith painting – To Swinehurst – Victory Cottage – On the Home Front – The Wartime Spirit – Rosemary's house – I shine at the Tabernacle – A traumatic night

I was to be sent to live with the working class! I could not believe my ears! I stared at my father, who had the grace to bow his head after pulling the rug of life from under me. Even the glass eyes of the elk, which had followed me all of my life, now avoided mine. Through the window the immense sky was appropriately clouded, great grey canvas covers pulled across. No bee buzzed; there was/were no Bile Beans to read this time.

'You have to understand,' my father had said, 'that life will never be the same again without your mother.' I had nodded solemnly, understanding, ready to shed a tear with him if called upon; even though Court Mourning, as Yasmin called it, was now over. I knew we had to pick up the pieces and go on.

My father, after a silence, got up from his treadle fretwork machine, bought in an attempt to assuage his grief in those first dark days, and took down a carrier bag from behind the door. From it he took – and I felt my senses swim – an extremely hairy check-tweed sports jacket. In oatmeal and white, with brown buttons, it had slits up the sides to accommodate the hilt of a sword; and buttons on the cuffs to deter the wearer from wiping his nose on the sleeve.

'Oh!' I said, deeply moved, putting out a finger to stroke the fuzz on the lapel. I took the jacket to be a gift for me in place of my mother – but no. It was for him!

I stood, burning face turned to the wall as he changed. 'You can turn round now,' he said; and then he walked, strutted, with long steps in and out of the furniture. Turning on his heel he raised a finger, and like a dutiful son I began to hum. 'A Pretty Girl Is Like a Melody' seemed to fit the occasion. Finally, exhausted, and because my humming had faded away into dumb insolence, he sat down at his desk. Dabbing at his brow with a folded handkerchief he asked me: 'Now what do you think of your father?'

I stared over his head, reading the framed certificate from The Independent Order of Oddfellows, knowing that the elk was now trying to catch my eye. I just couldn't find the words.

Miss Parkinson was now coming to stay for weekends, playing Snap with me in an attempt to build a relationship, and God knows what with my father. I met her once coming out of the bathroom and thought that she looked at me in a certain way; though I cannot be sure of that.

There was talk of course, especially among those on Mossies' window sill; and so I was forced to become a recluse. It was enough having to live down my mother doing you-know-what with Colonel Trewin, without the added shame of my father and his 'Houri', as Bernard had heard Miss Parkinson described at the chip shop. Beyond visits to the Riff tent, where, because it was Ramadan, we used marbles in place of sheep's eyes, my only outings were with Bernard in the early evenings, along the banks of The Drain.

We talked of many things, as boys do, but my mind was always on the end of summer. The return to Traggets, the Common Entrance Exam, and which public school I was to attend. Sometimes behind an old barn we practised the wall game, until Mr Frees the Scoutmaster, who had been watching us, took us into his shed and gave us a warning. But my heart was set on Eton, where Rufus Real was bound. I would eat no other pudding. Each night as I drifted into sleep, I mumbled how many buttons you were allowed to have undone each year; dreaming of dashing games of fives, of eating their mess, and poking the town urchins with the ferrule of my cane.

'You'll be living with Mr and Mrs Delius,' said my father. 'No relation. And you'll be going to a good Secondary Modern School.'

I stared at him. The elk had given up and was gazing fixedly at the wall. As I have said earlier, I could not believe my ears.

'I'm not going to get a big white stiff collar?' I asked in a daze. 'And have a butler?'

'No,' he said patiently. 'You're not going to get a big white stiff collar. Or have a butler.' He took a puff of one of the Wills Whiffs he had now taken to. 'You're going to live with Mr and Mrs Delius, in Swinehurst, and you're going to a Secondary Modern School. You're going to be an evacuee.'

'Swinehurst?' I cried. 'An evacuee?' The shock caused me to raise my voice. 'With a tie-on label on my jacket?'

My father nodded.

So, it came about that I was taken to London by a grim and silent De Kuyper, dressed as an Air-Raid Warden with a black steel helmet slung across her shoulder. There, on a platform at Euston Station, I was mingled with genuine evacuees from east of Aldgate Pump. Waifs called Ernie with purple heads and terrible trousers, holding the hands of infant brothers in broken boots, tears and snot running down their faces.

'Keep silent,' said De Kuyper. 'Try not to give away your class.' She pushed a packed lunch under my arm, put a quick kiss onto my cheek, then with a smart United Front salute she turned on her heel and was swallowed up in the crowd. I was alone.

It was like the Frith painting that Uncle Frank and I had done as a jigsaw. People in fancy dress milled around in the steam and the booming noise of the loudspeakers. I was bewildered by the whistles of the trains and the honking baggage trucks. The blues and greys and khaki of our fighting men, their clean-cut faces tired but resolute, Lee Enfields slung from their shoulders or propped close to hand. Boot toecaps filmed with dust, they slept on parcels of *Our Dogs* and *Sunny Stories*; or wrote hurried letters to loved ones in a quiet haven among the mail bags. White-belted military police pushed through in twos along the platform, concerned to ensure that everyone was wearing a hat. Bombed out families sat on pathetic bundles, placards on their chests saying 'Britain Can Take It'. Ladies in overalls and hats served rock cakes and tea; and there was the exotic touch of a foreign officer in operatic uniform, sallow skin and pungent breath. Even a black man dressed as a soldier.

Then into the train, the dark-red seats thick with dust, with Corfe Castle in watercolours to remind me of happier days. Twelve of us without a lavatory, under the control of a female Colonel Trewin in a tweed skirt and heavy chatelaine. We steamed back the way I had come. A long train of whimpering wretches torn from their mothers' arms, tears and lamentations trailing behind with the smoke, not knowing where they were bound. In my case I knew only too well. Before we had reached the Nabisco factory, and I strained my eyes for a glimpse of Rufus, out in the fields with his faithful ghillies, I understood everything. It obviously made sound economic sense for my father to mingle me with the evacuees. This was the cheapest way to get to Swinehurst, to Mr and Mrs Delius; my upkeep chargeable to King and Country.

I sat, tight lipped as De Kuyper had instructed me, as

the train pounded northwards. The female Colonel Trewin had produced a cluster of thick white mugs, and was pouring a brown liquid from what I believe is called a 'billy can'. I politely declined 'something to eat'. It would be, I was sure, the legendary 'cinder toast' left over from the tea, fit only for pigeons. Or possibly dripping, which I had heard about. I was pleased that I was able to sneak De Kuyper's brown bread and lemon cheese out of the paper bag.

'When did you last see your father?'

I choked on a crumb, prolonging the coughing to give me time to think. I knew the painting well of course, having it at home on a toffee tin, but why was she taunting me with it? Had she seen through my disguise? Realised that I was, not to put too fine a point on it, a cut above these head-infected street Arabs? I gave another cough, clearing the last of the Hovis.

'Beggin' yer pardon, mum . . . ' I spoke to her in the vernacular, down my nose, making my eyes shifty and evasive, hunching my shoulders and letting out some wind against the upholstery. I said that my 'farver' had joined up with his donkey at the outbreak of war, and 'me mum', the Pearly Queen, was taking in washing to augment the pittance from her job in the Blackwall Tunnel. As I picked my nose, working up my finger to the first joint, I could not help thinking of my real mother waltzing with a gin and Italian, of my father in his Jowett Javelin, honking his horn.

Emboldened by my obvious success – all eyes in the compartment were on me – I then went on to tell how I lay in a wide bed with fourteen brothers and sisters (Mrs Colonel Trewin's eyes narrowed at this point). Doped with gin-dipped dummies and laudanum, and tormented by the scampering rats as they crossed the rags that covered us to get to the midden. 'Then up we get at dawn,' I said, 'and off we go to pick oakum or sweep crossings, or 'old gen'lman's 'orses.'

'Swinehurst,' said Mrs Colonel Trewin, after a short pause, 'will be heaven for you.'

'Thank you, mum,' I said, raising my flat cap, which we had bought at Horne Brothers just outside the station. I accepted a small serving of the brown liquid ('Here,' she said, 'Child of the Jago'), which I poured out of the window as we went through a tunnel, seeing the platelayers' wet lamplit faces in the brick niche.

Thinking of all that lay before me, I settled back in my corner seat. Like slides from the Rev Eli Wannamaker's lantern my future appeared, alternating between the rush-strewn interior of the Swinehurst working-class home, and the scene at Gawain's on the first day of term when I failed to appear.

'Gosh!' Broomhead would say, tilting his hat to the back of his head. 'Corkie's not coming back!'

Boys supervising porters carrying in trunks; boys saying farewell to parents who kept the engines of their cars running; all came hurrying into the hall to crowd around Tonto at the notice board.

'Doesn't worry me,' said Wheelan, but he was silenced by a storm of hissing.

'Who's Corkie?' asked a maggot (a new boy) and was quite properly thumped into silence.

'Stand back!' cried the monitors, pushing people aside with their wands, as Dr Hazlit climbed onto a chair and prepared to address the anxious crowd.

'We shall remember him,' the headmaster began simply. There was a chorus of 'Hear! Hear!' and a section of the school orchestra started to play softly under the stairs. Unobserved, his face white and set, Rufus Real walked out past the round table into the gathering dusk. Alone under the Sitka pine he kicked a pebble with his patent pumps, unmindful of his tea.

As we approached the familiar landmarks of my home county, I began to see myself in a few years' time. For a start I would certainly be stunted, by a lack of fresh air and green vegetables. I was probably too old to develop rickets; but the strain on my eyes of the flickering candlelight, the shame of the earth privy, the infrequent bathing in the zinc bath, the diet of broth and pease pudding . . . I would turn out to be a sorry specimen. Wire bespectacled, pale and rough skinned, rotten toothed and round shouldered; my vocabulary restricted to 'Oh, cor! Fuck me!' in the thickest of regional dialects; certain to be passed over with a shudder for a position as a telegram boy.

We rattled through my home station without stopping, Pomfret's brother throwing the levers in his signal box. I thought I saw Pickersgill emerging from the urinals but could not be sure, having sunk down inside my muffler to avoid being seen. As we swung east away from the town, towards Swinehurst, I saw the blueish hills and caught a glimpse of the chimneys of Jasmine Villa. I could not help thinking how I would have turned out if life had been fair to me. Reflected in the window, rather than the endless potato fields, I saw myself. Tall and top hatted, pink faced and bright eyed, cane spinning through my fingers. The taste of frogs and champagne on my lips, a slim volume of verse in my pocket, in a foreign language, along with a silver flask of Vimto; and Rufus Real forever on the cocoa tin.

I sighed deeply as we slid into Swinehurst Central, the bumpkin on my left sniffing hard to clear his upper lip and shouting, 'We're 'ere!' We were indeed. Stepping onto the platform, attached like the others to a link on the chatelaine, I was given a cheese sandwich, compliments of the council. The town band played a selection from 'The Merry Wives of Windsor' while we waited for the Billeting Officer.

Though my troubles that summer were almost too much, there was still the war going on. Before I tell you about my reception into the Delius ménage, my traumatic first night with their daughter – the confirmation, as far as I was concerned, of the theory that the working class do not have the same standards as the rest of us – I will attempt to bring you up to date.

Food was now rationed, and each citizen was given a book of coupons which they exchanged for a few ounces of meat, or butter, or a bar of Fry's Motoring Chocolate. To ensure absolute egality, in line with 'The People's War' we were talking about, the Government decreed that no more than five shillings (25p) could be spent on a meal. 'British Restaurants' were set up throughout the land, intended for people who had not got 25p; and were cleverly designed to keep out anyone above the class of window cleaner. These moves were of course well intentioned, but led to bizarre scenes in the West End of London. Ladies and gentlemen, having eaten their bread while listening to the band, or absentmindedly nibbled their onion salad at Veeraswamy's while feeling the flock wallpaper, would find to their horror that they had spent their entire allowance. They were ruthlessly shown to the door.

'But the gel is *starvin'*, James! She's had nothing since her kedgeree this morning!'

'I'm very sorry, sir; but the Ministry of Agriculture Food and Fisheries regulations are quite clearly pinned up in the foyer.'

It was no use arguing with them.

It became a nightly sport of jolly Jews and Gentiles from the East End, carrying bundles of all they possessed, and hung about with placards bearing mottoes, to watch the upper classes milling around the darkened streets in their thousands, distraught and on the verge of panic. (They emerged – the jolly Jews and Gentiles – from the Underground stations, where they had 'knees ups' and lay in rows for Henry Moore – he, remember, who could so easily have been our maid.) Men in evening dress, white silk scarves against the fog, ladies in sequins and fringes, fox furs across their powdered shoulders – all of them in huddled groups under the gaslamps, desperately plotting how to obtain a meal. Sometimes a Cockney, the salt of the earth, one of those who lit fires for Jews and was grateful to get the *Empire News* in bed the following morning, would step out of the shadows, moved by compassion to forget for a moment his shyness and reserve.

' 'Ere, guv,' he would say, touching his forelock in salute. 'Can I do anyfing for yer?'

'What?' the gentleman would reply, helpless in the face of such altruism. 'What do you mean?' His education, his Latin and Greek and trigonometry, had not prepared him for this.

Tongue-tied, searching in his ill-educated mind for the words, attempting to explain the route to the nearest chip shop, the Cockney saw the gentleman hazily, through the yellow gaslight and fog, as a large white five-pound note. With which at that time you could make a down payment on a house at Ongar.

' 'Old yer 'orse, shall I, sir?' he would say, tightening his muffler in his embarrassment; and the gentleman, his lady beside him, her high heels silently scoffed at by the mums in men's boots, would bite reflectively perhaps on a canapé found in his tail pocket as they stepped into a taxi cab.

'You know, Muriel,' he would say, as they settled back against the leather upholstery, 'chaps like that . . . well, dash it, things just have to turn out right, haven't they?' And Muriel would murmur 'Yes' and give him a little squeeze, and as they passed Buckingham Palace they would both wave with their free hands.

The war was not at all bad. I have not actually read Clausewitz, but I am sure he has somewhere a chapter on 'Wartime Spirit'. This, at that time, was manifest throughout the nation. From the jauntily placarded East Enders dancing around the smoking ruins of their homes, to the Dowager watching, with only a hint of pain on her English Rose face, as the parkland was ploughed up for curly kale.

'Dobson,' she would say, as she entered the house

through the Doric portico, 'send out some jam jars of tea or whatever they drink.' And he would.

The city children moved through the streets of Swinehurst bewildered and lost, picking up sheep droppings from the pavement. 'You got a King 'ere, 'ave you, like we 'ave?' asked one; while his sister screamed and wet herself when she saw a tree. One by one they were unhooked from the chatelaine and led up a garden path by the Billeting Officer, a red-haired woman who kept well away from us. Mrs Colonel Trewin touched each one of us on the head with a gloved hand as we departed, something between a blessing and a thump. Finally, I alone was left. My hope that they had run out of families willing to accept us, or that I was being kept back to be allotted to the local landed gentry as a plaything for their daughter, was abandoned as we turned down a narrow lane to a row of cottages. At the first of these we stopped, and the Billeting Officer said, 'You can do this one.'

Mrs Colonel Trewin opened the gate. It was pale blue, wooden and shakily nailed together. Pushing me in front of her like a hostage, we walked down a path that was unusual, not to say interesting. Unlike my own at Jasmine Villa, with acanthus leaves and a Greek woman in tiles, this was composed of the contents of a thousand dustbins, spread and trodden into the ground. The cabbage leaves and sprout tops having rotted away, what remained was ashes from the fire, giving an overall impression of red, grey and blue; almost our national colours. Which went rather well with the painted notice over the low front door: 'Victory Cottage'.

My escort could not knock as the door was wide open, so she coughed and then cried 'Halloo!' while I held her skirt, feeling her suspenders, looking down the passage into the gloom. I had difficulty in placing the smell.

Before me was orange linoleum, a pattern of sunlit adobe wall, covered with clusters of purple grapes and bright green leaves. I could see the foot of a staircase, with what had been decent staircarpet now carefully nailed down. Some of the balusters were missing and had been replaced with firewood, but the whole ensemble was painted a pleasing shade of green, matching the leaves of the linoleum vine. On the wall, and going up the stairs like Number 10 Downing Street, were many pictures in dark frames. I could only make out the first one, which appeared to be Jesus Christ, though not as far as I could see doing anything religious.

Mrs Colonel Trewin was looking around for a bell on a hall table to jangle, when a very small woman appeared through the gloom from the direction of the smell. She wore a flowered pinny and slid along the linoleum, in furry slippers, as Yellowbellies of old had crossed the Fens in their wooden pattens. Her white blouse, the short sleeves showing her weathered arms, was open to the second button, revealing a pink glass crucifix and a rather daring expanse of vest. Her pleasant face, though small in keeping with the rest of her, was framed in chestnut curls; the rollers making me think at once (as a writer manqué) of brandy snap. She was covering these with a headscarf, tying it under her chin in the style of Marley's ghost. Mrs Delius, for it was she, dropped a somewhat perfunctory curtsey to the large person I was clutching.

'Good mornin' ' she said, being allowed to speak first as she was as it were on her own ground. 'Is this the little man?'

Mrs Colonel Trewin nodded, and obtained a slow wobbly signature in pencil, then looked down into my face. 'Be a good boy,' she said. I closed my eyes in expectation of the pat on the head, and when I opened them she had gone. I heard the gate close, as well as it could, and I was alone with Mrs Delius.

'Well,' she said, still a little excited after signing her name, 'aren't you a big boy?'

'Yes,' I said, taking off my cap to cross the threshold,

deciding that I would now resume my own persona. If Mrs Delius could not cope with an upper middle-class boy who had had two terms at a prep school, then so much the worse for her.

We went through into the kitchen and sat at the table, looking at each other across oilcloth decorated with yellow beehives.

'You are a big boy,' she said. She smiled to show me she really didn't mind this and put a kettle on the gas stove, next to the covered black pan from which the smell was coming. The kitchen, apart from the smell, was surprisingly clean; decorated in green paint left over from the hall.

My tea was served in a large cup painted with roses, its rim encrusted with twenty-two carat gold. (It said as much in blue underneath the saucer.) To be quite honest, I was impressed. I also had, on a matching plate, a slice of bread and dripping. I found that sprinkled with salt it was really quite good, but heavy I suppose in cholesterol. Mrs Delius sat down again, holding her teacup quite nicely I thought, considering who she was, smiling at me with just the slightest apprehension as she chose a topic for conversation.

'What size shoes do you take, Jeffrey?'

I told her. I was intent on putting her at her ease. I told her my collar and cap size, my glove size; even, with only a moment's hesitation, my inside-leg measurement. Maybe there was a complete outfit of working-class clothes laid out for me in my room? Or perhaps I was to be taken to an outfitter's and kitted out from top to toe, in woollen vests and heavy shorts, with a striped square-ended tie and a khaki balaclava. She sipped tea and smiled on as I gave her the facts. When I had finished my dripping, and a McVities digestive from the oak and chrome biscuit barrel (obviously a gift from a wealthy family she 'did' for), Mrs Delius asked if I would like to go upstairs.

I thought about this, pretending to read the label inside

my cap. She was at least thirty years older than me, but as the reader will have gathered I was well informed by now as to the facts of life. We were alone in the house, completely unchaperoned, and at first it seemed to me an act of indiscretion, of complete folly. Since Agatha Jennings had thrown the cow pat and taken up with Pickersgill there had been no one in my life; except for Bernard, and even in his best Riff clothes, his lips carmined for what he claimed was the Sidi Bel Abbes Harvest Supper, I did not, as people say nowadays, fancy him. I thought I would tread warily and let Mrs Delius make the first move.

The stairs creaked and the smell came with us as I followed her up, carrying my suitcase to which De Kuyper had strapped Sunny Jim, his hump turned outwards. Off a small linoed landing were two bedrooms, the door open to one showing a brass bed and a two-handed pot. (I was later to read the inscription inside, around a large eye: 'I See All'.) The net curtains, against bomb blast and mosquitos, blew gently in the breeze from the open window.

'You're in here,' said Mrs Delius, lifting the latch of the other green-planked door, as if offering me the whole of the west wing. Making sure that the door was left wide open, I stepped inside what was to be my room.

Mrs Delius put the thin towel she had been carrying on the washstand, next to the jug and bowl and the shaving mug. The room was small, rectangular, papered with cabbage roses, and had of course a dado. From the ceiling hung a parchment and silk-fringed lampshade that had almost certainly come with the biscuit barrel. There was, I saw at once, barely space enough for a boy's normal pursuits; and the room was made even smaller by the partition.

'This,' said Mrs Delius, knocking gently on the plywood, 'is where my daughter lives.'

It was like the Wendy House at Mrs Dooley's, in which I had first met Agatha Jennings. But opened out and dividing the room exactly in half. It had painted pink bricks, a little green ivy dabbed on here and there, and a cellophane window with (painted) swagged curtains to either side. There was even a painted drainpipe. This palisade ran down the centre of the room, stopping just by the door where its entrance was. Five feet high, it was topped, I noted, by a strand of barbed wire. The door, at which Mrs Delius was knocking, was set in a cardboard Doric portico, with a painted letterbox and knocker in more or less classical form. Inside a scrolled cartouche was the name 'Rosemary'. A note on the doorstep, held down by a sea shell, read 'No milk today'.

There was no answer to Mrs Delius's knocking, and I refrained from suggesting that she take a look over the pediment. I put my case on the narrow bed and held my breath as this new woman in my life squeezed past me to stand looking out of the window.

'Is your mother alive?' she asked, turning to look at me through the brass bars at the end of the bed.

I said yes, and waited for her to ask what size she was.

'What does she do?'

Tired, I was silent, not wanting to admit that she did the tango; but was then saved by the sound of footsteps ascending the stairs. Turning to face the open door, I forced a carefree smile; excuses and plausible stories rising readily to my lips, even at that early age.

'It's only him,' she said, 'Delius,' and I realised with shame that she had after all a clear conscience, a pure heart.

Fred Delius paused for breath at the top of the stairs, or to allow whoever was in the bedroom to adjust their clothing, then turned towards me with a faint squeak of his boots. He was a little taller than his wife, his skin even more weathered, and wore a blue suit, though without the stylish creases of the time. His face was smooth shaven and saintly, bright blue eyes regarding me with absolute trust and brotherhood. Raising the cucumber he held in his hand, he said: 'God made the land for the people.'

It was not a question, but I nodded and said that was certainly true. I had seen the legend painted on walls on my way from the station, so it seemed to be the general opinion in Swinehurst.

'This is Jeffrey,' said Mrs Delius. 'The evacuee. Isn't he a big boy?'

Mr Delius sat beside me on the bed, smiling fondly at the cardboard portico, while Ada (as he called her) went downstairs with the cucumber to see to the smell. He began to talk to me about Sir Stafford Cripps who, it seemed, although I had missed him, was hanging on the stairs. Was I a Christian Socialist? he asked.

'A Christian Scholar,' I gently corrected him, had been my early goal in life. Just now, although I did not say so, I only wanted to be upper middle class. Would I sing with him? he then enquired, to celebrate the joy of my joining the household. Yes, of course, I said, running through the verse of 'The Sun Has Got His Hat On' in my mind. Delius stood up, straightbacked, clasping his cap to the left strap of his braces.

'Last night I lay asleeping . . . ' his voice was loud though not unmusical, the happy face smiling at me and at Rosemary's house as he sang: ' . . . I dreamed a dream so fair. I dreamed I saw Jerusalem, beside the . . . ' Tucking Sunny Jim's head beneath the pillow, I quietly slipped down the stairs.

The front door was still open and I walked outside into the late afternoon sun, as the voice of Delius rang out overhead from the bedroom window. 'Jerooosalem, Jerooosalem, lift up your . . . ' From the kitchen, with equal fervour, Ada sang along with him.

It was quieter round the side of the house, though you could still hear them. At the very end of the garden, beside what I took to be an ornamental pool, I found what I was looking for, adorned with dog roses and the last of the green paint.

It was what Mr Lemm Putt would have called a

'One-family three holer', and I stood in the cool gloom, lit only by a shaft of light through a star cut in the door, and tears rolled unchecked down my cheeks. My face turned to the whitewash I sobbed uncontrollably; for there, at the end of the row, after the 'His and Hers' and the small oval for the property-owning daughter, a circle had been pencilled on the wood. A fretsaw and a sheet of sandpaper laid ready for use. Delius had been about to fit me in when he had gone upstairs with his cucumber.

Humbled, I walked, head bowed to avoid the washing, to the kitchen door; about to ask if I might call Mrs Delius 'Mum', or even Ada – to run upstairs and sing with full heart with Uncle Fred, as I thought of him now – but at that moment she lifted the lid from the black pan and the smell enveloped me.

'Come and sit down, Jeffrey,' she said, seeing me standing there, swaying. 'You'll be hungry, a big boy like you.'

It was of course a novelty to eat in the kitchen, and I sat looking at the yellow beehives, which had been laid with bone-handled knives and forks, waiting for my first High Tea. Uncle Fred, wiping his mouth and radiant from his sing song, joined us after washing his hands at the sink. There was no sign of the inhabitant of Rosemary's house. Holding my breath (it would have hurt their feelings to hold my nose) I watched Aunt Ada (as I had decided to call her) ladle the smell from the black pot onto willow-pattern plates. Looking back now, if only they had had the foresight to hang on to their china – the brass beds and the two-handed pot, the little boots from Hunstanton – they would have been worth a small fortune. But as someone once said, give the working man a horse and he will ride to hell. Sad, really.

The evening passed quietly and in typical working-class fashion. Uncle Fred went down the garden to finish his opening for me, then read aloud the local evening paper. I was surprised to learn that he was well known and respected in the area for the size of his cucumbers. Indeed, there was an item in that very edition telling how he had overcome opposition from just outside Spalding. We left Aunt Ada reading this, shaking her head in wonder as a pair of her husband's working trousers came to the boil, as we walked down to the Tabernacle.

It was my first evening in a large town and I was fascinated. Everything was closed of course, but families thronged the pavements, looking in the hat-shop windows, saying things like 'Hello' as they passed each other on the way to the off-licence. In Mediterranean countries, as I discovered later, this is known as The Volta.

It was a quiet night at the Tabernacle. Just a few of the elders, lending books to each other, plus a girl who could not be trusted. I was introduced as an up-and-coming Rechabite, evacuee and prep-school boy, and this caused an immediate hubbub in the gaslit room with its Xmas decorations.

'It's 'im,' cried a woman in a black cape, knitting, without so far as I could see looking up. 'It's 'im with the marks on 'im, like in Tibet!'

But most people were very kind, gathering round me but moving back when Delius shouted, 'Air! Give him air!' Mounting a mobile rostrum, he told them something of my background. (Salt of the earth that he was, he can surely be forgiven for wanting to show me off.) His mention that I had won a hardback copy of *Coral Island*, signed by the District Commissioner, for being the most likely lad in south west Lincolnshire for 1939 (something I have not mentioned), brought cries of wonder from the back of the hall. Then I answered questions as well as I could, Delius standing beside me, positively glowing. I told them about Euston, and the black man I had seen dressed as a soldier. ('Eye eeonkoh!' chanted a section of the choir which had filed in from the rehearsal room, lining up like the Mills Brothers, making paddling movements and grunting.) I told them about the Nabisco factory, which I had seen twice in one day, and there were Ooh!s and Aah!s and then a man in an engine driver's cap stood up to ask a question. Was I going to write a book, to be called *Down and Out in Swinehurst?*

I told him no, I had not considered doing that.

A man in a khaki overall stood up to point out that a Mr Hyndeman had dressed in frock coat and top hat when he gave out Social Democratic Federation leaflets at Belsize Park tube station. There was a murmur of agreement in the hall and Uncle Fred, catching my eye, encouraged me to join in.

A smallish man, though unaccustomed as he was to public speaking, then moved a vote of thanks which was seconded and carried by acclaim. A small crowd gathered around me afterwards, and I signed several evening papers and a programme. Quite carried away, I went on to answer supplementary questions about Traggets, explaining as best I could what prep was and promising to come back soon and see them all in my school blazer. Uncle Fred then said that I was tired and that it had been a long day for me, big boy though I was. As we left the choir broke into 'England Arise', the harmonium being furiously pumped into action, and the woman in the cape followed us into the street singing 'Will ye nae come back again'.

We walked home (how strange that already I thought of Victory Cottage as such) through the now deserted streets. At the corner of the lane was an air-raid warden to whom we said 'Good evening', and who clacked his wooden rattle in reply. Aunt Ada was at the sink, as we had left her, but I noticed with relief that the lid of the black pot was cold and still. We had cocoa, made half with water, and I was allowed as a special treat to take mine up to my room.

'Good night, Jeffrey,' said Aunt Ada, reaching up to ruffle my hair. 'You are a big boy, aren't you!' We bumped our foreheads together and I turned, in a turmoil of emotion, into the strong embrace of Uncle Fred.

'Good night, lad,' he breathed, smelling of the very soil

itself, putting a wet though manly kiss into my ear. 'God made the land . . . ?'

'For the people,' I finished. Picking up my cocoa, and my clean vest which had been airing in the oven, I hurried up the stairs. Bedtime at Jasmine Villa had never been like this.

I sat on my bed with the door closed, a strip of yellow gaslight showing underneath. Rosemary's plywood castle loomed, silent and dark, while from the brown Ekco wireless set downstairs the chimes of Big Ben rang out. 'Bong! . . . Bong!' Soon it would be Alvar Liddell reading it. I felt the tablespoon of Scott's Emulsion rattle against my teeth.

Undressing quickly and making my prayer short because of the lino, I got into bed. I could see the dark branch of a tree and a very small slice of the moon.

I must have slept, exhausted as I was by such a day, when suddenly the door was opened and a torch blazed into my face. I could see the filament of the bulb glowing in the yellow glare, and then it swung away from me, making frightening shadows on the ceiling. What appeared to be a tall dark figure opened the door of Rosemary's house. It closed again and I listened, for the click of a lock or the sliding of a bolt, but heard nothing. I breathed softly, keeping very still, feeling to make sure the cord of my pyjama trousers was securely tied.

Not a word had been said that evening about Rosemary, and I realised now that I had seen no photographs downstairs. No framed sampler or certificate on the wall, no buns brought home from school. I began to put two and two together. It was quite obvious that Rosemary was a mongol. By that of course I mean a gibbering idiot, not a descendant of Genghiz Khan. She would have a flat face and funny eyes, and go to the open-air school with Mossies' fat son. She was probably about thirty-seven, with ankle socks, her hair cut round a basin.

Mr Beeston had dealt with loonies in his Social Responsibility class, using apocryphal illustrations such as the one about the idiot looking over the asylum wall and seeing a man collecting horse manure.

Loony: 'What are you collecting that for?'

Man: 'I'm going to put it on my rhubarb.'

Loony: (after a pause) 'We put custard on ours.'

This was to point up the moral (quite widely held) that though these inmates dressed up as Napoleon, and sometimes had to be wrapped in wet sheets, there were, as people said, 'Wiser in than out.' 'Do not,' said Mr Beeston, who was a humane man, 'take the piss out of them.'

Anyway, I was certain in my own mind that Rosemary Delius was a loony, and very probably dangerous. Uncle Fred and Aunt Ada, deeply ashamed at what their excesses had produced, had incarcerated her like Mrs Rochester in a cell, albeit disguised as a Wendy House. Make no mistake I told myself, I was in a tight spot.

A creak. The door of Rosemary's house was opening!

There was no torch, no light, only mongoloid breathing coming towards me – the sliding of slippers on the lino in the Lincolnshire tradition. I drew up the sheets and the blankets, wishing that the shadow of an elephant's penis was all I had to worry about.

A finger touched my shoulder. I had turned to face the wall and lay in the foetal position. The finger moved, caressingly, over my shoulder and I shrugged, as if restlessly in sleep, turning over and throwing off the mongol's hand. Now there was no touch and I waited, breath held and eyes squeezed shut, ears distended as they took the responsibility of letting me know what was going on.

They heard nothing. I knew by *feel*! I felt the weight of the bedclothes lift from my shoulders, the night air on my bare midriff where my pyjamas had become disarrayed – then a lightening on my legs and my feet cool and free.

SHE WAS TAKING OFF THE BEDCLOTHES!

It was foolhardy to lay there, curled up and breathing through my nose. I was horribly vulnerable. Clutching the

104

bolster to cushion the impact of the first blow I sat up, saying, 'Hello? Is there someone there?'

There was no answer. Perhaps a grunt. Then panic overcame me as I realised that she – it – was putting up the blackout battens at the window, blotting out what little light came in from the segment of moon. Abandoning Sunny Jim, I sprang from the bed and dashed for the door. Did ever discretion prove the better part of valour?

The handle came easy to my hand and I wrenched open the door. Two strides along the landing I remembered, and then sharp left and down the stairs, or into bed with the Deliuses; the eye that sees all brimming below. I took the first stride – and was at once struck by a ping-pong bat between the eyes! Reeling back – I then remembered what I was reeling back into! No matter who barred my way, I was determined to get through. Looking back now I can only say, given the age and size I was, that it was an act of considerable courage.

Doubling my small fists I charged, head down, through the open doorway – and this time the sentinel, the mongol's assistant, struck me across the legs with an iron bar. I fell forward with a little cry onto a soft, feather-filled eiderdown, into the smell of attar of roses.

I lay, panting, realising that I had crashed into Rosemary's house, that I lay now on Rosemary's bed! As I sat up, taking breath to scream for Aunt Ada and Uncle Fred – for surely they would be able to control her with kind words and wet sheets – the lights came on. A forty-watt bulb in a fringe on the ceiling, and a candle-shaped pink thing in a ruched hat beside the bed. The light blinded me for a moment, as I switched from bad dream to nightmare reality – and then Rosemary entered through the plywood Doric portico!

She was not a mongol, but a tram conductress! She stood in her flyless navy trousers, regarding me, I thought at once, much as Miss Parkinson did when I met her outside the bathroom. Sliding my legs under the bedclothes (for I was in a state of deshabille), I waited for her next move, being pleasantly surprised to feel a hot water bottle in the shape of Don Ameche. I began to relax. It was unlikely that she was mentally deficient, employed as she was by the Lincolnshire Road Car Company. Though the fact that she was a tram conductress did not mean that she could be trusted. The newspapers of the time were full of them.

'You want a chip?' she asked, taking a grease-spotted parcel from her money bag and putting it at the foot of the bed. I felt the warmth on my feet, nicely sandwiched now between fried potatoes and the hot film star. 'There's salt and vinegar in there,' she said, nodding her peaked cap, the Swinehurst coat of arms, towards the bedside cabinet. Carefully wrapping the eiderdown around me I leaned over and opened the fumed oak door. There was indeed a full cruet; plus, and this quickened my pulse, a half bottle of Daddies Sauce.

Using fingers ('Nature's forks' she called them) we commenced what was to be an intimate dinner. Beside the chips there was a piece of cod in batter which we shared, and a carton of mushy peas which we ate, turn and turn about, with a medicine spoon. At a penny a small saucerful, inclusive of mint sauce, they were I believe a favourite of J. B. (Jack) Priestley.

'Sorry I woke you up,' said the tram conductress, licking the last of the bright green juice from her lips. 'I was on a split.'

'Oh, yes?' I said.

'Yes,' she said. 'Eight to ten, twelve to three, five to eight. You don't know if you're coming or going. I thought you were a lodger.' She made a face. 'I pulled the clothes down to see how big you were, and you stopped halfway. I thought you were wounded in the war – you know, just the top half of you. That's why I put the blackout up, so I could put the light on and have a look.' Her brown eyes, rimmed by black in the style of Queen Nefertiti and some maidens of today – though caused in her case by fingers

106

blackened by filthy pennies – regarded me in the nicest possible way.

I said that there really was no need for her to apologise. I explained that far from being a lodger, I was an evacuee; and as for being half a man – I blushed and lowered my eyes. Surely she had seen enough to realise that, though smallish, I was perfectly formed? She nodded thoughtfully, her cap badge glinting in the light. 'All right,' she said, 'What about a beer?'

I had to decline of course, as I waved aside the proffered Woodbine. I was a Rechabite I told her, and we did not do that kind of thing.

Why not? she wanted to know. What did we get out of it?

For a start, I said, a copy of *Coral Island*. There was silence then while we extricated the scraps of crisp batter from the folds of the paper.

'What about the other?' she then asked, licking the vinegar from the greaseproof. 'Is that allowed?' There was a smile on her red lips, the green being nearly all gone. I wasn't sure exactly what she meant, so I said yes, not wishing to be thought a stick in the mud. 'But only in moderation,' I added, wagging a finger.

Yawning in agreement, she started to undress, taking off her cap and shaking out her brown curls. Then the black leather crossbelts; first the money bag, then the brass machine that 'pinged'. She hung these on the end of the bed and scratched herself, and for a moment I thought she was about to do the other, right there in front of me! Already her epaulettes were undone.

'You staying there all night?' she enquired, starting to unfasten the embossed silver buttons of her tunic. I passed that off lightly as a joke, wondering if the buttons were made by the Broomheads, and said that of course I was just about to return to my own bed.

I did so rather quickly, not wishing to see the kind of underclothes issued by the Lincolnshire Road Car

Company, and returned the eiderdown over the plywood wall. As I called out, 'Thank you for the supper,' I was disconcerted to find that the tram conductress, when erect, stood head and shoulders above the house. 'Good night,' she said, in a voice which was slightly husky, and which I put down to the mushy peas. 'Sleep tight.' Pondering these last words I climbed into bed and lay there, fingering Sunny Jim.

The light on the ceiling went out and Rosemary's castle was in sharp relief, lit by the pink glow. To my shame I considered whether or not to creep across the lino and look in through the cellophane window. I knew of course that it was wrong; just as unwholesome as masturbating or drinking Guinness, and I finally brought Mr Beeston into my mind and decided to take his advice. He came at once, clear and vivid, grinning and swinging a stiff right forearm. I blushed as I quietly pulled the covers back and set foot on the cold linoleum. I say foot, because I was frozen in that position on hearing a gentle but persistent knocking at the door.

But which door? The tram conductress was surely not knocking to be let out! Was it a message? Like felons tapped along the prison pipes to each other? The Junior Rechabites did not demand a high standard of morse code, but I knew enough to realise that the tapping meant nothing. Except that someone wanted to come in, and it was coming from the bedroom door. I moved towards it, getting ready a plausible story, expecting it to be a Delius with nightcap and candle, come to see if we were safe and sound. Opening the door quietly, holding my pyjama trousers together, I saw in the glow of the pink light the tram conductress, fully dressed and accoutred, standing on the threshold!

My senses swam, as you will understand, and I took a step back into the room. Following me in, she closed the door behind her. 'Good evening,' she whispered, and I saw that she had grown a thin moustache, had her hair cut, and was smoking a short black pipe. My senses still swimming, the door in the Doric portico opened and Rosemary appeared. She was now in a pink nightdress to match the light. My eyes went slowly down to the flannelette hem. Mr Beeston's face and voice came to me again in full colour, in a cartouche in my fevered brain. 'Red hat, no drawers,' I heard him say. 'A chain around the ankle means she's a hooer . . . they wear nighties trimmed with fur to keep their necks warm . . .'

'Chester,' she said, 'this is Jeffrey. He's an evacuee.'

'Hello, Jeffrey,' whispered Chester, who I could see now was a tram *driver*.

'We work together,' explained Rosemary. 'He's my mate.'

'Like Tarzan,' I said, 'and Jane.' I was trying to lighten the mood, to save them from any embarrassment. I was also well aware that I had eaten his chips.

'That's right,' said Chester, and his pipe glowed as he sucked in: 'Ugh! Ugh! Ugh!' and he bent both arms and scratched under his armpits.

Tucking me firmly into my bed so that I would not fall out, they then went into Rosemary's house, putting out the pink light so that I could go to sleep. Chester went on making grunting noises for some time, bouncing up and down on the bed. I suppose he thought it would amuse me. Rosemary, being the kind of girl she was, took it in silence.

Chapter Seven

Home for a visit – Brother and sister again – Return of the Rev Eli Wannamaker – Dangerous behaviour on a commode – 'The Facts of Life' – The Brains' Trust – I am attacked by a clergyman

I had been at Swinehurst for almost a year. Indeed there was to be a small celebration at the Tabernacle the following week, with a cake and the little ones doing a dance. Having settled in well at school, rapidly reaching my old position of milk monitor, I had written several interesting letters to Rufus Real. In the first of these I had enclosed an essay for Dr Hazlit, giving my address as c/o Victory House, though as yet there had been no reply.

This was my first journey home, not counting the time there was nobody in. A food parcel packed by Aunt Ada on my lap, I was travelling, with a nod and a wink and on Rosemary's pass, by Lincolnshire Road Car Company. I could not help wondering what changes I would find.

It was early afternoon when I arrived, craning my neck to catch a first glimpse of the cardboard thermometer outside the wool shop. My sister Yasmin was standing with a poodle on a scarlet lead beside the horse trough. Lucille was having a drink, as was Pomfret, drinking from the far side of the iron mug to minimise the danger, and there was the usual small crowd to watch the bus turn round. As I crossed the road, giving a general wave to the tradespeople standing in their doorways, I saw with relief that Mossies' window sill was deserted.

'Hello, dearie,' said Yasmin. Her fox fur, with a face, reeked of Phul Nana; and I wriggled away from the embrace, disturbed, as her tongue entered my ear. She walked ahead of me along the London Road, pulled by the dog which wore a jacket tailored from the Stars and Stripes, and I noted the bracelet of silver threepenny bits around her slim ankle. Yasmin was a good-time girl. De Kuyper had hinted as much in her weekly letter, but I think I always knew. As I knew what my mother and father were (though not of course, at the time, what De Kuyper was).

Away from the centre of town, I fell into step beside her. She was very well she told me: 'Smashing' was the way she put it. Bernard had gone to stay with an aunt in Troon, in an attempt to get him off Riffs, and the cocoa tin had been disconnected. My father, having converted the Jowett Javelin to run on gas ('On chicken shit' as my worldly sister put it) now spent most of his time on the Scottish border in a campaign, backed by the Ministry, to bolster belief in the liberty bodice.

Mrs Dooley, almost certainly because of her work with the loonies, had been decorated. Yasmin said that it had come as a great surprise to her, but to no one else. Oh, and one of the Pomfrets had been killed, or had fallen as Dr Hazlit would have put it, at Dunkirk. Almost certainly he had gone mad and been shot out of hand.

Colonel Trewin, though already having done his bit, had been asked to do a bit more, and my mother had gone with him. Someone said they had seen her at Blackpool. Pickersgill had gone to an approved school – which was more, he shouted across the market place to me some time later, than I could say for Traggets. He maintained that they did prep there all day. Agatha Jennings had left school and gone into service; and somebody, nobody knew who, had bought Mrs Moss's doll. De Kuyper was a senior air-raid warden, responsible for the whole of the London Road; and Miss Parkinson was pregnant!

I found them on the lawn. That is, the air-raid warden,

the pregnant Miss Parkinson, and Sooty. Tea was laid on a cloth, the white of the napery setting off the deep yellow of the lemon cheese. Although Robinsons Lemon Barley Water was now almost impossible to get, it was as if I had never been away.

It was what we called at the time 'a pre-war tea', and when we had finished the last crumb, and Yasmin had been sent indoors to wash out her mouth with soap and water, De Kuyper wiped my chin.

'Are you a virgin still?' she asked quietly, as I gently stopped her from attending to my ears.

'I think so,' I said, blushing before the stern gaze from under the rim of the steel helmet.

De Kuyper picked up the last of the crumbs from the cloth with a wet forefinger, watching Aunt Ada's food parcel smoulder in the incinerator. I had sworn that I had brought it under duress, but she had been tight lipped as she pumped the Flit gun under my arms and down the front of my trousers. 'I hear they've got a daughter,' she said now. 'How old is she?'

'A daughter?' said Miss Parkinson, turning to smile at me. 'Is she pretty?'

'She's got black round her eyes,' I said, cautiously, and the two ladies exchanged knowing looks.

'Jeffrey,' said De Kuyper, after I had explained that Miss Delius was a young nineteen, 'you didn't tell us how many bedrooms they have.'

'No,' I said, 'I didn't.' I lay back on the grass and spoke to the immense sky. 'Two,' and then quickly, 'plus Rosemary's house.' I could feel them looking at me.

'Rosemary's got her own house?' They said it together, like two of the Andrews Sisters, the tone, of Miss Parkinson's voice at least, that of a believer in a property-owning democracy.

'With a Doric portico and a window,' I said, going on to describe something like the Petit Trianon, which we had done at school.

There was some light badinage about matchmaking, at which I smiled and blushed and hung my head, but it developed into a pleasant evening. After dinner we played De Kuyper's version of Mah Jong, with me discovering a talent for the West Wind, and I was allowed a small glass of Vironita. I was sipping this, realising for the first time what people saw in wine, dunking a custard cream that took the place of dessert – this you will remember was during the most arduous and stringent phase of the war – when Yasmin joined me at the fireside. Miss Parkinson had gone to bed with her cushion and a book of babies' names. De Kuyper was in the kitchen, and you can guess what it was that tickled our nostrils. Wrinkling them like The Bisto Kids, we smiled at each other; Yasmin, wearing a negligee and pink slippers, on the pouffe where the tango dancer had once sat. As Big Ben began to strike on the radiogram I twitched involuntarily in the gentleman's chair, opening my mouth for nine spoonfuls of Brylcreem. We laughed again. Then, like an elder sister should, good-time girl or no, she expressed an interest in Swinehurst and my new home.

No, I told her, we did not have a PX or a Rainbow Corner, not so far as I knew. In fact I doubted if we had any Americans in the town at all; though we had had, for a short time, a Free Frenchman seconded to the gun site on the sewage farm. There had been some talk of erecting, if that is the right word, a pissoir; but people had been against it, calling it 'the thin end of the wedge'.

Then we turned to Victory Cottage and my surrogate parents. Were they, she asked, what you would call a Christian family?

I found this difficult to answer. 'Of a kind,' I said. 'He sings, and he's had his name in the paper.' She was obviously impressed, and said that she had heard about his cucumbers.

We listened for a while to J. B. (Jack) Priestley, giving his Fireside Chat, and it led me to think, not unnaturally, of mushy peas. Then De Kuyper came in with Ovaltine on the gadrooned silver tray. Frothing it expertly with the plunger, she regarded us both with a fond smile. No doubt it brought back a time when we had sat there in the same firelight. I in my short grey trousers with the snake belt, and Yasmin with her Enid Blyton hair. Not to speak of the woman on the pouffe, dreaming of Colonels and the Big Dipper.

De Kuyper was wearing her green anti-mustard-gas cape, the white tapes properly starched, the goggles on her forehead, and we realised that she was going out. Later on, if it was a still night (what the Germans are apt to call a 'stille nacht'), we would be able to hear her rattle in the distance. As our father was exhibiting in Carlisle that night I was, in effect, the man of the house. I reached forward and poked the fire.

'You understand that Miss Parkinson's up the stick, don't you?' said Yasmin. 'In the club?'

'Yes,' I said. 'You told me.' I turned over the grey wartime pages of the *Radio Times*, admiring the garden sheds, waiting for her to go on. The air-raid warden, as she had been trained to do, had switched off the light on leaving and we were lit only by the glow of the fire. I thanked my sister for her delicacy, for the way she had raised such a difficult subject.

'In five weeks she'll have a baby,' she went on. 'It's growing inside her, getting bigger all the time. Fingers and toes and things by now; all curled up in her water.' She took a sip of the Ovaltine, her eyes wide, staring into the bright flames of the fire.

I had the picture, and I closed the *Radio Times* and replaced it with *Everybody's*, which Yasmin had moved on to from *Sunny Stories*. It was quite probable, I thought, in the absence of our father, and with De Kuyper safely out of the way – what with Miss Parkinson having almost finished her name book without finding anything suitable – that I was to be called upon to assist at an abortion. I noticed at this point the knitting needles on the carpet, next to the pouffe. How could I have been so blind?

'It's against the law,' I said flatly, as I sipped my Ovaltine. Our eyes met in the firelight, both of us with a ring of white froth around our mouth.

'What is?' she asked, a note of anxiety in her voice. 'What's against the law?' She rocked the pouffe a little nearer towards me – and I suddenly realised, naïf that I was, that it was not an abortion that was on the cards, with me passing knitting needles and bringing lots of hot water – but *incest*! I drew out my bag of sweets and offered her one, wishing that I had paid closer attention to what Mr Beeston had had to say on these subjects.

'That's against the law as well, you know,' I said. As you will have gathered I was much the widest read of the family, and I told her straight out that in our society it was terribly, terribly wrong; like masturbation and the drinking of Guinness.

'You mean the Rechabites?' she sneered, and that I'm afraid is the only word. 'Every bloody thing is terribly, terribly wrong, according to them.'

'I didn't mean that society,' I said. 'I mean that it's taboo.'

'Tabu the elephant boy,' she riposted, and we laughed together, dispelling the rather tense atmosphere.

'What I'm trying to talk to you about,' she said, taking a sweet, 'is sex.'

'Ah!' I said, putting the tips of my fingers together, carrying it off I thought rather well. I would much rather have had another go at the West Wind, but sex seemed infinitely preferable to the other business.

'Daddy asked me to have a word with you, about the facts of life. He can't do it himself.'

'That's a shame,' I said. There was silence while we stared into the fire. 'Why can't he do it himself?'

'Because he's in Carlisle.'

'Of course,' I said, nodding, waiting with interest, wondering whether I was expected to take notes.

'Sex,' began my sister, as if it were the title of a poem. 'Sex is a wonderful thing.' There was the utmost sincerity in her voice. 'But it is only to be done in wedlock.'

For a moment, genuinely, I thought that she said *Matlock*, and I stared at her open mouthed.

'The man,' she carried on, 'has what we call "a thing".' She paused as I nodded and said yes, I had one. It was her turn to nod.

'The woman,' she said, her voice becoming low and very serious, 'has a receptacle.' I stared hard into the fire, sucking my sweet and being careful not to nod. I heard her take a deep breath.

'The man takes his thing, at the right time and place . . . '

'In Matlock,' I whispered in fascinated horror.

' . . . when he is married. And puts it . . . ' She was holding out, I could see from the corner of my eye, a rigid forefinger, tipped with a scarlet fingernail. I shrank back into the gentleman's chair, closing my eyes. The knocking I heard over the pounding of my heart, I thought at first was the rigid scarlet tip against the carved walnut of the chair, and I swallowed my sweet. Then I realised that it came from the back door.

'I'll get it,' I said, doing a passable imitation of Barbara in 'Life with the Lyons'; moving swiftly across the room to switch on the light, and only then opening my eyes.

It was the Rev Eli Wannamaker, in clerical grey battledress. The Holy Ghost embroidered on each arm, and no less than three pips to give him the necessary authority.

'Come in, Padre,' I said, opening the door wide. 'You remember me, Jeffrey Cork? I was sent to live with the working class!'

He smiled at me, remembering me well of course, and crossed the kitchen to the gas stove. 'I came to have a word with you,' he said, lifting the lid of a pan, dipping and licking his finger. 'I heard you were home. I thought perhaps we could have a little chat.'

'Little chat?' I said, carefully closing the green-baize door; and then I let him have it. Senior Chaplain to the Junior Rechabites or not; man of the cloth and in the King's service: I remembered how he had taken my grand-mother's side in the matter of the blueish hills.

'Before you ask,' I told him, 'I am a virgin still!' I then went on to tell him how I shared a bed with Sunny Jim and the Panda. How Rosemary, as pure in heart as her mother, retired each night through the Doric portico. Though I did not mention the arrival of Chester as soon as he had put the tram away. I told him about Uncle Fred, though leaving out the cucumbers, and his insistence that God made the land for the people. But I did emphasise the extra hole he had sand-papered for me, expecting Captain Eli to note it as a prime example of Christian charity.

You could say that something had snapped, that I had been pushed too far. But it had been a long and emotional day, what with the travelling and the pre-war tea, and Yasmin going on about the other. 'And I didn't know you were on active service,' I finished up, frightened but excited at daring to talk to a clergyman in this fashion. 'Where's your wings?'

Captain The Reverend Eli Wannamaker straightened his beret and stamped his polished boots, so that the creases hung straight over his puttees. 'We serve,' he said simply.

'I didn't know you actually *fought*!' I said, looking at the blancoed webbing at his waist.

Unfastening his holster with a shy pride, the gallant Captain showed me a prayer book on a white lanyard. Illustrated by Arthur Rackham, the flyleaf was in the form of a polished steel plate which doubled as a shaving mirror. 'I let people who have been shot touch it,' he murmured; meaning the book, or Book, which had a washable cover. I said that was very good of him.

There was a pause and he cleared his throat, and then he said, 'Actually, I came to talk to you about your sister.'

'She's in the sitting room,' I said, pointing towards the green-baize door. 'By the fire. Talking about you-know-what.' He did not seem in the least surprised. 'Explaining the facts of life,' I told him, 'with gestures.'

He sat down on the commode and began to rock gently. 'I told you about you-know-what,' he said. 'Years ago.'

'You gave me a pamphlet,' I said, 'with disgusting diagrams in red and black.'

He rocked back and forward, squeaking before speaking. 'I think you will find,' he said, 'that that just about sums it up.'

I stared boldly back at him, knowing that he was lying in his religious teeth, and after a moment his eyes slid away from mine. Sitting in the twin commode I began to rock with him. 'I just came home for the weekend,' I said. 'You-know-what was the last thing on my mind.' He flashed me a smile of approval and we creaked together, like pilot and co-pilot taking a Dakota through a storm.

'All I was doing was having my Ovaltine!' I cried, really enjoying my first big helping of righteous indignation. 'Thinking about the West Wind; and then . . . what happened?'

'What?' he cried, clutching the wooden arms, showing the burnished studs on the soles of his boots as he rocked back.

'Abortion,' I said; and then taking a breath: 'And then incest.'

With surprising dexterity, the Reverend Captain stepped from the commode; leaving it creaking and rocking, moving away by itself across the kitchen floor. '*Abortion?*' he said, and he said it very well. '*Incest?*' He said that even better, and it brought Yasmin in from the sitting room.

'Not tonight, Vicar,' she said in the doorway, looking lovely with the light behind her. 'We're rather busy this evening.'

'So I understand,' replied the fighting clergyman, groping behind him for the commode which was slowing to a halt. He sat down again but kept still, bowing his bereted head.

'I was taking the opportunity to have a serious talk with Jeffrey,' said Yasmin. 'There are things that he has to know.'

'Of course,' said Eli, without looking up. 'You're quite right of course.'

'It's not a woman's job.'

'No, it's not. Indeed it's not.' He cleared his throat. 'I can't remember now if I gave you the pamphlet . . . ?' But Yasmin ignored this.

'So if I don't tell him, who will?'

There was silence. Then Eli spoke to the kitchen floor: 'His father?'

'He's in Carlisle,' I said, rocking slowly to a halt.

He raised both hands in despair and surrender. 'Very well,' he said. 'But I think I should insist on being present.'

So we all went into the sitting room and made up the fire. Yasmin made more Ovaltine and I sat, feeling rather important, on the gentleman's chair. To be the man of the house and allowed to poke the fire was one thing, but to be lectured by Yasmin and Eli on the facts of life was something else again.

'Put your finger out rigid,' I said, when we were ready. 'That's where we were up to.'

'I don't think so,' said Yasmin, glancing at Eli who had been given the pouffe. 'I think it's better if you just ask us questions.'

'Like The Brains' Trust,' said Eli, hugging his knees. 'What a good idea!'

'Right,' I said. 'We've dealt with things and receptacles.' I looked at Commander Campbell and Lady Violet Bonham-Carter, sitting there full of carnal knowledge, froth around their mouths. 'What's the difference,' I asked

– like the riddle-me-rees that ran across the top of every page in *The Dandy* – 'what's the difference between a cock and a dick, and a thing and a tool, and a hampton and a willy. *And*, as they say around Swinehurst, a pork dagger?'

'I don't know,' said the Reverend Captain, frowning. 'What is the difference between a cock and a dick, and a thing . . .'

'They're all the same,' cut in Yasmin, with complete assurance. 'Next question.'

'Thank you,' I said, inclining my head. 'The next question is from a young listener in Lincolnshire.' I was having a marvellous time. I sat back in the chair, feeling for my sweeties. 'Why two titties?'

'Pardon?' said Captain Eli.

'Why not?' said Yasmin.

I don't think adrenaline had yet been discovered, but I felt it surging through my blood. This was terrific! We were going better than Spit and Cough, the Flemish comedians that Uncle Frank always spoke about. 'Why can't they wear trousers?' I demanded.

'Because, as the Vicar would say, they're an abomination against the Lord.'

'Unto the Lord, I think,' muttered the commissioned cleric, putting his Ovaltine carefully onto the floor.

'Unless you happen to be a tram conductress,' I added, waiting for her nod of agreement. 'Can I ask anything I like?'

'*TITTIES*?' roared Captain Eli, before Yasmin could answer, loudly and suddenly and in a voice beyond abortion or incest. 'What are titties?'

'You're on the panel to answer questions,' I respectfully reminded him. 'Not to ask them.'

Being unable to rock the pouffe he was standing up, his face in the shadow beyond the firelight looking like the girl on the Biro calendar, only sans of course the white hat and spoon.

'Now,' I said, 'I would like to ask a series of questions that have been sent in by the boys and girls of Swinehurst Secondary Modern School.'

'Oh yes?' said Yasmin.

'Yes,' I said. 'They're all to do with the Spanish Fly.' I smiled at my sister, hoping that she had the answers on the tip of her tongue; for I had the feeling that The Brains' Trust was coming to an end. I should really have been watching the erect and enraged Eli.

The pouffe hit me full in the face, breaking the ear off my beaker. Then he was on top of me, pressing a cushion over my mouth and nostrils. Through my ears (which the cushion failed to cover, but through which I could not of course breathe) I heard him raving in his Vicar's voice.

'I'll give you titties!' he was shouting, and I tried to answer, 'Yes, please. Thanks very much,' just to lighten the mood as it were, but my mouth was full of cushion. This, I suddenly realised, was how the little Princes in the Tower had felt. The shadow of Crookback in the arched doorway . . . 'Now is the winter of our discontent . . . ' and before they understood what he was talking about – a pouffe full in the face!

But I fought back. I could see (it was a smallish cushion, not the kind Miss Parkinson used) that Yasmin had embraced him from the rear and was attempting to pull him off. In different circumstances I am sure he would have appreciated that. But he was too strong; and of course filled right now with the wrath of God. So, deciding that things had gone far enough – were indeed getting out of hand – I brought up my right knee, as taught by Uncle Frank, striking the two things which were to have been the subject of my next question, and which I was pleased to find that the Reverend gentleman still had. He crumpled onto the floor, though with eyes open and staring upwards. I motioned to Yasmin to move away at once.

'Phew!' I said, wiping Ovaltine from my pullover and

quoting, I think from the Duke of Wellington. 'A damn close thing!'

'Yes,' said my sister. 'It was the tits that did it.'

There seemed to be no answer to this, so I nodded, disappointed that I had been unable to ask why they do not lift the lavatory seat.

Chapter Eight

A ride to Hobbeycock Hall – Grave news from Rosemary –
A proposal – An emotional scene – I take a decision –
Swinehurst sleeps – I disappear over the horizon

My visit home had not been a success. I realised that as I
grasped the brass rail, as we raced through the outer
suburbs of Swinehurst. It was the day after my return, and
I was out for a ride with Rosemary. She came up the steel
spiral stairs, sliding open the door to the front observation
platform, where I knelt on the wooden seat. Eyes narrowed
and the wind in my face, I was playing at being a figure-
head. Below us, sock-wrapped hand on the throttle, toe
on the pedal that clanged the bell, stood Rosemary's mate,
Chester.

'How did it go?' she asked, leaning against the door to
keep it open, careful as always to maintain the proprieties.

'They tried to teach me the facts of life,' I said. The wind
whipped the words from my lips and I had to repeat them
as the tram slowed down.

'Bloody shame!' said Rosemary, pulling the chain, the
tram starting to gather speed again.

That's the way it was between us; an intuitive understanding. Both of us knew exactly where we were. But
Rosemary, I was to find when we got to the terminus, was
in trouble.

We were going to Hobbeycock Hall, the local stately
home, where someone had been murdered in the sixteenth
century. The bloodstain on the oak floor had never dried,

though you were not allowed to actually touch it. You could have tea there in the orangery, but it and the tram terminus outside, with its crush barriers for the Bank Holiday crowds, were deserted on this cold and windy day.

Chester was trying to light his pipe, after turning the tram round, while I assisted Rosemary in pushing over the backs of the seats to face the other way. I thought this was rather odd, seeing that Chester had turned the tram round, but it was no business of mine to question her professional expertise.

'Jeffrey,' she said suddenly. 'Can I talk to you?'

'Of course,' I said, 'but I don't think I want to hear about the facts of life. Not at the moment. Unless you'd like to tell me about the lavatory seat?' But she shook her head, meaning she didn't know I suppose, or couldn't be bothered to explain.

'I'm in trouble,' she said. A tear fell from her cheek onto her tartan wool scarf, tied like a stylish cravat and fastened with the badge of the Transport and General Workers' Union.

'I know,' I said. 'I don't know what you were thinking of.' And I smiled, trying to cheer her up. 'I'll help you,' I said. 'And I won't tell Chester.'

'You'd better not!' she said, quite forcibly, as I went down the aisle pushing the seats over the other way. Stuck in the metal grooves of the floor I found a workman's penny pink I had not got, and was bent over, excitedly retrieving it, when I felt her eyes on me. As I straightened up, somewhat flushed, she said: 'Jeffrey, what am I going to do?'

'You're going to the Bon Marche,' I said, 'in three minutes. Then you come back here again, and . . . '

'Shut up!' she said, even more forcibly. She breathed and shuddered and then said: 'I'm pregnant!'

I was surprised! All the seats shuddered as well as if in horror, as did the tram itself. Uncle Frank's watch must have been slow, for at that moment we started to move, to race back from Hobbeycock Hall to downtown Swinehurst. Rosemary, looking shocked herself by what she had just said, went downstairs to collect the fares; but found only Chester there, and of course he did not pay.

'I'm in the club!' she said from halfway up the spiral stairs, just her head and shoulders, like when she said good night to me over the Doric portico of her house.

'Just like Miss Parkinson,' I said, smiling and nodding, thinking that if she continued to work in her condition she would also have to have a cushion.

She sat down beside me, something I knew the Lincolnshire Road Car Company frowned upon. 'You're the only one I can talk to,' she said. Which I thought was obvious, seeing that there was nobody else on the tram but Chester; and a small enamel plaque said you were not to talk to him. She was holding my face in her mittened hand, squeezing my cheeks so that my lips pursed like a goldfish; but I managed to blurt out: 'How can I help, Rosemary?'

She said nothing for a moment, looking into my eyes, and I thought to myself, with a sharp intake of breath: 'Oh, my God! It's the knitting needles and the hot water again!' But no. Again I was wrong.

'Could you say you were the father?'

Gently pulling my face out of her hands, I attempted the sentence. 'You were the father,' I said loudly, upstairs in an empty tram. It sounded more than a little silly.

'No. *You!*' she almost shouted, grasping me by the shoulders with her verdigrised fingers; beginning to sound, I thought, a little desperate. Having no idea that she was interested in elocution, (something that was badly needed in Swinehurst), I tried again.

'Yah . . . yah . . . yooh,' I said, I thought very distinctly. 'Any good?'

She was about to strike me with her wooden ticket rack when Inspector Wallace, smart in his black raincoat and immaculate braided hat, swung aboard as the tram rounded a corner. I had seen him practise this on the Noah's Ark at the fair. I bought a half to The Parade, and Rosemary gave the impression that she was upstairs to keep an eye on me.

'Been to see the bloodstain, have you?' said Inspector Wallace as he scrutinised my ticket.

'Yes,' I said, my mouth still being fixed in that position.

Later that night it all came out. We had had, I remember, black pudding for supper, which I was now able to take in my stride. Aunt Ada had set off for the Tabernacle, it being Ladies' Night, taking Uncle Fred as her guest. Rosemary and I were doing the washing up.

'Well,' she said, as soon as we were alone. 'What do you think?' She had changed out of her uniform into quite a smart dress, and had made a point of washing around her eyes and scrubbing her fingers. I thought she looked rather nice. I dried the last of the plates and hung the tea towel over the oven door. 'About the black pudding?' I asked cautiously.

'No,' she said quietly. 'About being the father of my child.'

We sat at the kitchen table with a pot of tea, (after the day of my arrival the gold-encrusted china had been put away), and Rosemary put her hand on mine, moving aside the Daddies Sauce.

'Think of it,' she said. 'It can all turn out for the best. I can go back to work when we're married, and we'll be quite well off.' She smiled. 'We'll have our own little house.'

I stared at her open mouthed, letting the tea get cold. I had a sudden vision of yet another plywood house where my bed had been. With a bay window and a painted drainpipe, and me trying to get the pram through the cardboard door. 'When we're married?' I said, stupidly. 'In the Tabernacle?'

126

'Of course!' She squeezed my arm. 'Can't you see us coming out under the ticket racks, with the Road Car Company Silver Band playing on the steps?'

'And Inspector Wallace as best man?' I was feeling positively light-headed.

'If you like.' She was a little surprised, not knowing we were that close.

'With a carnation in his black raincoat? And live in a little house upstairs? You, me and a baby?' I removed my arm from the table. My voice had been steadily rising and my knees were now flexed, getting ready to run.

'No,' she said, in a soothing voice. 'Not upstairs. We'll find a little cottage, and Dad'll come and fix it up. And Mam'll give us some sheets.'

'Some *sheets*?' I said, unable to believe my ears. I stood up, leaving the tea, having no wish to hear about her dowry. 'I am fourteen!' I cried, taking out my Identity Card in its celluloid wallet and showing it to her. Without thinking I took off my pullover and began to wash my neck at the sink. I well knew that in some parts of the world I would have been a grandfather by now; I had heard all about child brides and swopping them for cows; but this was ridiculous.

'It's ridiculous!' I said.

'It's life,' she said simply, beginning to cry, the tears pattering onto the beehives. I watched her in the piece of mirror in the sink tidy, seeing her reflection alongside the carbolic soap. Suddenly I felt ashamed. The very least I could do was to consider the prospect. Rosemary undeniably cut a handsome figure, especially in her uniform, and I had become attached to her parents, Uncle Fred in particular. To spurn his daughter, to abandon her on a tram with a bundle in a shawl – I would be hounded from the house, from the Tabernacle, from Swinehurst itself. God might well have made the land for the people, but Uncle Fred would never rest until He had made me pay for what I had so manifestly not done. I completed cleaning my teeth and turned to face her.

'I have not yet reached puberty,' I announced. It was her turn to stare open mouthed.

'You haven't reached puberty?' she repeated, as if I were on her tram and had gone past my stop.

'Not yet,' I said. I think I had the idea that it arrived with your calling-up papers when you reached eighteen. I smiled at her with nice clean teeth. 'I'm sorry,' I said, 'but I don't think I can help.'

She went on staring, though she closed her mouth. 'That's it, is it?' she cried; so loudly that I drew the curtains and put the wireless on. 'Take your pleasure, and then piss off!' Not a nice way of putting it.

'That's it,' I agreed; taking an arrowroot biscuit from the barrel and, I must admit, a certain degree of enjoyment from the situation. As you know, I had a small part once in 'The Importance of Being Earnest', but it had been nothing like this.

'But what can I do?' she cried, starting to beat the Daddies Sauce bottle on the table.

'Please!' I said. 'Keep calm.' I took away the sauce bottle to prevent her from doing anything foolish. There was silence while I filled my hot-water bottle, making sure the teddy's head was dry, then I paused in the doorway. 'I think you're making an awful fuss,' I said. 'Miss Parkinson was in the club before you, but she didn't go on about it. *She* didn't ask me to marry her!' I thought that would make her smile, but it didn't. There being nothing more I could do I went upstairs, hoping to be asleep with Sunny Jim before the lights went on in the big house.

But of course, like all women, once they have an idea they won't let it go. Within minutes she had followed me up, breathing heavily, putting up the blackout. Switching on the pink light she sat out under the Doric portico, as if it were a summer evening. I could feel her looking at me as I tried to feign sleep, like Sunny Jim, his stuffed cotton head on the pillow close to mine. I was hoping that Chester would arrive to perform his amusing antics, putting out the light so that I could get some sleep. Indeed I said as much when I pretended to wake, stretching and yawning and blinking at the pregnant tram conductress in the strawberry glow.

'Hello, Rosemary,' I said. 'What time is it? Are you waiting for Chester?'

'It's time you faced your responsibilities,' she said, ignoring the second question. 'Time you became a man.'

I sat up in bed, plumping the pillow, fastening the top button of my pyjamas, recalling Bernard's postcard, in reply to my news that I slept, now, a bed length away from a beautiful unmarried woman. 'Oh cursed one, your time has come!' he had written in capital letters, quoting the last remark addressed to General ('Chinese') Gordon. The words had been spoken by an aide of the Mad Mahdi, as he hurried up the steps with a spear.

'Rosemary,' I said. 'Let us be sensible. What exactly is it that you want?'

'I want you to give my child a name,' she said.

'Yes, of course,' I said. 'If I'd known, I could have borrowed Miss Parkinson's book.' I gave a light laugh. 'Have you thought about Frederick?'

'Frederick who?' she asked, suspiciously.

'Frederick your father,' I said patiently. 'Fred. For a name.' She stood up in her pink flannelette.

'Jeffrey,' she said, 'listen to me.' She seemed to have calmed down, and I thought she might have put it all out of her mind and was going to tell me a story.

'Do you know how a girl gets a baby?' she began.

'Hang on!' I said. 'This isn't going to be about the facts of life, is it?'

She came and sat on the bed. This was something new, and in the context of the conversation a worrying departure. I drew my little legs up under me, so that I would not feel her through the counterpane.

'The woman . . . ' she went on, but I raised a rigid finger to let her know I had been properly briefed.

'Has a receptacle,' I said. 'I know.'

'I was going to say,' she said, 'that the woman always pays!'

'You mean on the tram?' I said, surprised.

'No, not on the tram,' she said; and then she reached for my pyjama case at the foot of the bed and gave a little scream into it. This seemed to do her good. 'Just shut up!' she said. 'And listen to me. Or I'll smother you with the fucking Panda!'

I half sat, half lay still, my legs doubled under me, not wanting another performance of Richard III; and of course I got a frisson from her use of the word.

'You don't get a baby by yourself,' she said, slowly, very much like Mrs Dooley reading Janet and John. 'You need a man. Do you understand that much?'

I nodded, tight lipped.

'In other words, it takes two to tango.'

I nodded again, my lips even tighter. Although she knew nothing of my mother and Colonel Trewin, I thought the remark in extremely poor taste.

'Now the man I tango'd with' – she was speaking even slower, each word hyphenated – 'already has a dancing partner. And if she finds out that we've been having a little rumba together, she will be very upset. Very upset indeed.'

She paused, and as my lips wouldn't go any tighter I rolled my eyes.

'So,' she continued, taking a deep breath and looking away from my face, 'the best thing is not to tell the man I tango'd with, that I'm going to have a little baby. Understand?' She lit a Woodbine, waving the smoke away from me. 'The best thing to do is to get someone else,' she smiled through a smoke ring, 'to tell everyone that he had a little rumba with me, and he's the baby's daddy. Okay?'

I hadn't the faintest idea what she was talking about.

'Now I know you're very young,' she said, 'but I've looked it up in *The Doctors' Book* and it's possible. We might have to wait a while to get married, and there will be talk of course, there's bound to be. But I can alway say that I forgot to lock my door one night. Or you came in through the cellophane window.' She knocked her ash into my pot, straightening up again with a grin on her face. 'You'll find that you'll get many a nudge of admiration,' she said. 'Even at the Tabernacle. And Mam'll start feeding you up. You know what they say: you can't do it on bread and jam.'

With a fixed smile, through tight lips, I felt compelled to murmur, 'But I haven't done it!'

There was utter silence. Our eyes held in the pink dusk. 'Would you like to?' Rosemary asked, softly.

'Rumba?' I whispered through aching lips. She nodded. 'If you want.' The Woodbine hissed as it went out. 'You do realise that we're not really supposed to do it before we get married?'

I nodded. It was all very confusing. That was what the Rev Eli Wannamaker insisted on. He used to hand out leaflets saying just that, that you were not supposed to do it before you were married; while the Junior Rechabites maintained that you shouldn't do it at all.

I watched as she crossed the room to her front door, passing with a smile and a wave beneath the Doric portico, listening for the sound of the bolt sliding home. But silence. Then her voice over the wall: 'I'm putting the light out, Jeffrey.'

She did, and I lay in the darkness, feeling the seam at the back of Sunny Jim's neck. Here was adventure indeed, beyond all that promised by Percy F. Westerman. I had only to rise and pass through the plywood portals . . . and mystery would be mystery no more.

But young though I was, do not think I was a fool. I knew that there was more to it than nudging admiration at the Tabernacle, and an extra slice from Aunt Ada. Mam. There would first of all be an urgent visit home, before the *Lincolnshire Standard* was read with incredulity at the breakfast table.

'Hello? De Kuyper – where are you? Guess what I've done . . . '

'Could I see my father, please? Yes, I know the way to the office. Hello, Daddy, have you heard the news . . . ?'

'Yasmin, meet your sister-in-law. One and a half please, Rosemary, darling . . . '

'Dear Mother and Colonel Trewin, There's something I think you ought to know . . . '

'Dear Headmaster, Because of my new responsibilities, I no longer wish to be considered for throwing the cricket ball . . . '

'Hello, Agatha. You must excuse me, the wife's waiting . . . '

'Bernard . . . really. It's not a subject one gentleman discusses with another. Yes, I daresay the Riffs are quite open about that sort of thing . . . '

'Dear Rufus . . . . '

All my plans, my dreams, my aspirations. Who would employ a married telegram boy with a child? My mind searched forward through time, and the future became brutally clear. The war was over, and England Merrie England once again. Because of my background, and what I owed to my short stay at Traggets, I would have a head start on my contemporaries at the Secondary Modern School. Not to speak of the shell shocked and one legged returning from the war. I knew that if I seriously applied myself I could be somebody in Swinehurst. In a pebble-dashed semi with a bay window. We would have a pouffe and a radiogram; the gentleman's chair if my father had slipped beneath the waves; and the child could play with my things. To the beat of Alvar Liddell I would stuff Scott's Emulsion into its mouth. Every Sunday Fred and Ada, Dad and Mam, would come for a Pre-War Tea; and he would dandle it on his knee and teach it to say God made the land for the people.

Like slides on the Rev Eli Wannamaker's lantern, the choices flashed before me in the dark bedroom. Rosemary and Jeffrey. Me in the elevator shoes they advertised in the classified section of *The Rover*. The white veil flowing over her silver buttons; the two of us waving from a decorated tram. The wedding photograph, with Yasmin's poodle at the front; and the gang on Mossies' window sill, eating chips or sucking sherbet.

' 'E married a tram conductress in Swinehurst. So much for 'is prep!' Pickersgill was saying, in a balloon over his head.

And in gold letters, on the varnished board at Traggets: 'Coram. J. St John; Captain, 8th Guards Division. Killed in action, Mersa Matrūh. Cork. J. Married tram conductress, Swinehurst.' At the going down of the sun we will remember them.

I sat up suddenly in the bed, startling Sunny Jim, my brow damp. I would run away!

Rosemary, though obviously excited at the prospect of having a rumba, seemed to be asleep. But Mr Beeston had warned us that these things loomed large in a girl's life, were more important than we might suppose. Even though, as he put it, they were pretty well insatiable, only having to lie there while we did the work. I suppose the nervous strain, plus up and down to Hobbeycock Hall all day, had been too much for her. I listened to her regular breathing and laid my plans.

I would leave at two o'clock, when I imagined Swinehurst would be at its lowest ebb, and head due south west. If I missed the Nabisco factory, I would still be on a course towards Traggets. Missing them both, I would stow away on a lugger at a Cornish port, bound for Los Angeles if possible. To cross the potato fields towards Jasmine Villa was out of the question. Running away was one thing; running home was the act of a maggot.

Uncle Frank's watch not being luminous, and the clock above the portico being painted at a permanent twenty past four, I had to guess at the time. Of course I drifted into my usual deep and healthy sleep, until I was awakened by the first sonorous stroke of the church clock. My mind instantly alert, every action clear and rehearsed, I seized Sunny Jim and the Panda and stepped out of bed. Only to crash to the lino and lay there, bloodless legs twisted under me like an Indian holy man. Indeed, I felt like shouting 'Fakir!'

I held my breath, expecting the pink light to come on and the plywood door to open. The beckoning finger. Or to hear any moment the shuffle of Aunt Ada, going downstairs in her khaki overcoat to fry me a sausage. But no, the house slumbered while my circulation returned. There had been no second strike of the clock, but I decided to wait no longer.

Opening the bedroom door I saw Uncle Fred's boots, left out for aesthetic reasons rather than with the expectation that anyone would clean them. Slowly I made my way down the stairs, each step seeming to creak louder than the last, until I reached the hall. The last rail of the bannister, the one that at home bore the pineapple finial, came away in my hand as it so often did. Deciding to use this to go over my shoulder, I hurriedly put my few possessions into a clean tea towel, knotting it at the end of my staff. Opening the front door I stepped out into the night.

The streets of Swinehurst were dark and silent as I followed the tramlines, glinting silver in the faint moonlight, towards the south. As I came abreast of the Home and Colonial a police constable stepped out of the tiled shadows.

'Evening, sir,' he said, his cape lifting as his fingers went to the brim of his helmet.

'Good evening, constable,' I answered, stepping onto the pavement, being unsure of the by-laws. I reflected, as the houses thinned out and the potatoes spread away towards the dark blueish hills, that Lord Trenchard had, by and large, done a good job.

Into the moon, like Charlie Chaplin, but without a hook at the end of my stick, I disappeared over the horizon.

Chapter Nine

*On the Great North Road – The Nabisco factory – My first
vista – Rufus Real at home – The Hon Wendy – A jolly
good breakfast – Fun with the Governess*

I had of course left my bolster in the foetal position, and
there was – unless Rosemary woke up and remembered
she had been let down – little chance of my absence being
discovered. Not until Aunt Ada knocked with the tea at
eight the following morning. Until then, until her and her
daughter's screams rang through the house, I was free.

My plimsolls padded past dark and sleeping farm-
houses. Sometimes a dog barked. Once a helmeted figure,
looking like De Kuyper, swept silently past on a bicycle.
Searchlights flickered long fingers of light across the sky,
but I doubted they were looking for me.

My plan was to stay on the main highway, offering a
thumb and a bright smile to passing cars. But it was a
civilian lorry which eventually stopped, its black tarpaulin
roped tight over something big. As it pulled in ahead of
me onto the grass verge, I ran after it and reached up to
open the door of the cab. The driver's seat was empty, but
still warm, a kind of motorised Marie Celeste. Then he
appeared from the hedgerow, buttoning up the front of
his trousers. A small man, in a cap, like one of the grass
roots at the Tabernacle.

' 'Ello then!' he said. 'What 'ave we 'ere?'

Realising what he had been doing, I was overcome with
embarrassment. (I am not an ecologist, but what a way for

the small furry creatures of the countryside to go!) But I decided to speak.

'Good evening, sir. Or rather good morning.' I laughed lightly to put him at his ease. I could see that he was a Londoner, salt of the earth; father no doubt of some of those children called Ernie, in their awful trousers, that I had met at Euston.

'Wot you doin' then?' he asked. 'This time a night, wiv a tea towel on a stick?'

I swung lightly aboard, thinking that if it had been the Hebrews' steam waggon I could have warmed myself at the fire, or made toast. Or had some of their tea, which they make with lemon and drink through a lump of sugar. While he tucked a sack around my knees I told him a tale of setting off to seek my fortune, my entire family having been wiped out by drought.

'Cor!' he said, just like in a comic. 'Fuck me! Wot drought was that then?' There was genuine concern on his homely face as he passed me his thermos flask. Pouring a little into the lid, I noticed the soggy toast in the glove compartment.

And so we sped south through the night. The driver, my benefactor, whose name was Chas, singing folk songs from east of Aldgate Pump. I hummed with him, and clapped, but the only line I recall now was: 'I painted her old tomata, over and over again'; collected he thought by Cecil Sharp, and arranged by Percy Grainger.

As dawn broke, silhouetting the impressive bulk of the Nabisco factory against the less than immense Hertfordshire sky, the lorry pulled again onto the grass verge.

'Okay, Squire?' said Chas. 'This do yer?'

I thanked him, deciding against giving him my two-shilling piece. More than likely he would have been offended. As he unbuttoned his corduroy trousers again I moved away in the long wet grass, the bannister and the tea towel over my shoulder.

'Bye, Squire,' he called, looking down.

'Bye, Chas,' I answered, staring straight ahead.

Streaks of dawn had given way to what promised to be a bright morning when I reached the high stone wall of the Reals' estate. I had spent some time at the Nabisco factory, watching Shredded Wheat lorries leave on their journeys to all parts of the civilised world. Indeed I had waved to the drivers, and some of them had waved back. Through the main gates I had seen cartons of the famous breakfast food, with overalled men and headscarved women busily at work. Hearing one of the ladies, who was bending over at the time, emit a peal of laughter, I decided to work there when I grew up.

But I had put the Nabisco factory behind me as I scaled Rufus Real's wall. First throwing over Sunny Jim and the Panda, then the tea towel, I tumbled down myself onto Rufus Reals' grass. Picking myself up I looked around.

It was very much like Swinehurst park really, but without a drinking fountain and a ruined lavatory. Thinking there would possibly be swings and a slide I set off along a gravelled path, marvelling at the rhododendrons and the pheasants hiding in the long grass. Then, suddenly rounding an oak tree in search of conkers, I looked up and beheld the first vista I had ever seen.

Grass smoother and greener than we had ever managed at Jasmine Villa rolled and sloped away from me. The gentle hillside, sculpted (I learnt later, when I saw the small overgrown cemetery) by forty thousand eighteenth-century salts of the earth, and carefully arranged with trees. Stone steps gleamed in the morning sun, as if scrubbed and whitened like those at Victory Cottage, and on each rise a stone vase of flowers; naked statues in various postures. A flash of water with the colour of the sky; ducks and a black swan, and white doves circling and calling in the silence. Then, ringed by privet clipped into the shape of triangles and balls, the home of Rufus Real.

It would be fair to say that I was impressed. The architecture reminded me at first of Rosemary's house, but there the resemblance ended. I laughed inwardly at my foolishness. There would be no note for the milkman at this front door, huge as it was for taking coffins and sideboards in and out. No painted drainpipes or cellophane windows. The house, I calculated, if set down in the centre of Swinehurst, would stretch from the Bon Marché to the Skegness Road. I could not begin to guess at the rates.

Feeling rather small, I set foot on the first of the white steps. I can see myself now, looking up, mouth open in wonder, the myriad windows in the grey stone twinkling in the sun. 'A thousand windows and a thousand doors . . . ' De Kuyper recited, and I could not help but reflect on the kind of reception the Hebrews would have received had they chugged in here in their steam waggon.

Slowly I made my way up the vista, touching the statues as my father would have done; thinking of breakfast. In a house such as this, war or no war, there was I knew a strong possibility of fried bread.

Suddenly, hearing voices, I hurried into a clump of trees. It was probably minions I thought, come down to whiten the steps. But no. Along an adjacent path, as Sunny Jim and I peered round the bole of a tree, came a group of figures. They were not minions, of that I was instinctively aware, and it was most unlikely that they had come down to whiten the steps. All male, they were heavily armed; and for a moment I thought they might be German para-troopers, grouping in the privacy of the park before attacking the Nabisco factory. Then I recognised the shortest of them as Rufus Real!

There were three men striding along the gravel, the biggest of them obviously Real Senior. They all wore tweed suits the colour of porridge, with patch pockets and matching caps. These were almost, but not quite, identical to those worn by the working class. Their porridge-coloured knickerbockers ended in socks, in a predominantly brown pattern, and stout brogues, rich with the same bull's blood that nourished Colonel Trewin's footwear. But of course it was not their outfits which had made me think at first of stormtroopers, but the guns they carried. Etched and damascened barrels glinted in the light, carved and polished stocks lay across their shoulders, in much the same way that I carried my bannister and tea towel.

The other two, on either side of the one I was certain was Real Senior, were thin and spoke like Mr Croxton, the master at Traggets who stared at you. I saw one of them pass across a silver flask, saying, 'Fency a spot of breakfast?'

The three were softly humming, in perfect harmony (like The Ink Spots but without the negro dialect), the Eton Boating Song. As you know, I had at one time set my heart on going there, but had always found the words – 'Pull, pull together, your bodies between your knees' – rather disturbing. Behind them, as I have mentioned, came Rufus. He was silent, in a similar porridge-coloured suit and cap, with a small shotgun under his arm. Though, as he told me later, a Purdey of the highest quality, it had twin corks at the end of its blued-steel barrels.

I was both deeply moved and excited. What would Rufus say when he found me in the woods with Sunny Jim? How his eyes would widen when I told him of Rosemary's proposition; about my being up after midnight; about my journey south with Chas. Almost beside myself with excitement, I leaned forward as he passed me, close enough to touch one of his little brogues.

'Pssst!' I said.

There was a heartbeat's silence. The crunch of Jermyn Street leather on the gravel had ceased. Rufus turned towards me, his mouth opening as our eyes met – and then all disappeared in a series of shattering explosions! Leaves and twigs fell about me, spiralling down from the trees; not to mention conkers, which I did not have the wit to collect. I was in the midst of smoke and the smell which, according to the Rev Eli Wannamaker, announces the advent of you-know-who. Face down in the leaf mould, covering Sunny Jim with my body, I was prepared to believe that the Germans had taken disguise to undreamed-of lengths.

A stout toecap turned me over and I opened my eyes to look up the barrel of a gun, bringing back a memory of my grandmother's nostrils all those years before. The mind plays strange tricks.

'It's Jeffrey!' came Rufus's voice, and with it the possibility that I would be spared.

'Thought you were a grouse,' said Real Senior, lowering his gun. 'I shouldn't do that again if I were you. Shoot anything that moves around here, don't you know; unless it's a dog or a horse.' A sniff, then 'HA!' he shouted suddenly, and he and his thin friends, gun butts into their shoulders, revolved slowly, barrels pointing at the blank blue sky. I stood up, brushing the dirt from Sunny Jim and picking up my bannister and tea towel.

'You're not the new boot boy, are you?' asked Rufus's father, wetting his finger and touching his foresight.

'No, sir,' I said. 'I'm a school chum of Rufus. I'm in – or I was in, before I had to leave – the bed almost opposite his.' I then spoke from behind my hand. 'We had some trouble at home,' I added confidentially.

The big man stared at me, hairs flaring from his nostrils. Though he was not certifiably deaf, I was to find that few of the words addressed to him actually got through.

'You're not the chappie with a thing on a string?' The others, who were still revolving, lowered their guns, taking an interest in me for the first time.

'No, sir. I'm afraid not.'

'Right!' he said decisively, after a silence. 'See you at dinner then.' He moved off through the trees, flanked by his friends, the three of them starting to hum.

'Jolly glad to see you,' said Rufus, putting out his hand. I gave him the two-shilling piece, which he looked at with interest before slipping it into his waistcoat pocket. Talking, as boys do, of what we had been up to, we walked towards the house. It turned out that Rufus was home on an exeat (something I later silenced Pickersgill with) and we planned to do great things together.

'Why don't you come back to Traggets?' he asked in all his innocence. 'It was never the same without you.' He told me that Wheelan had now got four maggots doing a Living Tableau after lights out. As we passed through the quiet sun trap of the rose garden, across the patterned brick terrace, men with string around their knees rose from the flower beds to salute the young master. I asked about Tonto, and Dr Hazlit, and the girl who was reputed to have 'Death Before Dishonour' tattooed just below her knickers.

Rufus said that Tonto was well; Dr Hazlit was having 'a good war'; and the girl from Guinevere's had disappointed many people by being expelled alive.

The sense of loss, the remembrance of that other world that I had left, was almost too much for me. In the formal Italian garden, well out of earshot of minions, I stopped and told Rufus about my opportunity of having a rumba on a tram.

'Well, not actually on a tram,' I said. 'In her house.'

'And her house was like ours? With a Doric portico?' His eyes were wide, as I had imagined, as he stared at me with respect over the sundial.

'Yes,' I said, irritated by the surprise in his voice, the way he said 'Doric portico'. People like Rufus, I reflected, though obviously better than us, had no idea of the culture of the provinces. What did he know of our horse trough?

'You've never even seen our horse trough,' I said, as he opened a door in a brick wall into the kitchen garden.

'I'm sorry,' said Rufus. Then: 'Is she a big girl?' I don't think he could quite grasp what a tram conductress was.

'Big enough,' I said, noting the pathetic girth of the cucumbers. A gardener's boy ran into a shed, closing the door behind him, as I picked and started to eat a nectarine.

'Shall I tell you about the late-night fish suppers?' I asked, wiping juice from my chin with a corner of the tea towel.

'Wow!' he exclaimed, his eyes widening again. 'Dorm feasts!'

'With mushy peas,' I told him, spitting the stone into the Cos lettuces.

Thinking I could smell the fragrance of Camp coffee I began to move towards the house, but he remained rooted to the spot, his mouth open. 'What are mushy peas?' he asked.

I shook my head slowly, with a patient and sympathetic smile. All this, and probably fried bread every day; but I, who had come through the maelstrom of a middle-class *and* working-class upbringing, was light years ahead when it came to the facts of life.

'Do you know the facts of life?' I asked, trying not to sound patronising.

'Yes,' he said. 'Of course. We're up to cunnilingus. But what are mushy peas?'

We were passing now through the orangery. Humming birds hovered over broad green leaves and orchids, while a Malay gardener, saronged and inscrutable, sprayed a mist of water. Waiting on the brass doorstep I could see the butler, arranging his face. Portly, straight off the Robinsons Lemon Barley Water label, he gave a small bow from the waist, showing the pink top of his head, before taking my bannister and tea towel. Against my better judgement, I also entrusted him with Sunny Jim.

As we entered the breakfast room, Rufus was still talking excitedly about mushy peas. We had washed our hands in a tiled and mahogany place, under the guidance of a man in a green frock coat, and I was, to be honest, extremely impressed. Not only with the tiles and the green frock coat, but this kind of breakfast came as something of a shock.

Through the windows – tall as Mrs Dooley's, though without the rope and pulley mechanism – was the vista.

But now in reverse. The white steps, the pools and the backsides of statuary, the manicured grass and trees leading away into the distance, though inexplicably with no sight of the Nabisco factory. Shafts of sunlight lit the room, and I realised at once that I was a guest of the impoverished aristocracy. The floor was simply bare boards. Clean of course, and strewn with mats, but lino was obviously beyond them. The furniture was old, though well polished, and the long table – its white cloth almost touching the floor – groaned under the kind of feast I had only seen before, in dream balloons, above the head of Hungry Horace.

At the head of the table, making short work of a muffin, was Mrs Real, who I learnt later was an Honourable. Rufus presented me to her at once. 'Good morning, Mother,' he said. 'May I present Jeffrey Cork to you?'

'Yes, of course, my darling. Anybody.' She was a very pretty woman, looking not a day older than Rosemary. Which meant, I thought, with a lift of an eyebrow, that she had given birth to Rufus at the age of four. I had heard at Traggets of certain Tibetan practices, involving yak butter, but was none the less disconcerted. She lay prone, covered with a silk sheet, on a flat trolley like an ironing board.

I shot a look of sympathy towards Rufus, standing with my hands behind my back, looking down at his mother's wheels. Possibly she was an inmate from the soldiers' hospital near Hobbeycock Hall, where they were lined up outside the gate on sunny days to watch the traffic, just the top half of them under blue blankets. But she had legs. Perhaps it had been the trauma of getting married at the age of three.

I later learnt that the Hon Wendy was simply passionate about breakfast in bed. Her husband considered this the practice of nancy boys, so a good old English compromise had been rigged up by Mappin & Webb. At the head of the trolley, with the muffin dish, stood the French maid.

144

She bent over now to wipe the Hon Wendy's mouth, as she did other parts of her as and when required, with a soft cloth.

'Tell me all about yourself,' said the pretty young mum. 'Any friend of Rufus . . . ' and she smiled, shaping her mouth for another muffin. Rufus nodded towards the food, so I made my excuses and backed away, to take a warm plate from the Lemon Barley Water man.

Moving down the sideboard, lifting the gadrooned silver lids, I thought I might just stay on there for ever as the boot boy. Although it was all, as the reader knows, so very strange to me, I proved to be a quick learner. I saw at once that if one took too many sauté potatoes and sausages, by the time you came to the end of the sideboard there would be no room to get your kidneys on the plate. If one had known of course, one would have brought along a twelve-inch plate, giving one a broad foundation. As it was, I saw that the trick was to select flat and squashable things, laying down a base of kedgeree and kipper, bacon and egg, then buttressing it with chipolatas and filling in the spaces with Oeufs Arnold Bennett. Mushrooms I ate as I went along, with butter balls and a fingerful of Gentle-man's Relish, heedless of the eyes of the retainer and the French maid. (The Hon Wendy of course, as she said herself in jest, spent most of her life looking at the ceiling.) I found space for two brown eggs, boiled in a silver contrap-tion reminiscent of the mine owners' sugar-winding gear in the Vale of Clwyd; but there was, to my disappointment, no fried bread.

The French maid left her mistress to help me carry my plate to the table, and I looked eagerly for the Daddies Sauce. There were three other people spaced down the snowy linen; two thin ladies I took to be the wives of the pair in porridge-coloured clothes, and the Nanny, wearing a felt hat and glasses. Rufus, being now at Traggets, was beyond the help of Norland training; but she had I supposed been a good and faithful servant, and was being allowed to stay on and eat muffins. They become, so they tell me, just like one of the family.

I cleared my throat. 'Could I have the sauce, please?'

Three heads turned towards me, as they chewed and swallowed, and I had a good idea where the fried bread had gone. The Kensitas man, the floor creaking under his measured tread, carried the cruet down to where I sat. But I saw at once, with disappointment, that though the silver terraces held within the filigree guard rails many kinds of mustards and chutneys, all the condiments and spices of the Orient (with the exception of powdered rhino horn and cantharides, which Rufus swore the housekeeper kept under lock and key), the one and only sauce was absent. After some thought, with all eyes upon me, I selected HP, which I knew the Deliuses had at Christmas, and was favourably impressed. Possibly a better shape of bottle, like Camp Coffee, which Bernard insisted on because of the Riffs on the label. But having said that, no one can seriously pretend it is the same.

The French maid turned a handle and the Hon Wendy was wound up into a sitting position. This was so that she could take a drink of chocolate and converse with me. It was the first time I had come across anyone actually *drinking* chocolate. I watched, fascinated, over my heaped kedgeree, as the French maid tested the temperature with the tip of her elbow, then held the fine china to her mistress's lips.

'Tell me now,' said the Hon Wendy, her wet chocolaty tongue searching out crumbs adhering to her face cream, 'all about yourself. Who are your people?'

'Yeomen,' I told her, hearing her add softly, with a sigh, 'The backbone of England.' I did not go so far as to mention liberty bodices, but I told her that my father was a Northern Manufacturer.

'What fun!' she cried, clapping her hands together, going on to say that in that case I probably knew J. B. Priestley.

146

I said no, I was afraid I did not, but we had the same taste in peas.

'Jeffrey had the offer of a rumba, mother,' put in Rufus from the other side of the trolley, the French maid feeding him an egg with a free hand.

'My!' said the Hon Wendy, admiring me over her cup. 'Maybe Jeffrey will do one for us this evening, after dinner.'

I mumbled something into my breakfast and the conversation turned somehow to gardening, it being just about the only thing she did standing up. She was proud of her expertise with scissors and a basket, and I told her about Uncle Fred, mentioning the size of his cucumbers. She sighed, asking if he came to town very often. I said no, I was afraid not, that he had had some trouble with fly posting. By this time I was wiping my plate, and it was time for Mrs Real's rest. So the curtains were drawn, the three remaining eaters being left in the dark, and Rufus took me upstairs to my room.

It was, I was pleased to find, one which overlooked the vista and had nobody's house next to my bed. I had half expected to find a rustic cottage with smoke curling from the chimney. Standing at the window, feeling a little like Lord North, I fancied I saw London in the distance, a dark smudge on the horizon. 'The Great Wen!' I said loudly, with satisfaction, slapping my young thigh.

'My father will shoot it if it stays in our garden,' said Rufus gloomily behind me. He was bored and wanted me to come to the nursery, to see his photos of the French maid.

The major domo had laid out my things on the bed. The tea towel had been ironed and folded, and the bannister stood behind the door, in a rack intended for gun or whip. Sunny Jim and the Panda, both of whom had been brushed and disinfected, were propped against the pillow; but the arrowroot biscuit I had kept in reserve was missing. I decided to say nothing about it.

Edward Arnold had also drawn a bath for me. I was

unsure whether or not to take this as an insult, but Rufus said he was always doing it; so we coloured the water and held a short replay of the Battle of Actium. The soap dish and an inflated French letter taking the parts of the opposing fleets. Yet another example of the firm grounding one got with a prep-school education. Rufus then politely asked for the return of the French letter, which he carefully deflated, dried, and repacked with a shake of talcum powder into its envelope. As I followed him along the corridor towards the back stairs he told me he was sending away for one with a feather at the end.

We reached the nursery floor in a scramble, the last to get there being a loony. Such was our speed that we caught the top-floor staff completely off their guard, the wet nurse hastily buttoning herself up. Eyes lowered, the nursery maid curtseyed on the landing, while the Governess scrambled off the rocking horse with a red face.

'Master Rufus!' she exclaimed, smoothing down her divided skirt, cockaded hat askew on her bun. 'We didn't expect you.'

Master Rufus, wagging a knowing finger at her, pulled a face as he glanced at the lunch menu. Having collected his mail and the latest issue of *Film Fun* from a gadrooned silver tray, he led me into his inner sanctum. This was a charming room, with a bright coal fire behind a brass guard, flanked by two young gentlemen's chairs and a specially shaped chaise longue, with an extra cushion and straps.

I was greeted by cries and piercing whistles from the grey African parrots, wicked eyed and each with its own obscene repertoire. Their Chippendale cages hung over the menagerie, a scaled-down replica of Bostock and Wombwell's, and Rufus assured me that all species would have been mucked out and fed by now. He waved towards the rack which held lances, handsome daggers and elephant guns, inviting me to try my prowess. But it was all too much for me. Crossing to the window, which was strongly barred to prevent Rufus being stolen by gypsies, I found we were too high to see the vista. But I was thrilled to be able to pinpoint the classic outline of the Nabisco factory. High among the chimney pots, (the family sweep waved in at me some time later), I looked around me in wonder. While Rufus fiddled with a zoopraxinoscope, watching images of the French maid leap and prance in the candle-light.

Stepping around the pedal-driven Bluebird – I noticed a signed photograph of Sir Malcolm Campbell – I browsed for a moment over the periodicals that hung over mahogany rods: the *Children's Newspaper*, *Our Dogs* and *My Land*. Then, breathing steadily through my nose, I began to move between Rufus's shelves. My fingers trailing along Hamley's scarlet boxes, printed 'Britains' in black; lingering over the Medical Corps, complete with horse ambulance and blood-spattered soldiers. I fired a small shell from a field howitzer before moving on.

The Camel Corps, numerous as those at Omdurman, were deployed on a sand table, the dunes of which stretched away into the shadows of the room, rising to the Atlas Mountains. Clockwork funiculars took sand up, tipping it out and coming down for more. I found it gratifying, if somewhat shocking, to find General 'Chinese' Gordon waiting for the end, halfway up the fretwork steps of the Residency at Khartoum.

At the window of the Foreign Office, in a scale model of Whitehall under glass, a tiny Lord North watched the Brigade of Guards, complete with band and King, troop the Colour. Rufus murmured 'Thank you very much' as I dropped a penny into a slot and a Wizard rolled his mechanical eyes, tapped with his wand, and began to do the three-card trick.

On a top shelf – lined with dark-green paper that hung down in a scalloped frieze – stood a fleet of tin ships, dry docked in teak; above them the De Havillands and flying boats of Imperial Airways. Frog monoplanes stood ready wound; the wings of gliders cast long shadows. Minuscule Huns peered down from the grey shape of the Hindenburg, held against the fine moulding of the ceiling by the whirring of tiny propellers. Bath-length battleships with vertical bows, sides bulbous with anti-torpedo protection, were manned by little German sailors in ribboned caps, under a tin White Ensign.

A fat, cigar-shaped submarine, dressed overall in tin bunting, floated in a tank beside a tugboat powered by the stub of a candle. On yet another shelf, above the recess for the Hobbies fretwork machine, (the next model up from the one my father had), with *Hobbies* magazines and blueprints in box files, and a man waiting quietly to help you with the tricky bits, were the steam engines.

Vertical engines, beam and pumping engines, the wicks burning in the boilers (and trimmed by an oily apprentice who lurked in the background), brass cranks and steel flywheels turning. The coloured lights of the model fairground shimmered in the burnished copper pipes. In attendance stood miniature steam waggons loaded with toy bags of coal, each piece fashioned by craftsmen and packed into tiny sacks by home workers in Widnes, Lancashire. I picked up and marvelled at the fire irons, no larger than my little finger, made in Cradley Heath, Staffordshire, the rake and the shovel complete in every detail. A tribute to British craftsmanship.

On a table by itself, just beyond the puzzles, stood the fort. I was delighted to see that this was set out for a replay of the alternative version of the Sudan campaign, in which General 'Chinese' Gordon catches the Mad Mahdi halfway up *his* stairs; and had what looked like ready dead Riffs lying in the wadis outside the walls. I made a mental note to tell Bernard if ever I saw him again.

Next to the De-Luxe size magic set by Maskelyne and Devant, under the shelves of leather-bound *Chums* and *Chatterbox*, was the toy theatre. With footlights, trapdoors and flies, and with bald automated musicians in the pit.

Wasp-waisted Gaiety girls thronged the spiral stairs to the dressing rooms, wearing finely meshed black tights that you could actually take off. The whole thing, heavy with red plush and gilt cherubim, authentic in every detail – down to the marks of fly buttons on the ornate ceiling – was completed by a little Florrie Ford in a yellow circle of limelight. There was also, so Rufus told me later, a wind machine.

'Do you *want* to see the photos of the French maid?' he asked now, pointing for me to pick up one of the inch to a foot mashers who had fallen over outside the stage door. He had become bored and was spinning slowly in a studded leather chair, chewing on a chocolate cigar.

'Not really,' I said.

Obviously disappointed, he put away the richly bound album that played a saucy tune. 'Do you want to see a book that moos and growls then?'

'No,' I told him politely, not at the moment, adding that perhaps I could take it to bed with me. But he had been brought up to amuse his guests, and now offered to let me paste some scraps into a book. Again I declined, telling him I was really not in the mood. By now things would be happening at Victory Cottage. Aunt Ada would be hammering at the Doric portico, yoo-hooing down the back garden for Uncle Fred, while a posse was hurriedly organised at the Tabernacle.

'I don't know what to do, Rufus,' I said, sitting down on a little milk float.

'You can play with the soldiers if you want,' said Rufus. 'Or would you like me to telephone for a magician?'

'I mean about home. They'll be worried about me at Swinehurst.'

'I suppose so.' He looked at me thoughtfully as he revolved in the chair. 'Those people you're with,' he said as he passed by, 'does the lady come down to breakfast?'

I nodded as he picked up speed, imagining him on a commode.

'The lady you met on a tram,' he said, his legs rising, his hands together like Mahatma Gandhi, 'Wheeeeeeeee!!!'

'The tram conductress, Rosemary?'

'Yes, her.' He came to halt, braking with his foot in the Riff rug. 'She said you could have a rumba?'

I nodded.

'And she lived next door?'

'No . . . well yes; all right.'

'So why didn't you go round and have one?' He looked me in the eye, frankly, in a manly way, all the innocence of his sheltered childhood, plus a good deal of Lord North's assurance.

I took a deep breath, waving aside the bag of treacle toffee. 'Because she was trying to trap me,' I explained. He nodded, understanding, having heard about that, as I had, from Mr Beeston.

'I think it's sixteen shillings a week,' he said, putting the tips of his fingers together. No doubt he had a solicitor's set in one of the wicker baskets in the corner.

'What is?' (This was when I saw the sweep waving in at the window, behind Rufus.)

'For a child.' He smiled, like Mr Rim does as you look up from reading his account with your mouth open. 'And you can see them on a Sunday.'

I stared at him, ignoring the sweep. 'See them on a Sunday?' I repeated.

'Friend of my father's,' Rufus explained. 'He's got several. I heard him say they were cheaper than polo ponies.'

'Just a moment,' I said, moving a little milk churn aside. This was important. 'You don't mean to say . . . you're not telling me you get sixteen shillings a week for each child you have? Who gives it to you?'

'The father gives it to you.' The ball of toffee appeared for a moment between his red lips, before audibly going back into his cheek. I stared at him, reaching out blindly for a piece, my fingers twiddling in the empty bag.

'The girl's father?' I doubted that Uncle Fred could afford

anything like that, but it certainly put things in a different light.

'*You* pay for it. Idiot!' said Rufus, rather rudely I thought. 'The one who had the rumba.'

Gripping the soft leather neck of the milk horse, I restrained myself from shouting at him that I had never had a rumba. 'Every week?' I asked.

'Every week.' He nodded with absolute certainty.

'Every week?' I said again. 'Until it grows up? Until it dies?'

'You'll probably die first,' he said, reassuringly, switching from solicitor to doctor.

I thanked him. I thought, as I had done when I was sent to live with the working class, that it was a lousy world. The man who washed out Pomfrets' churns certainly had a case. All those people who appeared never to do any work – like Colonel Trewin, before he had been asked to do a bit more – were obviously living on that kind of easy money. A postal order every week from an aged father somewhere. There was silence while Rufus changed the cylinder on the musical box; then, to a new tune, I said: 'What am I to do, Rufus?'

'But alas and alack, she came back, with a naughty little twinkle in her eye,' he sang in his pure clear voice, closing the glass lid of the box and watching the silver bells join in. 'I'm thinking,' he said.

I said that I appreciated it, but would he keep the chair still.

The fingers were together again, and he swallowed the butt of the cigar before speaking. If it had not been for the war, he said, I could have gone to the Continent. He could have given me a note for the lady on the Rue Mazarin. As it was, the best thing to do was to have a showdown with her, the tram conductress that is, making sure of course that my solicitor was present. Or change my name and join up as a drummer boy. Did I know that they used to help with the flogging?

153

I told him no, I didn't know that. But I was interested in his suggestion that I stay on as the boot boy. He said that he could put in a word for me, and we agreed to discuss the matter further that night, after dinner.

Chapter Ten

Dinner presented a difficult problem of protocol. Rufus, as a child, could not of course be present; whereas I, until and unless I spoke up for the position of boot boy, was undeniably a guest. So when I returned to my room, after nursery tea and a little fun with the Governess (who was, it turned out, a sport), it was to find laid out on my bed an immaculate suit of evening clothes. Everything but the crimson-lined cape, as worn by Mandrake the Magician. My tea towel was in a drawer of the walnut bachelor's chest, laid on crested shelf paper.

Although it was only five o'clock, I began to dress, enjoying the feel of garters for the first time as I relived the afternoon. Hearing again the whistle of the gauge-3 train as we thundered through the attics, Rufus in the driver's cap and the sweep as fireman. I had sat alone, a guest in the Pullman coach, as we sped past and under brass beds; startling girls in lisle stockings; picking up small red mailbags filled with sweets. Local children had acted as porters and eccentric passengers (and had been pleased to do so), as we rushed out into the sunshine, across a bridge by Thomas Telford, to draw up at a station below the clock tower of the stable block. As I put on my silk hat before the mirror, I still clasped the return ticket, clipped by the wet nurse, in the palm of my hand.

I looked at myself, moved a little and liked what I saw. All I needed was a cane. My eyes fell on the trusty bannister behind the door, and in a moment, patent pumps twinkling on the bare boards, I was pounding out a selection from 'Top Hat', which had reached Swinehurst the week before.

'Excuse me, sir.' With a cough into his pudgy hand, the stiff dickie stood in the doorway, and I shot him with my stick like Fred Astaire.

'There is a person wishing to see you.' This, like everything he said to me, was addressed to a point three feet above my head. He chassied to one side and I stared out into the corridor, across the faded carpet at the Sickert drawing and the fire bucket, waiting for the person to come into view.

De Kuyper? In black steel helmet and gas cape? *Rosemary?* In dress uniform, with the front let out? I grasped my stick tightly, easing my silk hat where it had become wedged just above my eyes.

It was a policeman; the local village bobbie. Quite obviously a bumpkin who had joined the force some time before Lord Trenchard. He drew back as he saw how I was dressed, then, nerving himself, taking a notebook from under his cape, he came into the room. 'I wonder if I might have a word with you, sir?'

'Of course,' I said. 'Sit down.'

'Not on duty, sir.' The reproach in his voice was gentle, and he thanked me for the human touch by inclining his helmet. Unlike those of the Clwyd Constabulary it bore no spike. I looked at the door, which C. Aubrey Smith had silently closed, and was sorely tempted, had my bannister been thinner, to shove it through the keyhole and into his ear.

'We have received a communication, sir,' said the standing policeman, 'from a place called Swinehurst.'

'Really?' I said, both hands folded on top of my stick. 'Whatever next?'

'As you say, sir.' He turned over the first page of his notebook, the one that told him what to do, and licked the stub of a pencil. It was what we called then indelible, and had made the tip of his tongue purple, like the head of the boy I sat next to in school.

'They report a boy – a young man, I should say,' he smiled at me, 'as running away from this place. This Swinehurst.'

'I can't say that I'm surprised,' I said, staring out of the window at the vista.

'You know it, sir, do you? This Swinehurst?'

'It's where boot boys come from,' I replied, easily, without looking at him.

'The name of this young man,' he went on, after breathing for a moment, 'is Jeffrey. Jeffrey Cock.'

'Cork!' I said. 'Surely.'

'Yes, sir,' he said, holding the page to the light. 'As you say. Does that mean anything to you, sir?'

'No,' I said, turning to face him, executing a routine with the bannister that I had often watched the drum major rehearse. 'I don't think so. My name is Franklyn.'

I watched him write it down in block capitals. Frank Lynn. Then underline it. 'Right, sir. Well, thank you very much.' He closed the notebook and smiled at me, showing his purple tongue. I inclined my head and showed him to the door, and with that characteristic touch of the finger to the helmet he walked towards the tradesman's entrance, boots silent on the dust sheet laid down for him. I saw a flash of boiled shirt pull back out of sight at the end of the corridor.

I thought I had carried off the whole thing rather well. They would probably carry on draining ponds and dragging rivers for a day or so, and of course there would be a Memorial meeting in the Tabernacle; but then it would die down. In a few years, in Swinehurst at least, I would be remembered only as a cautionary tale, told to children who rode alone on trams.

Thinking on these lines, musing on the possibility of the townsfolk putting up a statue, complete with stick and bundle and facing south, as Bradford had done for Philip Snowden, I cleaned my teeth, polished my hat, and thought with excitement of the coming evening.

As you can imagine, I was downstairs early, nodding to the parlour maids, handing my topper to you-know-who. Warming my striped backside before the great logs burning in the Gothic stone fireplace, I was once again impressed. The front room was large – big enough for several three-piece suites and two suits of armour. From behind one of these, Himself kept an eye on me. Canapé in hand, I was tapping the walls, looking for the secret passage, when the Hon Wendy made her entrance. In the light from the chandeliers she looked prettier than ever, wearing pink gems around her throat that reminded me of Aunt Ada's necklace. (Though there was of course no vest showing.) Blushing, as she beckoned me with a finger, I joined her on the chaise longue. She asked me about Traggets, about Wheelan, and I was holding my hands wide apart, to demonstrate how long it was, when Rufus was brought downstairs to meet his parents.

'Zees ees your muthair,' said the French maid, steering him towards us.

'Don't be silly, Honore,' said the Hon Wendy. 'He spoke to me this morning. Here I am, darling. Rufus!'

He looked sweet, though of course I refrained from telling him so, in pyjamas and dressing gown and with a clean teddy dangling from one hand.

'Good night, Mama,' he said, almost kissing her cheek. He then shook hands with me. 'Good night, old chap,' he said.

While Rufus paused on his way up the stairs, for some of the guests to snap with their box Brownies, cocktails were served. I took a small Green Goddess into the library; the previous night's loss of sleep and the excitement were catching up with me. Switching on a green-shaded lamp I wandered along the shelves. It was cool and quiet in there, and after climbing up and down the mahogany stepladders – mindful of my mother's warning not to touch old books – I thought it a good idea to take a nap until the dinner gong went. Carefully hitching my trousers, I curled up in a leather chair and fell asleep.

I awoke, not to a gong but to the sound of balls gently knocking together. It came from the billiard room next door, and without moving I found that I could see all that was going on through the open door. Reflected in the locked glass case that contained *The Well of Loneliness*, (a page of which was turned over every day), I saw what one of the men who had revolved with Rufus's father that morning was doing to the French maid. Naked and un-ashamed is the phrase, I think. His porridge-coloured trousers lay collapsed on the floor, as he had never been taught to leave them. Bare down to his reverberating garters, his pink bottom contrasted with the varnished edge of the table, as the maid's black-stockinged feet beat a gentle tattoo on the lampshade.

Though I had an extremely stiff neck, I did not move a muscle. I watched them, brilliantly lit on the green baize, a pink ball beside her ear, which I knew counted for six.

So this was it! The rumba.

When they had finished, the man put on his trousers and moved the brass bezel along the scoreboard. My French was good enough to translate their 'Thank you, very much' to each other. Adjusting her crêpe-de-chine knickers, the French maid picked up her feather duster and they left quietly through the double doors, turning out the light. Sucking up what remained of my cocktail, I adjusted my tie, all the while massaging my stiff neck, and rejoined the others in the front room. Just as Jeeves was thumping the gong and crying: 'Dinner is sarved.'

Being in a way, I suppose, the guest of honour, I was seated to the left of the Hon Wendy. Real Senior, who I had noticed appeared in affable mood when he nodded across the room to Rufus – he had obviously been successful in killing something – was at the far end of the table, beyond the cruet, the flowers and the silver figurine of Stanley Baldwin. I was interested to hear that he (Real Senior that is) was a Conservative Member of the House of Commons, and had once done well in a tournament at Le Touquet.

On my left was the wife of one of the men in porridge-coloured suits. (The sexes were seated like this, alternately, in a suggestive manner.) She was obviously hungry; her bib tucked in, rat-tailed spoon raised and mouth open ready as the soup came through the tall doors on a little cart.

'Is it ox tail?' she asked in an aside to me. 'Can you see?'

I told her it appeared to be brown. Of course I didn't know which of the two men – both now changed out of their porridge-coloured clothes – was her husband. Touching her quivering arm I asked: 'Do you have a servant problem?' I thought that was rather a clever ploy.

'Why?' she asked, turning to face me. 'Are you after the boot boy's job?'

I laughed this off, my chuckle turning to a subdued scream as Fluff Ears came up behind me, like the Japanese or the Mad Mahdi, and poured hot soup between my legs. 'No,' I said, 'of course not, I just wondered if you had a French maid?'

She said she had not; or a billiard table; and started to dredge up the Brown Windsor, like the steam shovel on The Drain.

It was social chit-chat like that all round the table, as Jowly drove in the scullions: girls in flat shoes, footmen with flat feet; platters, dishes and pigs' heads; the hot gadrooned edge of dishes appearing at your right ear. Tiaras and pomaded heads bobbed at the plates, knives and forks flashed in the correct order with practised ease.

Corks popped to laughter, faces distorted in crystal; carmined lips pausing while food was swallowed, to pass on a barbed jest or a wicked aside. A gentleman's hand disappeared under the damask linen to scratch himself, or to feel his next-door neighbour.

Then I felt my flies being undone.

I had a sprout on my fork at the time and I held steady, thinking that the boiling soup had rotted the thread and the buttons were falling off. But no; they were being unfastened by experienced fingers, and my shirt was being tweaked out. Remembering that I had on clean underwear, I maintained a smile and what I hope was a look of interest as I conversed across the table with the family Chaplain (who had his own marrow spoon); carefully estimating the length of his arms. It seemed unlikely to be the act of a man of the cloth, and I was relieved when he raised and waved both hands to indicate that he wanted more of the house wine. At the same time I felt more of my shirt being pulled out, and fingers twiddling among what later came to be called the short and curlies. I turned to look gravely at the Hon Wendy, who was toying with her food and had one slim white arm beneath the tablecloth. Surely not! But my left-hand partner was still on the soup and gesticulating for more.

'Hon Wendy,' I said quietly.

'Yes, darling?' She regarded me with wide blue eyes.

'I wouldn't do that if I were you,' I said.

She took a sprout from her mouth, in the nicest possible way, and put it on the side of her plate, on the gilt monogram. 'Why?' she whispered. 'Is there something the matter with it?'

At that moment warm fingers gripped me, having at last found it, and I lost all control. Heedless of noblewoman or curate, who were both watching me, I seized my dessert fork, like the Prince of Denmark's bare bodkin, and stabbed downwards at the Mummy's Hand!

*

'What's the matter?' I heard Real Senior shouting from a distance, from beyond the pain. 'Boot boy stabbed himself? More peas anybody?'

Yet again there was a circle of nostrils above and around me; hanging pearls and décolletage, masticating mouths.

'Give him air!' cried the Hon Wendy, kneeling beside me, supporting me in her arms. Gratefully I lay back against her bib.

'They're not pierced, are they?' I heard someone say. 'If they are, he's ruined.'

No, they were not pierced, but the punctures on my thigh had been very close. Footmen came in then with a five-barred gate, and I was carried into an ante-room, crying and trying to cover myself as best I could. There I lay on a day bed, unfastened, before most of my fellow diners, some of them still chewing sprouts.

As the next course was about to be served the crowd withdrew, one or two of them giving me sixpence as they passed, and one man leaving two pennies for my eyes. The Hon Wendy gave what she called 'the poor little thing' a kiss, which was more than I expected, and I was left to the ministrations of Honore, the busy French maid, who had changed her lacy apron for a starched bib with a large red cross.

'Eet ees a shame!' she said, as I sat up to see if there was a billiard table in the room. 'For someone so small.' I lay back, humiliated, becoming even smaller as she applied the Germolene with cold and chalky fingers.

Rejoining the company in time for the Cabinet Pudding, though walking rather oddly, I was greeted by several sympathetic comments. 'Here comes Jack the Ripper' and 'Look out! The young forker's back!' were two of them. As I passed the head of the table The Member asked me, not unkindly, whether I would not feel happier with a spoon and pusher.

Then of course the ladies withdrew. The port was circulated and the room began to fill with cigar smoke, some people putting the coloured bands carefully into their wallets, to mount when they got home. The butler, with a sneer, brought me a decanter of dandelion and burdock, and I relaxed with a liquorice pipe. After good food: good talk and the assurance that no one would interfere with one's flies. Almost an epigram.

In a pause in the hubbub of talk I said, quite loudly, standing up in order to free my pants from the ointment: 'I notice from my *Daily Telegraph* War Map this morning, that things look as if they are about to take a decisive turn.' This was not strictly true, as I had left my *Daily Telegraph* War Map behind in Swinehurst, but it made me the focus for all eyes. 'I think it is high time we opened a Second Front,' I added, lips twitching, a twinkle in my eye, knowing just how provocative I was being.

'What did he say?' asked The Member, in the silence that followed. Crumbs of Stilton dropped from his mouth as he stared at me. I stood up again. 'I notice from my *Daily Telegraph* War Map . . . ' but the moment had passed. They were engrossed in a packet of sepia photographs which was being handed round. As I was pointedly excluded from seeing them, I assumed them to be horrific scenes of war damage; an impression which was confirmed when I heard the Chaplain mutter 'Good God!' as he held one up to the light. Then everyone perked up; there was even a round of scattered applause, and people started to limber up and flex their fingers. Under the supervision of the major domo, two husky young men in green aprons carefully wheeled in a tall object, covered by a sheet, that ran heavy on the floor on castors. As the butler uncovered this, with an undeniable flourish, there were expressions of pleasure and anticipation around the table.

The machine, swathed with acanthus leaves and swagged garlands in relief, on ball-and-claw feet, was constructed of iron and painted a Swinehurst green. Inside, behind glass and before a painted background of a domestic interior, sat two baby dolls, not unlike the one so long in Mossies' window. Dressed in hand-knitted pink and blue respectively, they sucked dummies in their red pot mouths, a tube of revolting pink rubber leading from each teat to a bottle full of grubby-looking milk.

'Who's first?' cried The Member, flushed with excitement, being helped off with his jacket. Still munching his Croque Monsieur, he took up his position at one of the handles on the front of the cabinet. The Chaplain joined him, taking the part of the girl, blushing at witticisms from around the table. But most people were now forming themselves into two lines, going so far as to unfasten their bow ties and bob up and down, flexing their knees.

There was a sharp explosion as Edward Everett Horton fired a starting pistol, his eyes on me across the room, and I heard one of my fellow guests exclaim: 'The game's afoot!'

The contestants crouched, tailored backsides towards us, elbows a blur as they rapidly turned the handles, the eyes of both of them riveted through the glass on the choking babies. The faster they spun the polished brass, so the level of the milk in the bottles sank, pouring through the tubes into the elasticated bodies. It was close, but our host won by a soupçon, to a roar of applause, and therefore got his penny back.

We all had a go, (the bottles filled again as you put in your pennies), and then The Member, still surrounded by a small group offering their congratulations, said: 'Shall we join the ladies?' Relaxed and jovial we moved as a body into the music room, leaving bibs, crumbs, cigar butts and depleted decanters on the table. Looking back as the door closed, I saw two of the footmen bending over, determined to have their share of the fun.

The music room was a fine sight. Having seen my betters at play, I was now to see another facet of their rich lives. One of the porridge-coloured men's wives, with bare arms and bangles, was already singing at the grand piano. The other one, still chewing something, accompanied her on the harp. The tempo quickened as we entered the room, and I recognised the song immediately as one we had sung at Traggets.

'I know it!' I cried, hurrying to stand on the cartouche in the centre of the carpet, starting to beat time with my hands, 'Riding down to Bangor, on an eastbound train . . . ' I held the note, and thought I heard a glass shatter at the far side of the room. Then everyone came in on the next line, as if following the bouncing ball at the Pavilion De Luxe. Baritones in their boiled shirts, tenors stepping forward with a smile and a thrust of the chin; ladies suppressing nervous excitement, grouping together, arms around each other's waists. 'After weeks of hunting, in the woods of Maine . . . ' Until, like the massed Tabernacles at the Albert Hall, we thundered out the final line, heavily emphasised and hyphenated: *'An earwig in that horrid student's beard!'* Flushed, I bowed to the storm of applause and sat down, on the spot the Hon Wendy patted beside her on the chaise longue.

'You are a card, aren't you, darling?' she said, pleased that everything was going so well. 'Are you enjoying yourself?' Her husband (an impressive basso profundo) was going around showing people his trophy, while the Chaplain got his card trick ready. I said that I was, apart from the stab wounds, and that all in all it had been quite an evening. I then asked permission to retire, before the dancing and the indoor fireworks began, saying that I was very tired.

'You mustn't outgrow your strength, darling,' said the Hon Wendy, showing concern. 'Run along upstairs, and I'll have something sent up to your room.' As it was almost nine o'clock, I cautiously enquired whether this might be Scott's Emulsion; but she shushed me with a finger, as the Chaplain produced an egg from the back of her husband's neck.

I decided against going up to the night nursery, even though Rufus would probably be still awake. The French maid would be reading from the book covered with brown paper, and he would be waiting to talk to me about tram conductresses and my plans for the future. But I was utterly exhausted. My mind in a whirl from the rumba, and the food; not to mention the stabbing, and the game, and the sing song; and the egg coming out of The Member's neck.

Once in my room, I checked that the blackout was in place and switched on the light. Expecting of course to see sleeping apparel laid out on the bed. But no! It seemed that I was expected to wear the tea towel! No pyjamas, nightshirt or dressing gown. Only a face flannel, a cake of pink soap in the shape of a pig, with an inch of string for a tail, and an individual pot of Vaseline. Feeling more than a little piqued, and in my shirt tail and garters, I went along the corridor to the door marked WC.

Quite frankly I was again impressed, smiling at the cartoon, by Strube, of The Member in a pedalo. It was the first time I had come across toilet paper of quality, and I kept a piece, to take with me as a useful souvenir. A pale lilac, it was by today's standards far from soft, but between each perforation was a coat of arms. On the square I folded and pushed down my sock was: 'What I Have I Hold'.

Comfortable on the mahogany seat, which was in the shape of a saddle, I examined my wound for the first time. Should I ever return to Traggets, I thought it would prove every bit as interesting as the girl's tattoo. Before me, set into the wall, were bell pushes marked: 'Finished' and 'Send For Doctor', but I decided to let well alone. Feeling sleepy, and not wishing to be found there by the butler on his rounds, I emerged, leaving the ormolu chain swinging and the window open. As I did so, I caught sight of the dickie, withdrawing behind a wardrobe at the far end of the corridor.

Was it possible? Could it have been him, with the fingers, under the table? Stepping into my room with a shudder, I closed and locked the door.

Quo Vadis? I thought to myself; though this was long before the film. There I was in a four-poster bed, in a stately home not a stone's throw from the Nabisco factory. Throughout the land, at emulsion hour, Bruce Belfrage would be reading an urgent appeal for me to ring Whitehall 1212. While in two homes – albeit one ever so humble – a light would be burning in the window. It was too much for me. I decided to think about it in the morning, after breakfast, to perhaps talk to the Chaplain privately, and ask him how he did the trick with the egg. So with regret only that I had not borrowed the book that moo'd and growled, I drew the bed curtains and was asleep as soon as my head touched the brocaded pillow.

It was dark when I awoke, and I soon realised that it would be dark for ever unless I opened the curtains. Countless thousands must have passed on in this way in the fourteenth and fifteenth centuries. Putting on the light, I saw by Uncle Frank's watch on the night table that it was ten o'clock! Thinking this to be ten o'clock in the morning, in which case I had missed breakfast (for which I had planned to borrow a fourteen-inch platter from the nursery stillroom), I jumped out of bed, opened the bedroom door and stepped out into the corridor. To find the lights burning and to fall headlong over a butler's tray, which held a pot of chocolate, an assortment of Huntley & Palmers biscuits on a doily, and six Balkan Sobranie cigarettes, in red, blue, black and green, in a champagne glass.

'Jeffrey! Are you all right?' It was the soft voice of the Hon Wendy, who had opened the door opposite. She was dressed still in her white and puce off-the-shoulder gown, and I realised that it was only ten o'clock at night! I had not slept for half an hour. Behind her, his mouth open, stood one of the porridge-coloured men, dressed like me in his shirt tail and garters.

I said that I was quite all right, but tired and a little distressed. To the man, to whom I had not been introduced, I said: 'I see you have been treated the same as I. Seemingly they expect one to sleep in a tea towel!'

He did not answer, though his mouth remained open, and the Hon Wendy closed the door on him, bending at the lovely knee to bring her lips to my ear. 'We're playing hide and seek,' she breathed. 'You won't give us away, will you?'

I said that was unthinkable, and was thrilled by her trust; but at that moment spotted the large white kneecaps of The Member coming along the corridor. No one could seriously expect such a man to make do with a tea towel, so I could only suppose that everyone's trousers were collected at this time of night for sponging and pressing.

'Quick! Get inside!' I hissed, pushing the Hon Wendy into her room and closing the door. Then, with a bland smile, I turned to face the approaching Real Senior.

'Hello there,' I said. 'Are you it?'

I don't think he had seen me until then. 'It?' he said; and then he said it again: 'It?'

I smiled up at him, barring the way into his room, my hand behind me holding the doorknob. 'You're the boot boy, aren't you?' he said, bending towards me. 'Feller with his trousers open.' I nodded, a grin twisting my lips.

'You're getting warm,' I said.

'Warm?' he repeated, his eyes narrowing, wary, like Broomhead's when he saw Wheelan's thing rise. There was a silence. The Member coughed into his hand, looking up and down the corridor, and I saw a little pulse beating underneath his eye.

'Would you mind moving?' he said suddenly, flapping a hand at me. So I did him a few steps from Wilson, Keppel and Betty, first throwing down a handful of sand from the firebucket. The Egyptian Dance, with the back of one hand under the chin and the other on the kidneys, doing the snake charmer's music through my nose. This was unfortunately spoilt by the door opening and my falling into the Hon Wendy's room.

'He's got you, I'm afraid,' I said with a rueful grin, to the Hon Wendy as I sprawled on the carpet.

'Don't you believe it, darling!' she said softly, seated at her embroidery frame. 'One Alone' from 'The Desert Song', which brought back poignant memories of home, was playing on the lizardskin-covered gramophone.

'Come out, come out, wherever you are!' I cried, looking round for her friend, and then screamed as my thumb was impaled, like Rumplestiltskin's, on the embroidery needle.

'Do you *know* this chap?' asked The Member, standing over me like a Colossus in primrose garters, and I averted my head.

'His father's a Northern Manufacturer,' said the Hon Wendy, delicately picking at her petit point. 'He's a friend of Rufus.'

'*I'm* the friend of Rufus,' I said, taking my thumb out of my mouth, to save The Member from a foolish line of dialogue. There was the sound of a polite cough into a pudgy hand, and guess who was standing in the doorway with his heels together. Mercifully he had his trousers on.

'There's not another person wishing to see me, is there?' I asked, getting to my feet and snapping my garters. But The Member was nodding towards me and flapping his hand to the door. Quickly, with a zeal that did him credit, I was deposited in the corridor. 'Night, Hon Wendy,' I called as I went.

'Good night, Jeffrey,' called the Hon Wendy as the door closed.

Of course I was grossly overtired by now, and did a little shuffle in the sand. I think it was the first time I had seen nostrils actually flared. 'Four For Your Fucking Friends', (which is how someone had referred to him in chalk outside the main gate) took a deep breath. 'You're not the usual clarss of guest that we get 'ere,' he said. 'You're more like a boot boy.'

'Good night, lackey,' I said. 'After the war, when the boys come back, when we nationalise the means of production, distribution and exchange, what are you going to do then?' I had got that from a talk that Fred Delius had given to the Young Men's Movement at the Tabernacle.

'Fuck off!' said the butler, articulating well.

'God made the land for the people,' I told him, stepping across the custard creams into my room.

Again I locked the door and got into bed, but I was now unable to sleep. Staring at the carved oak above my head, at the E. Allan Poe machinery ready to rumble downwards at any moment, I murmured to myself 'Quo Vadis indeed!' Since I had gone to sleep not an hour before – content in the knowledge that my problems would be solved in the morning, by a few words after breakfast in the priests' hole – I had got up, thinking it morning; fallen over a supper tray; gone to the lavatory; joined in a game of hide and seek; and for some reason upset my host, the onlie employer of boot boys. What had I to show for it, beyond a piece of toilet paper down my sock? Just where was I going wrong?

Whether it was hearing the voice of John Hanson, I don't know, but I decided suddenly to run away. Again. This time abandoning Sunny Jim and the Panda, and making for the Free French Foreign Legion recruiting office. I smiled in the dark as I thought of meeting Bernard in the Soukh of Sidi Bel Abbes; saying 'Hello, Bernard' as I lifted aside his sheet.

There was that discreet knocking again at the door.

'Go away!' I called. 'It's too late!' Meaning of course that it was half past ten, too late to eat anything without it laying on your stomach; and also that my mind was made up.

The knocking continued. As I drew the bed curtains I thought I heard my name being called, but dismissed it as fantasy, pulling the tapestry wearily over my head.

The knocking ceased, and I heard whoever it was go away. Then, as I drifted into a troubled sleep, it began again. But now it had changed to a metallic tapping on glass. Sitting up I looked through a chink in the bed curtains, into the gloom of the room. The sound came from the window, from behind the Liberty's fabric, hand stitched to mahogany battens. Breathing through my nose to quieten my nerves, I crossed the room to take down the blackout.

Wide-eyed I stared out at the vista, then at a black shape against the moon, immediately before me, tapping insistently against the glass. It was a cocoa tin on a string. My shirt tail lifting in the rush of night air, I opened the window and spoke into the tin.

'Hello?' I said, pressing the Bourneville receiver to my ear and listening eagerly.

'Is that you, Jeffrey?' asked De Kuyper, and it was marvellous to hear her voice. 'Why aren't you in bed?'

'I was,' I said. 'I had to get up to answer the cocoa tin. Where are you calling from?'

'I'm upstairs in Nanny's room,' said the much-loved voice down the string. 'Pack everything neatly and come up here. Don't forget the Deliuses' tea towel.'

No, she said, there was no need for me to leave my bolster in the foetal position. So, pulling on my trousers, leaving the window open, the tin dangling and the bed unmade, I ran along the corridor and up the stairs. My bundle over my shoulder, and tears – yes, tears, I am not ashamed to say so – running down my cheeks.

De Kuyper was standing at Nanny's door when I got there, home in herself with the light behind her, and I buried my face in her gas cape. 'There, there,' she said. 'It's all over now. Let me spit on my handkerchief and wipe your face.'

We went into the small but cosy room under the eaves, where Nanny, who it later turned out was Rufus's mother (so she really was one of the family) sat staring into the fire. The books the Chaplain had left her to read lay on her lap, and opposite her sat a small solicitor, his spectacles reflecting the burning coals. The woman ('Cast aside like an old glove,' said De Kuyper in the car later) looked at us both wistfully, as my face was cleaned and my trousers fastened. Moments later we were descending the back stairs of the house.

On each floor we caught glimpses of guests, in shirt tail and garters, bobbing back out of sight at the far end of corridors. Some of them waved and beckoned to us. From the drawing room came the strains of music, the clicking of heels as gentlemen saluted their partners. I imagined the lady dropping a curtsey, the handsome pair advancing through an archway of white gloves. 'Listen! De Kuyper!' I cried, but she seized my arm and hurried me on downwards, my hand still cupped to my ear.

The cavernous kitchen was at rest, until the orders for bouillon and kippers came down. Hams hung from hooks on the ceiling; the giant flywheel of the mincer cast a shadow like that of a mighty beam engine. The fat cook, her misshapen shoes off, dozed in her chair by the fire. Gadrooned pies cooled on the window sills, and a large cat was eating what was left of the sprouts from a tureen. Waiting for us in this pantomime scene we found the butler, the Hon Wendy, and my father.

The Hon Wendy sat in a Windsor chair, itself standing on a square of red carpet that had been hastily put down. I saw that my father was wearing the hairy sports jacket beneath his raincoat and scarf.

'That's 'im!' said the butler, shooting his cuffs and pointing at me as we entered. All their faces, except that of the cat, were lit by the firelight.

'I knew right along, m'lady, he wasn't one of ours. Fuck off! I said to 'im, beggin' your ladyship's pardon. What am I goin' to do, 'e says, when they h'appropriate the whatsits; when they all come 'ome?'

'Clause Four,' said the cook, distinctly, without opening her eyes.

'Thank you,' said the butler, nodding in her direction, then turning back to his mistress. 'Fuck off! I told 'im, beggin' your pardon. Fuck off out of here, I said. We don't want your clarss 'ere, I said. "God gave the . . . " well, I won't tell you what he said then, m'lady, when he was jumping over the biscuits. Fuck off! I said to 'im . . . '

'Thank you, Gartree,' said the Hon Wendy, dabbling her fingertips in the bain marie before looking up, smiling at me. 'Well, Jeffrey. Or is it Mr Frank Lynn? It seems we have to say au revoir.'

I nodded shyly, keeping close to the gas cape. I was pleased to be going home, looking forward now to a farewell kiss from the Hon Wendy. I only hoped there would be the possibility, at the last moment, of my being able to kick the butler between the legs.

'So you are a Northern Manufacturer?' the Hon Wendy said to my father, who gave a stiff bow from the waist. At this moment the cook allowed her stomach to rumble.

'I hope the boy's been no trouble, your ladyship,' he muttered.

'Of course not. You can straighten up again now. It's been lovely to have him. He's had a very full day; haven't you, Jeffrey?' and she grinned at me.

'Thank you for having me,' I said.

She inclined her head prettily, her eyes and her necklace flashing in the firelight. 'He's had a ride on my son's train,' she said, 'and played with the Governess.' Her eyes met mine. ' . . . And watched his first game of snooker.' Her voice was even softer, our eyes still locked together.

'Snooker?' queried De Kuyper, sharply.

'A harmless game,' said the Hon Wendy, with the ghost of a smile. 'And he's had a good dinner . . . ' The cook, to show she was paying attention, bowed in her chair, ' . . . and some supper in his room.'

'I saw it outside the door,' said De Kuyper, grimly.

'And now he's going home,' finished the Hon Wendy, pressing her red lips together, squeezing a smile at me from her eyes.

'You've left out the hide and seek,' I reminded her, grateful to her for not mentioning the fingers under the table, or the fork in the thigh, or how I had cried out when I felt the Germolene.

'Ah, yes,' she said, 'the hide and seek. What fun, eh, Jeffrey?'

'You were nearly caught,' I said, wagging a finger.

'I'll bet she was!' said De Kuyper, and the smile and the blue eyes moved to her, though the Hon Wendy was still talking to me.

'When you are a big boy,' she said, 'a *really* big boy. When you have given up being chaperoned by big ladies in gas capes and steel helmets. You must come again and play with us.' Then, rising from her chair, she kissed me and chucked me under the chin.

Holding me in what Pickersgill called 'The Whore's Grip', De Kuyper marched me towards the tradesman's entrance; while my father walked backwards, bowing as he had seen them do in the Charlie Chan pictures, his hands up the sleeves of the hairy jacket. And thus we made our farewell, en famille as it were. As my father put my bundle in the boot, I looked in through the window of the servants' hall, seeing the cook, awake now and with her shoes on, enter and say something to the butler, who was picking his nose. She put a record on a cabriolet-legged gramophone, turning the horn towards the window, and as the chicken shit inflated and we moved off into the shrubbery, the strains of 'Little Man You've Had A Busy Day', played by Jack Payne and his Orchestra, reached us on the night air. 'Little man you're crying, I know why you're blue, someone took your kiddie car away . . .'

In the moonlight that entered the car, as the drive curved towards the main gate and the house came into view for the last time, I secretly unwrapped the package that had been pressed into my hand as we left. More by feel than sight; knowing that De Kuyper, if she had not thought

174

that I was simply playing with myself, would have flung it through the window at once. My fingers discovered an orange, a new penny, a packet of Japanese flowers that opened in a glass of water, and a small oval portrait of the Hon Wendy. On the back, with an 'X', (I was using my eyes now of course) was written 'We'll meet again!'

Part Two

Chapter One

A full moon hung over the blueish hills. The curtains of every house I passed were open, the light shining recklessly into the front gardens. It was May, but already many people had taken off their vests. I was walking home along the London Road, in long grey flannels and brown shoes, having that very morning had the chance – the absolute certainty if I played my cards right – of being able to dip my wick. (The term we used at the time.)

I had spent the evening with a largish crowd outside the wool shop, waiting to see, and to cheer to the echo, the lights come on again on the roof of the Railway Hotel. 'RAIL AY HOTE ' they said when they did; and we sang, wearing yellow and puce paper hats saved for the event, 'When the lights go on again, all over the world . . .'

It was VE Day, 1945. Even the King's Arms Inn, ('God save the Queen' we boys would add), and the off-licence, neither of which had neon signs, had been allowed to stay open until after ten o'clock, because of the end of the war in Europe.

We had won of course, and had accepted as we usually do that most Germans had not realised what was going on. A travelling exhibition had come to the library with photographs of Belsen, and De Kuyper had joined the long queue twice, the first time with me, in dark clothes and the whore's grip. What impact it had on the town I cannot say, for like the Londoner in striped trousers, the father of Mrs Moss's son, the subject was never mentioned again. Personally I kept my eyes closed, holding De Kuyper's belt to avoid bumping into things. I had no wish to suddenly come upon the Hebrews, stiff and nude in a hole in the ground.

As I say, I was going home in my long trousers, complete with crease and turn up, having left Bernard among the revellers in the back room of the chip shop. I had a letter to write, one that had to be posted the following morning and was to have a major impact on my life.

Three years had passed since the night I had been driven home from the Reals, the fumes of the chicken shit inflating the grey bag, propelling my father's car up the Great North Road. On arrival at Jasmine Villa my underclothes had been taken away and burnt, but there had been no recriminations. Soon I was tucked into my own bed, having looked in on Miss Parkinson and been asked to feel it kicking. As I looked around at the familiar shapes and shadows, listened to the scratching of the surviving mice, I thought of Rosemary's house, the pink light through the cellophane window. Though too tired for fear, I fully expected her arrival, along with Fred and Ada and the legal adviser to the Tabernacle, on the first bus in the morning from Swinehurst.

But no. I learned later that De Kuyper and Yasmin (my father, the bag billowing nicely, had driven straight back to Carlisle) had met the Deliuses over tea and toasted teacakes in the Co-op Café at Swinehurst. Because her tram was outside, Rosemary had not been able to stay for the whole of the meeting; but it had been agreed that I should now resume my life at Jasmine Villa. Uncle Fred was of the opinion that we should all forgive and forget, quoting Stanley Holloway's words that 'No one was really to blame.' Indeed, later, having been recognised by some people, he did the rest of 'Albert and the Lion', accompanied by the string quartet, under the palm tree on the bend in the stairs.

The next day he wrote to me in his careful copperplate, on Tabernacle notepaper embossed with 'God Made The Land For The People'. Beneath Joseph Arch addressing a crowd under a tree, with the sun coming up, Uncle Fred told me that His eye was on the sparrow; Lord Vansittart's days were most certainly numbered; and he (small h, Uncle Fred) would always think kindly of me. There was little space left, because of all the stuff at the top of the page, but he added that Rosemary was as well as could be expected, and was being taught by the Tabernacle how to knit. I had not seen or heard from them since. The baby, Chester J. Delius, as I learned from the *Lincolnshire Standard* that was silently handed to me at the breakfast table, would be romping by now in his tram conductor's set, in the garden of Victory Cottage.

My schooling had presented a problem. To return to Traggets I was told, though I pleaded with my father through the keyhole of his study, was out of the question, though I was allowed to receive the Old Boys' Newsletter for a time. In this I learned that Wheelan had been expelled, and Mr Beeston fined ten pounds, it being his first offence.

Finally I had been bought a bicycle, and a white-braided blue blazer and matching cap. Each morning I rode along the bank of The Drain, satchel across my shoulder, to the Grammar School. Where I did well; teaming up again with Bernard, who had gone off Riffs and had now taken to breeding rabbits. At least, he said, and in saying this you could see the man, there was money in rabbits.

But of course you wait impatiently to hear about my (very nearly) dipping my wick that morning. First though, about the letter I was going home to write. I had, a few months earlier, while at home with an earache, taken up philately. There was a club devoted to this at school, but their activities consisted mainly of counting the oranges, through a magnifying glass, on the trees of Mozambique. Rumour having it that if you found a tree with an odd number, the Portuguese Government (Britain's oldest ally) would pay you a thousand pounds. Or escudos. My interest in stamps was more serious. I had invested in a giant packet of mixed stamps of the world ('Unsorted') from Mossies. After checking through for tuppenny blues and Cape triangulars, I mounted them on sheets of paper, priced anywhere between threepence and a shilling. I advertised my services in *The Beano*, writing direct to The City of Jam. In short I was an entrepreneur, even though holding a sock full of hot salt to my ear at the time.

I had that morning received a letter, on lavender paper with a discreet gilt heading – a complete contrast to that of Uncle Fred's – requesting my approvals by return of post. The writer had gone on to say that she was a thematic collector, interested in scenes of May Day activities, 'with foreign people holding ribbons and dancing round the pole'. She was also, she told me, and this I found intriguing, a Nignog. (No 504.) The letter was signed 'Elspeth Garrowby (Miss)' and I had the idea that it could lead to something big. As indeed it did.

But now, at last, to the 'wick dipping', as we called it.

It was connected, as most things were in our town, with a Pomfret. The founder of the firm, a friend of Mrs Moss, had retired. The younger ones had returned from the war and, not being noticeably interested in Clause Four, had modernised, calling themselves a limited company and having the telephone put in. Not only had they replaced Lucille with an electric cart, and started to sell orangeade – which caused a certain amount of controversy – but they had taken over the sweet shop concession in the foyer of the Pavilion De Luxe, Captain Drew going rapidly downhill and having other fish to fry. In this, in starched white, with an embroidered 'P' on her breast, they had installed the widow of the Pomfret who had reputedly gone mad on the beach at Dunkirk and been shot out of hand.

Agnes, the widow Pomfret, pursed her red lips like the boy on the fruitgums' packet whenever I went up to the counter. In the same spirit I replied with a face like one of the 'Five boys' on the bar by Fry's, and within a matter of weeks she had invited me to her home, ostensibly to water the garden and tie up her peas. I suspected, rightly as it turned out, that there was a great deal more to it.

She lived in a bungalow (which in itself I have always found suggestive, what with the chance of opening a wrong door and seeing a bed). On her small lawn, on a base of old Swinehurst paving stones, there was a bricked-up grandfather clock, like a nun that had misbehaved. Its face was left bare so that one could see the phases of the moon.

When the day came – no less than VE Day itself, remember – I arrived in *new* underwear, ten minutes late in order to make her anxious. That had been Bernard's advice, garnered at Troon. Rolling up my sleeves, I watered and tidied the garden, weeding around the clock tower. Then, when she called for me to 'Come and get it' through the open window, went hopefully into the house.

Sitting across from her at the kitchen table, sipping my tea, I had a good look at her. In her own home, out of the hygienic overall, she looked different. She was oldish of course, perhaps mature is the better word; around twenty-five or six, with dark hair rolled under and ribboned in the style of Deanna Durbin. Fine bone structure, a generous mouth, and very big tits.

'Right!' I said, putting down the cup. (I had noted that once again the twenty-two carat stuff had been brought out for me.) 'Let's have our cards on the table. You're not in the club, are you?'

Her eyes widened with surprise. But how was she to know that, callow youth though I might appear, I was already wise in the ways of the world. I went so far as to leer at her, making one of Mr Beeston's gestures to get her going, quite different now from any of Fry's five faces. I was making it clear to her that she was fair game – 'A slice off a cut loaf is never missed' as Bernard's mother put it – and that I was much too sophisticated to be snared as the father of a posthumous Pomfret.

'I know all about the facts of life,' I said, accepting a Du Maurier from the red and silver box. Both Bernard and I, on resigning from the Rechabites the previous winter, had given up smoking string and gone on to Player's Weights.

'So if you've been having tram drivers here in the middle of the night . . . ?' I said this gently, smiling, not wishing to embarrass her.

'They don't have trams here,' she said. 'They have trams at Swinehurst.'

I nodded slowly. 'I'm well aware of that,' I said. 'I used tram drivers as an example. I don't know what kind of men you've been going with.'

'No,' she said. 'I don't suppose you do.'

It was very quiet, just the clock striking in the garden, and I heard her take a deep breath to settle her nerves. I took the liberty of refilling my cup.

'How old are you?' she asked, lifting the teapot but finding it empty.

'Sorry about that,' I said. Then I leered again at her, having to lay my cheek almost on the table so that she could see me, as she was staring at something between her legs. 'I'm old enough!' I said, with heavy emphasis; hoping she wasn't going to go on about what size I was.

Blowing a smoke ring I put my finger through it, though she wasn't watching. Just as well, I thought, that De Kuyper had put me through an intensive course in what she called 'What it's all about'.

Starting on the morning after my return from the Reals – her sleeves rolled up, Krafft-Ebing under her arm as she dribbled Dettol into the bath water – this had been no genteel question and answer in the firelight. Though she had dealt expertly with the laughable business of the lavatory seat, the first session had been devoted to 'Responsible Behaviour'. This had been more on the lines of Rosemary's 'The woman always pays', rather than Mr Beeston's 'Social Responsibility' classes. Thus, I was surprised to learn, they were entitled to say 'No'; being perhaps not in the mood at the moment, and you had to stop. While you were entitled to chance your arm, as it were, at the right time and in the right place – this coming under the heading of male assertiveness – it was wrong to kneel on them and tear their knickers off. They could be in serious trouble when they got home. Getting them drunk, according to De Kuyper, was both expensive and disgusting. In this she was with the Rechabites all the way.

There was, she said, a right way and a wrong way. Using audio-visual techniques well ahead of her time – the blackboard with chalk diagrams and arrows, handy little mnemonics to enable one to remember the erogenous zones – she sang with me a catchy educational song that included movements intended to help one in a shop doorway. Then she showed a short silent film, directed by Georges Méliès and starring the grandmother of the French maid. It had been at the bottom of her trunk, and she projected it on the ceiling, in a double feature with 'The Battleship Potemkin', while Miss Parkinson was at the ante-natal clinic. On the last day of the course, when we eased off – like Mrs Dooley used to allow us all to bring a favourite toy to play with on the last day of term – De Kuyper read me a short story, by D. H. Lawrence, entitled 'The Knee Trembler'.

It had all been pretty informal, but I think I can say that I was an assiduous student. As I always have been with a subject that interested me. From then on everything – or almost everything – had been crystal clear. Now, at last, I was about to heed De Kuyper's final maxim, one of those in pokerwork that hung in her room, that 'Theory without practice is sterile.'

Agnes, who had possibly been without it for four years, was still staring into her lap.

I realised that it was time to take command of the situation; to get on top of things, as it were. To let her know that she was moth to a flame, that she played with fire; that she diced with what some people were reputed to believe was a fate worse than death. Narrowing my eyes, I put out my cigarette in the saucer.

185

'Agnes,' I said, and it was the first time I had used her name, 'you're a very attractive girl.' I had been going to say woman, but I thought she might take offence.

'Thank you,' she said, looking at me across the table.

'That's all right,' I said, about to take another cigarette, but she put her warm hand over mine on the packet, possibly to stop me taking four for my friends.

'You're a nice boy,' she said, and I was surprised to see tears in her eyes. 'But you're very young.'

'Not *that* young,' I said meaningfully, giving her a big wink. At the same time feeling the bulge in the special pocket of my trousers. It was that same French letter which had sailed at the Battle of Actium, and which I am now ashamed to admit I had purloined from Rufus's desk as he changed into his engine driver's hat. After all, I had told myself, there was one in the post with a feather at the end. I had blown it up several times, and Bernard had borrowed it to try it on, but it was still as good as new.

Knowing that they were stirred by a man's reputation, I murmured, 'I lived with a woman once,' tickling the palm of her hand as I did so. Something I had been told that was as good as asking for it.

'Did you?' she said, withdrawing her hand and scratching it. 'What do you mean, lived with a woman?'

'At Swinehurst,' I said airily. 'She was older than me.' I was pretty sure that Agnes moved in a different circle from that of Aunt Ada. 'She was always saying what a big boy I was,' I added.

'Was she,' said Agnes, and I was glad to see that the tears had dried up.

'Yes,' I said. 'First thing she asked me – what size I was.' I smiled at her.

'And what size were you?' she asked, not returning my smile.

'Well,' I said, becoming uncomfortable, 'five foot three, at the time.'

There was a silence then; the house was so quiet

you could almost hear the ticking of the garden clock.

'Jeffrey,' she said.

'Yes, Agnes?'

'Do you want to go to bed?'

'I don't mind,' I said, standing up with some difficulty, and noticing for the first time a handsome veal, ham and egg pie on the draining board.

'It's in there,' she said, pushing open a door with a furry slipper. It swung inwards to reveal, as I have said they always do in bungalows, a double bed already turned down.

'Thank you,' I said. 'I see.' And then I had an awful feeling that perhaps she just thought I looked tired, that tidying up the garden had been too much for me and I should have a lay down.

'Are you coming in?' I asked.

'Yes,' she said, 'I'm coming in. You can't very well do it by yourself, can you.' The strain was obviously getting to her. She stood up, saying 'Undo me then' in a funny voice.

Taking deep breaths through my nose, I reached forward to untie the string of her pinny. As it fell to the coconut matting, I noticed that she used Daddies Sauce, the perfect accompaniment of course to veal, ham and egg pie. I couldn't help saying 'Wow!' softly.

'And wow to you,' she said, and then her hands were up my pullover, feeling me through my vest.

'Kiss me, Jeffrey,' she said, making her Rowntree's mouth, and I did. She had her eyes closed, and I wondered whether she imagined me as Clark Gable, or as the ghost of the one who had gone mad on the sands. Or was I no more than a plaything; all this merely a way of avoiding payment for my tidying up the garden. But my doubts were swiftly dispelled.

'Get your trousers off,' she said, her eyes wide open now.

'Yes, of course,' I said, looking nervously at the still-open window. It was not likely that she would have her own sweep, but anyone might look in. Working at the knot of my tie, I stepped into the bedroom.

She followed me with a loud sigh, taking off her earrings and closing the door. 'Don't let's mess about,' she said in the gloom.

'No,' I said, 'of course not. We're going to rumba, are we?' I just wanted to be absolutely sure.

'Rumba?' Her beads were off, and her bangle, rattling on the utility chest of drawers.

'You know – two to tango,' I said, giving up on my tie. It was a new knot, introduced I believe by King Edward VIII during his brief reign, and it wasn't as if it would get in the way.

'If you want,' she said, without enthusiasm, and switched on a battery wireless, next to a tinted photograph of Lucille.

The exotic sound of Edmundo Ros filled the room, singing in his light brown voice and shaking his maraccas. Her fingers were up my clothes again; this time caressing my belly button. I had heard that if the Gordian knot became unfastened, one could start to disintegrate like a cheap sausage. I'm not saying that I believed that, but, like eating apples late at night, it is better to be safe than sorry. So I stepped away from her, moving around the room in a Latin American kind of way, waving my hands in the air to the beat of the music. I was excited of course, and began to sing along with Edmundo.

'We're three Caballeros, three gay Caballeros, they say we are birds of a feathah . . . ' I revolved, singing, spinning round with my stomach held in, tossing her quilted nightdress case onto the floor and stamping round the ribboned edge with my heels. 'Olé!' I shouted, clapping my hands beside my left ear.

'Olé,' she replied, but it was hardly Carmen Miranda. Then she stamped her foot and, thinking she had caught the spirit of the occasion – and carried away by the beat of the asses' jaw in Señor Ros's orchestra – I snatched a spray of cloth violets from the lapel of a coat behind the door and stuffed it into her mouth.

She said something – it could have been another 'Olé' – and I stamped a provocative answer. A bit too close actually, catching her toes. Then I drew away, shouting 'Olé,' my heels drumming across the lino, eyes on my feet. Until I fell over a pair of sandals, and was able to note the fluff under the bed. Erect again, clapping, singing, shouting 'Olé's, I expected her to lift her dress to her knees and come stamping towards me. 'We're three happy chappies, without our serapes . . .' my voice, along with Edmundo's maraccas and the asses' jaw, faded into silence as the little bulb on the wireless set went out.

'Get your trousers off!' said the señorita again, picking the petal of a cloth violet off her tongue.

'Si, si,' I said, realising that the fun was over, and began to unbutton my braces, pushing the buttons through the stiff leather tabs. I could hear her undressing, white garments flying around the room like ectoplasm, though I tried not to look.

'Take them off over your shoulders,' she said; very much the married woman.

I stared at her. She was naked. Not even socks on, let alone a vest of a decent length. She was all dark shadows, into which she was spraying from a small net-covered bulb. Our eyes met.

'Not your trousers,' she said. 'I meant take your braces off over your shoulders!' There was that nervous tension in her voice that Mr Beeston had told us about.

Letting my braces dangle I began to unfasten my flies. 'I'll have to take my shoes off,' I explained, 'otherwise the trousers won't come over my feet.'

She was silent as I sat on the bed to unlace my shoes, but I could hear her breathing. Then I felt the bed move as she got into the other side, in Sunny Jim's old position.

'Have you any idea how long it is?' she asked.

'No,' I said. 'Not really.' Sitting there with my flannels

around my knees, my shirt tail thankfully the length that Mao Tse Tung should have gone for. What did she mean?

I was never to find out, for at that moment someone knocked on the back door in a familiar way: 'Tom tiddley om tom, tom tom.'

I won't repeat what she said. I said nothing; imagining the Rev Eli Wannamaker on the doorstep, checking his watch with the bricked-up clock, saying 'I know he's in there' as the door opened.

'Keep quiet and they'll go away,' she whispered. 'Have you got them off yet?'

'Yes,' I whispered. 'What about my socks?'

'It doesn't matter,' she hissed, so I decided to keep them on. I could not be certain of course that the bed had been properly aired. As I folded my trousers and hung them over a chair, not wanting my conkers to fall out, for some reason I remembered the sheet of quality toilet paper, with the printed motto, that I had tucked down my sock in the Reals' lavatory. I had long since put clean ones on of course, and wondered what had happened to it.

'Right!' I said, standing up, straightening my tie.

This was it.

I took a deep breath through my nose, and there came a loud tapping on the bedroom window.

Agnes repeated the word again, and went under the sheet, but I was quite annoyed as I strode purposefully across the room, fully expecting to find a cocoa tin on a string.

Of course it wasn't. Pulling back the curtains I found a man in a raincoat and a trilby hat. He held a leather briefcase under his arm, and the mid-morning sun flashed from his spectacles. He was of course a solicitor. I had walked into a trap. 'The old Badger Game' I said to myself.

'Good morning,' he mouthed at me through the glass, his eyes flicking down to my bare legs.

'Good morning,' I replied, opening the window, civility

costing nothing. If he dared comment on my dress, I would remind him that shirt-tail order was de rigueur in some of our greatest houses. 'I'm here to water the garden and tie up the peas.'

He nodded, as if that was all right by him. 'Provident Clothing Club,' he said. 'Mrs Pomfret?'

'No,' I said, 'I'm not,' smiling at him in relief, resisting a jest about her being in the club after all. 'Just a minute,' I added.

'Agnes,' I called out, 'the tally man's here.' But there was no answer. Crossing to the bed I poked the sheeted bundle, thinking she had not heard me. 'She can't have gone to sleep,' I said to the tally man. He had stepped up from the crazy paving and now sat on the window sill, his pointed black shoes dangling inside the room. 'Give her a tickle,' he said.

Smilingly reproving him with a wagging finger, I tried to sort out the bagwash on the bed. She was holding all the corners, so it was like trying to free a loony from a wet sheet; something I believe even Harry Houdini found difficult. 'How much is it?' I called over my shoulder.

'A shilling,' said the tally man. 'There's her leg sticking out.'

'Thank you,' I said, beginning to worry about her breathing. I felt bits of her through the sheet, but couldn't be certain what parts of her they were. 'I'll have you out in a minute, Agnes,' I shouted.

'Work up from her leg,' offered the tally man, whom I could see in the dressing table mirror, dying to help.

'It's all right,' I called, as I found an opening in the sheets and went right in up to my elbow. It was surprisingly warm in there, and as I began to move my hand about Agnes's teeth closed on it, like Lucille taking a mint.

As the reader knows, I was no stranger to pain, but this was far worse than a dessert fork in the thigh. Agnes bit and went on biting, as if she had started on the veal, ham and egg pie. I could only stand there, roaring with pain, startling the tally man who fell backwards out of the window.

I didn't see her again until the Victory Parade, and then long afterwards at the funeral. As she marched past in her snood and her white overall, representing those who had fought at home, doing a smart 'Eyes right' with a wobble of her embroidered 'P', our eyes almost met. I was up the horse trough with Bernard, and could not help thinking, as I looked at her seamed black stockings, of all that might have been.

But now, acting on her muffled and somewhat hysterical instructions, when she had chewed and spat out my hand, I pushed her patent leather handbag through the chink. A moment later, out came a shilling in a sweaty hand.

This I gave to the tally man, who luckily had not hurt himself, and who was leaning against the wall drying his spectacles with his handkerchief. Taking my clothes into the kitchen I got dressed, shouting in to ask if she wanted me to finish tying up the peas. There was no answer. Sucking my hand, thinking about rabies, I hesitated over the veal, ham and egg pie; but decided against it.

Chapter Two

My father had returned from Carlisle with the idea of liberty bodices *for men*! Working long hours, stripping away the broderie anglaise and using bigger buttons, he was assisted in his work by Miss Parkinson, who referred to him fondly as The Wizard of Menlo Park. She had had a son, introduced to me as my half brother, with whom I had little in common. As you will have noted from the previous chapter, I was now more or less mature, modelling myself on Donald O'Connor and often doing a routine in the privacy of my own room.

De Kuyper, because of her persecution of those who used the mustard-gas detectors in their gardens as bird tables, had been transferred to the Observer Corps. She now wore binoculars under her gas cape and I sometimes helped her scan the skies, looking for an ME 109, or the return of Bile Beans. In the Victory Parade she had been, quite properly, ahead of Agnes Pomfret and the people in clean boiler suits; just behind the band of the Potato Marketing Board.

Then, suddenly, came two major though unrelated events. Winston Churchill called an election; and my sister Yasmin had to get married.

It was a wet Sunday afternoon and we were all in the front room; the fire banked with slack, the rain coming down as hard as when the Hebrews had floated past so long before. My father was in the chair, the prototype of the masculine liberty vest twisted in his hands. On the pouffe sat Miss Parkinson, still looking as if she had just called in to get some letters signed and had stayed on for a cup of tea. Yasmin, the star of the show as it were, tried hard to look demure, while De Kuyper hovered just inside the door, reading her aircraft recognition manual. I myself, there in an advisory capacity only, sat on the chair that had been Sweeney Todd's, through the bottom of which the ketchup-smeared Bernard had dropped.

'What are we going to do?' asked my father, by way of an opening address.

It turned out to be months away yet. Then we learnt that the father, self-confessed and shameless, was a Lieutenant Cheeseman of the Duke of Lincoln's Second Foot. In charge of bedding for the Swinehurst garrison. Then, and this made everyone sit up straight, Yasmin announced that he – Lieutenant Cheeseman that is – was waiting at that very moment at the back gate. Some of us exchanged glances and licked our lips. My father, obviously thinking of adjourning the meeting and slipping out of the front door, wondered whether the Rev Eli Wannamaker should be invited to sit in, but received no support.

'So you're in the club?' I said to Yasmin. Until a few moments previously I had thought we were gathered together to play Mah Jong. So much for Lady Violet Bonham-Carter and all her advice, I thought.

My sister ignored me, and soon, if sluggishly, a discussion developed, out of which came several decisions. My father wrote these down. (1) Yasmin could get married in white. (2) My mother was to be invited, but my father wouldn't speak to her. (3) The wedding and the reception would be held in Swinehurst. (4) (This was Yasmin's suggestion) Lieutenant Cheeseman should be brought in before he got too wet.

Everybody cleared their throats and shuffled about a bit, until the suitor came through from the kitchen. He was brought forward like a new member of the House of Commons, De Kuyper still drying him off with a tea towel. The Speaker tried not to catch his eye.

Lieutenant Cheeseman was, by vocation, a salesman of

wholesale sweets and confectionery. He entered the room as if it were the back parlour of a newsagent's, with a greeting for everyone but eyes only for the boss, ready to snap open his fitted case and reveal his fossilised sugar novelties. Though at the moment of course in the King's Uniform, with brown gloves and a leather-wrapped stick, one could see him in a dark three-piece suit, a striped tie; hear his 'Thank you very much for your order' as he capped his Waterman pen and offered you a free sherbet lemon. On his flat face he wore solicitor's spectacles, a face which appeared to have partially melted before setting again, and which was not exactly weatherbeaten. He appeared to have shaved while waiting to be called; a scrap of toilet paper at the corner of his mouth; and there was talcum powder on the knot of his khaki tie.

'I understand,' muttered my father, examining the liberty vest, 'that you wish to marry my daughter?'

'Yes, sir,' said the Lieutenant, as if grateful for a large order of aniseed rock. 'It must have come as a surprise to you.'

'Not to me,' said De Kuyper. 'I always knew she had it in her.'

Miss Parkinson choked on a piece of fudge, and her coughing caused her to fall off the pouffe. 'You're in the sweetie business?' she said, when her back had been patted and she had regained her composure.

'Yes, ma'am,' he said, and she smiled at him; very much I thought as she had once smiled at me outside the bathroom.

Having nothing to add to this catechism, I watched the Lieutenant put his stick under his left arm and cuddle it. He was obviously very skilled in this and I could see that my father was impressed.

'Yasmin says that you have a good job to go back to,' said Miss Parkinson, Deputy Speaker as it were. 'Where will you live?'

'Prefabricated house, ma'am.' He stared straight ahead

at the ducks on the wall. (Daddy, mummy and a baby, like in the bath, but without red lips or a hole in their bottom.) My mouth hung open; my eyebrows rose. The word was new to me, and I saw 'Prefabricated House' as another version of Hobbeycock Hall or the Reals' pile. Of course I warmed to the man. But not for long.

'One of those that come on lorries?' asked my father, and the sweetie man agreed. Miss Parkinson asked him to make himself comfortable, and he put his legs apart, his hands behind his back and his stick across his bottom. The prefab house it seemed, when it arrived on the back of a lorry, was to be in Bradford; a place I knew then only by repute, and because of the black lady dressed as Queen Victoria. But when he said, lowering his head, his toilet paper falling off, that he had lost both his parents, my ears pricked up.

'To lose one parent, Mr Cheeseman . . . ' I began, eager to use what I had rehearsed so long at Traggets; but Yasmin turned on me, showing a side that I had alway suspected. 'Shut up!' she – and I do not exaggerate – snarled, behind the bridegroom's back.

'I've been to Bradford,' said my father. 'On business, of course.' He picked up the poker, and then put it down again, while I stared at him. I didn't know he'd been to Bradford.

'Well,' said Miss Parkinson to the happy couple, 'we'll come to visit you,' and I began to get mildly excited about a trip up the Great North Road. No doubt this would be soon, if we were to be there in time to feel it kicking.

There remained only the matter of De Kuyper's seal of approval. Something unspoken but awaited by all, except of course for Lieutenant Cheeseman, who had made the near-fatal error of tipping her a shilling at the back door. A silence was left for her, after we had watched my father fold the Beetle Drive invitation into an aeroplane, then clean his fingernails on the wing tips. De Kuyper then addressed the back of the gallant officer's head.

'What would you call yourself?' she asked. 'Wage slave or exploiter?'

'Or Nignog,' I added, it just coming to me, him being from Bradford. But of course I was totally ignored.

'Exploiter!' he said at once, eyes bright with belief turning towards De Kuyper, the fervent answer ringing out over the pip on his shoulder. Yasmin looked at each of us in turn, even me, lips pressed tight, the light of love in her eyes, bursting with pride.

Then, within weeks – for time was not of course on my sister's side – the wedding.

This was a big day, for me as well as for Yasmin and George. Not only had I a new suit, but I had been allowed to wear, behind the lapel, like a deaf aid, Uncle Frank's water container. Made of Britannia Metal it kept a carnation fresh for hours. I had also, unknown to anyone else, arranged to meet in Swinehurst my customer, Elspeth Garrowby, thematic collector and Nignog No 504.

You will remember that she had written to me at the end of the war, enquiring about stamps featuring May Days. (A point that did not escape De Kuyper, who until she actually met Elspeth did what she could to encourage the liaison.) I had posted my sheet of approvals that morning after VE Day, with difficulty because of my bandaged hand, and smearing Germolene on the envelope. Well, she had replied within the week, enclosing a postal order for six shillings and asking me to be her pen-pal. I had thought this a doubtful mixing of business with pleasure, but wrote back telling her some of my adventures, enclosing a sheet of further approvals. She had answered again by return of post, with a postal order for one and six, and asked for a photograph. I had considered sending her Don Ameche, but De Kuyper had thought that on a par with getting them drunk, and that it might frighten her. After some thought I sent her, rolled up like a medieval scroll, the Traggets school photo. You will remember that we all sat out in a field in long rows, the back rank standing and the Matron in front with the dog. Over the Sixth Form I put a vague cross in ink, in the sky, like Spot the Ball.

That seemed to have done the trick; though there were no more postal orders. The correspondence since then had been mainly on her side. A month before she had moved south from her home in Ilkley, where the moors are, ('No, not that kind,' I told Bernard) to stay with relatives in Doncaster. Then, a fortnight later, she turned up in Boston (England), staying with another branch of the family. With a feeling of unease, I noted that she was moving steadily closer.

As she had bought no approvals for some time, I wrote a short but firm letter explaining that I was giving up the business, and that my new – but unspecified – activities would leave no time for letter writing. I closed with a phrase current at the time: 'It's been nice to know you,' and got back, by return, what looked like a ransom note, in bold capitals: 'I MUST SEE YOU! IT IS VERY IMPORTANT!'

Life had taught me that she was almost certainly pregnant. I was of course, again, free of all guilt; but rather than find her being helped, swollen, off the bus one day in the market square, loudly asking the way to Jasmine Villa, I decided to meet her on neutral ground. In Swinehurst, on the day of the wedding. I selected the Pilgrim Fisheries (rather than 'a boarding house', which had been her suggestion) because in the back room, as well as tea and bread and butter, one could have privacy in which to talk.

After the wedding ceremony, we all posed on the steps of the Town Hall, my father stepping back into the shadow of the black Corinthian columns as the shutter fell. I stood at the front, like Matron's dog, keeping an eye on passing trams. The last thing I wanted was a scene. We then threw things at George and Yasmin ('George the First' she called him, which made people smile) and while they made their way to the Co-op Café for the reception, I slipped away up an alley. I was of course on familiar territory.

Elspeth was already there when I arrived. There was no need for the stratagems I had devised: that I would be wearing a white flower, holding my ear with my left hand, and blowing my nose. But, closing the chip shop door behind me, I did those things; hoping that she hadn't turned up yet, that the girl in the corner was a waitress having a sit down.

'Over here, Jeffrey,' she called. 'I've poured your tea out.' And as I sat down: 'I've put two sugars in.' I heard a faint echo of the Delius's maxim that one couldn't do it on bread and jam.

'I couldn't carry the evening paper,' said Elspeth. 'It's not out yet.'

'That's all right,' I said. It was quite obviously her. 'I knew it was you.'

What I meant, of course, was that there was nobody else there; just oilcloth-covered tables and bottles of dubious sauce. But it came out sounding like Don Ameche chatting-up Alice Faye, and I realised that I was starting to blush.

'And I knew *you*,' said Elspeth, husky already, 'even before you blew your nose.' She pushed a plate towards me, through a puddle of weak vinegar. 'Have a slice of bread.'

Ordering another pot of tea, thinking it the least I could do for a customer, I nibbled the pale yellow triangle while I studied her. You would not have thought her to be a philatelist, but it would be fair to say that I was impressed. She wore a shimmering orange and green dress; silk I think, modestly high at the neck and trimmed with what I believe are called flounces. Her accessories, white string gloves and a beaded handbag, were on the chair beside her. On her wrist was a bangle made from red, white and blue strands of electric wire. Pretending to check my flies, I managed to see her legs under the table. They seemed fairly long and straight, ending in white socks and black shoes with a little heel. Straightening up, smiling at her, I thought she looked like Dorothy on the Yellow Brick Road. She had a mouth like Judy Garland as well; generous they usually call it.

'Is she married yet?' she asked, in a low and holy kind of voice.

I said that since two o'clock my sister had been Yasmin Cheeseman, and Elspeth sighed and dabbled a pale pink fingernail in the vinegar. 'Think of her tonight,' she said in a whisper. 'Where are they going?'

'Clacton,' I whispered, then remembered that it was a chip shop and not a library. 'She's four months gone,' I said, raising my voice. 'Pregnant by him; George the First. It's not exactly a novelty to her.' I was sorry to be so hard, but I was determined to master the situation.

'I'm a virgin,' said Elspeth, her brown eyes fixed on me, still whispering. 'Like her in the Bible.'

I nodded, as if it were written all over her, dipping the crust of my bread in the vinegar. I then explained to her that it was perfectly normal and healthy for a girl to develop a crush on her first philatelic dealer. 'If things could have been otherwise . . . ' I sighed, shrugging my shoulders, rolling my eyes to signify what might have been, startling the woman who was coming round from the frying part to say that they were closing.

We stood outside, sheltering from the rain, while the bolts slid to behind us. Neither of us had a raincoat, but Elspeth carried an umbrella with a duck's head handle. She now erected this, and I felt a hand in a string glove slip through my arm. 'Where are we going?' she asked.

It had not turned out as I had expected. I had seen myself leaving her sobbing into a crumpled handkerchief, slipping a coin into the head waitress's hand with murmured instructions to see that she did nothing foolish. As it was, when we emerged from the entry, turning into the main road, I was in an odd position;

my cheek next to hers, our bodies touching from shoulder to elbow, breathing in face powder and the unmistakable scent of Phul Nana.

'My last bus isn't till nine o'clock,' whispered the perfumed one, feeling my biceps as we looked into the window of Freeman Hardy and Willis. I had her for another six hours.

Woolworth's was dry, and of course free, so we went in there. There was no one around that I knew, so I carried the duck's head umbrella. Several times we were pushed close together by the Saturday afternoon crowds; and once, by the gardening tools, under the hanks of raffia for tying up peas, we were squeezed face to face as someone tried to get through with a pram. Elspeth put her head on my chest, like Celia Johnson, and I held her close; because Uncle Frank's Britannia Metal vase had got caught in her cardigan.

Finally we came to the lampshades, and the back door. It was still raining and neither of us wanted to go round again. 'Where are we going now?' she asked, holding my arm, smiling at people as they passed. I looked down at the wet pavement, at her shoes and damp white socks, her bare legs. One could have done worse, I thought, from an advertisement in *The Beano*.

Her bus went from outside the meat market, which would be closed and dark at nine o'clock. I remembered what I had heard about the place, and of course the story by D. H. Lawrence. But until then, what could we do? Then I thought of taking her to Osrams, down a steep flight of steps in the next street. It cost a penny to get in, but for that you got a brass token which you could use in any of the machines. Nothing like a modern day amusement arcade, the only thing electric in Osrams was the light. No juke box of course, no music at all; just the sound of little footballers' legs going. Unless you put tuppence in for a short burst of 'Poet and Peasant' from the ghostly violin and drum. This was usually 'Out of Order', and all one could hear going down the steps was the creaking of the door in The Haunted House, as an automaton swigged from a miniature bottle of 'The Devil's Sperm', as the Rev Wannamaker had been known to call it.

The machines were spaced around a large low-ceilinged room, under glass like in a museum; but the real attraction was on a shelf which was just out of reach. Dozens of wax busts of murderers. Plus a man with an iron bar sticking out of both ears. This had been driven through his head by a mine explosion in British Columbia, and a card said that he had lived on for some time; though not for how long. Cards below the other busts detailed the stabbing, poisoning, smothering or otherwise putting away of wives. All the wax faces, even the one with the iron bar, looked rather pleased with themselves.

In a small room at the end, beyond the bicycle race in which the winner got his brass token back, reminiscent of the after-dinner sport of the upper classes, was a wax collection of the freaks of Barnum and Bailey. These were life size on plinths, and one could discreetly touch Eng and Chang; though moths had got the Pig Faced Lady. I wasn't sure it was the kind of thing that Elspeth would go for.

While I was thinking about this, she looked up at me from under her fringe. 'What time will they cut the cake?' she asked.

I had been thinking about that as well. The cake was coming down from Bradford, supplied by the firm that wanted George the First back, and was reputed to be of pre-war standard with real eggs. De Kuyper had flared her nostrils and walked out, slamming the door.

'I don't know,' I said, hesitating. It was of course a family affair, formal, with all the men wearing Britannia Metal vases. But as there was to be at least forty people there, it was not likely that we would be noticed. Then we could slip away to the meat market when it got dark; after the cake, while they were playing 'Pass the parcel'.

'Would you like to come to the wedding reception?' I asked her.

'I like weddings,' she said, nodding and sighing, leaning her head on my chest. She had been to seventeen she told me, as we walked towards the Co-op Café. Each had been recorded in a white silk-covered book from Timothy White's & Taylor's. First names of bride and groom; what kind of flowers (with pressed specimen); number of tiers on the cake; what the weather was like, etc. In a code (which I did not crack until 1955) she also noted whether or not she could see 'the bridegroom's thing' showing through his trousers. Seventeen nights she had lain awake, a bolster wearing a trilby clutched in her arms, trying to imagine what happened; what the happy couple were doing.

I was naturally embarrassed by this intimacy, and it was followed by silence as we walked through the back streets. As we reached the Co-op Café and I handed her the duck's head handle, I felt bound to say: 'Elspeth . . . what do you mean . . . what they're doing?'

'You know,' she said, as we went in through the bread shop, wiping our feet on the big mat. She lowered her voice under the illuminated Hovis sign. 'What they do when they get to the boarding house.' She turned away, but I could see her flushed face reflected in the glass case along with the bread rolls. A woman behind the counter said, 'Is it ordered?' and Elspeth turned to face me as I touched my Britannia Metal vase to show that I was a guest. Her face close to mine, her eyes closed, she whispered again, 'You know!'

I did indeed. I realised with something of a shock, but with absolute certainty, that Nignog Garrowby was a nymphomaniac; one of those that swarmed, according to Bernard, in the sleazier quarters of Troon.

Still thinking about that, certain now that tonight was to be *the* night, we made our entrance. We were just in time. No sooner had I got myself a brown ale, and an orangeade for Elspeth, when there was a roll on the drums, a clash of cymbals, and it was announced through the microphone that Yasmin and George were about to cut the cake. The bride had only time to hiss 'Who's she?' and 'What did you buy me?' before she was led off by the photographer.

'There is a tide in the affairs of men . . . ' and this was the crest of the wave for George Cheeseman. Never again would he be the man he was that afternoon, in the Co-op Café, the rain on the windows and the paper chains over his head. There was total silence in the room, but for the dramatic rolling of the snare drum, as he removed his shako carefully with both hands from the perfection and shine of his hair. An open-mouthed aunt from Ramsbottom took the helmet from him, parting the plume in order to watch what happened next. All eyes were on the gleaming boots, mirrored black and thigh high, and the tight white doeskin trousers that caused Elspeth to draw breath. Beneath the short cape hung the Victory Medal, among the starched lanyards on the braided and epauletted jacket. Understandably not wishing to spoil the effect by wearing his glasses, he waited for the silver bread knife to be put into his hand. This done, he was positioned facing the cake by the best man, a brother officer somewhat more soberly dressed.

'Good old George,' some wit cried, and we clapped as he sliced through the icing and marzipan, cracking and dislodging the name of his firm, which had been built up in Yorkshire Mixture and liquorice comfits. We all got a slice, and the lucky ones a sweet as well. Then we moved to the sides of the room, holding our paper plates; and at that moment I saw my mother.

It had been a long time since that day in the garden of Number 17. I had had several birthday cards since then, signed 'Mother', which I had not known what to do with. She lived now in London, alone 'among the dens and beauty parlours of Mayfair' as De Kuyper put it, since the

Colonel had been dropped into the Dordogne. Now she stood at one end of a trestle table, painted fingernails around a glass, wearing lime green and pearls. Beyond the dirty doilies and the crumbs of sausage rolls, at the other end of the table, my father fished a fly out of his pale ale, determined not to look up.

She was staring at me, across the floor on which the blind Ruritanian monarch and my sister were doing the foxtrot, his spurred heels kicking up the french chalk.

'Who's that?' asked Elspeth, aniseed rock in her mouth, looking around for souvenirs but missing nothing.

'It's my mother,' I said, feeling a fool, and Elspeth waved to her.

'Come on,' she said, and took me by the hand, pulling me round the edge of the floor; while the band – the resident trio augmented with drums and a spangled saxophone – played 'I've Got My Eye On You'.

'Hello,' she said, letting go of me and spitting the sweet into her hand. 'I'm Elspeth.'

'I'm his mother,' said my mother. 'Hello, Jeffrey.'

'Hello,' I said, looking down the table at my father. It would have been nice if he could have joined in.

'And this is your girlfriend, is it?' my mother asked.

'Yes,' said Elspeth, before I could say anything; then 'Excuse me' as she darted away to collect a sample of the confetti, before it was swept up.

'Well!' said my mother, making a face. 'I didn't know about her.'

I was tempted to reply that I didn't know about *him*, meaning Colonel Trewin, but kept quiet. If asked, I decided to say that I had picked her up in the chip shop. It sounded better than saying we had found each other in *The Beano*. We both nodded to the Rev Eli Wannamaker, dancing past with the woman whose husband had robbed the gas meter.

'Still,' said my mother, 'you're a big boy now.'

'Yes,' I said. 'I've been told that.'

There was a short silence.

'You'll have to come and stay with me sometime,' she said. 'We'll do something about your clothes. What are you going to do when you leave school?'

'I don't know,' I said, feeling instinctively that she would be against a career in the Nabisco factory. I pointed out that I had my National Service to do first.

'Yes, of course,' she said, raising her glass to me. 'You'll be a soldier like Hubert. Do you know what the Colonel always used to say?'

'Yes,' I said. I knew what the Colonel always used to say. My ears burned as I went to get her a gin and orange. 'Fuck off!' he'd said to me, as he'd raised his hat to the post lady. When I came back the band – the leader playing the bones and shouting through the microphone for everyone to join in – had broken into a South American rhythm. My mother, emptying her glass at a gulp and holding out her arms, said, 'Rumba?'

'No, thank you,' I said, backing away, colliding with Mrs Moss who was leading her fat son.

In the corridor, outside the toilets, I found De Kuyper dancing with the shop steward from the bakery. She could see that I was upset and came to me, brushing off the floury fingermarks. 'What's the matter with you?' she said. 'Your mother?'

I nodded; De Kuyper understood. 'You don't have to talk to her,' she said, waving to the baker as he went back into the heat. 'Why don't you get off somewhere with Miss Muffet?'

'She's just a friend,' I said. 'A Nignog actually. Interested in stamps and weddings.'

De Kuyper sighed. 'Do you know about the meat market?'

I nodded shyly, hanging my head, feeling myself starting to blush.

We slipped away as soon as Yasmin and George had left for the station. As Elspeth collected her cardigan and

206

duck's head handle from the cloakroom, Miss Parkinson began to sing. She had been sitting on the stage, to one side of the band, well out of reach of my mother; and now, stepping forward, she went into 'A medley of favourites, starting with "All Of Me" '. We hurried through the deserted bread shop, past empty shelves and neon-lit crumbs, to the amplified sound of: 'All of me, why not take all of me? Don't you know, I'm no good without you.'

The brown ale racing in my veins, my bladder was close to bursting. To keep Elspeth moving I held her arm, and we almost trotted through the dark streets. Under every gaslamp she smiled at me. Could she possibly know what I planned?

The meat market, as I had known it would be, was dark, closed and deserted. Washed down alleyways of locked shutters, the last speck of blood and suet swept away. At the cast-iron arch at the entrance, topped by a contented cow, I could go no further. The lavatories by the bus stops were also washed down, closed and locked up. Telling Elspeth to walk on, I made for the kiosk which opened at dawn to sell tea and toast to the meat market porters. It was dark, deserted, but behind it was darker privacy still.

'I'm not going in there,' said Elspeth, loudly, standing under the contented cow and pointing into the blackness of the meat market. 'Not by myself.'

I forget what I said to her, possibly something quite abrupt, and stepped smartly round the back of the kiosk. Within seconds I was washing down the wooden wall with bliss, spraying in an arc and with great joy, when I heard a bus pull in to the pavement. Through the kiosk window, looking through the dark silhouetted interior, I saw that the bus was empty. The engine stopped and then, predictably you may say, I heard a voice that I knew well.

'Hobbeycock Hall, love?'

'No,' I heard Elspeth reply, 'I'm waiting for somebody.'

'Despite the shock, the brown ale made me start to sing softly, as I swung sideways to avoid splashing my suit.

My stream, golden in the glare of the bus headlights, ran down a Zebo sign and onto the pavement like a yellow river in flood. 'Are you going to Hobbeycock Hall? Parsley sage, Rosemary and thyme . . . ' Holding it, swinging it down, I hit part of the kiosk wall that was patched with tin and drummed like Edmundo Ros, like the monsoon sweeping from the east. Turning into the darkness, back to the kiosk, I raised a high trajectory, like a Thames fire boat, but it made a loud splashing like Lucille the horse. Two streams now ran round the sides of the toast emporium, across the broken pavement and into the gutter, to rot the nearside tyres of the bus.

At last it came to an end, dribbling down like a fireman's hose. Not bothering to shake it, I put it away quickly and called out, 'Elspeth. Come here, please.' Disguising my voice of course. I could see her through the kiosk, standing on a delta of pavement, a snaking stream on either side of her. The bus conductress was smoking a cigarette and watching her.

'No!' I heard Elspeth say, her back to the kiosk, from under the umbrella, which she had put up when she heard the brown ale drumming on the Zebo sign. 'I won't!' There was a faint splash as she stamped her foot.

Impasse, is, I think, the word. You will understand that I did not want her round the back of the kiosk in the wet; I simply thought that we could climb through the up-ended porters' barrows and weeds and over a spiked wall, and get into the meat market that way. Anything rather than walk out onto the lamplit pavement, pretending that I had merely stopped to fasten my shoe laces.

The bus driver was eating a bap and watching. Very soon a crowd would gather, crying 'Come out, let's have a look at you!' And then the Meat Market Police, whom I had heard about. An impasse indeed. Racking my brain for a way of escape, I considered tying a handkerchief around my face; but thought that it would upset Elspeth, and make the bus crew think they were under armed attack. So, finally, taking long deep breaths through my nose, I came out fast; my hand extended to take Elspeth's arm and rush her away.

'Hello, Jeffrey,' said the conductress as I emerged into the light, feeling the last few drops run down my leg.

'Hello, Rosemary,' I called out gaily, shaking my leg, with a wave of the extended hand, as I seized my girlfriend and hurried her away into the darkness.

'Who's she?' asked Elspeth, as I pulled her into the deep doorway of a wholesale pork butcher. 'Is she married?'

I took several more deep breaths. It had been a nasty shock. I had no idea that trams had given way to buses on the route to Hobbeycock Hall. Thank God she had not had the child with her.

'She's the past,' I said, which I thought was rather good, and running my hands up the back of her cardigan I brought my mouth down, crushing the lips of the philatelic Nignog.

As you will have gathered, Elspeth was willing. But when I urged her to open her lips she spread them, like stretching the wrist of a rubber glove, keeping her teeth tight together. I knew that it was hardly the response I would have had on the Rue Mazarin.

Wary of being bitten, of having to go to De Kuyper again for the Germolene, I went for her neck; nibbling along her shoulder until – surprised and oddly moved – I came to the broderie anglaise edge of her liberty bodice. I had decided not to go for her chest, having looked closely in the chip shop and again at the reception, thinking there was no point in feeling for what wasn't there. She would probably, I thought, have taken offence.

'How long have we got?' she whispered into my ear.

It was too dark to see Uncle Frank's watch, so I struck a match. (I had brought Player's Weights so that we could have a smoke afterwards.) 'We've got half an hour,' I told her.

'Then hurry up!' she said, sounding a little strained,

standing braced against the pork butcher's shutter, as if expecting me to hurl knives and tomahawks at her. 'And stop spitting!' she added, as I moved in, as it were, for the kill.

Nonplussed by this, I then realised that each time I bent over her, a measure of carnation water slurped out of Uncle Frank's Britannia Metal vase. Her chest was quite saturated, so it was just as well that I had left it alone.

This was it, I thought, getting into the prescribed position; concentrating hard, not wanting anything to go wrong this time. Elspeth had her right hand up the back of my jacket, exciting herself by sliding the metal adjusters of my braces up and down, and by leaning my left shoulder against her arm I pinned it to the shutter. So far so good. Then, with my left hand I grasped her left wrist, holding it in the correct position above her head to do the paso doblê. At this point I noticed that several cats, or rats, had gathered to watch, sitting around us in a half circle. Ignoring them, and smoothly, with expertise and assurance, remembering at the last moment to put the box of matches back in my pocket, I thrust my hand up Elspeth Garrowby's skirt.

They say that shock can kill you; and they are probably right. Frozen in flamenco posture against the rattling shutter, our eyes held each other's in the darkness, slightly crossed because they were so close. 'What's the matter?' whispered Elspeth, the flounces of her skirt raised high, bare knees exposed to the watching rodents.

'You've got trousers on!' I said, letting go of her hand, which came down to fondle the lobe of my right ear.

'I know,' she said.

She was wearing short grey flannel trousers, to just above the knee. My fingers discovered that the flies were sewn up with strong thread, but otherwise they were just like a boy's, though I could feel no conkers.

'*Boy's trousers?!*' I was not only shocked, and of course unprepared and bewildered, but naturally outraged. For

210

an insane moment I thought that perhaps she *was* a boy. Bernard had a book about them. Or a freak escaped from the back room of Osrams; something between Eng and Chang and the Pig Faced Lady. I released her, feeling her pluck wistfully at my braces.

'Why are you wearing boy's trousers?' I asked, regaining control of myself, stepping back from her, out of the pork butcher's doorway into the light of a pale moon that had appeared through the clouds.

'My Aunt Doreen said I couldn't come if I didn't,' she said. And then, in fairness to Aunt Doreen, 'Because she didn't know you.'

'She's sewn up the flies!' I said, in case she didn't know.

'I know,' she said. 'She said I wouldn't have any use for them.'

There was a silence, as you can imagine. The mood had been shattered. I lit a Player's Weight and walked up and down, wondering if she was wearing braces. One does not think rationally in such circumstances. The cats or rats had given up and gone.

'I can take them down.' Her voice came from the darkness of the doorway, but it was hopeless and she knew it. Quite frankly it was more than I could face. Even with eyes closed and in the dark, the thought of the grey flannel – with God knows what kind of underpants collapsing around her white ankle socks – was too much for me.

'You'll miss your bus,' I said, pretending to read the pork butcher's name.

Somewhat chastened, we emerged from the meat market, attracting knowing nods and nudges from the people in the queue, Elspeth still apologising for her Aunt Doreen. Thankfully the bus to Hobbeycock Hall had gone. Elspeth's was in, so kissing her forehead, giving her what was left of the cake which I had in my pocket, I promised to write every day. The flannel trousers did not show as she went upstairs, but they accounted, once you knew about them, for her shape. We waved to each other, and she blew kisses; then, just as the engine started and the bell rang, she slid open the window. 'My umbrella,' she called down, 'I left it.' Calling back for her not to worry, I waved until the bus turned the corner. A man waving to someone else winked at me and I winked back, walking away as if hurrying off to a well-deserved mixed grill.

As I entered the meat market again I thought I would have a rest from girls for a while. At least until I was in the army. In uniform, away from home, things were bound to be different.

The umbrella was in the corner of the pork butcher's doorway, and I lingered a moment, thinking of what might have been. Then, out of the darkness, a voice spoke to me.

'Wot you doin' then?'

Shielding my eyes from the blaze of a torch, I said, 'I came to get my umbrella.'

'Oh, yes?' The voice was sceptical, to say the least.

Coming out into the moonlight I saw that it was a Sergeant with bright buttons and numbered collar, lacking the spiked helmet of the Welsh Constabulary, but with all the majesty, and it was enough, of the Meat Market Police. Obviously realising that I was not one of the usual run of idlers to be found on his patch, he reached out to touch the carnation in my vase, rephrasing his opening question.

'What you bin doin' then?'

Only then did I realise that Elspeth had unbuttoned my braces at the back. I now felt them sliding over my shoulders and my crutch starting to droop.

'You know how it is, officer,' I said, my knees together, lighting a cigarette; not offering him one because of the laws against bribery, and because it was the last of my packet of five. 'I've been to a wedding.'

'Oh, yes?' he said again, clipping the lamp onto his belt, probably watching my crutch sag with interest. 'Wot were you then?'

'I was a guest,' I said, not caring for his tone. 'At the Co-op Café.'

'The Co-op Café, eh?' He swung his heavy torso, so that the lamp shone into the pork butcher's doorway. 'And then you came round here? So where is she?'

I was silent, both hands in my pockets to steady my trousers.

'Where's the bride?' There was a count of three, then he opened his mouth and laughed out loud. You could hear the cats and rats running away, the laugh echoing up the empty alleyways. I let him go on, thinking that he couldn't have much to laugh at, being on duty in there all night.

'Come on then,' he said, the lamp on his belt rising and falling, the light flickering across my face as his stomach settled. 'Where is she?'

'Clacton,' I said.

'Clacton?' I saw a ghastly grin in the gloom. 'Wot you doin' 'ere then?' He was probably a light comedian with the Meat Market Police concert party.

'My sister is in Clacton,' I explained. 'She's the bride. George is the bridegroom.'

'George who?' he asked. 'George the First?'

'Yes,' I said, surprised that he knew. 'That's what she calls him.'

'Does she,' he said, after a short pause. 'Clacton are they?' A cloud was across the moon and I couldn't see his face, but I knew he wasn't laughing. I decided to come clean.

'I did have a girl in there,' I admitted, thinking about nudging him but deciding against it, 'but I didn't do anything.'

'Didn't do nothing?'

'No.' I wanted to tell him that I had done nothing because she had been wearing knee-length grey flannel trousers, but some sixth sense held me back. 'All right,' I said. It seemed the only way out. I pointed to the precise spot with the duck's head handle. 'We did it. There.'

He swung the light in again, to see if we had left our mark, and now his voice softened. 'That's better,' he said. 'How many times?'

How many times? I wasn't sure what to say. Once would seem feeble; a brusque and casual way of treating a girl. More than six, given my age (and his of course) might seem like boasting and would only antagonise him. 'Three,' I said. Then nervously, because he didn't say anything, 'I think.'

'You think?'

'Yes,' I said, starting to walk away, one hand between my legs and the duck's head handle under my arm. 'It might have been four,' I said, when I was a few yards away.

'Or even five,' he suggested. He was just a light now, four feet off the ground, like Tinkerbell. 'Yes,' I called, still backing away, 'it could well have been five.'

'Or six?' I heard, as I reached the corner of the alley and saw the gaslamps at the entrance.

'Yes,' I shouted into the darkness, and heard the dreadful laugh begin again.

Chapter Three

Having posted the duck's head handle to Ilkley – thereby wiping out any profit I had made in my relationship with Elspeth Garrowby – I settled down, in the months that remained before I was called to the Colours, to try my hand yet again at being an entrepreneur. But jewellery this time, rather than stamps. Or at least a plaster of Paris profile of a lady wearing a pillbox hat.

It had been a plastic brooch of Yasmin's, left behind in the scramble to become Mrs Cheeseman, and the idea had come to me at school. That very evening ('Son of the Wizard of Menlo Park' as Miss Parkinson put it, her hand on my shoulder) I had made a mould out of an empty Germolene tin. Within hours, with the aid of a little Vaseline, I was turning out brooches, each with a small gold safety pin set in the back. Mrs Moss, who had the local franchise, had them pinned in rows on a sheet of cardboard, headed 'The Latest Thing'. They were reasonably priced at one and six, a third of which was hers.

Engrossed as I was, though aware of the election called by Winston Churchill, all talk of politics washed over my head. Soon I had four Germolene tins going, and planned to introduce a two-shilling model in gold paint. I knew of course that we came into the Swinehurst constituency; that our MP lived in a large house that was later turned into a mental home, but I had no idea, nobody had told me, who the Labour candidate was to be. I knew nothing of the Labour Cavalcade.

You can imagine my amazement, coming out of Mossies, my retail outlet, having delivered some stock and collected two and threepence, half in pineapple rock, when the Cavalcade entered from the far side of the market place. I had of course noticed quite a few people hanging about on the pavement, but assumed them to be the usual boulevardiers taking in the sunshine. The off-licence now had a chair outside, and though you were not allowed to consume drink on it, it gave a distinctly Continental flavour to the town. Several people had commented on it.

Then I heard the music, heard the slap of sandals as children ran towards it; saw the scarlet and the gold braid, the sun flash from the brass instruments, as the Swinehurst Temperance Band wheeled around the corner, marking time outside the newsagent's in their polished black shoes.

'England Arise', a tune new to me then – and never heard before in our area – caused the pigeons to wheel in alarm over the roof of the wool shop. There was the rattle of shutters being secured from the Conservative Club and the Lincolnshire Penny Bank.

Then singing, in broad daylight, from the throat of a man halfway up the horse trough. 'England arise! The long long night is o'er'. I had seen him before in the Co-op grocers, but never like this. 'Faint in the east, behold the dawn appears' he sang, and was joined by a little woman looking up at him, possibly his wife. 'Out of your age-long dream of toil and sorrow' they belted out together, and he took off and waved his cap as the band marched towards us.

'Hurrah!' shouted the little woman, though she couldn't see much. 'Come on!' she said, nudging me. 'You know it.'

I didn't of course, and my mouth hung open as the bandmaster led the Temperance Band across the cobbles, stick tight under his arm.

Singing came from the far side of the market place – from outside Pomfrets' and the ironmonger's people threw their caps – rising high and falling back above the roof of the Railway Hotel, like flat balloons against the sky. There was a splash beside me as one fell into the horse trough. As I moved away, from the singing and the caps falling from the sky, Carton the policeman, a one-time friend of Bernard's mother, went past in the middle of the road. Wheeling his bicycle, the pole for pushing bodies across The Drain tied to its crossbar, his cape in a neat bundle on the handlebars. He blushed as he waved the bread van out of the way.

The market place now had a thin rim of crowd around the sides, as people hurried down from the council houses, where my mother didn't like me to go, singing and dancing and some of them wearing curlers. The man who washed out Pomfrets' churns was there of course; and as the band passed, between the euphoniums, I saw Agnes come out of the dairy, clapping, her embroidered 'P' heaving. I hadn't known until then that she was that way inclined.

But my eyes were on the flags, the banners streaming in the breeze. Most of them were red, though there was one Union Jack which everyone said was upside down. They were carried by youths mounted on decorated bicycles, going of course at the pace of the Temperance Band, but not many of them fell off. A prize was to be awarded to the best of these, and I marvelled at the crepe paper wound so merrily between the spokes of the wheels, festooning the pumps and the handlebars. But they were quickly past, and forgotten, for now came the Swinehurst Maidens, home-made dresses swinging around their socks, bearing sheaves and sickles, waving aloft dried flowers. Several of them looked at me, and I felt it only right to begin to clap. I had seen nothing like it before.

The music changed to 'I'm The Man, The Very Fat Man, That Waters The Worker's Beer' as the fifes and drums of the Woodland Folk swung past. The little woman was crying between my legs. The crowd sang and cheered as the children, holding hands and throwing flowers, stopped and did a little dance. In their midst was a black

217

boy on loan from Nottingham. Someone fell off the horse trough, but no one turned round to look.

It would be fair to say that I was, until that day, apolitical. Like my father I had accepted, broadly speaking, Lord Beaverbrook's view of world affairs. But now, as The Socialist Clergy of Swinehurst went past, their sandals slapping the cobbles together, I abandoned both the dream of becoming an entrepreneur and the prospect of a career in the Nabisco factory. 'When Adam delved and Eve span, who was then the gentleman?' they chanted. 'Who indeed!' said the little woman between my legs.

'And what do I care if it makes them ill, if it makes them terribly queer . . . ' I recognised the voice. Turning in surprise I saw Bernard, the red rosette he had got for the best of his rabbits in his lapel, singing with the crowd. We smiled at each other and I moved beside him, taking one of the song sheets which were being passed from hand to hand. 'I've a yacht and a car and a big cigar, and I water the worker's beer' we sang together.

'Look!' cried Bernard, in wonder and amazement, pointing. But I was too moved to answer. I began to punch his other arm, which was our way of expressing deep feeling at the time. Blinking back the tears I hooted and whistled, jumping up and down and squashing the little woman's finger. For here, a lumbering juggernaut, swathed in green and yellow bunting. It had a faint smell, and cinders and cabbage leaves fell through the floorboards as it hit each cobblestone. The shire horses that pulled the float of the Swinehurst Tabernacle were dressed for May Day, scarlet ribbons and glittering brass, bells between their pricked ears and with braided manes. At the rear of the dustcart the choir sang 'Jerusalem', while at the front, next to the driver, in clean shirt and red tie, was the candidate. 'VOTE FOR DELIUS! VOTE LABOUR!' said a banner over his head.

'*Uncle Fred!*' I shouted, turning to Bernard in frantic excitement. 'I know him! I know him! It's Uncle Fred!' But he couldn't understand what I meant, pointing to the place on the song sheet and starting to sing again. A man on my left, his head bowed and cap pressed to his waistcoat, was already into 'And shall those feet, in ancient time . . . ' But I left them, running alongside the huge iron-shod wheels, shouting to attract Uncle Fred's attention. It was hopeless of course, my voice was lost in the music and the singing, the cheers of the crowd. Even Aunt Ada, seated behind him, holding his coat in case it came on to rain, failed to notice me. Then the Cavalcade swung into the centre of the market place. The crowd surged forward, and as I tried to fight my way through – smoothing over an unpleasant incident in which I was mistaken for the class enemy – I saw the decorated bus.

It had gone directly to the centre of the square, to form the hustings for the speeches. As I approached I saw the two of them, but I was beyond surprise now. On the platform of the bus, dressed as Marie Antoinette, was Rosemary. She looked stunning, with bare shoulders and with her black eyes properly done. Up on the roof of the bus, saying 'Testing . . . one, two, three, four' into a microphone, was the chairperson of the meeting; De Kuyper herself.

'Comrades and friends,' boomed out over the market place, after little Mr Freeson from the wireless shop, in his brown overall and trilby, had gone up with a screwdriver. 'We are gathered here today to face a new dawn.' The choir, which had been humming in the dustcart, started to swell, but De Kuyper waved them into silence. 'A spectre is haunting Europe,' she announced, pausing to let it sink in. She was wearing her warden's trousers tucked into boots, a trench coat, and a bigger rosette than any of Bernard's rabbits. She then read out *The Mask of Anarchy*, 'By Percy Bysshe Shelley', taking it from her handbag as if it had arrived from him in the post that morning. It was strong stuff, several people around me 'tut-ting'.

'Rise like lions after slumber, in unvanquishable number'

rang out, metallic and loud, from the grey loudspeakers; then she went on to read a pamphlet by Rosa Luxemburg, who Mrs Dooley – unexpectedly turning up next to me – said had no connection at all with the Ovaltinies.

'Bloody 'ell!' said someone behind me, as De Kuyper castigated and damned the bourgeoisie. 'Aye,' said another voice, 'that's tellin' 'em.'

There was an awkward moment when the candidate attempted to get up the ladder to be introduced, while Mr Freeson insisted on getting down first, being heard over the loudspeakers to say that he hadn't realised what it was all in aid of. Then Uncle Fred faced the populace, with De Kuyper beside him, bosom still heaving.

'Comrades and friends,' said Uncle Fred, 'I'm a simple man.' That was true enough, so we all clapped again and shouted 'Hear, Hear!' 'God gave the land to the people!' cried Uncle Fred, and as the cheers rang out, as those who had found them threw their caps again into the air, I felt a hand on my arm and looked into the dark eyes of Louis the XVI's wife.

We sat inside the decorated bus, having moved her 'Let them eat cake' placard from the seat, while Uncle Fred spoke over our heads about free hearing aids and freedom for the Indians. Outside the window was a sea of upturned faces, mouths open, daring to believe it would come to pass.

'How are you, Jeffrey?' asked Rosemary, who had of course heard it all before.

'All right,' I said. 'I didn't know about Uncle Fred.' She looked fondly up at the roof, smiled at me and nodded.

'I'm engaged now,' I said. That wasn't exactly true of course, but on the principle of being cruel to be kind, I thought it the best method of getting the past out of the way, so that we could talk politics. For I had decided to become a Socialist. There had been no sign of him, in his tram conductor's set, but I didn't want the embarrassment of Chester J. Delius blocking my application to join the Labour Party. I thought it best to make it plain that we had moved on, grown up, started fresh lives.

'Was that her in the meat market that night?' she asked.

'Yes,' I said. 'A Miss Garrowby,' hoping that she had not spoken to the Meat Market Police Sergeant.

'She looked nice,' said Rosemary, taking it very well, as I always knew she would. 'What is she?'

'A Nignog,' I said. 'And a stamp collector. Thematic, actually.'

'I mean, is she Labour?'

'I shouldn't think so,' I said. 'Not in Ilkley.' I wondered what Rosemary would say if she knew about the grey flannels.

Outside the bus the crowd had started to sing again, to the tune of 'The Lincolnshire Poacher':

Oh, Hitler's a non smo-o-ker, and Churchill smokes cigars, but they're both as keen as mustard on Imperialistic wars; but your Uncle Joe's a worker boy, and a very decent chap . . .

I joined in heartily with Rosemary on the next line, watching her lips, as I had once done on the tram to Hobbeycock Hall: 'Because he smokes a pipe and wears a taxi driver's cap!'

Grinning at each other we applauded ourselves, as the crowd outside cheered and whistled, and red balloons printed with a profile of Sir Stafford Cripps drifted up out of the town and across the countryside.

'What have you been doing?' I asked, the sing song having helped to clear away any embarrassment.

'I had a baby,' she said.

'Yes, I know,' I said. There was a pause. 'How is it?'

'It's three,' she said, pushing a finger under her curly white wig to scratch her head. 'Do you know what it's called?'

'I saw it in the paper,' I told her. 'Thank you very much.'

'Just think,' she said, staring at me, 'if you hadn't run away.'

'I didn't actually *run*,' I said, reading the by-laws on the ceiling; remembering her that night in the glow from the cellophane window. The promises she had made about the admiration I would get, and the feeding up. There was no going back now of course, but I knew that Aunt Ada would have been more than generous.

'Still in the same house, are you?'

The wig nodded. 'Dad built on a wing.'

That was the kind of thing he would do, I thought. And then he arrived through the emergency door halfway up the stairs. First his boots, then his honest face and bright eyes.

'Jeffrey!'

On the platform, the spit from his speech still on his chin, heedless of the crowd which called his name, he opened his arms and I went into them, very close indeed to tears.

'Now, lad!' he said into my ear, while the Labour agent fretted anxiously in case there were reporters around. But Uncle Fred defied convention, keeping his strong arm around my shoulder until Aunt Ada had been passed over the heads of the crowd, along with the potted meat sandwiches and the flask.

Rosemary put the leather-covered chain across, and we had a very pleasant little tea party. Just me, the candidate and his family, and the Socialist Clergy, who said a few words with his eyes shut.

'My!' said Aunt Ada, looking at me with obvious approval. 'He's grown! Isn't he a big boy, Fred?'

Outside, all around us, the market place was en fête. Some people were looking through the window to watch us eat, but most were strolling about, wide-eyed and excited. There was a long queue at the stall where De Kuyper was selling the day's special offer: one each of a book by John Strachey, Harold Laski, and Michael Foot under a false name; with an unframed photo of Sir Hartley Shawcross, suitable for hanging. They were going like hot cakes.

Later, when the Cavalcade had gone, I walked home with De Kuyper. In my hand I clutched a copy of *Left Wing Communism: An Infantile Disorder*, in the Little Lenin Library, which had been reduced. I didn't know where to begin.

'De Kuyper,' I began, as we walked along the London Road, my brain still fevered by the excitement and colour of the afternoon, the warmth of my reunion with the Delius family. 'Will he get in? Uncle Fred?'

She smiled at the pavement ahead. 'You know my feelings on bourgeois democracy,' she said. And of course I did.

Arriving home I went straight into action. As I said to Bernard over the hedge, until now the philosophers had been concerned with understanding the world. The point however was to change it! De Kuyper had said that if I could convert my father, we were probably home and dry. So, pinning on my new yellow badge depicting a shovel, next to the blue and gold Nignog on my lapel, I made straight for the study.

'Come in,' my father called when I tapped on the door, but looked surprised to see me. I sat down facing him, having said, 'Good afternoon.'

'What do you want?' he asked, after a silence in which I marshalled my facts, deciding on which front to attack. He picked his nose and his eyes were wary. I came straight to the point.

'Do you think it's fair?' I challenged him. 'The factory?'

My father quickly buttoned up his waistcoat and tightened his tie. 'What do you mean?' he parried. 'The factory.' Then, while I was trying to recall a quote from *The Theory of Surplus Value*, 'Are you worried about your inheritance?'

Shaking my head slowly, with a sad smile, I said, 'No, it wasn't that.' I broadened the smile, for rather than simply winning a debate I wanted him to vote Labour. 'I wanted to talk to you about the ethics of owning the means of production.'

He slipped a mint into his mouth and looked around the room, doing the Lone Ranger's tune with his fingers on the arm of his chair. 'Now?' he asked, but I had my fingers spread, ready to tick off the facts.

'Take your raw materials,' I began, 'your cotton and your rubber buttons, and your broderie anglaise.'

'*If* you can get it!' he put in.

'Indeed!' I was warming up. 'Now let us say that each item costs sixpence. All right?'

He had either narrowed his eyes still further, or closed them altogether. I waited, and at last he gave the slightest of nods.

'That's one and six,' I told him. 'For the cost of a liberty bodice.' I raised my hand to let him know there was more to come. 'Plus,' I went on, 'the cost of labour. Shall we say a shilling?' I waited until he nodded. 'That's for sewing up a liberty bodice, and packing it in tissue paper.'

'If you say so,' he said, starting to pick his nose again.

'So that's one and six for materials; a shilling for labour. That's half a crown for a liberty bodice,' I summed up.

I waited for his comments, and when he said, after a while, 'Well?' I was ready for him.

'I know you have overheads; like rent and rates, and string, and depreciation on the sewing machines. Shall we say another penny? Or tuppence?' I tried again. 'Threepence?'

'What are you driving at?' he asked, his eyes open. 'What are you trying to say?'

I raised my hand again, meaning that all would become clear in a moment. 'That's two and nine,' I said, 'or two and ten.' I was determined to be generous, to leave no loophole for him. 'Now; how much would I have to pay?'

'What for?' he asked, opening his mouth no more than was necessary.

'For a liberty bodice. If I wanted to buy one.'

He moved about in his chair, then suddenly bent forward to unlace his shoes. 'From me?' he asked, from down there.

'No, from a shop,' I said, though I wondered what discount he would have given me.

Having retied his laces he sat up. 'Which shop?'

'It doesn't matter which shop!' I said, I hope not testily. 'How much would I have to pay?'

'What size?' he asked, starting to crack his knuckles, his head bowed in thought.

'It's not *for* me!' I said. 'I just want to know how much they sell for. Retail.'

There was a long silence, which surprised me. I thought he would have had these statistics at his fingertips. Finally he said: 'If you were to shop around, you might get a medium, middle quality, for somewhere between eighteen and six and a pound.'

'Thank you,' I said, with a sigh. I had him. After a pause of just the right length, during which I took a deep breath and licked my lips, I said: 'A long way from two and tenpence, isn't it?' Sucking in my cheeks I pretended to study my fingernails.

'You mean we ought to put our prices up?' he said, almost at once, hesitating then pushing the packet of mints towards me. He was clearly interested.

'No,' I said. 'What I mean is, how much profit do we – do you – make? On each one.'

Glancing from door to window he lowered his voice. 'Elevenpence,' he muttered.

'*Elevenpence!*' I couldn't help it. I almost spat the figure back into his face. He half rose in the chair, then sat down again, crossing his legs and poking a finger into his right ear.

'Elevenpence,' he said again, now clearly distressed; so

much so that he was actually looking at me. 'It's not enough, is it?'

'Not *enough*?' I cried, outraged of course, but he had turned away, to take out a Board of Trade pamphlet from the drawer of his desk. Holding it before me, moving his finger below the heavy black print, he recited: 'New Trends in Undies'; and then the sub-title: 'The End of the Liberty Bodice; A Study Document.' There was a silence.

'What are we going to do, Jeffrey?' he said, putting the pamphlet face up on the blotter. I laid my Little Lenin on top of it, like Master Bun the Baker's Son.

'A spectre is haunting Europe,' I told him, and he nodded in agreement. His eyes were still on me, his eldest son; hoping no doubt for me to outline plans to renew and revamp the firm, to enable it to face the post-war world; like the Pomfrets had done with the dairy. I took another mint.

As you will have guessed, I was about to tell him that he should refund the elevenpence per liberty bodice extorted from his employees. Backdated the seventeen years since the firm was founded, with interest. Then to ask him for a contribution to Uncle Fred's Fighting Fund, and his assurance that we could rely on his vote. I didn't think he would actually put a red and yellow 'VOTE FOR FRED' poster in the window of Jasmine Villa, but I thought he might lend us his car on polling day.

'What about a co-op?' I said, sitting back to let him think about this; but he seemed puzzled.

'A co-op what?' he asked.

I realised what had come into his mind: the South Lincolnshire Co-operative Society that did all the milk and most of the funerals in our area. 'No, not *the* Co-op,' I said. 'A co-operative. With the workers owning equal shares; all meeting every Monday morning in the board room, deciding what to do.'

'What board room?'

In his office then, I told him. Yes, of course he could sit

at his desk. It didn't matter that there weren't enough chairs; they wouldn't be in there all that long.

'They wouldn't do it,' he said, shaking his head. 'Not without wages.'

I told him no, he'd got it wrong. They would get wages as well.

A stranger might have thought that he'd died with his eyes open. I heard Rupert run down the hall, shouting that he was 'Going wee wees', and the Andrews Sisters singing in the kitchen. Finally he spoke.

'I don't get it,' he said, (the first time I remember him using American slang). 'What's the catch?'

There was no catch, I explained; they would all have shares. Like a cake, I said, drawing one on his blotter.

'*Shares?*' he said, quite loudly for him, not even looking at my drawing. 'There aren't any *shares*! It's all mine!'

Yes, I pointed out; it was *now*, but the idea was to give them all equal shares, so that between them they would own it.

'And they get wages as well?' he repeated, in a funny voice. He seemed to have difficulty with that point.

'Yes,' I said. 'And an equal share of the profits.'

I heard him muttering the word, as he went off to the lavatory, passing my half brother who was shouting that he'd done his wee wees. When he returned he stopped in the doorway, as if it were my room. '*Why* do I give them equal shares?' he asked. He was not angry; distraught is probably the word. He kept his hand on the brass door-knob, his feet on the coconut matting, as if about to lock me in and phone for the people with the wet sheets. I decided I should broaden the picture; get away from the particular.

'The whole country will be run like that soon,' I said. 'When Uncle Fred's in.'

My father looked up and down the corridor, to make sure we were not overheard. 'Run like what?' he asked.

'When Uncle Fred's in where?' Then, as if dreading the answer: 'Who's Uncle Fred?'

'Run like our factory,' I said, feeling I was getting some-where now. 'When Uncle Fred's in Parliament. Uncle Fred Delius. Swinehurst.'

He nodded, to say that he remembered. 'Him with the cucumbers,' he said, staring down at his shoes. Then: 'Where did you hear all this, Jeffrey?' he asked quietly.

I had the sense to leave De Kuyper out of it. 'Mainly from books,' I told him. 'Karl Marx, and Lenin; Little Lenin as they called him; and Sir Hartley Shawcross.'

'And the man who cleans out Pomfrets' churns?' With-out waiting for an answer, shaking his head in despair, my father walked down the hall to put on his overcoat. Coming back to the doorway he pointed his stick at me. 'Are you smoking opium?'

'No,' I said, 'Player's Weights.'

'Drinking?' He knew that I had left the Rechabites.

'Not yet,' I said.

He looked again up and down the corridor, came into the study and closed the door, standing with his back to it. I thought for a moment that he was about to pour me a large sherry from the bottle in the bookcase, followed by a large cigar, to make me sick. But he didn't. 'What about women?' he asked, his chin on his chest, his hands on the hook of his cane; like a Swiss Guard at a lying-in-state.

'What about them?' I said, cautiously. Perhaps he knew of a local equivalent to the establishment in the Rue Mazarin, and had put on his coat to take me along there.

'I've been meaning to speak to you,' he muttered.

'That's all right,' I assured him. 'I've had a pamphlet.' Adding: 'From the Reverend Eli Wannamaker,' in case he thought it was another from the Board of Trade.

'Are you – have you – you know. Are you sleeping with them? Women?' His head still bowed, he muttered this down the front of his waistcoat, but I heard him.

'Not *sleeping* with them, no,' I said carefully, allowing a smile to play around my lips.

Suddenly he looked up, his eyes full on me. 'Do you believe in God, Jeffrey?'

It was a question that deserved a moment's thought. 'No,' I replied, after a moment, then quoting my grandmother, despite the business about the blueish hills, 'but I believe in keeping clean.'

He stretched forward past me to the desk, and for a moment we were almost close enough to touch. Then his hand closed over the mints and he left the room, hesitating, his back to me, in the doorway. 'What about the Church of England?' he asked.

'I'm not sure,' I said. One could only go so far, and I was never an extremist.

Chapter Four

Uncle Fred did not get in. Some people put this down to his election address – 'God Made The Land For The People', in red on shiny paper – rather than my father's refusal to lend us his car. But we, the Labour Party that is, won the election nationally; though Elspeth wrote that we had failed (as I think I predicted) to take Ilkley. I had a new *Daily Telegraph* map on my bedroom wall and worked hard, putting in the coloured pins as the results came through, having a lot of yellow ones left over. When Sir Hartley Shawcross stormed to victory in Lancashire my cheers rang through the house and, leaving my post, I raced for the stairs. Hammering on De Kuyper's door, shouting that the long long night was almost o'er, I got no response; heard only The Laughing Policeman, and what sounded like someone crying.

The Victory Meeting was held in the Tabernacle at Swinehurst, chaired by The Socialist Clergy. I sat in the front row as Uncle Fred rose to speak, beside Aunt Ada, who held his scarf between her legs to keep it warm.

'Brothers and sisters,' he began, 'comrades and friends.' I shifted uncomfortably, thinking of the plaster of Paris brooches which were selling well. Only that morning a cardful had gone off to Ilkley, with threepence commission for Elspeth, which she planned to put towards her bottom drawer. It was difficult to reconcile being a successful entrepreneur with the wearing of a badge that depicted a shovel; let alone the pithier bits of Little Lenin.

'We didn't win this time,' said Uncle Fred, and there

230

was a murmur around me of 'No, we didn't,' and 'We didn't win last time, either!'

'But we will!' he said, simply, with belief. Everyone there believed with him, and clapped and whistled and stamped their feet on the wooden floor.

'Have faith,' said Fred Delius, who hadn't finished, 'in people like Sir Hartley Shawcross, and Harold Wilson.'

'We have, we have!' called out several people, and then the chairs were moved back for dancing, to Joe Loss, and the Red Army Choir, conducted by A. Alexandrov.

'We're not downhearted, you know,' said Rosemary as we took to the floor. A scatter of applause came from those who remembered me as a prep-school boy and leading Rechabite, a little colour I suppose in their lives in the dark days of the war. We were doing a foxtrot, to Glenn Miller's 'Take The A Train', preparing to fishtail down the long side of the room.

'I heard about Ilkley,' she said into my ear, as we hovered on a patch of french chalk, our pointed toes darting in the intricate pattern before gliding forward. 'It was a shame.'

I knew what she meant. Ilkley had been a disappoint-ment, and by implication Elspeth was at least partly to blame. Or had Rosemary heard about the plaster of paris brooches? Feeling her bosom against me, (a great improve-ment on Elspeth), I thought a lime-green brooch would look rather well there. 'Fabergé,' I breathed into her ear.

'Pardon?' said Rosemary.

But I spun her into a turn outside the toilet door, thinking Fabergé, the Master Jeweller, with his own shop in Swine-hurst; the smartest women in the Western World beating a path to my door. We danced on, under portraits of Uncle Joe and Uncle Fred, while I resolved to find more Germolene tins and to double my production.

During a break in the music, while the needle was changed and the buns brought in, Rosemary suggested that we got some fresh air. As we made our way to the back door, I noticed one or two nudge each other and nod towards us.

Behind the Tabernacle it was dark and quiet. We strolled along a cinder path, bringing back memories of Victory Cottage, with chicken runs to either side. It was a beautiful evening, the moon as full and as silver as on that night I headed south, running away from Swinehurst. The wheel had turned full circle and we were together again.

'What are you going to do, Jeffrey?' Rosemary asked.

'I don't know,' I said. 'You mean now?' I was cautious, as you will understand. Though now mature and well able to handle the situation, I did not know – literally – where the path led; what Rosemary had in mind. She was an attractive woman, and it was true that we had unfinished business together, but I was not sure that I wanted to get involved again. After all, I had come to Swinehurst that day to celebrate the overthrow of capitalism, and I had all the way to cycle home.

'I mean life,' she said, 'in a Socialist Britain. The world's open for you, like an oyster.' And she mimed the opening of a large shell with her hands. 'You can do anything you like.' She looked at me in the moonlight, the shadows of the chicken wire like a veil across her face, like Margaret Lockwood, and I realised I had just received a double entendre.

'Not *anything*,' I said, realistically; meaning I suppose that we had our duties and responsibilities. 'I've got my National Service to do, and,' I cleared my throat, 'I'm going into the firm. Starting at the bottom, of course.'

I had to break off then to step over a couple doing the rumba, right across the path. 'You were talking about starting at the bottom,' said Rosemary, rather loudly. She had walked round them, looking up at the moon.

'Excuse me,' I said, and went back to have a look. I was right; they could be doing nothing else. It was shadowy, but I could see well enough. He was on top, and appeared from his back and his boots, which quivered between a pair of mauve court shoes, to be of a similar type to Pickersgill. I could see no more of the lady, except for one white hand clutching the khaki wool of his pullover. Quite frankly I was amazed, and of course extremely interested. 'Rosemary!' I called, but she had walked on.

I caught up with her at a bend in the path, and she was still looking up at the moon, stepping carefully in case there was anyone else lying down. 'Rosemary,' I said, a little excited of course. 'Did you see . . . ?' But she cut me off, rather rudely.

'Let's go for a drink,' she said, and led the way through an allotment. Following her, retaining all the detail I could in my mind, I realised that she had been this way before.

My second rumba! First on a billiard table; now under the stars. People were doing it everywhere, all over the world. And now my first pub!

For I had assumed of course that we were making for the High Street, for Farmer Giles's Milk Bar. But no! Before I had time to consider my position we were entering the back door of The Boy on the Barrel, a public house I had once seen Bernard's mother come out of. Rosemary – as if she had been there before – led me down a wet passage and into the Snug. We sat on a bench, under a big mirror, and I breathed in the smell of beer.

'Go and get them,' she said. 'I'll have a gin and orange.'

The hatch opened at my polite knock and a moustached man, informally dressed like the one in between the mauve court shoes, asked me if I was eighteen. Not wishing to tell a blatant untruth I turned to Rosemary, who was lighting a Turkish cigarette.

'Yes,' she said, blowing out smoke, the blueish cloud rising in the mirror, 'he's old enough.'

There was no mistake this time. That was surely the second double entendre of the evening.

'Only asking,' said the man. As he went to get the gin and orange, I took the opportunity of looking through into the public bar (where I was to find later it was a penny cheaper). Men and women were playing shove ha'penny, sipping beer, feeling for the salt in their crisps. 'A vision of hell, should you ever be damned and degraded enough to see it!' The words of the Reverend Eli Wannamaker rang faintly in my ears.

'What about you?' said the man, who I presumed was the landlord, putting the gin in front of me. I had of course been thinking about that, breathing through my nose. It was a momentous occasion. To resign from the Rechabites – mainly to be allowed to smoke Player's Weights in peace – was one thing; it was a far bigger step to actually take to strong drink. Assuming an eighteen-year-old voice, I spoke: 'A Guinness, I think,' I said. But as mine host turned to the shelf behind him to pick up the familiar bottle, preparing to open it, I stayed his action with a raised hand. 'Can I see the bottom?' I asked, smiling so as not to give offence.

'Bottom?' said the landlord. 'Bottom of what?'

With a 'Pardon me', I took the bottle from him and held it against the light. It was a dark liquid of course, and there was a coating of dust; but so far as I could tell there seemed to be no sediment, no residue of boiled-down Irish pets. With an approving nod I passed it back to him to pour. Watching, I asked if he knew the old story about the brewers founding their untold millions on the froth in every glass; but he closed the hatch in my face.

'I keep forgetting,' said Rosemary, when we were seated together and I had swallowed my first mouthful, 'that you're only seventeen.'

'I'm a big boy,' I said, going so far as to nudge her, lighting a Weight and lounging back, as well as one could on a bench. Did I have to remind her that I had been thought eligible for husband and father three years before? I sipped the fiery black drink, which I thought not unpleasant, something like syrup of figs in fact.

We were alone in the Snug. People were singing outside

in the wet passage, punctuated by the banging of the lavatory door. I looked around me, at the surroundings in which the Rev Eli Wannamaker maintained some people spent all their time. At the bench which continued round another two sides of the room; at the large mirrors, engraved with the name of the beer. At another beer's name on a rubber mat on the floor, and two more iron tables with tin ashtrays.

'So you're going into the firm?' said Rosemary, who had already finished her drink. 'I thought you were against capitalism?'

I was, I assured her. Absolutely.

'God made the land for the people,' she reminded me, keeping her voice down, as we faced a pokerwork sign saying 'No politics or religion'.

Indeed, I said, but things could not be expected to change overnight. We were taking over the means of production, distribution and exchange; starting with the coal mines, then steel and the railways. The liberty bodice, as I saw it, was a long way down the list. Until then, I thought I could play a part in both ameliorating the conditions of the workers, and helping in a peaceful transition to state ownership. I told her that I had almost won my father round to setting up a co-operative, giving everyone equal shares; but he had not yet agreed to give them wages as well.

'I should think you'll do very well,' said Rosemary, taking half a crown from her bag for another round. 'When are you thinking of getting married?'

'Not for years,' I said. 'I have to go into the army, as you know; and I might be an officer.'

She spun the half crown on the table and we watched it strike the tin ashtray and come down heads.

'Why might you be an officer?'

I explained to her that prep-school boys were automatically selected for Sandhurst. It was simply a matter of leadership. There was no question of my being a militarist, or anything like that. Pushing the coin towards me, Rosemary told me to finish my froth.

The landlord made no comment this time about my age, and I smiled when he asked if I would care to examine the bottle's bottom. 'Now let's talk about you,' I said to Rosemary, as I sat down again beside her. It was a line that Clark Gable had used to effect with Barbara Stanwyck, the one with the funny mouth. On a sudden whim I began to suck my Guinness up the side of the glass, trying to lower the froth, untouched, to the bottom.

'I suppose I'll just go on,' she said, 'bringing up little Chester.'

'Yes,' I said. 'Yes, there's him, isn't there.' I knew that big Chester had long since left town. I had seen the infant on two or three occasions but, except for when he wore his tram conductor's outfit, there was no obvious resemblance. As a matter of fact I quite liked him. Though the same age as Rupert, he wasn't always going on about his 'Wee wees'. 'You could always get married again,' I said.

'What do you mean, again?'

Not knowing what to reply to that I looked around to see if there was a shove ha'penny board handy, but there wasn't. Winding Uncle Frank's watch, I said that I would have to be going soon, and that I was worried about my rear lamp. But she wasn't listening.

'Who would have me?' she asked sadly, pushing her glass and another half crown towards me.

This time I knocked on the hatch like they did in ITMA, saying 'Dis ees Funf speaking!', but the landlord didn't seem that amused. Sitting down again with Rosemary, I put my arm around her shoulders, to cheer her up. 'There's a lot of people will have you,' I said.

'Yes,' she said, and I detected bitterness, 'like Doris Allerdyce!' She nodded to the rear wall of the Snug.

'You mean . . . ?' I said, interested of course. 'Her on the path?' She nodded vigorously down at the table top, and I wondered how she had known who it was. Perhaps she had recognised the shoes. 'I didn't know her name,' I said. 'Where does she live?' But she ignored my question.

'Just because a girl's had a baby,' she said, 'they think she's easy!'

'Yes,' I said, 'I suppose they do.' I had never thought of it like that before. 'A slice off a cut loaf' went through my head. Sucking up the last of the froth, I decided that syrup of figs wasn't quite right; it had a distinctive taste of its own. Then I had an idea.

'Can I take you home?' I said into her ear, taking her hair out of my mouth. I had to speak rather slowly to get the words out. 'Pardon me!' I said, fingers to my lips, annoyed with myself for not examining the second and third bottle. It appeared that I had swallowed a good deal of sediment.

Suddenly Rosemary stood up and went to the door. Hurriedly I grabbed her handbag and gloves which she had left on the bench and stood up to follow her. 'Wait for me!' I called.

'I'm going to the toilet,' she said, and a moment later I heard the door bang in the passage.

'A slice off a cut loaf,' I said to myself, always having had a great respect for proverbs and sayings; then I noticed the landlord looking at me. Framed in the open hatch, he looked like the drawing of 'Teecher' that Lord Snooty did sometimes on the blackboard.

'Time!' he shouted, and slammed shut the hatch. I thought he was right; it certainly was. My elbows on the wet ledge I knocked on the hatch, my feet starting to dance on the lino.

'How old are you?' I asked him when he appeared, tea towel in hand. I won't repeat what he said, it was an establishment that I never set foot in again, but I smiled and said, 'Only asking.' Thinking that was rather good, I twirled away from him, only to fall over a table and hit my head on the bench. The door opened, and I said, 'Baby!'

– playing it like Clark Gable – 'I don't look down on you because you've had a baby!'

'That's very good of you,' said the landlord, who was a lot taller when you could see all of him.

What a scoop, I thought later, if the Rechabite Documentary Film Unit had had a crew outside in the allotment that night. The holder of an inscribed copy of *Coral Island* being run out of the back door of a public house. 'Lackey of the beerage!' I shouted, from behind an empty dog kennel; but he had gone.

'Are you all right?' asked Rosemary, who had followed us out after collecting her accessories, telling mine host in no uncertain manner to put me down. I said that I was, but thought it advisable to lie still for a few moments.

'Good night, Jeffrey,' she said, walking away into the darkness.

Then she came back, to ask if I felt able to ride a bike. Not only could I do that, I told her, but first I would see her safely home. For all she knew, I said, Teecher's loose-bowelled Great Dane could be roaming the cinder paths. We had a short argument over this, and then Rosemary helped me up and we set off; only to find that Miss Allerdyce had finished and gone.

'It was about here, wasn't it?' I said, but Rosemary said, 'Shut up!' and walked on. As she took the torch with her, I was unable to examine the spot.

'You go that way,' she said when I caught up with her at a fork in the path. 'It comes out at the Tabernacle.'

'I insist on taking you home,' I said, quite forcefully. I don't think I had ever taken anyone home before. (Bernard, of course, but that's not quite the same thing.) Agnes Pomfret had been already at home when I got there; and Ilkley was of course much too far away.

'I don't want Dad to see you looking like that,' said Rosemary, whatever that meant. 'Not after losing the election.'

'All right,' I said. 'Give us a kiss then.' Just like that; like an older and much more experienced man, like David Niven might have done.

'You smell of beer!' she said, wrinkling her nose and turning away; which I thought was a little unfair, seeing that she had paid for it all. Then she gave me a quick kiss on the cheek and started away down her fork of the path. But I caught hold of the belt of her camel-hair coat. It came off in my hand, but she stopped; not wanting to go home without it.

'Just a minute!' I said; the dominant male now, my voice making her eyes widen, her mouth open: 'A proper kiss!'

She had never seen me like this. Though, as you know, the mother of a three-year-old child, she was a little over-whelmed. Pushing her up against the wire netting, I took her into my embrace; and felt at once that it was going to be an improvement on the pork butcher's doorway. Instead of Elspeth's teeth, the stretched wrist of a rubber glove, I felt Rosemary's tongue probing right into my mouth; some-thing I didn't know that you did. Made bold and reckless by this, and of course the sediment in the Guinness, I slid a hand inside her coat and began to play with her cardigan buttons.

'I waited for you,' said Rosemary, into my ear. 'Till I fell asleep. You had your chance then.' And then she bit me. That was something else I didn't know you did, and I much preferred the tongue business.

'I had to go somewhere,' I muttered, my nose in her ear. Quite frankly I was now ashamed of that episode, when I had decamped by the light of the moon, with a tea towel on a bannister.

'I know,' she said. 'You had to go see the Shredded Wheat factory!' I think she was about to bite me again, but just then the wire netting gave way and we fell into the chicken run.

'Christ!' said Rosemary. 'The chickens!' She was lying

beneath me in the long grass, in the style of Doris Aller-dyce, and we both closed our eyes, expecting bantams to flap and squawk over us as they made their escape. But all was silence. Except for faint music coming from one of the houses that backed on to the allotments. The jaw bone of an ass, the voice of Edmundo, came to me out of the darkness. Remarkably calm in the circumstances, and breathing through my nose, I moved aside a tin plate that had held a chicken's dinner, in order to give myself enough room.

I think I did rather well. Once I had made sure that there was no question of grey flannel trousers, nothing sewn up with strong thread, there was no stopping me. It is not, of course, something that a gentleman is prepared to go into detail about; but I think I can claim that a good time was had by both.

Because of the alfresco nature of the event, it was not possible to relax afterwards and have a cigarette, and then a bit more. Rosemary had laddered her stockings in the melee, and I had lost my tie pin, the one with the horse shoe, but I thought it a small price to pay.

As there was no point now in my taking her home, Rosemary walked with me to the Tabernacle, where my bicycle waited in a patch of moonlight. 'Thank you, very much,' I said, as I took my clips from the saddlebag: hoping that it did not weaken you, like it did with boxers. I had after all a good distance to go.

'Will you write to me?' she asked, and I noticed her hand caressing my racing saddle.

I suppose she meant some kind of 'Thank you' letter, but I knew instinctively that it was the end of a chapter. It was, I thought, as I checked my rear lamp, the beginning of the rest of my life. Once, under such a moon, I had left Swinehurst as a boy; now I was leaving as a man. Wobbling out of the cobbled yard, ringing the bell, I raised my hand in salute.

It was not until I had turned into the silent High Street,

under the bright lamps, policemen looking at me from Lipton's doorway, that I realised that I still had her change in my pocket from the three half crowns.

Chapter Five

'I never thought I'd see the day,' said De Kuyper; though she didn't really look that surprised. Brushing a thread from my shoulder she stood back to look at me. I was wearing the suit bought for Yasmin's wedding, the one with the stained lapel, with black shoes and a clean hanky. My father was waiting outside in the car, a Vick inhaler up his nose, and Miss Parkinson and Rupert were at the gate to see me off. It was the morning of my first day at work.

The evening before, at dinner, my father had said a few words.

'You're starting right at the bottom, remember,' he had said, from behind the *Lincolnshire Standard*. 'And no talk about giving shares to people!'

I had promised. What with Marshall Aid, and the regeneration of Europe, the bottom had fallen out of the plaster of Paris jewellery market. I was now a member of the Young Conservatives, mainly because of Lillian Braithwaite, whose father had, reputedly, two cars. We – the YCs that is – met in each other's houses, rather more informally than the Tabernacle crowd, and without so much singing or marching about. There was also less emphasis on reading. We played tennis and Canasta, and on St George's Day went in a charabanc to hear John Hanson sing. There had been an attempt to get punting started on The Drain, with hampers and portable gramophones, but it had come to nothing.

I had avoided Swinehurst since the episode in the chicken run. Though I had kept a newspaper cutting of

Uncle Fred and the decorated bus, with Marie Antoinette on the platform. I had had Guinness several times since, but not the other, and had heard via De Kuyper, her back to me at the gas stove, that Rosemary had married a man on the railway. Lillian Braithwaite and I had played 'Murder' in her house, when her parents were out, but I had got no further than her throat. Elspeth, a trainee hairdresser in one of Ilkley's smartest salons, wrote every week.

What did people make of me, I wondered, as I sped that morning towards the city, towards the heart of commerce and industry that was now beginning to beat again. 'Merchant Adventurer'; that is how I had been told to regard myself, by the man who had called round for my subscription to the Junior Chamber of Commerce. De Kuyper had bared her teeth at him when he had tried to sell her a ticket for their dinner and dance.

'Keep yourself to yourself,' muttered my father. 'Remember what you are.' The yellow plastic hand outside his window went stiffly up, brooking no argument, as we turned into the mercantile district, between high Victorian warehouses, to the bombed site where we left the car. People like ourselves, of the business class, were hurrying along the street, and one of them said 'Good morning' to my father.

Our name, 'Cork & Son', encrusted in Brasso on the granite pillars of the entrance, moved me. I had been there before of course, but mainly as a child, being fussed over by the elder ladies, one of whom I recalled had kept a lock of my hair. I thought it might have been the notorious Mrs Skinner, ('Maude' as the girls called her), the shop steward whom my father warned me about while taking the Vick out of his nose, but he doubted that.

We were on the second floor, over a brush maker, who I was told had a Government contract which stipulated square-handled brooms for Holloway Prison. In my father's office, while he took off his scarf and driving gauntlets, I looked through the glass partition into the work room. At the rows of hairdos and bare elbows, hearing 'Music While You Work' – Troise and his Mandoliers – coming from a loudspeaker hung from a beam. Though never able to grasp the theory of equal shares *and* wages, my father was a paternalistic employer.

Noticing me, despite the music, some of the girls looked up from their machines and smiled. Though in doing so one girl stitched a button to her thumb. As her workmates pushed her head down between her knees, one of them said something to her friend, who looked up at me, and then they laughed. I thought I might do very well there. No question of course of 'Droit du Seigneur'; as the man from the Junior Chamber of Commerce had said, to take advantage of my position would be unthinkable. But there was the undoubted cachet of being the son of the house, of being something new and sophisticated, bringing colour and excitement into their lives. The girls modestly lowered their eyes as my father led me through the work room, singing out in unison 'Morning, Mr Cork.' (Though in the argot of the back streets it sounded like 'Mr Cock'.) I said 'Good morning' and 'How are you?' to all the good-looking ones on either side, until my father told me to shut up.

At the rear of the room, under the Health and Safety Regulations, was the bench cum office and revolutionary cell of Maude Skinner, head cutter and close associate of the man who washed out Pomfrets' churns. She was slicing through mounds of soft white material and made a point of not saying 'Good morning.' My father, who had changed into a khaki overall, touched the brim of his homburg to her.

Down a passage, past the cloakrooms and the string room, was as far as I remembered going before. I was enjoying the tour, ('That's yours,' my father said, nodding at the door marked 'Men'), and looked around in the dispatch department with interest. It was all unpainted wooden racking, around a large bare table, with rolls of brown paper and big balls of string. Mr Grandidge, the packer, a faithful employee of many years, in a cap and a khaki overall, was unpicking knots in a length of string. He went so far as to say, 'Good morning,' and bore an uncanny resemblance to the grandfather of 'Oor Wullie', Scotland's version of Lord Snooty. The stubbly white whiskers, not a lot of teeth, the stained waistcoat and heavy watch chain; but he was not, as far as I know, given to joining in games of 'fitba' with the bairns.

'This is him,' said my father, a different man on his own ground. 'Don't stand any nonsense.'

'I won't,' I said. 'You can be assured of that.' Then realised that he had been talking to Mr Grandidge. Shaking his head, my father left us alone.

To be quite honest, I was somewhat disappointed in the khaki overall I was silently handed. I had expected, like Traggets's round table, some kind of embroidered badge of rank on the breast pocket. Then I smiled at my foolishness. What need, when everyone knew what I was? Mr Grandidge, being too shy to address me, handed me two white mugs and pointed the way; out of the back door, down the fire escape, and across the street to the Empire Cafe.

'You're new, aren't you?' said the woman in a white coat, filling the mugs with orange tea. I told her that I was the owner's son, come to learn the business from the bottom up. 'From the bottom up, eh?' she said, while I stirred my tea with a spoon on a string, going on to inform me that they did dinners. We, that is my father and I, never got round to providing a works canteen. We should be 'With them, but not of them' was one of my father's sayings, and until we could run to a directors' dining room, with waitress service for middle management and Maude Skinner, he took his lunch in the Queen's Head, where he used to take Miss Parkinson before they were married. Everyone else brought sandwiches.

Mr Grandidge had his elevenses (it was actually ten past nine) out of a white cloth. He ate them with his back to me, sitting on a large soft parcel addressed to Messrs Marshall and Snelgrove. I drank my tea and then, quite naturally, was keen to get started. In fact I said as much: 'I'll start, shall I?' I said, and began to stack the flat grey cardboard boxes, wisps of tissue paper showing around their lids, onto the table. I was strong for my age, despite being a Guinness drinker and no longer a virgin; but to be honest, liberty bodices are not very heavy. They were packed a dozen to a box, and working with a will I began to count to myself. Twelve elevenpences were a hundred and thirty-two; eleven shillings profit per box. Having emptied a tall basket on wheels, I pulled in another waiting in the passage. There were at least fifty boxes in it. Fifty times eleven shillings = twenty-seven pounds ten. Clipping my new fountain pen into my breast pocket, I carried the boxes to the table and pushed them along towards Mr Grandidge's back. I didn't really wish to be rude, but it had been five minutes at least; and time was money. (That was framed in the Braithwaite's bathroom.) I coughed into my hand, and then again, but Mr Grandidge was dunking his crusts into his tea.

'Mr Grandidge,' I said, 'when you're ready.' I hadn't realised that he was deaf, and I gave him a bit of vigorous mime, until he shook his white cloth out over the fire escape and folded it away.

'What's yer name?' he said, lighting a cigarette that he took from an embossed brass box that Queen Mary had sent, filled with chocolate, to all the troops in the trenches in the First World War. It was too big really for a cigarette case, without an elastic strap inside to hold his Woodbines, but he liked it when people noticed it, and he could say that Queen Mary had sent it to him, full of chocolate, when he was in the trenches in the First World War. Pathetic really.

But what was my name? The reader will understand the quandary I was in. It was in effect the first test of my ability to manage men. I almost blurted out 'Jeffrey Cork', but

246

then recalled my father's words about being *with* them rather than *of* them. I was hesitating between Master Cork and Master Jeffrey, (the young scion of the house, a good part for David Niven) when Mr Grandidge put a round-handled broom into my hand.

Thinking that because of his war wounds, and his deafness – inflicted while he sat with his brass tin of chocolate in the trenches of the Somme – he was now unable to use a broom, I made no fuss. Our generation did indeed owe his a debt. While I swept the floor, brushing the dust out of the back door, where Mr Grandidge had shaken his crumbs, he put all the cardboard boxes back to where I had taken them from. It was only later, after a gentleman from the brush factory had called in to see what Mr Grandidge was doing at Kempton Park, that we got down to work.

'This is the life, eh, Mr Grandidge?' I said, as I stood by the table and watched him wrap up liberty bodices. I proved to be what he called 'a natural' and, after I had been across to the Empire Cafe for some more tea, I was allowed to put my finger on the string while he tied the knot. Then the railway came to collect the parcel for Marshall and Snelgrove, and I went down the fire escape and swept up after the horse. Then it was dinner time, as they called it. I thought the time had passed quickly, and that my first morning at work had gone rather well.

Mr Grandidge, still in his overall and without washing his hands, went across to the Empire Cafe. Had he asked me, I would have joined him, but of course I could understand his shyness. There was a huge gulf between us. I wondered if my father would come for me, to take me to the Queen's Head, but then realised that it would have been damaging for him to show undue favouritism. I should have thanked him for bringing me in the car that morning. Opening my sandwich tin, I made a seat from the parcels we had packed and unscrewed my flask of tea.

Against it I propped my *Sexton Blake's Weekly*, which I found much easier going than Little Lenin.

I had just finished a story where Tinker, disguised as a butcher's boy, had foiled a plan to steal our latest torpedo, when I felt that I was being watched. Looking up, I found that several girls had come in from the workroom, and stood now by the baskets looking at me. More girls joined them as I swallowed the last of my Hovis, jostling and giggling in a group, all of them looking at me.

I should of course have known that they had spent the morning thinking of me, humming along with The Big Ben Banjo Band, imagining how I looked in my khaki overall. All with a single mind, they had watched the clock crawl towards noon, to when they could make my acquaintance.

'Hello,' I said, smiling to put them at their ease. I was of course no longer the gauche youth of yesteryear.

The girls all wore pinnies, and two of them were knitting. I was glad to see that Maude Skinner was not amongst them. A dark-haired girl in fur-trimmed slippers, who seemed to be the spokeswoman, smiled at me. 'How are you getting on?' she asked.

'Very well,' I answered. 'I'm starting at the bottom, you know,' and they broke out in a fit of nervous laughter. There was great strain, because of the enormous gap between us.

'We've got something to show you,' said the spokeswoman, stepping aside and pushing the other girls so that they formed a passage to the door.

I was embarrassed. It was obviously going to be a presentation of some kind, something they had had a whip round for. As I had done no more as yet than sweep up, bring the tea and hold my finger on the string, I thought they had gone a little too far. But of course they were looking forward to the day when I would be installed in the front office, eating at the Queen's Head. They also wished to make me welcome; to show that they appreciated my being with them, if not of them. In short, it would have been churlish to refuse.

'Thank you very much,' I said, combing my hair, then walked forward nodding and smiling, hands behind my back; very much like the Duke of Edinburgh.

'Jeffrey's your name, isn't it?' asked the spokeswoman, as I moved amongst them, breathing in their Phul Nana.

'Yes,' I said. After all, one can surely be informal during the lunch hour, especially when one is about to receive an award.

'I'm Janet,' she said, and pushed me in the chest with the flat of both hands.

I was of course totally unprepared, and taken off balance I fell over backwards. Fortunately there was an empty basket behind me, and I fell into this. The girls all gave a cheer, pleased of course that I had not hurt myself, and then I felt the basket begin to move.

'It's all right,' I called. 'Let me get out now.' But I was pushed through the swing doors and down the corridor, my feet in the air, trying to stop my trousers falling back and exposing my leg. Then we bumped through another door, and Janet was smiling down at me.

'Out you get, Jeffrey,' she said, and then someone, trying to be helpful no doubt, tipped the basket up at one end and I fell out onto the floor.

I was in the ladies' toilet!

Scrambling to my feet I straightened my tie, averting my eyes from the drawings on the wall. It seemed an odd place in which to make a presentation. The girls were standing in front of the door, arms folded, though several had their hands on their hips; akimbo I think it's called. I cleared my throat.

'You said you were going to show me something,' I said.

They laughed; all of them. It sounded very loud in there, almost menacing. I noticed a poem, dedicated to my father and blatantly signed 'M. Skinner'.

'You got it wrong,' said Janet. 'It's more like you showing

us something.' And they all laughed again. You will understand what I mean, when I say that I began to hope for Mr Grandidge, or my father, to come through the door; though seeing where we were it did not seem likely.

They laid me down on the floor, on my back; two of the girls holding my arms and another, a fat one, sitting on my ankles. I had my eyes closed, because I found that when I looked I could see up Janet's pinny.

'Get it out!' I heard her say, and for a fleeting second I hoped they were unwrapping some piece of electro-plated tableware, suitably inscribed. But no. As at the Real's dinner table, but this time with all caution thrown to the wind, I felt fingers tearing at the buttons of my flies.

It felt cool in the air of the ladies, and was mercifully small. (Detumescent, I think, is the word.) Once again I gave thanks to De Kuyper, for having laid out clean pants for me that morning, though she could never have imagined anything like this.

'Touch it, Doreen,' I heard Janet say. 'It won't hurt you.'

'You leave it alone, Doreen!' I said, loudly. 'Or I'll tell my dad!' I risked a quick peep to identify Doreen.

Someone breathed on it, possibly noticing how chilly it was in there, and someone touched it tentatively with a knitting needle. Then Janet said, 'Give me the brush.'

I opened both eyes. *They were going to paint it!*

She was kneeling beside me, holding a scrubbing brush, and the fat girl was opening a tin of Cherry Blossom boot polish.

'Don't forget his balls,' said someone, but that was the only really vulgar note in what Janet explained was an initiation ceremony, like they did at the Masonic Hall, as she opened my trousers wide and lifted my shirt and vest. She blacked it, thick and all around it; a serious look on her not unattractive face. I took it like a man; though I swore to myself that if they followed the directions on the tin and started to polish with a soft cloth, I would scream.

But they didn't. They took me into a cubicle and held my head down the bowl, possibly thinking that I felt faint. When I came out, they had all gone, except for Janet. She handed me a towel, then lit a Woodbine for me.

'You all right?' she enquired.

I told her that I was. I also said that though I was all for tradition, for keeping the ancient customs alive, they should not have pulled the chain. Turning away to re-arrange my clothing, I wondered what De Kuyper would say about the state of my vest.

'You got a girlfriend?' asked Janet, moving her head like a Balinese dancer for a last look as I buttoned up.

'Of course,' I said, combing my hair. She was undeniably handsome, and without her pinny and fur slippers, and but for the warning from the Junior Chamber of Commerce, I might have been interested. But I had also heard a J. B. Priestley play on the wireless, about the consequences when a son of the property-owning class has a rumba with one of his father's employees. They end up drinking Jeyes Fluid, and no good can come of it.

'She's in Ilkley,' I said. And then to elaborate, to let her know that we were rather more than pen-pals: 'She came to my sister's wedding, at the Co-op Café in Swinehurst.'

'Did she,' she said, not over-impressed, though I doubted that she'd ever been to the Co-op Café. Certainly no further than the bread counter. 'When's she coming again?'

'I don't know,' I told her. 'She might be joining us for a weekend house party soon.' I lied only to emphasise that I was well and truly spoken for.

'You'd better start washing it then, hadn't you!' she said; and she was gone, the door swinging.

A moment later I emerged from the ladies, to find my father waiting. He held his watch cupped in his left hand, as if timing a racehorse that had just galloped down the corridor.

'It's two minutes past,' he said.

'Is it?' I replied, hurrying past him with my legs apart.

'Jeffrey!' he called after me, rather sharply I thought: 'Come to my office.' I stared after him as he walked away.

Sacked? On my first day? By my own father? Surely not! Was there no justice I wondered, as I hurried through the packing department, ignoring Mr Grandidge's call for my finger. Out of the back door and down the fire escape, waving a negative to the woman in the Empire Cafe. At the end of the block I met the racing correspondent from the brush factory, who asked if I was all right. Coming out into the High Street, opposite Woolworth's, and feeling conspicuous in my khaki overall – not to mention the way I was walking – I turned left, past Macfisheries and Halfords, then left again, and ran as if in a three-legged race to our front door. Dashing up the stairs, past the one hundred thousandth liberty bodice in a glass case, I entered my father's office looking both contrite and flushed.

But he wasn't there. He had gone with Mrs Farrer (the one with a lock of my hair) to see what had happened to me.

'Which way did you come, Jeffrey?' she asked, when they appeared in the doorway, staring at me. I had sat down to regain my breath, and waved a khaki arm.

'Round by Woolworth's and Macfisheries,' I said, and my father and Mrs Farrer exchanged glances. (Rumour was that she had dined at the Queen's Head prior to Miss Parkinson.) With a nod and a jerk of his head, which she understood as an order to go to the string room, my father closed the door. Asking me to get up, he sat down at his desk, looking into his handkerchief. Then he spoke: 'How did your first morning go?'

'Very well,' I said, telling him how I had brought the tea from the Empire Cafe, about the spoon on a string, and how I had held my finger for Mr Grandidge. 'We sent a parcel to Marshall and Snelgrove,' I told him, wanting him to realise that I was taking the job seriously, that there was nothing dilettante in my approach.

'What did you think of Bert?' he asked, opening a drawer in his desk, looking inside and closing it again. Bert was Mr Grandidge; I had seen it painted on his coat peg. Despite my concern about the boot polish setting hard, I felt responsibility settle on my shoulders. Quite obviously my father was asking for an assessment of the man, so that he could be promoted, possibly given a clock.

'He's very nice,' I said. 'He's got a brass box that he got from Queen Mary, when he was in the trenches. It had chocolate in it.'

'I know,' said my father.

There was silence. 'Worker's Playtime' was just coming to an end. My father stood up and put on his homburg hat, which he wore to distinguish him from others in khaki overalls. 'I'm going to the bank,' he said.

We went down the stairs together, but he did not speak until we had reached the pavement. Then he asked: 'Where are you going?'

'Back to work,' I said, noting the concern in his voice, realising of course that, in a sense, I was in charge while he was away. We began to walk towards the High Street, and when we got to Macfisheries he spoke again: 'Are you all right, Jeffrey?' he asked.

'Yes,' I said, 'I know the way.' I was thinking that I would hurry back and have a good wash. Perhaps the Empire Cafe would oblige by drying my vest and pants in the oven, now they had finished dinners. I watched my father cross the road to the Lincolnshire Penny Bank, then hurried along past Halfords, round the corner and up the back street to the fire escape. The railway horse was there, his head in a bag, but had not yet done anything.

The carter, in his silver-buttoned waistcoat, was sitting on the table, talking to Mr Grandidge and drinking out of my mug. 'I'll be with you in a moment,' I called; thinking: 'While the cat's away . . . !' as I went into the gents' toilet.

Taking off my trousers, I tried to roll up my shirt and vest; but they kept coming down, so I took them off.

Someone had wedged a piece of mirror behind a pipe, like in the kitchen of Victory Cottage, and in this I could see myself, and by jumping up and down what they had done to me. Then I put on my overall, though it was cold and rough to my skin. I thought there was a possibility of someone from the brush factory, if they climbed on top of a wall, being able to look in on me through the window. By standing on an upturned bucket I was able to get the affected part into the sink. There was no soap, only a scrubbing brush. I was looking at that, wondering what the procedure was when a new girl joined the work force, when the door opened and Mr Grandidge came in.

On tiptoe on the bucket, the part that Bernard had impaled on the cold edge of the sink, I watched him, via the mirror, enter a cubicle, leaving the door open and standing for a long time in silence with his back to me.

'I am not doing it in the sink!' I felt compelled to say. Not that it was any of his business. He came out, adjusting his clothing, then lit a cigarette, tapping it first several times on Queen Mary's embossed toque.

'You've got black stuff on your vest,' he said.

'I know,' I said. 'Can you get me some soap?' Adding, 'Please.'

'There's some in the ladies',' he said, making no move to get it, and not explaining how he knew. Perhaps he had been wheeled in there as a young man, just back from the Somme, the chocolate still fresh in his brass box.

'I can't go in there like this, can I?' I said, stepping off the bucket. I watched him think about it, or at least I thought he was thinking about it.

'You're ballock naked,' he said at length; having looked from my crumpled clothes to my bare legs several times and put two and two together.

I admitted that I was, under my overall. I did not wish to pull rank on him, as they say, to order him next door into the ladies' toilet to get the soap; but I was fast losing patience.

'Ballock naked,' he said again, shaking his grizzled head in wonder; then he looked at his watch, saw that it was almost tea time, and left me.

I couldn't believe it. Opening the door I shouted after him: 'Mr Grandidge!' Then 'Bert!' Then ran in my bare feet to the packing department. The back door was wide open, and through it I could see the old bastard going into the Empire Cafe, one white mug in his hand.

In the workroom, Geraldo (Gerald Bright, remember?) was going strong, as I crept up to the door of the ladies' toilet. My heart beat fast as I listened carefully (at the door, not to Geraldo), feeling the draught as you can well imagine. The sink, I remembered, was on the left, next to the drawing of Miss Parkinson (faint but still actionable). One quick foray, eyes closed; grab the soap and out again. Breathing through my nose, mouth and eyes tight shut, I pushed open the door – and heard the loud voice of the vulgar Doreen!

'Eh! Look who's here again!'

Safe in the gents', a mop handle against the door, I considered my position. There was no question of my putting on again my vest and pants, thick as they were with Cherry Blossom, and wet now from the lavatory floor. I did what I could inside the crutch of my trousers, with the scrubbing brush and a little Vim I found, and hung them from a pipe. I could hear De Kuyper asking how and why I had returned home in lederhosen.

Woolworth's, I knew, sold vest and pants. There was also, supervised by a girl with a stiff white face, a counter full of soap. I put on my shoes, pulling the socks as high as they would go. They met, just, the hem of my overall. Turning up the collar, hands in the pockets to keep it together, I stepped out into the packing department. Grandidge had drunk his tea, and for want of anything better to do was tying up a parcel. Taking my real leather wallet from my jacket, which hung next to his herringbone over-coat, I went out of the back door.

'Going for your tea?' he enquired, ingratiatingly I thought. He was trying to make amends for not getting me the soap, and I ignored him.

Halfway up the back street I met my father returning from the bank. Seeing me approach he stopped, looking at the high walls to left and right.

'Where are you going, Jeffrey?' he asked, when I was within earshot. 'To my office?'

'No,' I said, 'to Woolworth's, actually.' We stood for a moment, two lone figures in an empty back street. There was not much to say, and after all we would be travelling home together by car, when we could discuss how the day's business had gone. 'I'll see you later,' I said, moving away with a wave, then pausing to pull up a sock; though in raising a leg in order to do so I revealed more than I intended.

'You've got no trousers on!' my father said.

'I know,' I said.

'You're not going to Woolworth's to buy trousers?' The shock in his voice was unmistakable.

'No, of course not,' I said, smiling at the idea. No one we knew would be seen dead in clothes from Woolies. Giving him another wave I walked away. As I crossed the High Street a policeman swivelled to follow me with his eyes.

I bought vest, pants and sandalwood soap, and also a face flannel, which I enjoyed tremendously, rubbing away and working up a good lather. I was doing that, mounted again on the old grey bucket, when Mrs Farrer knocked on the door and asked if I was there.

'Yes,' I said loudly. 'And you can't come in!' Holding each end of the soapy flannel, I was drawing it backwards and forwards between my legs. I was completely en-grossed.

'Your father wants to see you,' she called out.

Telling her to wait, I set to work with the roller towel. A few minutes later, wearing my new undies, my shirt with the black tail and my damp trousers, I emerged from the toilet to find Mrs Farrer smiling anxiously at me. She had obviously been briefed.

'This way, Jeffrey,' she said, nodding and gesturing down the corridor towards the workroom, where community singing was going on. She made little movements forward to encourage me.

'I'll race you!' I said, and shot into the packing department – my legs moving freely now – only to find that Grandidge had sold the pass, had locked and bolted the back door. He had of course got his tea from the Empire Cafe before he did so, and stared at me now over the rim of his mug.

'Come on, Jeffrey,' said Mrs Farrer, behind me, reaching to take me by the hand. As if I were the fat son of Mrs Moss, home from the open-air school.

'Thank you,' I said. 'I know the way.' My brain whirred, and I began to breathe through my nose.

'He went out ballock naked,' said Grandidge, revealing the side of his character that had so endeared him to Queen Mary.

'Do you want anything from Macfisheries?' I asked Mrs Farrer. 'Or Halfords?' It was my last throw.

'No,' she said, 'I don't think so.'

'Right,' I said. 'Well, we mustn't keep him waiting, eh?' I smiled at Mrs Farrer, cutting Grandidge dead.

Politeness costing nothing, I opened the door for her into the workroom. Keeping close behind her, my nose in the clean corner of my handkerchief, I held my stiff index finger in the small of her back. Of course she knew that it wasn't a real gun, but she moved more quickly, giving out little giggles and cries of 'Oh, Jeffrey!'

The singing died away. There was just the whirr of the machines, and I felt all eyes upon me. Only Mrs Farrer's giggles and her 'Oh, Jeffrey!' and our feet on the bare floorboards. Otherwise silence. We had almost made it to the office door, indeed I was starting to breathe again through my mouth, when the voice of Janet, the spokes-woman, rang out.

'I'll be with you in Cherry Blossom time,' she sang; and then the vulgar Doreen joined in.

'I'll be with you to change your name to mine.'

Then the whole room, a choir, conducted by Maude Skinner waving her shears. I pushed Mrs Farrer aside and ran.

'Church bells will chime; you will be mine; in cherry blossom time!'

Closing the door of the office, leaning against the partition, I found my father looking out of the window, expecting Mrs Farrer and I to come round the corner from Macfisheries.

'Hello, Father,' I said.

He turned, looking through the glass into the general office and meeting the proud smile of Mrs Farrer. Then at me, down below my overall, to see if I was wearing trousers. He then nodded towards his desk, on which stood a hatbox, from J. Dunne the hatters.

'That's for you,' he said, slipping a mint into his mouth.

'Thank you,' I said. 'Thank you very much.' Over the years he had brought home several empty boxes for me to play with, but none quite as good as this. A whole chapter in *101 Things a Boy Can Do* was devoted to what you could construct from such a box.

'Open it,' he said. 'Go on.'

Mildly excited, I lifted the top, thinking that perhaps it still held tissue paper, which I could use for tracing. Behind the partition I heard the creaking of stools and knicker elastic, as the workforce stood up to look.

It was a homburg hat. Black and with a youthful line to it, as worn by the young Sir Alec Douglas-Home. Or indeed Tonto Broomhead at Traggets. Inside, the gleaming leather band was stamped in gilt with my size, six and seven eighths.

'Put it on,' said my father, sucessfully concealing his emotion.

I did so, adjusting it in the reflection in his framed copy of The Factory Act. There was a ripple of applause from Mrs Farrer and her colleagues, then the sound of Janet, and Mrs Skinner, and the vulgar Doreen, sitting down again. They were not easily impressed. Like most workers of the time – only just out of shawls and clogs, still singing along with Our Gracie – they had been infected by the heady rhetoric of Sir Hartley Shawcross. One or two of them may well have had the works of Little Lenin in their handbags. But they recognised authority. They were, I think, like children, grateful to be firmly led. As I turned to face them, my father having quickly pushed the hat the right way round, they knew without a shadow of a doubt exactly who and what I was.

From that day on I was 'Master Jeffrey'. Until my father slipped beneath the waves at Bognor, when I became 'Mister Cork'.

Chapter Six

'Red sky at night, shepherd's delight' quoted Bernard, with a raised finger, as we strolled along the bank of The Drain looking for women.

'I know,' I said, glancing up at the enormous sky striped in orange and gold. Being country boys, we were of course full of ancient lore like that. But I had just put a question to him, and was awaiting an answer.

'If I were you,' he said, 'I'd book into a hotel. That's what people do.'

'Thank you,' I said, rather caustically. 'How much would that cost?' Though middle management, I had learned that I got a pound less than Grandidge, and had been toying with the idea of discreetly approaching Mrs Skinner.

'Not a lot,' said the man of the world, who hadn't the faintest idea. He was wearing his Sea Cadets' uniform, with HMS Swinehurst around his hat. 'Just for an hour. They couldn't charge a lot for an hour, if you didn't have any meals.' He kicked a stone into the stagnant water with his black sailor boy's shoes. 'Mind, you'd have to have a suitcase with you.'

I stared at him. At his whistle on a white string; at the seven creases ironed across his bell bottoms; signifying, so the seagoing Pomfret said, the seven seas of the world. All I had asked him was what I should reply to Elspeth. Foolishly, I had written that I was to be in Bradford the following weekend, on a visit to Yasmin and George. Of course she had replied by return that WE COULD MEET!, Bradford being within striking distance of Ilkley.

'What's the suitcase for?' I asked. 'If you're only there

for an hour. Or less,' I added, remembering how long it had taken in the chicken run.

'You're not allowed in without one,' said Bernard, who had picked all this up at Troon. 'And she'll have to wear a wedding ring.' He nodded to me with utter certainty, defying any argument, while I cooled rapidly towards the whole adventure.

'Anything else?' I asked, for future reference as it were.

'I don't think so,' he said. 'You've still got your thing in your wallet. You'll just want a tip for the pageboy.'

He saw the look on my face.

'He comes when you bang the bell,' he explained. 'To pick up your suitcase, while they're looking at her fingers.'

I thanked him for giving me the benefit of his experience, and we stopped to have a cigarette by a wall that had fallen down.

'Dry stone walling,' said Bernard, as we kicked away stones until we found a smooth one to sit on, 'is a traditional English craft, using no cement or mortar, which makes it easier to repair when it falls down.'

We sat side by side in silence, looking back at the town as the sun slid down behind the blueish hills. Silent as they say only good friends can be. In fact, the longer we knew each other, the less we had to say; until we finally stopped speaking. Though as I have said, we still exchange Christmas cards.

We must have looked an odd couple. He in his sailor suit, in the hope that any girls we met would want to touch his collar for luck, and me in my homburg hat. My father had said that there was no need for me to wear it all the time, especially with an open-necked shirt, but I liked it. That very morning, by registered post, my calling-up papers had arrived; and it was possible that in eighteen months' time my head might be too big.

The War Office had ordered me to report, a week after my return from Bradford, to Swinehurst barracks, regimental headquarters of the Duke of Lincoln's Second Foot.

This was almost certainly, I had told Bernard, in order to be measured for a uniform, issued with brown boots and a stick, before going on to Sandhurst.

Bernard, five months younger than me, and despite his Thursday evening flag waving and his dancing in the garden – climbing invisible rigging hand over hand to the 'Teedle oot toot toot' of his mother's mouth music – was interested in the Palestine Police. While I took his point about the smart hats, the swagger sticks and the Alsatian dogs, I had drawn his attention to the short trousers and the likelihood of the Jews throwing things at him.

'When I come out,' he said, 'I'm going into the post office.'

I stared at him, with just a tinge of envy, recalling the day we had set out to get Pickersgill. Bernard had said then that if he didn't explore, he would become a telegram boy; and nowadays they had red motorbikes. He clenched both fists, bending his wrists and going 'Vroom, vroom!' though I pointed out, dryly, that one 'vroom' was more than enough for 125 cc.

'After that I might be a telephone engineer,' he said. 'Up a pole with a belt.' He babbled his lips to keep his engine ticking over. 'My mother says there's more of a future in it.' I nodded my hat, in rare agreement with his mother; and there was of course his early grounding in setting up the cocoa tin on a string.

'You'll be a factory owner,' he said, and I detected a trace of Stafford Cripps in his voice.

'A Northern Manufacturer,' I said. 'Yes, I will.'

There was a silence then, both of us realising that we were growing up, and apart. To cheer him up, to lighten the mood, I said: 'When I take over, I'm thinking of going into knickers.'

We laughed so much we fell off the wall, my homburg and his sailor hat rolling in the grass, until some girls came past and we got up, in case they wanted to touch Bernard's collar.

'What about Lillian Braithwaite?' he asked, as we began to walk home.

'What about her?' I parried. We had had an awful row the week before, at the Tramps' Supper, and I didn't know if Bernard was aware of this. He had lapsed from the Young Conservatives, being slightly left of centre since hearing from De Kuyper about the Invergordon mutiny.

The Tramps' Supper, as far as I was concerned, had been a fiasco. Having kept some of Uncle Frank's clothes for such an event, and sent away to Ellisdons for a cardboard abscess and a pair of hairy ears, I had arrived at the Braithwaites early and lit a fire of twigs on the raked gravel – only to be told by a woman in elastic stockings that the others were inside with the apéritifs.

Lillian, with lipstick on her nose, wore a brand new sack and wellington boots. The boys had soot on their cheeks and baggy trousers, and some of the girls wore top hats; one with a bird's nest made of shredded paper in the brim. And that was it! We were served baked potatoes from a gadrooned silver dish, and when I attempted to talk like a tramp, modelling myself on the one Rufus and I had met in the Somerset churchyard, I was asked to leave. Lillian had followed me out with a red face.

'They don't call them effing spuds!' she shouted. 'That's not how they talk!'

'That's exactly how they talk,' I told her. 'And they don't have maître d'hôtel butter, or flags in their sandwiches!'

She had started to cry, standing under a Chinese lantern; not exactly one's idea of political leadership. 'We meant it to be like Judy Garland and Fred Astaire,' she snivelled, her nose coming off in her handkerchief. 'Walking up the avenue. Funny!'

I tore up my membership card, dropping the pieces into the pond, in which I had intended to tickle a goldfish. 'Thank you for having me,' I said, swinging stick and bundle over my shoulder. 'You can take my name off the trip to Whipsnade.' And I walked out of her life.

'You didn't get anywhere with her then?' asked Bernard, making that movement with his fingers that his mother didn't like. On this subject I was still the recognised authority, having given him a rough outline of what had happened in the chicken run. As far as I knew, Bernard had got absolutely nowhere; and this had nothing to do with his accident. Hence the sailor suit, I suppose. Leaving him at his gate, I walked home, deciding to slip quietly into and out of Bradford, leaving Miss Garrowby on the far side of the moors.

Quite frankly I felt uneasy about her. She was perfectly acceptable as a pen-pal, but there was a disturbing – and increasing – emphasis in her letters. They came every week, arriving always on Tuesday morning with *The Wizard*. ('Another one from Mrs Simpson,' De Kuyper would say, holding it by the corner.) Four or five pages about what had happened in Ilkley, and usually ending with a long passage about her going to bed.

'Dear Jeffrey . . . I have a peach-coloured eiderdown, and on it is my nightdress case. It is a darker peach colour, round, with a flower in the middle and ruffles. My nightie is white, with a yoke collar and little blue *forget-me-nots* [her italics] down the front. My little dressing table is painted white, with Bambi on it, and your photo in a silver frame.' (This was the snap taken by Mrs Farrer, on the afternoon of my first day at work, after I had been given the hat. My father's feet were behind me on the fire escape.) 'There are no other photos in my room, just Stewart Granger, and some kittens playing with balls of wool. I turn you round when I get undressed, then I turn you back again so that you can see me drink my milk. I have blue *forget-me-nots* on my pillow . . . ' If she had been to a wedding there might be eight or nine pages. On the back of every mauve and perfumed envelope was SWALK. Tongue in cheek, I printed CAPSTAN (a strong cigarette of course, but also an acronym for 'Can A Prick Stand Twice A Night') and was surprised that she did not enquire what it meant. De Kuyper, as she took one of my letters to the post, said: 'I see you've put it without a question mark. Like the Webbs did with the second edition of *Soviet Communism: A New Civilisation*.' Not sure whether she meant the swimming Webb or the lettuce people, I gave her an enigmatic stare.

As luck would have it, Elspeth's mother rang up two days later, to say that the little hairdresser had mumps and was under the peach-coloured eiderdown. 'Have you had it?' she shouted down the line. 'You know what it can do to a boy!' In a moment of relief, and sentimentality, I sent Elspeth some stamps I had left over; mainly Swiss and boring; telling her I would write from Sandhurst.

Thus, free of any pressure, we left for Bradford on the Saturday morning. My father driving, Miss Parkinson beside him, and me in the back with Rupert. On the outskirts of Doncaster, while Miss Parkinson held my half brother over a drain, my father took the opportunity of speaking to me.

'You're going into the army,' he said, staring ahead at the mascot on the bonnet, his leather gauntlets still holding the wheel.

'Yes,' I said. 'I know. I told you. It was a registered letter . . . '

'If there's anything you want to know . . . anything you want to ask me?' Sunk into his motoring scarf, he waited. This was obviously planned, and I was surprised.

'You haven't been in the army,' I pointed out. 'Not as far as I know.'

'Your grandfather was at Rorke's Drift,' he said. 'Only a week after.' If he had turned round then he would have seen my mouth open. I hadn't known that. 'The blackies came at them from all sides,' he went on, as if reading a story on the wireless. I bent forward, waiting for him to continue, but that was it.

'Did they kill him?' I asked.

265

'No,' he said. 'They'd all gone when he got there.' There was a pause.

'I don't think I'll be fighting the blackies,' I said, considering touching his shoulder to reassure him. He half turned in his seat, though still looking out across the fields, as if watching for a ululating Impi moving through the potatoes, and lowered his voice.

'If you're in a barracks,' he said, then speaking faster, because we could hear Rupert shouting that he'd done his wee wees, 'there's usually a little room or cubicle near the entrance. It will have "Prophylactic" on the door. You can get a tube of ointment there.' Then the fawn wool was over his mouth and he was starting the engine, the illuminated hand rising stiffly to announce our leaving the lay-by.

'Been having a nice talk?' asked Miss Parkinson, who didn't miss much.

'Yes,' I said, as we bowled along, and leaned forward to whisper into my father's ear. What was the ointment *for*? Did he mean Germolene? But he was concentrating on his driving, on operating the illuminated hand, now that we were approaching a built-up area.

'Don't put your father off,' said Miss Parkinson.

So I asked Yasmin later that day, when she was getting the tea ready in the kitchen of the prefabricated house. She had drawn the curtains in case anyone looked in and saw the tin of salmon.

'How would I know what kind of ointment soldiers get in a tube?' she said, while I buttered the bread.

She had matured since marrying and becoming a mother. Gone was the poodle, and the bracelet from her ankle. Her black roots were now halfway down her hair, which was in curlers under a chiffon scarf, because they were going out for a drink that evening. In her pinny and cardigan, her pink fur-trimmed slippers, she looked every inch a housewife. I was surprised that she hadn't heard about the ointment.

'Are you happily married?' I asked.

'Yes, I sodding well am!' she said.

I said that I was glad to hear that, arranging the three-cornered bread neatly on a doily, while Yasmin stared at a calendar from the sweet firm that hung on a nail, clear of the damp. George, standing on a chair in the back row, waving Happy New Year with the other executives. I thought that was touching, seeing he was in the other room; in the flesh as it were.

'Elspeth's got mumps,' I said, changing the subject.

'Has she,' said Yasmin, soaking up the salmon juice on a piece of bread, something she had always liked to do as a young girl.

'And I'm going in the army next week,' I told her, not without pride.

'You'll find out what they use the ointment for then, won't you?' she said, handing me the trifle to take in.

'Well done,' said my brother-in-law, who was already at the head of the table, pointing to where I should put it. My father was in an armchair, behind the *Telegraph & Argus*, the Nignog's newspaper.

George smiled at me, presumably for bringing in the trifle. 'What's it like to be a worker then, eh?' he asked, parting the lace curtains with a spring onion to have a look at his motor car.

'Very nice,' I said. 'Thank you.' I sat down opposite the cake, which had 'Victoria' written on top in liquorice comfits (it was the child's birthday), wondering if George – who had been a commissioned officer – knew anything about the ointment.

'After victory,' said my brother-in-law, eating the onion. Then, thinking I did not understand, he nodded to the cake and to the play pen in the corner. 'Victoria. We called her after Victory.' He stared at me as if I were stupid. 'We won the war!' he said, loudly, as if I didn't know. My father looked over the top of the adverts for a moment, then sank back out of sight.

The last time I had seen George had been at his wedding

267

reception, at the Co-op Café in Swinehurst; a fine sight in his dress uniform, laughing and carousing with his brother officer. It was difficult to believe now that it was the same man. He gave the impression of not living there, in the prefabricated house; of having just called in. The insurance man invited to join us for tea. Rather than homely slippers, and no collar, his black pointed shoes tapped restlessly on the stained concrete beneath the table. He wore, in his own home, a blue business suit, with a propelling pencil at his breast. Beside his cork mat was a buff file and his fountain pen, and throughout the meal he examined invoices; tightening his lips and grunting over each one. He was, we all saw, a man who was going places.

It was what we called then, still in the days of rationing, a 'pre-war tea'. As well as the salmon, (George, with a light in his eyes, told of people who had lived out the entire war in Harrogate, eating five-shilling chicken sandwiches), the trifle and the cake – a portion of which, with comfits, was wrapped to take home to De Kuyper – we were each given a bag of 'Victory Vs'. These were off ration, being classed as medicinal, and hence almost impossible to get.

'Leave it to me,' said George, right forefinger along his nose, like my solicitor. 'I can always get them.'

We sat around sucking them afterwards, while we discussed current affairs. Yasmin and Miss Parkinson were washing up.

'Personally,' said our host, as if it were on his territory, (he had told us that he covered Odsal, Wibsey and Idle, and went as far as Cleckheaton on a Wednesday), 'I am not prepared to give away India.'

'No,' said my father, nodding, because George was looking at him. Yasmin had taken the *Telegraph & Argus* for the cat's box, and he didn't know what to do with his hands. He stared now at me, and I realised that he wished me to debate on his behalf. I lightly cleared my throat.

'You don't think,' I ventured, 'that the Indians should rule themselves?'

'No, I bloody don't!' said George. 'They're not ready for it.' He was still looking at my father, who had found a copy of *Blighty* under the cushion and was turning the pages.

'Ah!' I tried not to smile too broadly, settling back in the utility chair. 'You think they should, when they are able to.' It was a good debating point that would have won nods and nudges all round at the Tabernacle. My brother-in-law turned to stare at me.

'Your Indian,' he said, pointing the mottled blue fountain pen at me. 'Your wily Oriental gentleman, your wog, is a good fighting soldier. Especially your Gurkha and your Sikh.' I nodded agreement, having seen them in action at the Pavilion De Luxe. 'Under British officers,' he emphasised. 'So long as you don't go greasing his bullets with pig's fat. And your upper-class Indian, those that have been to school over here, can turn out to be good at cricket.' He came close to smiling. 'Though of course they couldn't play for Yorkshire.'

'Ranjitsinji,' I said, still nodding agreement with him.

'Jig a jig!' he replied, raising a fist and slapping his blue serge bicep with his other hand, looking to see if the kitchen door was closed.

'Char wallah,' said my father, and we paused in our Hindustani conversation to look at him. 'It's what they call the man who takes round the tea,' he explained. 'Char means tea.'

'I know,' said George. 'We grow it there!' He looked with pride from my father to me, daring us to contradict him. 'Lipton, Tetley's, Brooke Bond.' He ticked them off on his fingers. 'You never heard of an Indian tea, did you? Binga Bangerwaller's tea?' He paused so that we could all imagine the funny writing on the packet. 'You don't think Earl Grey was Indian, do you?' He was staring at me, so I shook my head. 'We *plant* tea,' he said, enunciating clearly, as if my father and I were from the open-air school. 'That's what they call it, *planting* it. We give them bushes, and tell them how to plant it. And then they pick it, when we tell them to. They don't know what it is.' He went on staring at me, until I murmured that we had had a picture at Mrs Dooley's of them doing all this.

'We have to take the choicest buds off and test them,' he said, the fountain pen wagging. 'Make tea out of them and spit it out. You're not allowed to swallow it.' He stared at my father and me, until we both nodded that this was beyond dispute.

'We run the post office,' said George, putting down his pen and starting again on his fingers. 'And the civil service. And the railways. And the police.' There was a pause on his little finger. 'Can you imagine?' His voice rose with each of the five syllables and he stood up, blotting out the light from the window. My father put his handkerchief over his face. 'Can you imagine what they'd've been like if we'd never gone there?'

No, I admitted; I couldn't imagine that.

'Howdah.' It was my father's voice through the Irish linen. 'That's what the mahout sits in. On the elephant.' But George ignored him.

'I'll tell you something . . . ' He stepped forward and brought his eyes, behind the steel spectacles, down level with mine; his backside just in front of my father's face. 'Can you imagine it the other way round?'

Not knowing what he meant, I kept quiet; just opening my mouth to exhale, because of the 'Victory V'.

'Can you imagine *them* coming over here?' George said slowly, making three words out of 'imagine'. 'Can you im-ag-ine them coming to Bradford? Eh? Walking into Bombay Station, saying "Two and two halves to Bradford, Forster Square?" Eh?' he said again, loudly, turning for some reason to address the handkerchief. 'Could they do what we did?'

'You mean plant tea, and run the railways?' I asked, to help out my father; but unsure of my ground. The Tabernacle and Lillian Braithwaite's organisation had taken

270

differing views on this subject. Feeling my brother-in-law's hot breath on the top of my head, I assumed that he was staring at me.

'Do you know what I'm talking about?' he demanded. I thought it best to shake my head and say no, not really. I was only waiting for him to move out of the way, so I could get to the toilet.

'I'm talking,' said George, 'about devoting a whole life to a country. Do you know what I mean?' I wasn't sure I did, but having just learnt of the family's involvement with Imperial history, albeit a few days late, I waited for him to go on.

'You take it the other way round,' he said, willing me to look up at him. 'Can you see them coming over here? Like we went there?'

'It's too cold for them here,' I said.

'It's too hot for us there!' George riposted. 'But we went!' He poked my shoulder pad. '*And* we took a way of life with us, when we went. They had bugger all!' He started on his fingers again, right in front of my face. 'Religion, sport, football and cricket, bagpipes, card games, Rose's Lime Juice . . . '

'Robinsons Lemon Barley Water,' I suggested.

'Yes,' he said. 'Robinsons Lemon Barley Water. And marmalade.'

'Robinsons marmalade?' I asked, interested.

'They didn't have any marmalade,' he said, ignoring my question. 'Or bread. Not like our bread. We had to take it all out there. Port out, starboard home. Posh.'

'Well,' I said, in the silence that followed, reaching for the *Radio Times*. 'I wonder what's on Saturday Night Theatre?'

'Never mind Saturday Night Theatre!' he said, staring at me now with definite dislike. 'Do you know what I'm talking about?'

'Yes,' I told him again, nodding vigorously, while he took deep breaths through his nose.

'And you're saying,' he said. 'You're saying that they'd come over here? With their mangoes? That you'd be able to see them going to work in their sheets, down Great Horton Road?'

I held up my hand, but he wasn't stopping.

'You're saying they'd work here? In the combing? Their wives, with spots on their heads, burling and mending?' He had a finger to his forehead, to show what he meant. 'On the trams?' This last was so loud that the child of Victory began to whimper in the corner.

'Not on the trams,' I said. This was fantasy.

'And they'd have their own shops?' he shouted, heedless of his daughter's cries. 'They'd have to. They couldn't go in ours! They wouldn't know what to ask for!' His eyes widened as his im-ag-ination ran riot. 'Sari shops? Cafes? Curry cafes?!' he shuddered, opening his mouth wide to breathe out. Whether this was the 'Victory V', or a mime of eating curry, I wasn't sure.

'George,' I said, intending to distract him by telling him about my homburg hat; but it was hopeless.

'Did you know they get married when they're ten?'

'No,' I said, I didn't know that.

'*And*,' he said, 'they don't eat sweets like we do!' This, to him, was obviously far worse than getting married at ten.

'How do they eat them?' I wanted to know, but was ignored.

'And pictures!' he said. 'They'd have to have their own picture houses!' He was really scathing now. 'You can see it, can't you?' Now he was a talking poster. 'At the Regal next week: the Three Stooges, talking Indian!' He turned to my father, but he was pretending to be dead.

'And fish shops!' he said suddenly, turning back to me. He drew a shop fascia in the air with a finger. 'The Bombay Fish Shop,' he announced; then in a funny voice: 'Fish and five, twice. Do you want anything on?' He was now the Aga Khan in a white overall, turban in the steam, salt and

272

vinegar poised over the parcel. Now he was the customer, (he was quite good at this, really). 'Just a bit of curry sauce, please, Gunga Din.' Then he was himself again, withering me with a long look. 'You want your head washed out,' he said. 'From the inside!'

'I'm sorry,' I said, still wondering how they ate sweets in a different way. Though if they were married by the time they got any worthwhile pocket money, they probably had other fish to fry. I smiled at the thought.

'It's not funny!' he snarled.

'What isn't?' asked Yasmin, she and Miss Parkinson rejoining the gentlemen as it were.

'Him and his Indians!' said her husband, turning on her. 'They're all coming over here, according to him!'

I wasn't quite sure how I had got into the position of advocate of mass immigration, responsible for an unending stream of rickshaws and bullock carts pouring over the curve of the earth, winding down the Manchester Road like the March of Time. Wistfully, I recalled the harmless after-dinner games of the Real household.

'All I said was,' and I raised my hands for calm and reason, 'all I said was – don't you think they should rule themselves?'

'And all I said,' said George, 'is no! I bloody well don't!'

'I was reading about an Indian doctor,' said Miss Parkinson, the peacemaker. 'In Leeds.'

'Witch doctor!' said George.

'I don't remember his name,' said Miss Parkinson.

I was looking at my father, his head back and covered with the handkerchief, like the sleeping Miles Malleson in the film of the handbag play. Now I saw it move as the mouth twitched, rise with a gust of air, and realised that in the privacy of his little tent he was laughing.

Chapter Seven

'Hands off cocks! On with socks!'

It was the morning of my second day in the army, and nothing more different from Mrs Hazlit's 'Do come along boys, please!' can be imagined. The Corporal marched down the hut, beating his stick on the iron bed ends, shouting the traditional if rather coarse form of good morning.

I lay on a straw-filled palliasse, in a khaki vest with enormous holes for my arms, grey blanket to my chin, staring up at the loudspeaker on the roof truss. The evening before we had listened to Jack Jackson, first of the disc jockeys, who scorned Troise and his Mandoliers and pretended to have in the studio a cat called Tiddles. It was generally agreed, at least at my end of the hut, that he made the noises with his mouth.

Civilian life already seemed an age away. The week since we had returned from Bradford had been a blur. De Kuyper, who continually referred to me as 'cannon fodder', reading to me nightly from an anthology of mutinies. At work, Grandidge, who had my departure date ringed on the calendar, instructed me in bayonet drill. ('*In . . .* in 'is guts! Across . . . rip up . . . *out*!' He chanted, while I jabbed with a broomstick at a Hun resembling my father that he had sketched on a bale of cloth. 'Up with yer butt to break 'is jaw! In again when 'e's down . . . boot on 'is chest to pull it out . . . boot on 'is face, and *forward*!') I had of course asked him about the ointment, but he couldn't remember. He had told me about an instrument known as 'The Umbrella', because it opened out like one, and which was quite disgusting. I took it that he was joking, or that it was peculiar to The Great War; like brass boxes of chocolate from the Queen.

On my last day, Mrs Farrer had cried, plucking at my overall and showing me my hair. As I lifted my hat in farewell, standing on a parcel so that all could see, the girls had cried 'Goodbye Jeffrey!'; the vulgar Doreen adding something, some kind of valediction, which a burst of laughter from the other girls prevented me from hearing. Because of his interest in my future ('Keep yer 'ead down, and yer arse against the wall!'), I looked into the packing department to shake Grandidge's hand; but he was over the road at the Empire Cafe.

'Look after yourself,' my father muttered, on the morning I left, as he was going into the downstairs lavatory.

'I will,' I said, then lowered my voice. 'And I'll ask about the ointment as soon as I get there.'

'Goodbye, Jeffrey,' Miss Parkinson called from the kitchen. 'Come back and see us, won't you?'

'Thank you,' I said, taking a last look round, hearing Rupert shout from upstairs that he'd finished. De Kuyper was waiting at the front door with my suitcase.

'No tears now,' she said, smiling through her own. 'Have you been?'

Embracing her, assuring her that I had, I told her that it was not a time for tears. We had talked the night before about what I would do in a General Strike; and I repeated my promise to fire over the heads and then to vote with my feet. Kissing her, I picked up my case, and the carrier bag which held the sandwiches and the letter for the sergeant.

Outside the gate, in mufti, Bernard was kicking a stone about on the pavement. 'I thought they'd come for you in a staff car,' he said. 'With a flag on the bonnet.'

'Goodbye, old man,' I said, extending my hand. 'I'll see you when I get leave.' We shook hands, and he asked me to keep the cartridge cases of all the bullets I fired, as he collected them.

'On holiday, then?' asked the Pomfret who worked on the railway, as I walked into the booking hall.

'On His Majesty's Service,' I said, opening the registered envelope and presenting my free pass.

As the signal dropped with a clatter, and the train puffed around the curve, Pomfret wheeling out the empty fish boxes for Swinehurst, I thought back to the day I had rattled through without stopping. En route, I had thought then, to a life of squalor and servitude. Now I saw myself reflected in the mirror of the Nestlé's machine. Reasonably tall and smartly dressed, my hair was beginning to wave naturally. Touching the folded white handkerchief, arranging the pen and pencil set at my breast, I felt the wallet that held three pounds ten, and the freshly talcumed memento of Rufus Real. Things had, I thought, as I moved forward into the steam, hearing Pomfret shout 'Swinehurst! Non-stop to Swinehurst!' not turned out too badly.

Of course I had expected the railway to make an effort, to put crossed flags on the front of the engine, and a placard of some kind, but no; its name was 'Beryl'. Neither was it crowded with chaps like me, eager faces at every window, cheerful badinage as they reached for my luggage and helped me aboard. In the small hours of the previous night I had pictured the scene in the compartment. There would be one in the corner – possibly up on the luggage rack – playing a mouth organ, and we would all sing, swaying with the movement of the train, arms around each other's shoulders, as the countryside flashed by. There would be a small working-class cynic – possibly the one tapping his foot on Corfe Castle – and an inhibited and twitchy one, who needed to be watched. There would be a fattish, always hungry one, the butt of our jokes (but defended against bullies from other platoons), and a tall one with wavy hair who did well with girls. I would either be him, or the quiet one who surprised everybody at the end. The cynical mouth organist, the twitchy one and the fattish one, were almost certain to get shot.

Disappointingly, there was no one in my carriage who looked as if he were off to join the Colours. Reading my Sexton Blake, I wondered if the regimental band – fronted by the shampooed goat, and playing of course 'The Lincolnshire Poacher' – would be on Swinehurst platform, as the train slowed under the bunting. They would smoothly change to 'The Eton Boating Song' as we detrained and lined up, raincoats over our arms, to be inspected by a gruff but kindly officer with a moustache, before being regaled with tea and buns from a mobile canteen.

A blackboard on an easel, beside the ticket collector, told new recruits to take a number seven tram.

I sat upstairs, my mind full of memories as we turned off the High Street, away from Victory Cottage and my old haunts. Farmer Giles ('Tom Soup 6d' chalked on the window); the Boy on the Barrel; the Pilgrim Fisheries; and the back street leading to Osrams. Then the broken window of the Tabernacle; a smiling Uncle Fred blocking out the draught. As we crossed the bridge I could see into the chicken runs; see the cinder paths, a duck in a puddle beside the still-collapsed wire. Feeling a little sad, I read the by-laws on the ceiling of the tram.

At Swinehurst Barracks another young man alighted with me, raincoat over his arm and suitcase in hand. As the tram rattled away we nodded to each other, walking between the white-painted stones and ropes to ring the bell at the wicket gate. 'First Battalion, Duke of Lincoln's Second Foot' said the noticeboard, on the smooth grass beside the moat.

It was like a real fort, with lots of what I knew were called crenellations, and slits to fire arrows through. Though the date carved over the gate, 1910, was I thought a little late for a drawbridge. The flag of the regiment flew from a tower, showing they were in residence; and I saw on the wall, somewhat faded, the painted slogan 'God Made The Land For The'. A friend of Uncle Fred had obviously been disturbed by a sentry. I recalled the green-painted message I had read aloud from the brick wall of Armley Jail, on our way back from Bradford: 'Hang Lady Astor, The High Priestess Of Fascism'. My father, drawing in breath between his teeth, had put the hand out and his foot down.

'Mock,' I said, smiling and nodding at the sandstone walls.

'Croxley,' said my companion. 'Albert.'

The gate was opened then by an extremely smart Sergeant. He wore a flat hat, stiffened at the front like the Palestine Police, so that the burnished peak pressed against his nose. His patent boots had the gloss of Victor Sylvester's shoes, his spats and belt were snow white. He carried a stick with a silver knob, and he stepped through the gate with a smashing of steel studs on the gravel, with a loud cry of 'Shit on the doorstep!'

'Shit on the doorstep, Sergeant!' came the answering cry, from a Corporal dressed, whitened and hatted exactly the same, though his stick was shorter and knobless. He also stepped through the gate, his head thrown back in order to see us.

'Good morning,' I said, impressed by my first contact with military tradition. This ritual probably went back to Bannockburn, or the scaling of the heights of Alma. 'We've come to join.'

'Good morning,' said the Sergeant, loudly. 'We've come to join.' Exactly the words I had used. He was staring at Croxley Albert. When you could see his eyes they were tiny, like fly buttons, in a flat face like my brother-in-law's. 'What do we do with shit on the doorstep?' he shouted now, and the Corporal, who besides being knobless was apparently hard of hearing, slammed his boots together, rattling loose gravel against the gate.

'Sweep it up, Provost Sergeant!' and he began to touch me – quite against both letter and spirit of King's Regulations – behind the knees with his stick.

'Get 'em up! Up! UP! yelled the Sergeant, galvanising my

new friend Croxley to run on the spot. In this fashion we entered Swinehurst Barracks, home of The Foreskin Fusiliers, as someone had chalked above the veranda of the guardroom. Tickled and prodded in a quite outrageous way, we galloped past geraniums and antique cannon, and into a hut which appeared to be a waiting room. Having picked up a degree of speed, Croxley and I ran twice around the table, bumping into the folding chairs, being joined in this by several young men who were already there. Dropping their raincoats they ran with us, assuming it to be the first training session, until the Sergeant shouted for us to halt.

'When the hofficer comes in,' he roared, 'stand hup!' Then they left us, both doing manoeuvres with their sticks as they turned smartly about. Ron told me later that they were bastards, and if the officers knew how they abused their authority it would not have been tolerated for a moment. Already suspecting as much, I had decided against giving the Sergeant the letter from De Kuyper, or asking him about the ointment.

Still rather nervous, Croxley and I sat together, smoking the Passing Cloud cigarettes I had bought for such a special day. He told me he was going to be a fishmonger. His womenfolk made Christmas crackers at home, in the front room: 'Me gran and me mum and me Aunty Else. They come in a van.' We didn't have a lot to say after that.

Gradually the room filled up with young men, with suitcases and raincoats over their arms; all of them running when they came in. I moved away from Croxley, promising to have a look at his knife later on, to sit next to a chap in a sports jacket who looked as if he might have had a prep-school background. As they say, appearances can be deceptive. It turned out that he had been employed in taking loaves of bread off a moving belt. But he was an amateur boxer, with three medals and a cup, jogging out of the bakery at dawn for the five miles home to Dewsbury; wherever that was. He confided to me, over a Passing

Cloud (he was not at the moment in training), that he intended to be another Rockfist Rogan, keeping his vest on and not turning professional. Not that he scorned the material world, or had a desire to move bread about for the rest of his life, but because he had been told that the blackies would always be world champion; their heads and chins being naturally harder, and their not feeling pain like a white man.

At that moment, happening to glance out of the window, I saw a bevy of officers, all with leather sticks, gloves and briefcases, heading towards the door. I did not hesitate.

'Room – shun!' I called, standing on a chair so that they could see me. Feet together, left arm across my body with my raincoat, my right stiffly at my side, thumb in line with the seam of my trousers. There was a hush as the officers paused in the doorway, surveying us, though no one else had moved.

'Good morning,' said a Captain, three pips on his shoulder like the Rev Eli Wannamaker. He was staring at me, the only one of course in the correct posture. 'Very good,' he said, after a pause, licking his lips. 'What's your name?'

'Cork, sir. Jeffrey Cork.' I anticipated his next question. 'Junior Rechabite, sir. Leading hand and quartermaster. *And*,' I got in, as he opened his mouth, 'Cadet Corps, Traggets School, The Isle of Avalon.'

There was a silence, and I saw the officers exchange glances, before they went into another room and closed the door. Rockfist Rogan was staring up at me.

'The Isle of Avalon!' he said, awestruck. 'Fuckin' hell!'

I think that just about summed up the opinion of everyone in the room. Though the buzz of conversation resumed as soon as the officers left, I saw several glances thrown in my direction. One or two even went so far as to applaud when I jumped lightly down from the chair.

We were then (like peas one could say) processed. A trestle table was set up and we gave our names, addresses, religion and next of kin, to an educated Sergeant in a green tie. One could choose between C of E and RC, though a boy from Leeds was adamant about being put down as 'Jewish'. Refusing, for some reason, what the Sergeant thought the more concise 'Jew'; but still qualifying, so I was told, for special margarine.

We then had lunch, in a large hall kept scrupulously clean. Every fifteen minutes, at a warning cry of 'Feet!', diners lifted their boots as a wave of water surged under the tables, followed by a line of trained soldiers pushing squeegees. In cafeteria style, one took a tray and got soup and bread, a portion of pie, a ball of mashed potatoes from an ice-cream scoop, and a spoonful of vegetables. This was served by chefs in vests, all in a line, the last one of whom poured on the gravy. One then took a piece of jam tart, already under custard, and a mug of tea from a bucket. Ample portions, and no doubt nourishing, but as this was not – as we were frequently reminded – a holiday camp, one was not allowed to object to custard skin. We sat on benches, at long tables, lifting our feet as I have explained, while we speculated as to whether they put anything in the tea.

'They have to,' said a Scottish chap, who wore what had once been a cricket pullover. We watched him mash up his soup and bread, pie and veg, jam tart and custard – all in the same plate – adding Croxley's carrots and thinning the mixture with a little tea. 'Otherwise, you'd be all wanked oot the morn!'

I had of course expected a certain amount of lewdness, rough soldierly humour, and I smiled at this as I looked round to see what the chap from Leeds was having. There had been no overtly Jewish food on the hotplate, and I couldn't see him, but Rockfist Rogan said that they probably had their own dining room.

It was after lunch, while washing my cutlery outside in an oil drum, that I first made the acquaintance of the Corporal. A squad of soldiers had marched past – not very well I thought – and half in jest, and because I meant to take my duties seriously from the start, I called out 'Hup, two three!' Several of my colleagues, scraping their plates into the next oil drum, smiled at my knowledge of military terms. But the Corporal, whom I had not noticed marching behind the squad, halted them and came over to me.

'Who said that?' he barked, stick tight under his arm.

'Him,' said Croxley, pointing to me with his knife. 'Mock.' (He had been in the toilet when I had introduced myself from the top of the chair.)

'Jeffrey, actually,' I said, smiling at the Corporal, knowing how useful it could be to have friends among the non-coms.

'Right!' he said, standing very close to me, eyeball to eyeball as they say nowadays. I offered him a Passing Cloud, but of course he could not smoke on duty, and a moment later he marched away with his men.

'Bye, Corporal!' I called after him, not realising how soon we were to meet again.

Then it was time to collect our uniforms. They were not an awfully good fit, but the storeman told us that he could box-pleat our jackets for seven and six. He was also offering lead weights on a string, for our trousers, at the reasonable price of a shilling a leg. I had brought wire from the brush factory, to stiffen the front of my peaked hat like the Palestine Police, but was given a beret. This was at least an advance on the forage cap, though a little loose after we had been to the barber's.

It felt cool now where my hair had been as I sat on the edge of my bed, remembering Bert Grandidge's stories about lice. (The reason of course for HM the Queen packing her chocolates in such a stout container.) As I scratched and yawned, looking down the hut at my platoon coming to terms with the morning, I was grateful to the Corporal for leaving the door wide open.

Hut Number One was, I think, where they placed those who would nowadays be called 'high flyers'. Croxley, there just to make up the number, had the first bed on the left – on which he spent most of his time, waiting to throw his knife into the door as it opened – but Rockfist Rogan and the uncouth Scot had been directed to Hut Number Three. I was in the far corner beside the fireplace, and had already settled in. The evening before, while my colleagues caroused in the NAAFI, I had carefully arranged my pack and ammunition pouches. Stuffed with newspaper, lined with cardboard to make nice sharp corners, their brass buckles gleaming, they stood proudly on the shelf over my bed. Beside them was my felt-covered water bottle with its cork on a string, as used in the Sudan. My Lee Enfield .303 was close to hand in its clip on the wall. Wrapped in one of De Kuyper's yellow dusters were my best boots, polished already almost to glass. With them under the bed was a box, like the tuck boxes we had at Traggets, painted green like everything else at Swinehurst Barracks, in which I kept most of my possessions. I opened this now to take out my sponge bag.

'Does she do a turn?' asked Ron, rising on his elbow to look at the photo of Elspeth, which I had stuck inside the lid of the box.

'Good morning,' I said, taking the remark in the right spirit, and replying that yes, I thought it fair to say that she did a turn.

'Shag like rattlesnakes!' said Ron, lying back and blowing smoke at the ceiling; meaning of course all of them, not just Elspeth.

He had arrived late the evening before, in cavalry twill trousers, having called in at the Swinehurst Regal to see Deanna Durbin. ('She's had more than I've had hot dinners,' he told me, along with a précis of the plot) and had been surprised to find me spitting on my boots in the dark. Other than his plans to become a film star, and that he was the child of a mixed marriage – his father being an intellectual and his mother an idiot – I knew nothing about him.

Then – and I found it quite stirring – Reveille came through the loudspeaker; a bugle, just like at Sidi Bel Abbes. Then – 'Eh!' The Corporal who had been banging his stick and shouting 'Hands off cocks, on with socks!' had reached the end of my bed. It was of course the very same one.

'Hands off cock, Jeffrey Mock,' he said, rhyming cleverly. 'Remember me?'

'Yes, of course,' I said. 'Good morning.' He had a sheet of paper clipped to a board.

'Hup, two, three, four!' he said, and in leaning against the end of my bed caused it to collapse. Taking it in good part, I was attempting to fit it together again when he marched to the centre of the room, shouting, 'I'm going to read out the names!' As if announcing that he was about to leap sixty feet into a tank of water, with his clothes on fire.

'When you hear your name, you say "Corporal". Right?' Everyone agreed, as they pulled on their socks, that they would.

He read them out, moving his finger down the page and his lips in practice before each one, and everyone answered 'Corporal'; as we had cried 'Sir' at Traggets, when Dr Hazlit did a spot check to see if anyone had run away. 'Corporal!' I rapped out when he came to Cork, and he stopped, his mouth ready to pronounce Croxley.

'You 'avin' me on?' he asked. 'You're Mock!'

'Cork,' I said, smiling. 'Jeffrey.'

'Cork Jeffrey?' he said, not smiling. 'You taking the piss?'

I assured him that I was certainly not 'Extracting the urine', as we had phrased it on the Isle of Avalon; and of course we soon had it sorted out. I laughed, saying that it was just like Eton and Marlborough, addressing each other formally by surnames; while the Corporal knocked all the things off my shelves, apologising as he did so.

An interesting start to my first full day under the Colours, I thought, as we marched off to breakfast. (Bacon, and a perforated spoonful of beans, the legendary 'cowboy's breakfast'.) I was looking forward to manoeuvres; to riding on a tank with leaves on my head; or to us all marching through Swinehurst, bayonets fixed and bands playing, which we were entitled to do. But we went instead to see the dentist. Then back into the cafeteria, for a talk from our Commanding Officer. Hurrying to take a seat in the front row, I settled down to hear my first lecture, an exercise book open on my knee.

'Good morning,' our CO greeted us, putting his leather stick and gloves on the table before him. A Colonel, he in no way resembled my mother's seducer, the one who had been dropped into the Dordogne. His face was kindly, almost that of a younger Uncle Fred; but I sensed instinctively that he would have no truck with the theory that God made the land for the people.

'I want to talk to you this morning,' he began, 'about your National Service; and, more specifically, about the six weeks' initial training you will receive here with us.' There was a soft buzz of excitement behind me, mainly from people asking each other what specifically meant.

'As you know,' he said, 'the war is over.' He paused, casting a clear grey eye over the assembled troops. It happened to meet mine, and I nodded, to show that I was with him, if not yet of him.

'Why then, you ask, do we need an army?' He paused again and I smiled at him, though failed to catch his eye this time, to let him know that I was no stranger to rhetoric.

'To guard both the home country and the Empire,' he said, and I wrote that down.

'Would you mind not writing home, while I'm talking?' he said, quite pleasantly, though with an edge to his voice. With something of a shock, I realised that he was addressing me.

'I'm taking notes, sir,' I said, standing up and to attention of course.

He nodded, and there was a pounding of boots from the back of the room. Then the large hand of the Provost

Sergeant snatched the exercise book. Stick under his arm, head thrown back so that he could see, he held it at arm's length and read out, loudly: 'CO's speech. Why do we need a harmy? To guard both the 'ome country and the Empire!' He flicked through to make sure that the rest of the pages were blank.

'Thank you, Provost Sergeant,' said the Commanding Officer, blowing his nose on a civilian handkerchief. 'You can sit down,' he said to me. Waiting until the Provost Sergeant had done his about turn and marched to the rear of the room, he then resumed.

'Here, you will be assessed and selected for the specialist branch or regiment in which you can best play your part. You will be given a basic training in drill, fieldcraft and weaponry, but,' and here he smiled and fingered his moustache, 'we do realise that all work and no play, tends to make Jack a dull boy.' There was an appreciative murmur through the ranks, and Ron said later that he thought we were about to be given the opening hours and tariff of a mobile knocking shop, like the French took with them into action.

'So,' said our Colonel, 'there will be five-a-side football, every evening; and . . . ' he lingered on the word, 'I am informed that there is a ping-pong table in the NAAFI.' The Provost Sergeant began to applaud, stick between his legs, and we all joined in, realising as the Colonel sat down that the lecture was over.

'Oh, yes,' he said, remembering and half rising, 'are there any questions?'

Silence. The odd shuffle and cough, as everyone but me examined their finger nails. I thought it prudent to wait, to let someone else go first.

'Questions for the hofficer!' bellowed the Provost Sergeant, slamming to attention and doing a manoeuvre with his stick. But nothing; fresh-cut heads stared down between open knees. It was clearly up to me. Rising to my feet, I cleared my throat.

'Yes,?' said the Colonel. 'Your name?' Beside him a young Lieutenant opened a wine-coloured diary, licking the little pencil, about to make a note.

'Cork, sir,' I said carefully. 'Jeffrey Cork.'

'And what was your question?'

'Answer the hofficer!' roared the Provost Sergeant, as I drew breath.

'Thank you, Provost Sergeant,' said the Colonel, encouraging me with a smile.

'It's about the ointment, sir,' I said, sensing heads rise with interest all around me.

'The ointment?' The Colonel waited for me to elaborate.

'In a tube, sir.' I was standing rigorously to attention, and you could have heard a pin drop.

'Ah, yes,' said the Colonel, licking his lips. The Lieutenant had replaced the pencil in the diary and now had his hands over his face. 'You mean from the prophylactic room?'

'Yes, sir.'

'You want to know what it's for?' The Colonel was gathering together his hat, stick and gloves.

'Yes, sir.' He was staring at me, noting how my shoulders were held back, my thumbs in line with the seams of my trousers; marking me down no doubt as the type of lively and enquiring mind that Sandhurst was crying out for.

'Actually,' he said, his hat and gloves on, and tapping his stick into a leather palm, 'you'll be having a talk on this subject from the MO. With a film, I believe.' He paused, and a look of concern came onto his face, charged as he was with the moral and physical welfare of so many young Englishmen. 'No special reason for asking, have you?'

'My father mentioned it, sir.'

'Did he?' The Colonel glanced at the Lieutenant, who already had his hat on and was holding the door open for him. 'You're an army family, are you?'

'Rorke's Drift, sir,' I said.

'Rorke's Drift, eh?' he said, impressed, walking backwards.

'Yes, sir,' I said, honesty compelling me to add: 'The week afterwards.'

'The week afterwards, eh? Good.' He felt behind him for the doorway. 'Well, thank you very much.'

'Stand hup for the hofficer!' screamed the Provost Sergeant, and of course everyone did, but with a wave of his stick he had gone.

Outside in the sun, the Corporal took us off to march up and down for a while. Then, before lunch, an unexpected treat, to the regimental museum.

This was in the tower, with a little cannon outside the door. Removing our berets as a mark of respect, we followed the curator, our boots making an awful noise on the polished floor. Behind us came two trained soldiers – no doubt welcoming the change to dry feet and Mansion polish – with blankets wrapped around their squeegees.

The curator was a pear-shaped private, old enough to have in his kit a brass box that had once held the Queen's chocolate. He was known as Kitchener, because he had met him. 'Stood right there,' he used to say, pointing. ' "Carry on," he says. "Yes, sir," I says.' Of course I thrilled to this, and made a mental note to tell Bernard. It was as close as either of us were likely to get to the Mad Mahdi and Lord ('Chinese') Gordon.

Private Kitchener, as you could see from the good conduct stripes which ran the length of his arm, had already done thirty-eight years. All of them in Swinehurst Barracks, except for a period in the Thirties when he had fed the monkeys in Gibraltar. ('The Rock' he called it, and later showed us a story by James Joyce, typed out by the educated Sergeant, in which a lady did things with a banana.) The monkeys, he maintained, were 'like the fuckin' ravens. When they're gone – we're finished!' Allowed to wear gym shoes, because of his age and the floor, he gathered us round him at the first glass case.

'This is a body,' he said, pointing with his stick, (*Everyone*, you will note, had sticks at Swinehurst Barracks, except us!). 'Of the first man killed by the regiment.'

We pressed around the glass, our eager faces lit by the bulb which shone through the mummified stomach, showing the holes inflicted by the Second Foot. The actual grapeshot was neatly displayed below on a card. Kitchener had seen it all before of course – had probably been there when they brought it in, still warm – but his big face shone in the glow with ours, as we regarded what might be called the end product with utter fascination.

'He was Spanish,' said Kitchener, who had very early army teeth – themselves no doubt destined for a glass case when he faded away – that moved of their own accord, whether he was talking or chewing, or not. 'We was with the French,' he explained, as we moved on.

'This is a good one,' he said, pointing to a bayonet hung on the wall. The weapon had serrated teeth along one edge of the blade. 'How it works,' said Kitchener, taking the thing reverently from the wall, 'is . . . you stuck it in. Right?' He looked at our rapt faces. 'Then, when you pulled it out – you pulled out 'is guts!' Even the squeegee pushers, leaning on their handles, were fascinated; and I made another mental note to tell Bert Grandidge.

Whispering, because of where we were, Croxley asked if he could touch it. Kitchener let him, with a finger, then wiped the blade with his khaki handkerchief and replaced it on the wall, giving it a final pat to keep still. We filed past, most of us touching the teeth now that Kitchener wasn't looking.

He had shuffled to the centre of the room where, behind whitened ropes, on a platform covered with greengrocer's grass, a tableau was mounted. Three dummies, with moulded orange hair and brown lips, late of the Thirty Shilling Tailors, stood back to back. (I realise that three people can't, but you know what I mean.) Dressed in old-fashioned uniforms, they were defending a flag on a pole that could have done with a good wash. Crawling towards them was another dummy, painted black and with a rug-wool wig, holding a spear and a lionskin shield. One chipped hand (realistically showing him to be pink underneath, like we are all supposed to be) was almost touching an Englishman's foot. As Kitchener volunteered no information, we stood looking at this scene in silence.

'Who won?' asked Ron, finally.

'We did,' said Kitchener, turning away to point out a group photograph of the first battalion. As at Traggets, they were arranged in a field in long rows, the back rank standing and the CO seated in front in the Matron's chair. In place of the Hazlits' dog, they had piled half a dozen drums on the grass. When asked where he was, by Croxley, Kitchener took a snap from his wallet that showed him playing with the monkeys at the time.

'Should think we fucking did win,' said Ron, who was still looking at the tableau. 'Three to one!'

We went on to look at the medals, and the shrunken heads, and the Duchess of Lincoln's gravy boat, which she took with her to the garrison church. The cup given by Eastern Command for five-a-side football was interesting, and I would have liked to have been able to take home a dum dum bullet for Bernard. Then we came to a row of busts, with their exploits on cards below them, looking very like the wife killers in Osrams.

'Him,' said Kitchener, tapping a moustached bust that wore a solar topee. 'He was captured in the mutiny.'

'What mutiny was that?' I asked eagerly, delighted to have something to tell De Kuyper in my letter home.

'What mutiny was that?' repeated Kitchener, his stick falling slowly down to his gym shoes as he stared at me. 'The fucking Indian Mutiny!'

Of course I apologised, blushing and falling to the back of the crowd, while Kitchener carried on with his enthralling story. About a subaltern called Smythe, chosen for a dangerous mission because of his having been circumcised in an affray with the founders of the Tabernacle. After staining his body all over with walnut juice, growing his hair long and discolouring his teeth, he had crawled out through a sewer one night to see what the sepoys were up to. Captured at sun up, in Kitchener's words: 'His balls were delivered at the gate, tea time.'

'Probably forgot to take his sun hat off!' said Ron, who I suspect did not get as much out of the museum as the rest of us.

We moved away from the conducted tour, to look at a series of daguerreotypes showing men being tied over the muzzles of guns and blown apart.

'I'm putting down for The Army Film Unit,' said Ron. 'What are you putting in for?'

'I'm not sure,' I said, looking at a relief model under glass of the section of the trenches held by the regiment at the Somme. Little officers (converted from Hornby railway porters) sat in dugouts writing poetry, or led the way towards the barbed wire, carrying nothing more lethal than a tiny stick. While the soldiery kicked footballs about and generally played the fool. On the wall behind was a framed cartoon, showing two balaclava'd soldiers opening a tin. 'What, plum jam again?' one of them was saying.

'You could wet yourself,' said Ron, over my shoulder, 'looking at jokes like that.' We walked down the room to join the others, who were filing out past Kitchener, his beret held upside down at waist level.

'Either an officer, or the Intelligence Corps,' I said to Ron, answering his question as we marched off to lunch; only to discover, with mixed feelings, that it was jam tart again.

Chapter Eight

There was indeed jam tart again for lunch, the plums an unmistakable shape under the yellow rubber. We were also just in time to see a fair-haired youth from Skegness claim to be a vegetarian. Lillian Braithwaite had taunted me that many of Uncle Fred's crowd were that way inclined, but I had never knowingly met one. He was in Hut Number Three, with Rockfist Rogan and the lewd Scot, and had not been seen the day before because of his refusal to wear boots. He stood now at the cafeteria, in gym shoes, spoon and fork in hand, drawing back his plate as the chef attempted to give him a portion of braised liver.

'SALAD??!!' The cry stilled our hubbub of conversation, mainly about Lieutenant Smythe's foreskin, and we craned our necks out of the queue to see what was going on. The Sergeant Chef, with stripes on his vest so that you knew who he was, had been brought from the oven to adjudicate.

'I'll give you fucking salad!' we heard him shout, and saw him take the Skegness youth's plate and put on it – not salad – but a generous helping of braised liver. 'That enough?' he asked, perforated spoon poised. There was an envious intake of breath along the queue.

'I don't eat meat,' said the vegetarian, politely enough, putting the plate down on the zinc counter.

'Don't eat fucking meat?' shouted the Sergeant Chef, in an awful state now. His white-hatted platoon had gathered behind him, arms folded and ladles all over the place; while his customers, even those lucky enough to already have their liver and jam tart, hung on every word. Grimly he shovelled on more liver, picking out the choicer bits with severed arteries still attached.

'Is that enough?'

It was more than enough, and there was really no need for him to shout as he did. The man was just in front of him, and on a diet of grass could not have been long for this world. Looking at the chef with compassion, as if he were a pig, he now picked up a clean plate and moved along to the mashed potato man. But he, standing open mouthed, pretended that he couldn't see him.

'Oh, *no!*' said the Sergeant Chef. 'No fucking potatoes without meat!'

It was an impasse. For a moment I thought the vegetarian was going to try his luck with the jam tart; but no, he put back his plate and turned away.

'Thank you, Sergeant,' he said, and we drew back as he passed us, going pale and empty towards the door.

'*EH*!!' and with the outraged cry came the banging of the perforated spoon on the counter. 'Eh, you!'

'Me, Sergeant?' The vegetarian had stopped and turned round, possibly expecting to find a lettuce being waved at him.

'Your fucking dinner!' said Escoffier, holding up the heap of liver, gravy dripping over the thick edge of the plate.

Growing boys as we were, all eyes were on the khaki lumps. But the vegetarian stood his ground; shaking his head, lips pressed together. Realising that it was, as I say, an impasse, the master chef lowered the plate down onto the counter and sucked his thumb.

'Eat your dinner – or you're on a charge!' he said, and a thrill of horror ran round the room. But the vegetarian (made of stern stuff, we all agreed) went on shaking his head. Then there was the crash of the doors opening, and a complex pattern of steps as black glass boots slammed to attention.

'Whassermatter, Cook Sergeant?'

The Provost Sergeant stood tall and rigid, his fly buttons taking in the scene with anticipation, shaming the 'whites' of the cooks with his accoutrements. While the Cook Sergeant, wise in the ways of doctoring tea, but uneasy in the face of radical ideas, relaxed inside his vest with noticeable relief.

'Man won't eat his dinner, Provost Sergeant,' he reported.

'Man won't eat his dinner?' repeated the Provost Sergeant, in amazement, twirling his stick and pointing as he marched forward. 'This man?'

'Yes, Provost Sergeant,' said the cook, licking a spot of gravy off his tattoo.

'Eat your fucking dinner!' demanded the Provost Sergeant, addressing of course the vegetarian.

'I'm sorry,' said the young crank, standing to attention. 'I don't eat meat.'

'Don't eat meat?' repeated the Provost Sergeant, blankly.

'What's the matter, Provost Sergeant?'

This was the Officer of the Day, coming in to ask if everything was all right. He wore a red sash, like we did at Mrs Dooley's when playing team games with the bean bags, and took in the situation at a glance. 'Some kind of problem?'

'Man won't eat his dinner, sir!' shouted the Provost Sergeant, whipping his stick under his arm and crashing to the salute.

'Won't eat his dinner?' repeated the officer, unable to believe his ears, staring at the vegetarian.

'No, sir. Says he don't eat meat!'

'Don't eat meat?' said the Officer of the Day. 'Is this true?'

'Yes, sir!'

'I was asking him,' said the Team Leader, standing in front of the vegetarian. 'Is that correct? You won't eat your dinner?'

'Yes, sir. I won't eat meat. But I'll eat mashed potatoes and jam tart.'

'Mashed potatoes and jam tart?' said the officer, with a curl of his lip, stepping forward to regard the cooling plateful of braised liver. 'Is this yours?'

'No, sir,' said the Cook Sergeant. 'His.'

'I was talking to him,' said the officer, showing I thought a commendable calm. No doubt they were taught to handle situations like this at Sandhurst. Removing one chocolate-brown glove, he held out an open palm, like a surgeon awaiting an instrument; and the Cook Sergeant placed a fork in it. With the edge of this, the officer sliced off a well-done piece of offal, speared it and carried it to his mouth. We watched intently, it being the first time most of us had seen an officer eat.

'Very nice, Cook Sergeant,' said the Officer of the Day. 'Very nice indeed.'

'Thank you, sir,' said the Cook Sergeant, holding out a bowl for him to spit in.

'Now, let's have no more of this nonsense,' said the officer, wiping his mouth delicately and turning to the vegetarian. 'Come and eat up your lovely liver.' Holding out a whole cross section of a pig's filtering system on the fork, he waved it slowly and temptingly.

'They'll have to charge him,' whispered Croxley, as the vegetarian shook his head, eyes turned upwards and his mouth tight shut.

'Fucking shoot him!' muttered Ron, from behind the sepia pages of *Picturegoer*. He had nothing against vegetarianism, but, like the rest of us, was sorely in need of his dinner.

'Right!' exclaimed the officer, his patience exhausted. He handed back the fork to the Cook Sergeant, who detached the lovely liver and put the fork in a weak solution of Milton until the following day. 'Put him on a charge, Provost Sergeant.'

'Sir!' said the Provost Sergeant, letting out his breath

with pleasure. Two of the squeegee men were called in as escort, before and behind, and off went the vegetarian.

'I'll have that one!' said Ron, as the queue began to move again, grabbing the plate with the tepid but double portion.

But I was more thoughtful, not having realised that one could be charged for declining to eat one's dinner. I went hot and cold at the thought I had been toying with all morning; of politely refusing my custard.

Conduct prejudicial to good order and military discipline; refusal to obey an order; dumb insolence; wanking in the army's time – for he had earlier turned his head away from the adulterated tea. The list of charges to be brought against the vegetarian was almost endless, according to Kitchener. He was unable to go into more detail, having the lavatories to finish cleaning, but he thought it unlikely that the youth would be tied over the muzzle of a gun.

None the less, though liking my meat as much as the next man, I was pleased to see him the next morning.

Hut Number One ('The Daredevils' we had chalked over the door) were out on the square, about to march up and down, and I had been selected as 'right marker'. The Corporal had done this to atone for a jape he had carried out that morning. Tiptoeing in amongst the sleeping Daredevils he had taken my bed to pieces; with me still in it. As I marched out onto the hallowed tarmac, fists rising level with my braced shoulders, arching my brows to prevent my beret slipping over my eyes, I thought back to an earlier time; to the day when – in smaller boots, and with a cap buttoned under my chin – I had crossed the market square towards Mossies' on my return from school. As I stood alone, ramrod straight, awaiting the Corporal's command that would bring my comrades hurrying to join me, fists to shoulders, shuffling into line, I caught sight of the vegetarian.

Silhouetted against the sky, he ran round the battlements in full kit. Rifle held high over steel helmet and large pack, small pack and ammunition pouches, full water bottle, gas cape and bayonet. After each circuit of the wall, he would hurry down the steep steps and run on the spot painted outside the guardroom, bringing his knees up high, shouting out, 'I must eat up my dinner.' Then, at a tap of the Provost Sergeant's stick, he would climb back and run round the wall again. Though it was said that he was allowed to vary the monotony by going the other way. To show that he was not being persecuted for his beliefs, there were other wrongdoers marking time by the geraniums, all dressed as if slogging up to Arras. Some were shouting that they were 'Shit on the doorstep'; while others chanted in chorus: 'I must learn to leave it alone.'

'Eat up your dinner' was, I suppose, the moral of that story. And your custard as well. I thought about it, as we learned how to turn round all together. But then, after our mid-morning snack of bread pudding and doctored tea, came the moment I had been waiting for. The interview with the Personnel Selection Officer, known as 'the PSO', who turned out to be none other than the officer of the previous day, the one who had done his best to tempt the vegetarian.

'Do sit down,' he said, waving to a folding chair, opening my dossier before him on the desk. Lighting a pipe that was, like his stick, wrapped in leather, he said: 'Now then,' with a smile through the smoke, waving his Swan Vesta: 'Cork, isn't it?'

'Yes, sir,' I said; wondering if, as it seemed to be an informal interview, it would be all right for me to light up the last of my Passing Clouds.

'The chap who asked about the ointment.'

'Yes, sir.'

So they had been talking about me in the mess!

Actually Kitchener, after he had finished the lavatories, had shown me the prophylactic room. Screened by a bush, at the rear of the guardrom, it had been locked, a notice telling one to apply to the Provost Sergeant for the key. I had decided to wait until a real need arose before doing so.

'Well,' said the PSO. 'the purpose of this interview is to find out something about you. To find out what you'd like to do. So that I can decide what's best for you. Is that all right? You do understand what I've said?' I said that I did, and leaned forward attentively.

'I see that you're a county man,' he said, reading the form I had filled in.

'Yes, sir.' I mentioned Uncle Frank's application to be High Sheriff of Lincoln; explaining that he had died before it was sorted out.

'Really?' he said, relighting his pipe, having been so impressed he had forgotten to suck. 'Your father's in trade, I understand?' he went on, and I agreed. We were Northern Manufacturers, I told him; and when I took over I was going into knickers as soon as possible. After a decent interval of course.

'Of course,' he said, the match burning his fingers. 'You mean, you are on the board?'

I nodded, looking modestly down at the coconut matting. I knew that however unprepared he was to find a company director on the folding chair, his reaction would differ from that of the Corporal, who had said that the only board he could imagine me on was the one on which, in his words, 'The monkey fucked the duck.' Relaxing and crossing my legs, showing him the two shillings I had invested in lead weights, I handed him the photograph that Mrs Farrer had taken, the one of me wearing my hat on the fire escape.

While he stared at it, I chatted of my time at Traggets. I thought it possible that he might himself have been an Old Traggetian, which would of course have helped enormously. But it turned out, to my utter amazement, that he had never heard of the school. Quite frankly, I began to doubt the man's background.

'Do you read?' he asked, turning over a page in the file.

'Yes, sir,' I said. There was a silence. Through the window I could see the vegetarian pass along the battlements.

'What kind of books do you read?' he asked, drumming his fingers on the blotter.

'Mainly Clausewitz, sir,' I said. I had gone to the library, over the museum, to ask for him, to look up a good quote; but Kitchener, who did that job as well, had said he was out.

'Clausewitz, eh?' the officer said. 'And Wittgenstein?'

'Yes, sir,' I said. 'Him as well.' Anyone who didn't know his prep schools was hardly likely to catch me out.

'I see,' he said, writing something down, then moving a paper over it so that I couldn't see. 'What about sport? You play any games?'

'Yes, sir,' I said. I was looking at a poster behind him, showing the joys of serving with the Military Police. Two sun-bronzed figures in splendid hats, mounted on khaki horses and smiling benignly, held pennanted lances against a bright blue sky.

'What games do you play?' he asked, loudly. In some way I had unsettled him; probably by exposing him as unlikely to have been to a decent school.

'All kinds of games, sir,' I said, knowing that fitness was one of the things they were looking for. I told him of my regular walks with Bernard along the banks of The Drain. 'He's going into the navy,' I said.

'Is he?' he said. 'I meant team games.'

'Not since school, sir,' I had to admit; going on to tell him about the bean bags.

'The bean bags?' he enquired, after a short silence.

'Yes, sir.'

He got up and opened the window, because of all his smoke. 'The bean bags,' he said again, his back to me.

'Yes, sir.' Of course I knew that they didn't have bean bags in the army; at least not in my regiment. I couldn't understand why he went on about them. Sitting down again at his desk, he wrote something in my file, with a flourish, then closed it.

'What did you want to be?' he asked, looking at his watch.

'You mean in the army, sir?' I grinned, having almost said, 'You mean when I grow up?'

'Yes,' he said, starting to clean out his pipe. 'The British army.'

I grinned again at his joke, then even more broadly as I recalled the words pencilled on the wall of the waiting room: 'Toodle oodle oodle oo, they're looking for monkeys in the zoo; if I had a face like you, I'd join the British army.'

'I'd like to be a subaltern, sir,' I said; first wiping the smile from my face, then adding, 'please.'

He scraped the black stuff out of his pipe with a pearl-handled penknife, onto a buff form, then shook it into the waste paper basket. Then he blew through the empty pipe, in my direction.

'You mean you'd like to be a batman?'

'No, sir,' I said. Grandidge had been one of those. 'Not a batman, sir. An officer.' I was tempted to add 'Like you', but decided against it. I smiled at him, frank and open, like one more than willing to soak in walnut juice at the word of command.

'What makes you think that you'd like to be an officer?' he asked, finding something interesting in the bowl of his pipe. 'The prospect of ordering men about?'

'Not only that, sir,' I said, not liking to mention the greenish shirts, with epaulettes and breast pockets, and of course the stick.

'Well,' he said, suddenly, after staring at me for a moment, assessing me. 'Thank you very much. Would you send the next man in?'

I said that I certainly would; and at the double. At the doorway I hesitated, clearing my throat to catch his attention.

'Yes?' he said, looking up from his pipe. 'It's not about

the ointment, is it? It's really not my province, you know.'

'No, sir,' I said. 'The bean bags.'

'The bean bags?' he said quietly. 'Yes?'

'I don't think I told you I was team leader.'

'No,' he said. 'No, I don't think you did.'

'The blues,' I said. Not that it was important.

'The blues, eh?' he said. 'Well, thank you very much.'

'Not at all, sir,' I said, my hand at the salute as I closed the door.

'They're going to let me know,' I told Ron, when I rejoined the Daredevils, who were still marching up and down.

'And me,' he said. 'Two three four,' as we turned round and marched back the way we had come. Ron thought his chances were pretty good, and told me that stars of The Army Film Unit were automatically given rank, to enhance their authority, like doctors, Vicars and the military police. So we were both feeling rather pleased with ourselves as we ate our lunch, and looking forward – at least in my case – to an academic afternoon. No less than two lectures, by the Medical Officer and the Chaplain.

The Padre, as he liked to be called, (along with the customary 'sir' of course), was on first.

'What I want to talk to you about this afternoon,' he said, half sitting on a table and dangling a brown boot, showing that this was to be a pretty informal affair: 'Is – are – the opportunities that have been presented to you by your period of service.' He paused, wrinkling his eyes to see if there was any comment; but as both the Jew and the vegetarian were absent, there was only respectful silence.

'Firstly, then,' he went on, 'I want you to regard these barracks as a school.' His lips twitched, showing that he realised how provocative – even waggish – he was being. 'A school,' he said, 'with the Commanding Officer as headmaster, the officers as housemasters, and the non-commissioned officers as groundsmen, cricket professionals, fencing coach – you know the kind of thing. All right?'

On my usual folding chair in the front row, I met his smile with a nod. I liked the analogy with a prep school, but was having difficulty in placing the Corporal and the Provost Sergeant. Traggets, whether the chap who couldn't cope with his pipe had heard about it or not, would have treated vegetarians in a more liberal manner.

'Out there,' said the Padre, pointing to the window, 'is the quod.' There was the scraping of chairs, as everyone tried to have a look.

'Where, sir?' asked Croxley, but the fighting clergyman (who wore wings) was not to be interrupted.

'In the Admin block,' he said, still pointing. 'In the Pay Office, you will find the Bursar. In the Medical room,' his finger moved a vague compass point, 'you will find the . . . ?' He waited for the answer, his mouth open and his other hand cupping his ear.

It came from an unexpected quarter. Ron, whom I would not have thought to be interested in religion said, loudly, 'Medical Officer.'

'Very good!' said the Padre, smiling and nodding at him. Then the twinkle returned, and he wagged a finger. 'Not to be called Matron!' Somebody laughed at the back of the room, and we all turned round to see who it was.

'In fact,' went on the man of the khaki cloth, becoming serious, 'we can extend this example to the whole nation. So that His Majesty the King becomes Headmaster; Sir Stafford Cripps becomes Bursar; and the outposts of Empire become houses, with gentlemen like Mr Smuts and Mr Mackenzie King as housemasters.'

As they say, there is a tide in the affairs of men; and I took it at the flood, rising to my feet and holding up my hand.

'No, you can't,' said the Chaplain. 'You only congregate in there and smoke. You can wait like everyone else.'

'Sir,' I said, not to be denied, 'we could take the whole

302

world as a school. With Mr Trygvie Lie as the Headmaster, and all the countries of the United Nations as houses.'

He stared at me, picking his nose, as did everyone else (stare at me I mean, not pick their nose) and I thought I would stay behind after the lecture and give him the Rev Eli Wannamaker as a reference. It could well lead to a flying start at Sandhurst. Then Ron rose to his feet beside me.

'Sir,' said Ron, 'we could take the whole universe as a school. With God as the Headmaster, and all the planets as houses.'

A chair scraped, and out of the corner of my eye I saw Croxley stand up, licking his lips.

'Be very careful what you say,' said the Padre, in a level voice.

'Can we have the window open, sir?' asked Croxley, still anxious to see the quod.

'No,' said our spiritual adviser, decisively. 'You may not!' He put on his hat, tucking his stick under his arm and pulling on his gloves. Pleased that I had made my mark, I sat down; followed by Ron and the anxious Croxley.

'Are there any questions?' asked the Padre, facing us with the door open, duty getting the better of him.

There were no questions. Those that had watches looked at them. It had all gone much quicker than we had expected.

'Right!' said the Medical Officer, or Matron as we had been told to think of him. 'Sit up, shut up; and let's get on with it!' He took a deep breath, swelling his smart shirt. 'Crabs!' he announced; as one might begin, 'I must go down to the seas again.' At a snap of his fingers the lights went out, and on the screen on the wall appeared a lavatory seat, tastefully shot from above by The Army Film Unit.

'You've all read the poem,' said the MO in the darkness, referring of course not to the opus by J. Masefield, but to the one he recited in his Scots brogue: 'It does nae guid to stand on the seat, the crabs in here can jump six feet.'

I have to admit that most of us thought this an improvement on the theory that all societies were like a prep school.

After the film had ended, with the badge of Ron's regiment filling the screen (and it had been strong stuff, hardly the kind of supporting programme that Captain Drew would have booked into the Pavilion De Luxe), the Medical Officer came straight to the point.

'I'll come straight to the point,' he said, rapping his snake-entwined stick on the table. 'Crabs are one thing. In fact ye could call me an expert on crabs.' He paused, obviously feeling the same about these as the vegetarian did about cows and sheep. The light now being on, his sharp Celtic eyes moved over us, possibly looking for his speciality. 'But I dinna want ony mon saying to me that he caught anything else frae a lavatory seat! Or a telegraph pole! I've heard it all before, ye ken!'

You really could have heard a pin drop. The only sound was of Croxley scratching under his arm.

'If ye've been wi' a lassie in the toon,' went on the MO, 'ye report to the Provost Sergeant,' (this with a great rolling of his Rs), 'and sign the wee book. And then what do ye do?'

Hand on Ron's shoulder, my chair falling over with a crash, I scrambled to my feet, unable to contain myself. 'The ointment, sir!' I cried.

'Very guid,' he said, nodding towards me. 'The ointment, as the laddie says.' I elbowed Ron in delight, nodding back to the Captain, and taking out my propelling pencil to write it down at once.

He nodded again to me later on, remembering me, when we were touring an exhibition set up in an adjoining room.

'Is that it, sir?' I asked, stopping before an iron gadget, something like an egg whisk.

'Aye,' said the crab expert. 'That's it. Yon's The

Umbrella. A fearsome beastie!' We formed a small circle round him while he demonstrated its use.

'It goes up your Hampton,' he began, then paused as our mouths fell open. 'Did ye think it went in your ear?' He started again. 'Ye put it in like this, ye see – then ye open it!' The scraping edges sprang out as he touched a lever. 'And then – ye pull it – *doon!*'

He went through the motions with what I can only call pleasure on his face; as if a Gordon Highlander stood before him with his kilt raised. We were, quite frankly, appalled; a groan like the Red Army Choir filling the room. There was a rush for the door and the fresh air, many people holding themselves like Girl Guides; while from behind us came the callous laughter of Matron.

Chapter Nine

'Wake up, Ron!' I said, shaking him, lifting the beret off his face. 'You'll miss it!'

I should really have roused him in time to see the two wooden painters and decorators in a field. What would he say if he now missed the Nabisco factory? Cleaning the windows with sleeves and handkerchiefs, people craned their necks and held up their children to see the famous factory for the first time. I had of course seen it before, twice, and though far from blasé my eyes followed the road I had travelled along with Chas, searching for a pinnacle of the Reals' house. But all was hidden by trees in leaf. Then there was a ragged cheer along the length of the train as the factory came into sight; several people lowered their windows and waved.

'Did you see it?' I asked Ron, turning to him excitedly.

'Yes,' he said, his boots still on the seat opposite, the beret settling again over his face.

It was five weeks since, as soft and somewhat naive civilians, we had passed through the wicket gate of Swine-hurst Barracks. We were now hardened soldiers, trained almost to a hair's breadth; able to turn round together on the move as one man. Our passing-out parade was only a week away – for all of us that is except for the vegetarian, who had missed so much, because of his tours of the battlements, that he was having to start all over again. As the band played, the shampooed goat chewed, the Commanding Officer saluted and Kitchener waved from the museum window, we would march off to glory. Or, in the case of Ron and myself, Elstree and Sandhurst respectively.

This weekend was our first leave, from after Saturday morning duties to midnight on Sunday; and I had agreed to spend it in London. To meet Clark Gable, and nurses in black stockings and gaberdine raincoats, who were, according to Ron, 'avid'.

We had risen early that morning, to prepare for the weekly inspection. The night before we had cleaned out the fireplace, scrubbing the hearth with a toothbrush in the traditional way, then painting white lines on a scarlet background to simulate bricks. After cleaning the windows and washing the walls, shaving the broom handles, black enamelling the fire irons, painting the bed ends and the fire buckets and changing the water, we had each trimmed our soap to the regulation size with a razor blade. Then we had polished the studs on the soles of our boots, blacking in between and attempting to raise a patina on the instep. To save time in the morning, we had stacked the three biscuits of our palliasses, sandwiched like a liquorice allsort with our meticulously folded bedding; then spread Mansion polish under and around our beds, before rolling ourselves in our gas capes and going to sleep on the floor.

As dawn came over the battlements, we buffed up our buttons and folded our overcoats, packing them with cardboard so that they stood wasp waisted, beside the bed. After polishing the brass and assembling our freshly blancoed webbing, we then squared off the corners of our packs, having passed the set square round the room in comradely fashion. Then, having pulled oiled flannel through our rifles, we began to lay out our kit. Best boots at the front of course, then gym shoes, the soles blackened, but leaving white the maker's diamond; the laces ironed and coiled, the metal tips burnished. Next the blue, knee-length PT shorts, and the pullover, its arms crossed in memory of an earlier Colonel who had slipped beneath the waves at Salamanca. Three and a half inches to the right, the scoured and Brasso'd mess tin in which the inspecting officer would expect to see his face. With crossed knife and fork, surmounted by custard spoon and mug, which had been steeped in bleach to remove the stains of tannin and chemical additives.

Now the housewife; the tapes bleached and ironed flat, the bobbins of thread to either side of crossed needles, with the spare buttons formed up as the square at Inkerman. Then the shirts and socks, the spare vests and pants, all folded the correct way, showing a stain-free crutch and in perfect line down the room. We checked that with a long piece of string.

There was a certain satisfaction to be gained from all this, and working with a will I had finished by half past eight. This had meant my missing breakfast, but gave me time to shave (which I was now having to do every day). I was drying and trimming my shaving brush, about to balance it in the centre of my face flannel, when the Corporal marched in, waggish to the end, and tipped everything all over the floor.

I told the officer, who came in with his stick and his team leader's sash five minutes later, that I had overslept. The Corporal, who was shouting out for us to stand by our beds, fixed me with a beady eye.

' 'E's got a bad back, sir,' he said, now one pace behind the officer. 'Can't get it off the bed.' It was a joke.

'Can't get it off the bed?' repeated the officer, who didn't look much older than Bernard. He stared down at me as I knelt with an apologetic smile, attempting to refold my underpants.

'And 'e wanks, sir,' confided the Corporal, behind his hand; but I heard him and made a mental note to remonstrate with him later. All this could have a serious impact on my career.

'Wanks?' repeated the officer, whose father was probably in the War Office. He took a step backwards, holding tight to his stick, as the Corporal demonstrated with a rapid jerking of his hand; as if pulling on the grip of a cricket bat. Shaking his head sadly, quite obviously another one who had not been educated at Traggets, the officer moved along to have a look at himself in Ron's mess tin.

'I would have cut his head off, and stuffed it up his arse!' said Ron later, referring to the Corporal of course, as we hurried between the white-painted lines to the guardroom. I smiled, appreciating his sense of humour, saluting the CO as he came out of his office, though I wasn't sure he could see me at that distance.

'No,' said Ron, an hour later, 'as you were. I'd stuff *his* head up the Corporal's arse!' He was referring this time to the Provost Sergeant. We were in what Kitchener and Croxley called 'the karzy', sharing a cigarette to calm our nerves before asking again for our weekend pass.

'Do you think you can leave 'ere,' our old friend had enquired the first time, 'with your arse 'anging out?'

'No, Provost Sergeant,' we replied in unison, having learnt enough to trot away at once, shouting out that we were a disgrace to the regiment. After half an hour in the canteen, which was full of people who had given up and were going to bed for the weekend, we tried again. As we approached the guardroom, swinging our fists shoulder high, we heard the 12.30 tram rattle past on its way to the Central Station.

'Go 'ome?' cried the Provost Sergeant. 'Looking like that?' I blushed for both of us, staring straight ahead at the pick-axe handles on the guardroom wall. Surely Ron must have noticed that one of his laces was an inch longer than the other!

But, finally, our luck changed. While the Provost Sergeant was in the prophylactic room, checking his stock before the busiest night of the week, his deputy was kind enough to take ten cigarettes, rather than keep us hanging about.

Now we were in the Home Counties, golf courses

flashing past, fast approaching what used to be called The Great Wen. I stared across at the sleeping Ron, then opened my suitcase. Moving aside a towel, a clean khaki vest and a tube of the ointment (purchased from Kitchener), I took out a small and a large paper bag.

The white lanyard looked smart against my box-pleated jacket, as I slipped it under my shoulder strap and fastened the end to the button on my breast pocket. I would get a whistle at Selfridges. Looking again at Ron, to see if he was still asleep, I opened the large bag and took out the hat. It bore the brass badge of the Second Foot, and I had already stiffened the front with the wire from the brush factory. After breathing on and rubbing up the rampant goat, I put it on and pressed the peak against my nose. My head back against the horsehair cushion, I saw myself reflected on the ramparts of Corfe Castle.

'Oh, dear me!' said Ron, the beret slipping off his face. 'How are you, General?'

I smiled at him, fixing the brass letters on my shoulders, and the crossed rifles of a sniper to my sleeve. At the bottom of the bag, on elastic, I had whitened stripes; but I thought it prudent to leave these until later.

'All you need is a stick,' said Ron. Dispassionate is, I think, the word for the way he was looking at me.

'A cane,' I corrected him. 'Not a stick, sir – a cane,' the man in Horne Bros had said; though declining to sell me one – with a pair of pips and a brown leather belt – unless I brought a note.

After more witticisms, all of which I took in good part, Ron fell asleep again, quoting under his beret lines from a film, asking me to stay as I was and never change. Waiting a moment, and after walking my fingers lightly up his thigh, I took out from the back of my pay book the cardboard portrait of the Hon Wendy. The one she had pressed into my hand the evening we had parted. Though I knew that Ron carried a sepia Anna May Wong in his Rexine wallet, I doubted that he would understand.

310

The new penny and the Japanese water flowers had of course long since gone; but this I had always carried with me. Even during the episode in the chicken run, the lovely Hon Wendy had been there. (It had been the reason I had not opened my wallet, not wishing to expose her to Rosemary in such circumstances; and why I had therefore refrained from using the Corinthian fleet.) Looking at her now, I heard again the servant's gramophone playing: 'I know why you're crying, I know why you're blue', and the chicken shit expanding in the bag on top of the car. While I held her beside my right ear, so that we were both reflected in the Cornish landscape, she seemed to nod graciously with approval; though of course it was just the movement of the train.

Ron stirred, mumbling something about Vivien Leigh, so I tucked the Hon Wendy away, next to the pink and black packet I had borrowed from her stepson. Not enough to stop an enemy bullet, perhaps, but one day . . . in Soho or Mayfair . . . 'Jeffrey!' Even the French maid, walking behind with the dogs, would be radiant. 'Hon Wendy!' Halting my men, crisply, on the right foot, ordering them to 'Stand easy' and not to look – taking her perfumed elbow, looking into her blue eyes, as a flunkey unlocked the door to a private dining room . . . with pink chaise longues, where the food was left outside the door with a discreet cough . . . Taking down my trousers, I sighed as I began to add extra lead around my ankles.

But Soho, strangely enough, is where we found ourselves later that evening. After walking down Wardour Street, Ron pointing out the offices of the film companies, saying that if they had been open he would have gone in and made himself known, we had stopped at a window to admire a slowly revolving Olivia de Havilland.

'They put glycerine in their eyes,' I said, having read that in his *Picturegoer*, and Ron agreed; saying that it was a hard life, but it was the only thing he wanted to do. He then told me a rumour concerning Miss de Havilland, which, if true, put her on a par with Doris Allerdyce. Her with the mauve court shoes.

We were looking, of course, for the Savoy Hotel, where we knew Clark Gable and The Three Stooges stayed when in London. Ron said there was no hurry, as all the best people would be dining at this time. So we went into a restaurant in the Charing Cross Road. After dinner, said Ron, if I didn't fancy Clark Gable, we could either look around for some nurses or go to The Bag of Nails, an underground night club recommended by his father.

I doubted that we could afford an underground night club, or that they would let us in wearing boots. But I said nothing as I helped myself to more Daddies Sauce; something conspicuous by its absence at the home of the Second Foot. Ron, as if sensing my doubt, explained that no one would allow us to pay for anything. We were in uniform, and so far as they knew responsible for saving them all from Nazi tyranny. 'And,' he added, 'when we're introduced, call me Melvyn.'

'Melvyn Brackenbury?' I asked, nudging him to observe a man looking at us, possibly about to send over a pot of tea and insist on paying our bill.

'Yes,' said Ron, smiling at the man as he wiped his plate with his bread. 'Like Melvyn Douglas. Haven't you noticed the resemblance?'

Of course I said that I had, deciding to be Alan (Ladd), whom I respected for his quiet good manners and manliness. The man who had been looking at us then left, with a woman who came out of the lavatory, and we decided that we should look for a bed. We could always, said Ron, come out and walk about after we had registered.

I had been thinking about this. Not the coming out and walking about, but the cost of a hotel. I recalled Bernard's briefing on how expensive they were, even for a short time; and the obligatory tip to the bellboy. London hotels, I realised, were unlikely to be cheaper than Troon. So I was pleased to be able to produce from my pocket a leaflet that had been handed to me by a religious maniac as we got off the train. Agreeing that we were not likely to run into Clark Gable, let alone The Three Stooges, in the Holy Ghost Hostel, I said that it was certain to be cheaper, and probably more informal, than the Savoy.

'He's probably in bed now, anyway,' said Ron, explaining that film stars began work very early in the morning. They had to be made up, ready with glycerine in their eyes, before Rockfist Rogan jogged out of the bakery in his vest.

'We can see him tomorrow,' I assured him; privately thinking Clark Gable somewhat over-rated and flashy. Adding that we could also go to Hyde Park. Ron maintained that Hyde Parke seethed with nurses on a Sunday.

So by half past ten – early of course for The Great Wen, but we had had little sleep the night before – we arrived at the Holy Ghost Hostel, just as they were closing the doors.

'Posh!' exclaimed Ron, pulling his mouth down, rather overwhelmed I think by the fine exterior of what had been a London town house.

'Port out, starboard home,' I told him, pointing out the Doric portico and the pole for the family flag. But, unfortunately, the Holy Ghost people having entertained the forces for the duration of the war, the interior was something of a disappointment.

'Here,' I said, stopping by a marble head which had no nose, but wore an airman's forage cap, 'would be a gadrooned silver tray, on which you left your card.'

'Syph!' said Ron, pointing to the missing nose. He then adopted a pious expression as we passed beneath the dangling feet and entered the hall.

This, beneath the handsome ceiling, was a mass of khaki and shades of blue; soldiers, sailors and airmen, all wanting to lie down cheaply. Crowded together, they stared into what had once been a ballroom, and was now, its gilt and cherubim covered with pea-green paint, a dormitory.

Where the doors had been there was now a chain; and behind this, mounted on a harmonium in the aisle between the beds, the religious maniac from King's Cross pedalled and led the singing. What we took to be his wife, in an overall and a hat, moved amongst us in the hall; stretching her neck to smell our breath, to make sure we were giving voice. Those found to be drunk, or silent, or mouthing rude versions of the hymns, were expelled through a side door by a big religious helper. We then had prayers, led by the organist, who revolved towards us on his stool. His eye fixed on Ron, who was at the front and had been singing loudly, he shouted for Him to look after the King and Queen and the two Princesses; not forgetting those set in authority over us. Then, when we were expecting an urn of cocoa to be wheeled forward, the chain was let down and we were allowed in; one to a bed, as the wife kept shouting.

'I don't know about you,' said Ron, indistinctly because the camp bed had collapsed around him like a cigarette rolling machine, 'but I'm in the Savoy next time!'

I agreed. The Savoy might well be expensive, especially by the hour, but with guests of the stature of Clark Gable and The Three Stooges, religion would surely be kept to a minimum. Sitting on my bed, I wondered if I should take my clothes off. I was tired, mainly because of the weight of the lead around my ankles, and concerned that Sandy Macpherson was going to play on through the night. But no. After a final lullaby, and a certain amount of badinage with two sailors, he locked the harmonium and covered it with a black cloth.

I fell asleep in my hat, the leather band under my chin to deter pilferers, dreaming of waltzing with the Hon Wendy to the strains of Rock of Ages. Only to wake at dawn, not knowing where I was, and to find Ena Baga rousing us with a religious medley. Ron, who was not musical, said that no film star who stayed there would be late on the set. I had to free him from his bed, so he could get his trousers on, in case the wife came round shouting, 'Hands off cocks!' etc.

We then went out into a yard, to wash under a tap, though Ron warned everyone that it was probably some kind of baptismal ceremony. Morning tea, again according to Ron certain to be heavily doctored, was after hymns in the hall and another address from the resident organist. So most of us, though having nothing against religion, left.

We found that, like Swinehurst, there is very little going on in London on a Sunday morning. Though we did catch sight of a horse and cart delivering Twinings Tea. I waved to the bowler-hatted driver, plaid rug across his knees, who civilly raised his whip in reply.

'Where've you lads been?' enquired a rubicund police-man, who was trying door handles in the Strand.

'We,' said Ron, who had surprised me by changing into his cavalry twill and sports jacket, 'have spent the night with the Holy Ghost. And his band.'

We heard the policeman chuckling behind us, his cape thrown back as he wrote it down with an indelible pencil. I imagined him telling a plump cook, as he wolfed her pies, 'The 'Oly ghost and 'is band!' and her big bosom heaving with mirth; until they were interrupted by the bell ringing for tea and toast, and she had to get off his lap.

By half past seven we were crossing a bomb site towards Ludgate Hill, with the same thought in mind. Tea, two or three rounds of toast, with perhaps an egg and fried bread. All that, according to Ron, free to the needy in the crypt of St Paul's; with possibly bacon and something in the hand as we left, for veterans of the Eighth Army. Religious again, of course, possibly the odd chorus to be sung before you were fed; but no pea-green paint, or the wife in the overall and hat. As we walked, I looked around for Roman artifacts, which Bernard collected along with bullets. Ron was playing at film directing, using finger and thumb as a viewfinder. 'Action!' he cried, his hands now the clapper board, closing in front of his nose; but I wasn't listening. I had just set eyes on the Queen!

She was in an open carriage (very much like the one Yasmin rode in at Blackpool, when she ran away with the man in the RAF blazer), and was escorted by a troop of the Household Cavalry. I recognised them at once – as I did her, of course – having them at home in lead, though most of them with their heads held on by matchsticks. They were waiting for the traffic lights to change; and the Queen, there being no one else around, smiled at us as we climbed a low wall and stood on the pavement.

'Fuck me!' said Ron, and he can surely be forgiven. 'It's the Queen!' This was said sotto voce of course, so she was unable to hear; and I have never heard lip reading included among her many accomplishments. Not content with a smile, the Queen (and it really was her, with a white-fringed thing around her shoulders) graciously nodded towards us. The horse of the trooper nearest to me danced sideways, the way that horses do, then did its business right there in the road. In front of us, and of course in front of the Queen, who took it very well; probably having seen a lot of it before. The trooper stared ahead under his plume, the sun catching the sword in his white-gloved hand; obviously too embarrassed to look round.

'God save the Queen!' cried Ron, getting out his handkerchief, and I moved away from him; not so much because of the royalist fervour, but because of the state of his handkerchief. If this had happened a year or so earlier, before I had met Lillian Braithwaite, I would probably have shouted some slogan like 'God made the land for the people!'; and been cut down by the blade of the embarrassed trooper, anxious to make up for his animal's faux pas. As it was, I gave her a friendly wave and came to the salute; hoping that she might throw out a bag of gold. But of course she didn't, and I was told later that they never carry money.

'I didn't fancy yours!' said Ron (referring of course to

the Lady in Waiting), as the lights changed and the carriage rolled away like Twinings Tea.

We stood there, the proof that it had really happened still steaming in the road. It was an auspicious start to the day, so we abandoned the idea of the feed at St Paul's and headed for Hyde Park. Our luck was obviously in, and we wanted first pick of the nurses.

We were there by eight o'clock, having had a wash and brush-up on the way; but a man who seemed to take a fancy to Ron – offering him a position as kitchen porter – said that there would be no nurses yet for hours. For nostalgic reasons, seeing it for the first time since leaving Victory Cottage, I had bought *Reynolds News*, the Socialist Sunday paper, and settled down on a bench to read it, ignoring the man until he went away. Ron had gone for a stroll down Park Lane; on the lookout for Anna Neagle.

It was the first time I had ever been spoken to by someone on a horse. Not on a cart, or in a carriage, but actually astride one. So it was a moment or so before I realised where the voice was coming from. I had felt a waft of hot and fetid breath in my ear, but had assumed that the man had come back.

'Hello, Jeffrey,' the voice said, from mid air. 'It is you, isn't it?'

'Yes,' I said, looking around, then up, and seeing my mother.

She was in jodhpurs and boots, the full outfit that Lillian Braithwaite would be married and buried in, with a check jacket and white lace at her throat. Her hair, more blonde than I remembered, was pulled back and tied with a black ribbon.

'What on earth are you doing here?' she asked, as the horse nuzzled my paper, slavering over Hannen Swaffer.

'I'm on a visit,' I said. I couldn't get up because of the horse's face.

'How super!' she said. 'Were you going to surprise me?'

'Yes,' I said, folding up what was left of the paper. 'I

317

was just finishing the *Reynolds News*, then I was going to surprise you.'

To be quite honest, it had never crossed my mind. I was a little dazed. What with the religious medley, and then the Queen, and now her. And it wasn't yet nine o'clock. By giving the horse the paper to eat, I was able to stand up; so that she could reach down and pat the top of my hat.

'You look very sweet, darling,' she said. 'What are you?'

'I won't know until next Friday,' I told her. 'Then I might be a subaltern.'

'I say!' she said, and the horse showed its big yellow teeth, dancing sideways, so I stepped back hurriedly. When she had calmed it down, (calling it 'Colonel', believe it or not!) I told her that I was waiting for a friend. 'He's just gone for a stroll,' I said, without any mention of Anna Neagle. I didn't want her to think of us as licentious soldiery, on the lookout for you-know-what.

Then Ron came through the bushes, shouting that he thought he'd seen Herbert Wilcox getting onto a bus. There had been no sign of Anna Neagle. I said that she was probably making the most of the lie in, and introduced him to my mother, who he said later was 'the spit' of Greer Garson.

Ten minutes later, after taking back the horse, she returned, looking smaller on her feet, and rather odd with the inside of her thighs reinforced. Taking my arm, saying how much she liked my hat and the white string, she raised her smart leather riding crop to hail a taxi. Ron sat between us in the back, telling us that the studio sent an American car to pick up people early in the morning.

My mother lived in a block of flats in Maida Vale. These I naturally assumed to be council, her being on her own, and her solicitor always writing to Mr Rim about money. So I was surprised when the front door was opened by a man dressed like a night-club attendant. 'Good morning, madam,' he said as we crossed a marble hall; no prams or dustbins, only vases of gladioli. In the lift, Ron whispered that it was because London had a Labour council.

The flat was furnished and decorated in greys and greens, with crinoline ladies, a small chandelier, white carpets and little jars of violets. Making Ron comfortable in a green silk armchair, with an ashtray on a strap, so that he could watch for celebrities from the window, I followed my mother into the kitchen. Having taken off her riding habit she now wore what I think is called a twin set; a paler green than the armchair, with pearls and a clean white pinny.

It was not a kitchen that De Kuyper would feel at home in. The stove was electric, and there was a refrigerator containing butter, and a bottle of foreign wine. There was also a hatch in the wall, through which you could put the rubbish; accounting of course for there being no dustbins in the hall. The kitchen cabinet was painted daffodil yellow, and as my mother opened it I saw that it was crammed with tins of John West. She chattered brightly, but I was silent; partly because I had not seen her for so long, and because I was wondering whom she knew in Harrogate.

'We'll have chops,' she said, her face lit by the light inside the refrigerator; as it had been by the sun that day she had slept between the gnomes. 'Petits pois?' she enquired, looking at me with a smile.

'Little peas,' I translated, taking it that she was testing my French. I had determined in the taxi that though I would talk to her, eat with her, even take money from her, I would remain loyal to my father and Miss Parkinson; and I would show her that I had turned out well, despite being cast aside like an old glove. We sat at the kitchen table, and like Aunt Ada on my arrival at Victory Cottage she began with my size. 'You really are a big boy now, aren't you?' she said. Her lipstick was purplish, and she looked at me through spectacles on a gold chain.

'Yes,' I said, 'I am.' To tell the truth I was a little embarrassed. Sipping my sherry, I answered her questions about the family. She had heard about Yasmin's baby, and though I didn't know whether my sister had had a hard time, I was able to tell her that George was now so highly thought of that he was entrusted with Odsal, Wibsey, Idle and Cleckheaton. Victoria, I told her, named to commemorate the defeat of the Third Reich, didn't really look like anybody. My mother was pleased to hear that I had started at the bottom, saying 'How super!' and I showed her the photograph of me in the homburg hat. She held it up to the light, saying at once: 'Those are your father's feet!'

After a pause, I apologised for not spending more time with her at Yasmin's wedding; explaining that I had to see Elspeth to her bus. My mother said that she understood perfectly, with a grin that would never have crossed Mrs Miniver's face. Of course I became embarrassed again, bending over to adjust my weights, realising that she and the Colonel had probably known the darker recesses of the meat market well. She said she had left the reception as soon as Miss Parkinson had started to sing.

Still fiddling with my trousers, but determined on loyalty, on which I have always put a high price, I said that was a little unfair. Miss Parkinson was only an amateur, just doing it in her own time.

'How true,' murmured my mother, pouring more sherry for both of us. I then took a glass and a little mat in to Ron, who said that he had just seen Stewart Granger with a woman, to ask him if he wished to play Canasta or listen to 'Forces' Favourites'.

We had lunch at a round dining table with green candles, though my mother said that she didn't want them lit, thanking me and blowing them out. She coaxed Ron, who was cautious about exotic food, to try a little mint with his new potatoes; and produced for me, with a flourish from behind her back, a bottle of Daddies Sauce. There was a lump in my throat as we moved on to the Harrogate pineapple, with Carnation milk whipped up and topped by a sugar violet. I could see that Ron was impressed.

As we were leaving my mother slipped a ten-shilling note into my hand ('In case you meet any nurses'), and said that next time, when I was a subaltern, I must bring a brother officer; someone who was more at ease with herbs.

Not wishing to embarrass the night-club attendant by crossing his palm with too little, or too much, we walked down the steps, meeting on the way a man of the same type as the Colonel. He wore a short fawn overcoat, and carried a bouquet in cellophane. I nodded to him, but no more.

As the reader will doubtless know, the Savoy Hotel is a goodish walk from Maida Vale. We were of course strangers to the area, but eventually found it down a side street, behind a theatre. One of us, I must say, more excited than the other. Taking our position on the pavement, we waited for Clark Gable, Ron bending down and waving into all the cars as they came out.

By two o'clock, when there had been no sign of the ears and the striped suit – and I said he could hardly be in bed already, no matter how early they had to get up – I was keen to move on. We had, after all, the The Great Wen at our feet, and I wanted to go to Ellisdons, the firm that had been kind enough to post to me my cardboard abscess. Ron, though wanting to buy a Melvyn Douglas moustache, agreed reluctantly, maintaining that he'd just seen The Three Stooges in a Rolls-Royce. I pointed out that if what I had heard was true, that one had gone mad, another married, and the third died, this was unlikely.

We had originally intended, when planning our week-end – if we had the time that is, if Ron had not been asked to take a screen test by a talent spotter – to stand outside Buckingham Palace. But we both felt now that if the Queen looked out of the window and saw us again, she would think that we were following her. So we set off for the National Gallery, a place that Ron said was packed with nurses on a Sunday, all pretending to look at pictures, but with their minds only on one thing. It was while we were taking a short cut, in an alleyway off the Haymarket, that a lady said to us as we were passing – without so much as a 'Good afternoon' – that she would do us both for a pound.

Around the corner at the end of the alley, in a deep doorway, we discussed the offer. Risking a peep back, I saw that the lady was quite definitely not a nurse. Noticing me peeping, she smiled and made certain movements with her fingers. Waving, to show that no offence was intended, I hurriedly drew back out of sight.

'How about it?' said Ron, straightening his knitted tie. He was pale and breathing through his nose. 'Eh? If you will, I will.' His back pressed against the wall, he also took a quick peep, saying that one did not have to look at the mantelpiece while poking the fire. A little brusquely, I told him that I knew the proverb. What I wanted to know was if, when she said she would do us both for a pound, that meant ten shillings or a pound each. If the first, then it was undeniably reasonable; though I didn't think my mother had given me the ten-shilling note to spend in such a way. All things considered, I said that I really would prefer to wait for an avid nurse.

'I'll do you for a dollar, darling!' she said in her thick London accent, appearing suddenly round the corner and trapping us in the doorway.

She was a very big woman. A diamanté butterfly in her banana-coloured hair caught the sun, her lipstick touching both nostrils. She wore a trench coat – as Ron pointed out later, very similar to that worn by James Mason in 'Odd Man Out'. She opened it now, like the cloak of Mandrake the magician, blocking out the daylight and showing us in the dusk, with a heavy waft of Phul Nana, huge stockings held up by white straps and knickers embroidered with the Royal Warrant.

We stopped to catch our breath in the doorway of

Hamleys' toyshop; me pretending to look at teddy bears with a beating heart, while Ron looked back down Regent Street to see if she was following. Then, while lighting much-needed cigarettes, comparing notes while the memory was still fresh, we were trapped again.

'Wot you doin', then?' asked the military policeman. A vision in snow-white belt and gaiters, he must have had at least a pound and a half of lead in his trousers. His boots were beautiful, and he wore a real brown-handled revolver on his hip. His colleague, also with a white stripe of authority, and of course with the red top to his immaculate hat (which, according to Traggets legend, meant that their private parts rubbed free and disturbingly on the inside of their trousers), squinted under a peak as steep as the Eiger as he took out his notebook. I had heard that they always went around in twos; the theory being that at least one of them would be able to write.

'I'm just looking at the teddies,' I said, bending to see the price of one sitting in a little chair. I could hardly say that we were resting, having fled from a big woman who had exposed herself just off the Haymarket.

'Thank you, mate,' said the quick-thinking Ron, adopting one of his character voices, sucking hard at his Weight as if he had just stopped me for a light. With a friendly nod to all he attempted to leave, but was halted by a large hand, the sharp-eyed MP noticing that though in cavalry twill and sports jacket, he wore a khaki shirt. They were not fools.

I gave, I think, a good account of myself. Standing to attention, I explained that though, technically, I had not yet been assigned to a regiment, and therefore should not be wearing the hat and badge of the Second Foot – let alone the white string and the crossed rifles – there was more to it than that. They waited while I cleared my throat. Not only was I the scion of a county family, I pointed out, (having to spell the word 'scion' for them); a name still bandied about by the older residents of Rorke's Drift; but I was destined for the Royal Military Academy before the month was out. I looked at them hard at that point, intimating that our paths might well cross in the future. In other words, I said, though in their eyes I might appear to be 'dressed like a pillock', I was in fact showing what I would have thought was a commendable pride in my regiment: ie I was *with* them, if not yet officially *of* them. As I reached my peroration, the vision in white, obviously impressed, returned my pay book; having discovered and ogled the Hon Wendy with pursed lips. Behind me I could hear Ron denying that he was improperly dressed, saying that he wore boots only because he had forgotten to bring his suede shoes.

'It's been a good weekend!' he said later, with feeling, as we stood outside Ellisdons, the retailers of hairy ears. They were of course closed. The MPs, after labouring with their indelible pencils, had let us go; shouting for us to straighten up as we marched away towards High Holborn. I pointed out to Ron my cardboard abscess in the window, between the black face soap and the realistic fried bread, coated with bitter aloes. 'Laff, Laff, Laff!' it said on the card.

'A fucking good weekend!' repeated Ron bitterly, loudly enough to startle a man who was trying the door. Probably desperate for a rubber pencil, or a floating sugar cube, he gave up and walked away. 'Him on the organ last night!' went on Ron, 'and her with the knickers! And now we're in the shit!'

'And no Clark Gable,' I said, leaving the nurses out of it, agreeing with him that things could have turned out better.

We caught the six thirty train, getting us into Swinehurst in time for the last tram to the barracks. In a corner seat, on the side facing the Nabisco factory, I packed away my hat and white string, reflecting on how different it would all be when I was at Chelsea Barracks, or in the little hut outside the Palace.

'Hup, two three,' I murmured to myself, marching my company along the Mall, gaily waving my cane to debs out shopping for strawberries. ' 'E's a good 'un!' the men would say to each other, under their bearskins. ' 'E's a right card, 'e is!'

'What did you say?' asked Ron, lowering his *Film Fun*. Behind it he had been glueing on the David Niven moustache he had bought in Shaftesbury Avenue.

'Nothing,' I said. We stared at each other.

'It's not the same, is it?' he said.

'No,' I said. 'Not really.'

'I wish I'd gone home,' he said, putting his boots up on the seat. 'Him on the organ, and her with the knickers . . . !'

'Shut up!' I said, still feeling that The Great Wen had rather more to offer than we had found.

'We should have sent a note up to his suite,' said Ron, dropping his beret over his face.

Chapter Ten

That's what I quoted to my father a week later, when I was home on leave. 'We should have sent a note up to his suite,' I said. I was telling him about Ron, and our weekend in London; intending to lead up gradually to the meeting with you-know-who. He had grunted, possibly sympathetically, twiddling his thumbs and sucking a mint, as I explained about film stars having to get up early in the morning to have glycerine put in their eyes.

The past week had gone by in a blur of activity. It had been exciting, but had led to bitter disappointment.

On the Monday, more than making up for any adverse report the Royal Corps of Military Police had put in the post, I had again caught a tide in the affairs of men and risen in my folding chair. It was a lecture, under the auspices of the Army Bureau of Current Affairs – an outfit charged with reminding those reading *Film Fun* of the wider world around them – entitled 'Know Your Enemy'.

'Here he is,' said the officer, the one the same age as Bernard, who hadn't heard about wanking. With his cane he tapped the green part of the map, marked USSR. 'Have any of you any idea what the Kremlin's strategy is?'

'Cairo, capital of the wogs,' I began, turning sideways so that those at the rear of the room, the present-day Outhwaites as it were, could hear. 'If they get the pyramids and the Sphinx, we're in the . . . ' I hesitated, selecting an alternative.

'In the shit,' said Baby Face, somewhat surprisingly. 'Yes, indeed we are.' He was nodding, slowly and heavily, as Mr Pelham had done when Rufus first put forward this theory.

'Once they've got Cairo, and cut the canal, sir,' I said, 'they're down into the Red Sea, running amok in the Indian Ocean.' I took a deep breath, partly for dramatic effect.

'Thank you,' he said. 'What's your name?' But I raised my hand.

'The lifeline to India is threatened,' I concluded. 'Cork, sir. Jeffrey Cork. One nine one six double eight nine six.'

The educated Sergeant, the one who had written down our religions, sat next to him reading a Pelican book. He grinned at me and I smiled back, inclining my head.

That was Monday. Tuesday was taken up with putting the finishing touches to our marching up and down, in preparation for the passing-out parade. The goat was brought out for the final dress rehearsal, but was certainly not shampooed. Wednesday, because of the danger of becoming over-trained, we relaxed at another showing of the film 'The Lavatory Seat'. There was also the finals of the five-a-side football. (Daredevils 0, Hut Three 5; R. Rogan 1, Lewd Scot 3, Croxley og.)

Thursday was quite an exciting day, when we went into a field to fire live bullets. But Friday was a disaster. In the morning the eagerly awaited postings were pinned on the noticeboard, and as the others drifted away, Ron and I were left alone, staring at our shattered dreams.

If the reader was expecting – having heard of the perverse way in which the mind of the War Office works – that Ron was to go direct to Sandhurst, while I was to report to Anthony Asquith in his hut at Elstree – I grant you that would have been mildly amusing. As it was, Ron was posted to the Army School of Hygiene, Aldershot. While I, though promoted as a sop to the rank of Gunner, was to join the Royal Artillery at Dover Castle.

'You got two good 'uns,' said Kitchener, coming up behind us silently in his gym shoes. ' 'Igene,' he said, reaching between us and tapping the typewritten sheet with his lavatory brush. 'We didn't have that in my time.'

'I don't want hygiene!' said Ron, almost as upset as I was. 'What do I want hygiene for, when I'm going to be a film star?'

Kitchener attempted to comfort him. He had once escorted some infected mattresses to Aldershot, and waxed almost eloquent about the place. Except for many more squeegee men, marching about the dining hall behind a tidal wave – something you would expect in a place like that – the Harmy School of 'Igene had, he said, a lot to offer. For instance, he told Ron, there was a whole field full of 'karzies and pissholes'.

'Karzies and pissholes?' queried Melvyn Douglas loudly.

Kitchener nodded solemnly. (The visit had been the high spot of his long life, on a par with playing with the monkeys in the Mediterranean.) A whole field he told us, line upon line of field latrines and urinals, every known example of mobile bath house and delousing equipment. Officers were seconded, he said, lowering his voice, from foreign armies, just to come and see it. 'And filums,' he added.

'Filums?' asked Ron, his forehead against the green baize. 'What filums?'

Filums on scabies and ringworm, said Kitchener, and an animated short on crabs; recalling with a smile the double feature that had been showing when he was there. 'And you, mate,' he said, turning to me, his teeth moving about with envy, 'you might get to play with the fucking monkeys!'

'I don't want to play with the fucking monkeys,' I said, walking away and leaving them both. I wanted only to be by myself.

'What do you mean, you don't want to play with the monkeys?' said the Colonel, motioning to the Provost Sergeant that it was quite safe to leave us alone.

'Permission to speak, sir,' I said, when the sound of the boots had died away. I realised that I had not made a good start to the interview, being understandably distraught, and getting tangled up with the CO about Gibraltar. He of course thinking of the Lord Kitchener who had sunk beneath the waves, and me referring to the museum and lavatory custodian.

'Yes,' he said now, with a sigh, 'speak, Cork, by all means. What is it? You've cleared up the matter of the ointment, I take it?'

'Yes, sir,' I said. 'Thank you.'

'And your back?' he enquired. 'No more trouble with that?'

'No, sir,' I said, thanking him again.

'Well, what is it?'

'My commission, sir.'

He blew his nose on a civilian handkerchief, then revolved away from me in his chair. 'What commission, Cork?' he asked, talking to the wall.

'The King's Commission, sir,' I said, surprised that a man in his position should be so obtuse.

'The one you expected to be posted up in Part Two Orders this morning?'

'Yes, sir,' I nodded. 'That one.'

'Which wasn't there?'

'No, sir. It wasn't.'

'And you thought there'd been a mistake, in posting you to the Royal Artillery at Dover? And you're here now to straighten it out?'

'Yes, sir,' I said, having known all the time that he would understand.

'Sit down,' he said, revolving to face me again.

'Pardon, sir?'

'Sit down,' he repeated. 'Stand at ease, then stand easy, then pull up that folding chair and sit down. For two minutes, while I explain to you that you are not going to Sandhurst.'

329

'Where am I going, sir?' I asked when I had sat down, leaning forward eagerly.

'You're going to Dover,' he said. 'To the Royal Artillery, as you read this morning.' He opened a drawer in his desk, the one Edgar Lustgarten kept a loaded automatic in, taking out a little fruit pie in a box and throwing it into the waste paper basket. 'Did you really expect to become an officer, Cork?'

'Yes, sir,' I said, suspecting this to be an OCTU character test. Then I felt myself start to colour as he stared at me, realising that it was how my parents had stared at Uncle Frank across the breakfast table, when he had announced his intention of becoming High Sheriff of Lincoln.

He did a turn in his chair, taking his cane with him this time and playing with it. 'The fabric of our society,' he said, speaking quietly, almost gently for a soldier, 'is maintained by us all knowing our correct place; our station in life as it were. Do you understand that?' He went so far as to smile at me.

'Of course, sir.' I smiled back and quoted remembered lines from Mrs Dooley, about the rich man in his castle and the poor man at the gate.

'Absolutely,' the Colonel said, nodding. 'So there must be officers, and there must be men. You do see that?' He smiled again. 'It would be a jolly peculiar army composed entirely of officers, wouldn't it?' We grinned at each other across the desk, sharing the joke.

'You mean somebody's got to be the men, sir?'

'Absolutely,' he said.

'And I'm a men – a man – you know what I mean, sir.'

'I have never,' said the Colonel, playfully taking aim at me along his cane, 'seen a better example.'

'Thank you very much, sir,' I said.

'Thank *you*, Cork,' he said. There was a short silence as we stared at each other. I knew that if only Colonel Trewin had been more like him, I would have been more than happy to have been carried along to Number 17 with my mother's soft blue suitcase, making only a pretence at a struggle. My whole life would have been different.

'Sir,' I said at the door, 'I realise that there has to be officers and men – and as there are more men, they're probably more important – ' He gave a very slight nod. 'But what was it that stopped me being an officer, sir? Was it what the Corporal said?'

He had the telephone in his hand, just about to dial; possibly to speak to the War Office. 'What did the Corporal say?' he asked.

'You know, sir,' I said, embarrassed, then jerking my hand up and down as if pulling on the grip of a cricket bat. I did not like to say the word to him. 'What he said I did.'

'I don't know what he said that you did,' he said, putting down the telephone and shaking his hand in time with me, then faster, more as we used to shake an aspirin bottle full of milk at Mrs Dooley's, trying to make butter. 'But he didn't say it to me.' He stopped shaking his hand and laid it on his desk, holding it down with his cane. 'I can assure you, Cork, that any decision I came to was not influenced by what a Corporal said, or by anything you do, or do not do.' Freeing his hand he gave another little shake of the aspirin bottle. 'Or, for that matter,' and he moved a buff form across the blotter with the tip of his cane, 'by you appearing dressed like a pillock in Regent Street!'

'Thank you, sir,' I said, backing out and closing the door.

So to Saturday. The Passing-Out Parade. The sun already over the battlements in an immense blue sky as we packed our kit bags. A final cowboys' breakfast to sustain us for the journey, then a hurried round of farewells. Without his clipboard or his merry morning cry, the Corporal stood in the hut doorway to wish us God speed. He said that never, in all his experience, had he had an 'intake' like ours. I thought he had done his job to the best of his abilities, though I declined to put my loose change into his hat.

Then the stirring sound of the drums being tuned; the bleating of the goat as it was combed. A tremor of excitement in all our stomachs. Even Ron – who had drafted a letter to J. Arthur Rank the previous night, asking him to do what he could – even he smiled at me as we lined up, fist to shoulder, for the last time.

A roll of the side drums; the start of the beat of the big drum; a clash of the cymbals; and as the clock above the guardroom came to nine thirty, precisely, the band began to play. On the word of command, to our regimental march, shaved and pressed and gleaming, all in step, we emerged from behind the hut. 'Oh, 'tis my delight on a shiny night, in the season of the year . . . '

'Shut up!' hissed the Corporal, and I did so. But I was moved, having to blink back the tears as we marched onto the square, wishing only that I could have worn my white string and illegal hat. Chin and stomach tucked in, as we had been taught, I swung my fists high, bursting with pride in my county and regiment.

I had expected some kind of crowd. I knew there would be no presentation of swords, or riding horses up steps, but thought to see local women holding up bundles or biting tear-stained handkerchiefs. A knot of pressmen, tickets in their hat bands; the clicking of camera shutters as ragged children ran alongside us, pleading to be taken along as drummer boys. But the square was empty, except for the band, and the mascot, and the Colonel standing to attention. He was raised on a box so that we could see him, clear of what the goat was busy doing. Behind him stood Baby Face, holding his cane and gloves; and I observed Kitchener at a small window in the tower, watching us and having what he would call 'a crafty smoke'.

'Eyeees . . . right!' Our heads turned as one, as the Commanding Officer came to the salute. For a moment I though that our eyes met. 'There,' he must have said to

332

himself, seeing me pass to the beat of the music, straight backed and head twisted, fists swinging high and beret down to my eyebrows, 'goes Cork. Did I do the right thing?'

Outside the gate we stood in line, waiting for the chartered trams, lifting our knees slowly in time with the music. The band had been allowed out too, onto the grass beside the moat, where they sat on folding chairs and gave us a selection from 'Chu Chin Chow'. 'I am Chu Chin Chow from China . . . ' sang Croxley, hands up his sleeves, safe in the knowledge that the Corporal, like the Provost Sergeant, never set foot outside the gate.

With 'Special' wound up at the front, the trams were decorated with bunting, cardboard crowns and red, white and blue light bulbs. Gay as the London omnibuses that ran direct to the Somme, packed with happy soldiery clutching their brass tins of chocolate.

The Daredevils took posssession of the upstairs platform, hanging over the rail to wave goodbye to the home of the Second Foot. The regimental standard streamed above the battlements, but only the slim figure of the vegetarian waved back.

'Goodbye, Provost Sergeant,' we called, some people going further, as the wicket gate was closed and the heavy beam dragged across. In case sepoys made a rush, or we tried to get back in again.

The Transport Officer looked at his watch, then waved his cane, jumping aboard as the bells clanked and we began to move. With a whine, a roar and a clatter, we picked up speed, swaying towards Swinehurst; a tear in many an eye at the thought of saying goodbye to each other at the station. But we sang. Some brave spirits, carried away, even standing and dancing on the roof; like the girls kicking their legs on the aéroplane wings in 'Flying Down to Rio'.

'Wish Me Luck, As You Wave Me Goodbye' we sang, punching each other's shoulders in fellowship, and people came out of shops and public houses to see what was going on; and then went back inside again.

Ron – because I had said I would introduce him to Captain Drew, though I had pointed out that I could promise nothing – had agreed to come home with me for the first half of his leave. He was in no hurry to tell his parents about the 'karzies and pissholes'. I had informed De Kuyper by telephone, so that she could prepare Uncle Frank's old room; and she had informed me that Elspeth was coming to stay for the following weekend! Seemingly she had become, by post, a friend of Miss Parkinson, and they were planning to look at the shoe shop together.

Although it was Saturday, half day at the factory, my father had not yet returned home. But Miss Parkinson was at the door to meet us, looking rather flushed I thought, and wearing her Katherine Hepburn suit.

'How nice of you to come,' she said to Ron, nodding to me, taking his hand and leading him into the house; while I ran upstairs to talk to Bernard.

'We'll go down The Drain after tea,' I said. 'Then you can meet him.'

'What's he like?' came the faint voice of my old chum, sounding somewhat grudging over the string.

'The spit of Melvyn Douglas,' I told him, hanging up the tin and grabbing my homburg to show Ron.

As it turned out, because it was cordoned off – the police being engaged in pushing a body from one side to the other – we were unable to go down The Drain that evening. Bernard was a little annoyed, having put on his sailor suit, but we stayed in and did a bit of a jigsaw. Then, when Miss Parkinson had taken Ron to see the photos outside the Pavilion De Luxe, utterly fascinated with his talk of glycerine and how film stars had to get up so early, I told De Kuyper about the meeting with my mother. My father had still not returned, and it was assumed that he was still in the Queen's Head.

'On a horse!' exclaimed De Kuyper. 'I thought she'd have a motor car!'

I explained that it had been in Hyde Park, a recreation area for nurses, where one could just as easily find one's mother in a rowing boat. It was no indication as to her prosperity or social standing. I went on to describe the flat in Maida Vale – De Kuyper's eyebrows climbing when I mentioned the silver epaulettes of the night-club attendant – and she gave a loud 'Ha!' when I got to the crinoline ladies, and the wine in the fridge. I thought it best to draw a veil over the John West, and the man in the short fawn overcoat.

Bernard was to join what he called – and now smoked – the Senior Service, in three weeks' time. He was working hard at his hornpipe and his knots and told me that he hoped to start, because of his experience with the seagoing Pomfret, as a midshipman.

'We're called "Middies",' he told me, and described their uniform ('a bum freezer and a bow tie'), with a glance verging on the contemptuous at my gaitered boots.

I told him to wait until he had some service in; showing him the disc which hung on a string around my neck, so that I could be identified and buried quickly. His mouth hung open as I recounted some of my adventures.

'Wow!' he said, when I paused on hearing the front door close, and a stick rattle into the elephant's foot. 'Do you really think she meant ten bob each?' But further discussion was prevented by my father looking into the room.

'Hello, Jeffrey,' he said, going on to add that he thought I was bringing a soldier friend home. I told him that this was Bernard, whom he probably remembered better as a Riff. Ron, the soldier, was out with Miss Parkinson.

'Well,' said my father, expansive after so long in the Queen's Head; thanking me, but saying that he wouldn't come in as it was late. 'How do you like the army?'

'It's very nice,' I said, putting on my stiffened hat and

standing up, so he could see me better. De Kuyper had put my white string in the wash.

'You've got something in your trousers,' he said, pointing.

'It's lead,' I told him. 'It makes them hang better.'

He nodded that he understood, then good night to Bernard.

Giving the sea dog all the bits of straight edge I had, I followed my father along to his study. He was at his desk, looking tired and trapped as I closed the door.

'It's not about giving profits away again, is it?' he asked, feeling for a mint.

'No,' I said. 'I've something to tell you.'

'Oh yes?' he said, and there was a pause. 'Did you find out about the ointment?'

'Yes,' I said, and there was another silence while he sucked and waited. 'I'm not going to be a subaltern,' I told him, looking over his head, into the dusty face of the elk. I heard him (my father that is) bite right through the mint and swallow the pieces.

'Aren't you?' he said, feeling for another one.

'No,' I said. 'At least not for a bit. Unless I'm commissioned in a field.' I waited for him to say something. 'Ron's going to the School of Hygiene,' I said, telling him about the acres of toilets which were known all over the world, and adding, 'I'm a Gunner. It's a slightly higher rank than private.' Going on to explain that my regiment, the Royal Artillery, was the senior regiment in the British army. I then hummed him a few bars of our tune. As he was taking this in, I said: 'I went to London last week.'

'Did you?' said my father, his thumbs now revolving.

'Yes,' I said, 'with Ron. He's interested in film stars.' I heard Bernard go yo-hoing down the corridor, and De Kuyper locking the front door behind him. I then went on, as I began this chapter, to tell my father about calling on Clark Gable at the Savoy. 'We should have sent a note up to his suite,' I said.

336

'Yes,' he said. 'Yes, you should have done that.'

'He – Ron – he said he saw The Three Stooges in a Rolls-Royce,' I told him, grinning, but I don't think my father had heard about their respective fates and seemed more interested in his thumbs. 'Then I met her,' I said. 'On a horse, in the park. My mother.' The thumbs stopped dead, like a lathe switched off.

'Your mother?' he said. 'In London?'

'In jodhpurs,' I told him.

'Did she say anything?'

'Yes,' I said. 'She said, "Hello, Jeffrey. What are you?" ' I grinned, and he stared at me. 'Then the horse ate the *Reynolds News*', I told him, still hoping for a smile.

'Was she by herself?'

'Yes,' I said. 'Except for the horse.'

I then told him about Ron seeing Herbert Wilcox getting onto a bus; and the two of us going with my mother – no, not all on the horse – to her flat in Maida Vale. Sparing no detail, I told him about the Carnation milk and the sugar violet, though not of course about the man in the short fawn overcoat.

'And I showed her the photo of us outside the factory,' I said. 'She recognised you.'

'Did she?'

'Yes,' I said. 'She said, "Those are your father's feet." '

I left him cleaning his finger nails on the wrapper from the mints, probably trying to decide just where he had gone wrong.

Before I knew it, the first week of my leave had gone. Saturday had arrived, and with it Elspeth at the station, in a hat of orange and green birds' feathers, with a short stiff veil. That night we were going as a foursome – Elspeth and I, Ron and Miss Parkinson – to a Grand Dance.

The week had not been uneventful. We had finished the jigsaw by Wednesday, and then the three of us, Bernard, Ron and myself, had roamed the countryside; walking down The Drain and sitting on Mossies' window sill. Or at least Ron and Bernard did. I stood nearby, a cane I had filched from the allotments under my arm, eyes open for a red-capped vision in white by the name of Pickersgill; for rumour had it that he was now one of them. On the Thursday, on the 'slice off a cut loaf' principle, and because of what I had hinted at one evening in Hut Number One, Ron set his cap at Agnes Pomfret.

Bernard and I watched from across the market place as he strolled into the dairy, wearing the Melvyn Douglas moustache that had arrived from Ellisdons that morning. I had advised him that perhaps it would be better not to mention my name. Privately, I thought he was wasting his time; but a rebuff would be character forming. If and when he became a film star, he would have too much of a good thing.

'He's away!' hissed the virgin sailor boy, nudging me, as Ron emerged from the dairy with a leer on his face. On the open pavement, in broad daylight, he made the kind of gesture one associates with the Haymarket.

De Kuyper, as always the soul of understanding, brought tea forward so that Ron could be at the dairy when it closed. So that, as she put it, he would not have to do anything on an empty stomach. When he returned – the young Hornblower having irritated me for three hours with 'What do you think he's doing now?' – Ron gave us, over a good supper left for him in the oven, a précis of the evening. Apparently they had gone straight down The Drain and into a field; Agnes informing him, as she turned round the swinging cow to read 'Closed', that she had her knickers in her handbag.

We stared at him, most likely with our mouths open, as he wiped his plate with a slice of bread; seemingly unaware that half of his new moustache had been lost at some point in the evening. God alone knew where it was now.

'Do you mean . . . ?' I said, leaning forward over the table, not sure that Bernard was able to follow all this.

'Do you mean – that you –?' Melvyn Brackenbury smiled lopsidedly, the pips of a fried tomato on his chin.

'She told me about you,' he said.

'Did she?' I replied, yawning. Standing up I took off my tie, directing Bernard's attention to the time, which was well after nine o'clock; motioning him to finish his cocoa.

'Yes,' said Ron, crossing his cavalry twill, so that we could see the green stains on his knees. 'She said you'd been up to her house.'

I nodded curtly, to intimate that a gentleman never tells. 'I've seen her clock,' I said. Bernard gaped glassily at me as I added: 'It's bricked up.' This of course was for Ron's benefit. Whatever else she had told him down The Drain, before her starched overall went over her head, she was unlikely to have told him that. Bernard already knew, it being common knowledge in the town. 'You didn't get any pie then?' I asked Ron.

'Pie?' queried Ron, after a pause. 'What kind of pie?'

"What kinda pie ya want?" quoted Bernard, who had done Steinbeck at school. 'We got cream pie, chocolate pie, blueberry pie, vanilla pie . . . '

'Veal, ham and egg,' I said, shutting Bernard up, and causing Ron's eyes to widen. I shaped the size of it with my hands.

'No,' admitted the leading man, somewhat subdued. 'I didn't get any pie.' Then he winked, recovering quickly. 'But I'll tell you what we did have . . . '

'Daddies Sauce,' I said, which brought the head of the literate tar swivelling back to me. 'I know,' I said, casually, as if brought up on nothing else. Taking Bernard's uniformed elbow I steered him to the door. 'Good night, Bernard,' I said, watching his little white hat move away uncertainly in the darkness.

It must have preyed on his mind, leading him to make a beeline for Agnes at the Grand Dance. Avid for experience, he had passed us in the London Road with no more than a nod, hat on the back of his neck like a Trebor mint. Now he stepped across the floor with the merry widow, while she fondled his woggle; looking around over his head for someone with rather more to offer.

We saw them as soon as we came in, while Elspeth and Miss Parkinson were in the lavatory. They were doing the quickstep (Agnes and Bernard that is); and she made the old fruitgums face at me over the sailor boy's brilliantine. Ron raised a hand to her, which I thought was the least he could do; both of us noting the capacious handbag on her wrist.

But we of course were the centre of attraction, as we stood waiting for the ladies. Except for Bernard (and the people selling *The War Cry*), we were the only ones in uniform. De Kuyper had come up with a replacement for the nude half of Ron's face, and we were both smartly turned out. Ron had his beret rolled under his epaulette; but I, unable to do that with my stiffened hat, and not trusting the hobbledehoys who leaned against the radiators, kept it on. With the lead removed from my ankles, and having already drunk two pale ales, my feet were tapping and ready to go.

The band were playing 'In The Mood'; the brass section standing, both of them waving bowler hats in front of their instruments before sitting down again. The band leader – a Pomfret who had once played with the Junior Rechabites – waved his cane to me, and I inclined my head. Then the music changed to an Al Jolson number: 'When The Red Red Robin Comes Bob Bob Bobbing Along', and out of the lavatory door came our partners; Miss Parkinson into Ron's arms, and Elspeth into mine. Straight backed, hands clasped high, we fishtailed down the floor; little Mr Freeson from the wireless shop moving backwards before us with a tin of french chalk.

'I'm sleeping in Melvyn's room,' said Elspeth, making my breast bone vibrate like a kazoo. 'And he's sleeping in yours, isn't he?'

I said that he was, moving a wisp of brown hair out of my mouth with my tongue. She smelled of something I couldn't put my finger on. She told me she had brought with her the nightie with the forget-me-nots on, complete in its peach-coloured flounced case; and – this for the fourth or fifth time – that she wasn't leaving until after Sunday lunch. 'One Night Of Love' she sang, eyeballs turned upwards, though that isn't what the band were playing. As we moved into a slow foxtrot, showing off with with some deft footwork, I took the opportunity to feel her, my fingers searching for the seams and the bulk of the chastity garment. Tonight, I thought, inflamed by the pale ale, could well turn out to be *the night!*

'Hello, Jeffrey,' said Agatha Jennings, and I took my hand away from Elspeth's thigh as if she were hot. As indeed she was.

Agatha Jennings! Sweetheart of my youth! She was smiling at me, as she had once smiled in at my window as the banana crate came to a halt. She was moving away from me, her face above a blue serge shoulder, beside the back of a strange head and a boil plaster. We moved together down the floor, she going backwards of course like Elspeth; only Agatha and I able to see each other. She had grown since going into service, and with her red snood and her lipstick, no one would have taken her for a maid.

'Who's that?' said Elspeth, noticing my smile, trying to look round and missing her step, so that I had to drag her along.

'Just a girl,' I said.

'A girl!' she said. 'Were you in love with her?'

'Not really,' I said, raising my eyebrows to Agatha, trying to see if carrying hot water upstairs had developed her chest. 'Calf love. Nothing more.'

'I bet!' said Elspeth, surprisingly vicious for an apprentice hairdresser. 'Who broke it off?'

'I did,' I said, remembering and whirling her away, but whispering the sordid details into her ear.

Which was one of the reasons that we left early. Before the mirrored ball began to spin, and young Pomfret led his combo into 'Who's Taking You Home Tonight?' I knew that Agatha was waiting for a ladies excuse me; and Agnes was still looking at me over Barnacle Bill's head. But the main reason was Lance Corporal Pickersgill. Off duty, but dressed as I feared.

'I shall always remember this,' said Elspeth, as we strolled home along the London Road, her birds' feather hat a sickly green under the gaslamps. She looked into the allotments, breathing deeply.

'Why?' asked Ron, taking one of her chips. 'Why would you remember this?'

'These things,' said Elspeth, mysteriously, to the pavement, 'mean a lot to a woman.' She exchanged secret smiles with Miss Parkinson, flushed and wobbly on her stilettoes, who raised a fishcake in response.

Chapter Eleven

The house was in darkness when we arrived; only the usual lamp burning in De Kuyper's window. With whispered 'Good nights', we tiptoed up the inside treads of the stairs.

'Do you want to go first?' asked Ron, when we were in my room.

'No,' I said, not sure where he was going.

'Right,' he said, at the door in shirt-sleeve order and stockinged feet. 'I'll go shake hands with the wife's wedding present.'

I lay on the bed, musing on his ready wit, when the door opened again. 'That was quick,' I said. 'Not exactly a handful, eh?' I thought that was rather good.

'Shhhhh!' said Miss Parkinson, dressing gown over her pink bed jacket. 'Where is he?'

'He said he was going . . . he's gone to the bathroom.'

She was also in stockinged feet, a painted big toe bursting through. Turning to open the door, her finger to her lips, she came face to face with Elspeth.

'Shhh!' they said, both together, and giggled. Elspeth was wearing her forget-me-not nightie and her birds' feather hat.

'I'm looking for Ron, to see if he's all right,' whispered Miss Parkinson. Elspeth nodded, as if that was a good idea, keeping her finger pressed to her lips.

I heard the door close and was alone again. All was silence. Taking off my shoes, like everyone else seemed to have done, I opened the bedroom door. The house slept

– or so you would have thought, if you hadn't known better. There was a strip of light under the bathroom door, which went out when I tapped softly in Morse code: 'Dah, di di dah di, dah dah.'

'Who's in there?' asked my father, emerging silently from the master bedroom in his mulberry dressing gown and slippers.

'I don't know,' I said. 'That's why I was knocking.'

We stared together at the bathroom door for a few moments, then his hand came out of his dressing-gown sleeve, knuckled ready to knock; but he decided against it. 'I'll go downstairs,' he said.

He padded down quickly, showing a glimpse of blueish bare ankle at the bend in the stairs. I heard him knock, a pause, and then the homburg hat was coming up again.

Opening the door of the spare room (now the nursery, with Epaminondas on the wall) I saw Rupert's head on the pillow, in the glow of his night light. So it wasn't him. But as I tried to softly close the door I became aware of someone holding the handle at the other side. I was startled, realising that my half brother could hardly reach that far from the bed, even if shamming sleep. Then a hand came round the door and pulled me into the room.

'What are you doing?' hissed Ron, raising a finger, begging me not to wake the little sod, as he called him.

'I'm not doing anything,' I told him. Which was true. 'My father's trying to go to the lavatory. What are you doing?'

'Going for a shit,' said the suave Melvyn Douglas. 'Your Elspeth came down in her nightie, so I nipped in here.' We heard the cistern flush downstairs, and I opened the door a little, enough to hear my father shuffling fast down the stairs.

'Now's your chance,' whispered Ron. 'Get up to her room!' He gave the appropriate grunt, the clenched fist on the swinging forearm, as he pushed me out onto the landing. Deciding that it was a good idea, I hurried up the uncarpeted stairs and tapped softly on her door, not bothering with Morse code. There was no answer. Disappointed, I turned to descend again, and walked right into De Kuyper. She was coming up, dressed like everyone else, with her hair loose on her shoulders.

'Where are you going?' she whispered.

'Down,' I said, squeezing past her, smelling the coal tar soap. I heard the bathroom door open and close, but when I got there the landing was deserted. Going to my bedroom door, I found it locked. Surprised, I tapped and listened. The key turned and it opened a fraction.

'Is that you?' whispered Ron, in honeyed tones.

'Yes,' I said, trying to push the door open.

'Fuck off!' he said, annoyed about something, keeping the door where it was with his foot. 'I thought you were going upstairs?'

'There's nobody there,' I said, pushing. 'Let me in. It's my room.' Though we were, as Kitchener had sung at the canteen piano, 'Comrades, comrades . . . ' if not quite ever since we were boys, I knew he would be unable to resist playing with my things if given the opportunity.

'Shhh!' said Miss Parkinson behind me, yet again, and I felt her fingers on my waist as she moved me aside. 'Mel-vyn,' she crooned, and the door swung inwards like Ali Baba's cave. 'I'm just going to see if he's all right,' she whispered, patting my bottom, and then the door was closed in my face. Quite frankly, I did not know what to do.

'Hello?' I hissed, my mouth to the keyhole. 'Can I go to bed, please?'

I was listening for an answer of some kind, my ear to the panel of the door, when my nostrils were filled again with that smell I couldn't put my finger on.

'Shhh!' said Elspeth into my other ear, her warm breath followed by the tip of her tongue. We were crouching like that, on the level of the keyhole, me drying my ear with my handkerchief, when we heard the cistern flush again downstairs.

'Quick!' said Elspeth, seizing my hand and pulling me into the bathroom. As I slid the bolt, and she pulled the string for the light to go on, we heard my father go past and into his bedroom.

'You're a bad boy!' said Elspeth, her whisper loud with the bathroom acoustics. 'Dragging me in here like this!'

She was standing by the washbasin, both hands behind her, staring down at her white-socked feet. There was silence, except for the cistern refilling on the floor below. Just her smell, and the shimmering green of the hat in the mirror behind her. I thought it was a good opportunity to give her a kiss.

Moving in close, remembering Ron's advice to use your knee, to observe if they closed their eyes, I put my arms around her. She gave a wriggle, asking me not to tickle, but keeping her hands behind her on the washbasin. I was just about to raise her veil, behind which her eyes were closed and her face set, when someone tried the handle of the door.

With a single bound I crossed the room, pulling the chain and shouting in a strained voice over the rushing waters that I wouldn't be a minute. The cistern began to refill, squirting and hissing, and Elspeth let out a trembling breath. Then, whoever was waiting outside began to kick at the door.

'I wanna wee wees!' said Rupert, as I opened the door and pulled him in. He was naked from the waist down, but said 'Hello' to Elspeth, looking with interest at the feathers on her head. She gave him a kind of a twisted smile. Sitting him on the lavatory I gave him a yellow duck to rub up the wall, to simulate a Dakota taking off.

'Are you in there, Rupert?'

It was my father, Rupert's father, tapping softly on the door. Elspeth's eyes were wide open, and she was losing colour. I gave Rupert a poke with my finger, to make him say something, and he fell off the lavatory seat.

'What's the matter?' called out our father, as Rupert screamed, wanting to fish the duck out from its little pond. To placate the child, and because it couldn't be left there to frighten people, I reached down for the duck – just as Rupert, who was standing on the back of the seat, pulled the chain. The duck came up to meet me, and the water soaked my sleeve up to the elbow.

'Come on out,' said my father, quite loudly. 'If you've finished.'

'Yes,' I called. 'We're just coming.' As I unfastened the door, Rupert revolved the bristles of the lavatory brush in the ear that Elspeth had licked. Putting him out onto the landing, I switched off the light and followed, pulling the bathroom door to behind me. 'He wanted to wee,' I explained.

'Who's that?' asked my father, as my bedroom door opened and Melvyn, with his hair in a mess, looked both ways to see if the coast was clear.

'That's Ron,' I said. 'My soldier friend. From the Army School of Hygiene.'

'Hello,' said Ron, coming forward, buttoning his shirt, having closed my door behind him.

'Hello,' said my father. There was a short silence. The only sound was of the toilet water dripping from my sleeve onto the carpet. 'Did you want to go?' my father asked Ron, pointing to the bathroom door.

'No,' I said, firmly, transferring Rupert's hand, the one not holding the lavatory brush, into that of our father's. 'I'm going.'

'You've just been,' he said.

'That was Rupert,' I corrected him, slipping into the bathroom quickly and locking the door. As I pulled the string, I had mixed feelings about finding Elspeth still there. There was a tapping on the door, and Ron's voice, deep and low.

'Don't be long.'

I listened, waiting to hear the door of my father's room close, but they were engaged in a hushed conversation.

'Jeffrey tells me you're a Northern Manufacturer?' began Ron, always good at what he called 'the moody'.

'Yes,' said my father.

While Ron thought up some more dialogue, I became aware of Elspeth shivering. She had had the sense to move away from the washbasin, but accustomed as she was to the warmth of the Ilkley salon, her ankles were turning blueish like my father's.

'You can go downstairs,' I heard my father say; the perfect host.

'Thank you,' said Ron.

The stairs creaked, the door of the downstairs toilet opened and closed; we could even hear the seat go down. Then complete silence. I waited, for what seemed a long time, hardly breathing, but could hear nothing. Only a faint moaning sound from the hairdresser, seated now on the edge of the bath. Putting the bathmat round her shoulders I pulled the chain, watching the duck rise with the foam, bottom first, then switched off the light and opened the door. To find my father, and his son, hand in hand, staring at me.

'You can't use it,' I said, pulling the door to and holding it closed. 'There's a duck down the lavatory.'

'A duck?' said my father, who really should have been in bed.

'Yes.' I thought it time to take charge of the situation. 'Let's get him into bed,' I said, picking up my half brother and carrying him into his room. I tucked him up, while my father watched from the doorway.

'Come inside,' I said, motioning him into the room.

'What for?' he said, warily, but doing as I asked.

We stood looking at each other, beneath the water-melon smile of Epaminondas, as he groped in his dressing-gown pocket trying to find a mint. Rupert was already asleep, the lavatory brush beside him on the pillow, and I listened to my bedroom door open and close, the door of the master bedroom open and close, and, after an embarrassing wait, the door of the bathroom open – and the chain being pulled. Above the weary sound of the cistern I heard frozen feet racing up the stairs to the attic.

'Who was that?' said my father, hand to his ear.

'The duck,' I said. 'It'll keep doing that.'

We came out of the nursery together, walking across to the open bathroom door. The white pot handle was still swinging on the chain. Together we looked down the lavatory, at the yellow duck bobbing the right way up. My father lifted it out and put it into the bath with its parents.

'Good night,' I said, covering a yawn, going to my bedroom door.

'Good night,' said my father, going to his, but not taking his eyes off me. We stared at each other across the landing, and then Ron pulled the chain in the downstairs toilet and we both opened our doors. I heard Miss Parkinson say, sleepily, 'Wherever have you been, Alfred?'

I waited for Ron, but declined to speak to him, avoiding his nudging elbow and slipping out as he entered the room. Noting how late it was, how much time had been wasted, I tiptoed quickly up the attic stairs. As I reached for the handle of Elspeth's door, De Kuyper's opened and I was trapped, blinking in the light that shone from her room.

'Who keeps pulling the chain?' she said.

'It's all right,' I told her. 'It's finished now.' Behind her I saw a bright coal fire in the little Zebo'd hearth. The wireless was on, very low in a foreign language.

'Do you want to come in?' she asked. 'I can make you a sandwich.'

'No,' I said. 'No, thank you.' I appreciated the thought, knowing she had no cooking facilities up there.

'Do you want to borrow a book? Or ask me something?'

Her eyes narrowed in concern, as she reached out and squeezed the water from my sleeve.

'It was the duck,' I murmured.

'Of course,' she said. Then she reached past me to turn the handle of Elspeth's door. 'It's open,' she said, and I felt her lips brush my ear, the one that hadn't been touched so far that night. Though the fumes of the pale ale still urged me on, I would have liked to have gone in with De Kuyper then; to have sat by her fire drying my sleeve, sipping her cocoa, while she told me stories.

'Good night,' I whispered.

'Go on,' she said, pushing me gently, in the way that men punched each other's biceps. Then the door closed quietly on her smile, leaving me in the dark.

In Uncle Frank's room a theatrical shaft of moonlight slanted through the dormer window, divided by rusting iron bars into stripes across the bed. I could always smell his pipe, even after everything had been burnt, and he had been taken away, turned sideways to go down the stairs. It would have been no surprise to see his cropped grey head on the pillow; though of course it would have been to Elspeth. I smiled. I had once heard him telling Bernard's father, when he was still around, that he'd had three in a night. 'One of 'em a blackie; with legs up to here!' I had not been able to see where he was pointing, but I recalled the feeling of pride that I could do the multiplication when he added: 'And each of 'em three times!' Though I hadn't the faintest idea what 'without uncunting' meant. 'Bloody 'ell!' Bernard's father had said, obviously impressed.

One of the small window panes – held by rusting nails, the putty dried and gone – was blocked by cardboard, with a black letter 'T' on it. That had been Typhoo, when De Kuyper had cut it from a box in the kitchen. The hole it filled was once the way in, and out, with a plywood threshold and a bell, for Alfredo, Uncle Frank's pigeon. 'Fly, you bugger!' he would whisper, chin on his hands, watching Alfredo swoop and flap, circling to gain height, too fat with corn and split peas to go far. No, he'd told me, there was no message on his leg; and he brought no message back.

The pigeon's food was kept in a Bemax tin, and its drinking water in a white enamel jug piped with red. Once I had come into the room as Alfredo was going – my mother was shouting, and the door slammed far below us as my father went out. Uncle Frank was hunched in the window, watching the bird, still whispering to it as it wheeled against the evening sky. In the last light of the sun it became a white dove.

You could hear each fall of its pink feet on the window sill, on the green woodwork, rotten where the rain came in. It would brush its seeds and turds onto the floorboards, cooing, its head moving from side to side, looking for Uncle Frank.

'Is that you, Jeffrey?' It was Elspeth, sitting up in the bed, fastening the top button of her nightie.

As I sat on the edge of the bed, I saw the furry kittens from Ilkley with their balls of wool. She had hung them on the nail where Uncle Frank's certificate had been. 'I'm sorry about the toilet,' I said. 'And Rupert and the duck, and all that.'

'That's all right,' she said, reaching out to touch me. Her arm was very white in a stripe of moonlight. Then: 'You're all wet!' The bed creaked, and now I could see her face, frowning, concerned. She was feeling me all over with her open hand, like Blind Pew. 'Take your clothes off,' she said, in a hoarse whisper, then touching me by accident: 'Sorry! And your trousers.' She said this urgently, as if they were smouldering rather than just slightly damp.

This of course was it, I thought. Her concern that I might catch rheumatic fever because of a splash of toilet water was nothing but a pretext to get me into bed. And no abortive knee trembler in a pork butcher's doorway this time. One night of love indeed. Eight hours of it at least, as breakfast was late on Sunday morning. As I took off my shirt I tried to divide nine into eight.

'Do you love me?' she asked, sitting up anxiously, bathed in the moonlight. Pathetic really; as if I were likely to say no at a time like that!

'Yes, of course,' I said, dropping my trousers.

'I won't look,' she said, turning away to smile at her furry friends. A moment later, naked except for vest, pants and socks, and of course the disc on a string which I had to wear at all times, I slid into bed beside her.

The house was silent. Just the hiss of a cistern, and some faint martial music as De Kuyper's foreigners signed off for the night. Our shoulders almost touching, we lay looking up at the stains on the sloping ceiling, as Uncle Frank and Henry Moore had done.

'My Uncle Frank died in this bed,' I said.

'What of?' she asked, her voice muffled by the sheet.

'The class system,' I told her. 'According to De Kuyper. He used to keep his teeth in a glass. Where your hat is.'

'Did he?' she said, raising her head to look, as if they'd still be there. They had gone into the dustbin, along with his glasses and his magazines, and the body of Alfredo. Wet tea leaves on its breast. De Kuyper had told me not to look.

I heard Elspeth take a deep breath, probably to calm a wildly beating heart. As a virgin of course, like the one in the Bible as she put it, this was a big moment for her. Then I felt her touch me.

'You've got clothes on,' she said.

'Only underclothes,' I said. Then: 'Ooh!'

'Sorry,' she said. 'Cold hands, warm heart.'

'That's all right,' I said.

'I never knew how men's knickers opened at the front,' she whispered.

'Didn't you?' I said, not recognising my own voice. She was holding it as if it were the handle of a pint pot.

352

'It's big!' she said, obviously impressed.

'I know,' I said, flattered of course, as any man would be. 'It gets bigger still,' I said, not boasting but warning her. The last thing I wanted was hysterics; her screaming and tripping over her nightie on the stairs, De Kuyper tut tutting and all the bedroom doors opening again.

'How do you know?' She was up on one elbow, looking down at me, but without letting go. 'Have you been with another girl?'

'Of course not,' I said, smiling at the thought; but remembering then for some reason, possibly the pale ale, soft fingers tweaking out my shirt beneath the Reals' double damask.

'Nobody?' she asked, threateningly, squeezing suddenly. 'Not her at the dance? In the snood? The one who threw pooh at you?'

'Threw pooh?' I repeated, starting to laugh. 'Ooh!' as she squeezed harder. 'She's a maid,' I said.

'I'll bet!' said Elspeth. 'What about her with the little sailor?'

'I don't know her,' I said, wondering how Bernard had got on.

'Yes you do! Her from the dairy. She was pulling faces at you.'

'Not at me,' I said. 'At Ron. All right, Melvyn then.' And I told her about them going down The Drain on the Thursday. The act of a cad, of course, but not to her. For a virgin, especially like the one in the Bible, she was extremely interested.

'Tell me what they did,' she commanded. 'With all the words.' She was now using a corner of her nightie, a patch free of forget-me-nots, in the manner advocated by the makers of Cherry Blossom. So I did. I lay back in the moonbeams, a big black Elspeth on the wall above me, like Epaminondas, and I spoke to her freely, in the tongue the Provost Sergeant had learned at his mother's knee. And when I couldn't imagine anything else that Melvyn and

Agnes had done to each other, I told her of Doris Allerdyce, hem in her mouth, flat on her back on a public right of way. 'Mauve shoes!' said the dark shadow, with a shudder of distaste. She changed her position, the bed creaking enough to bring a smile to the face of the sleeping De Kuyper, and I could see her elbow moving on the wall.

'Go on!' she said, no whispering now. 'More! Use the dirty words!' But I was silent; the pale ale having turned to acid, as the Rechabites always said it would. My eyes were closed, and there was the sound and light of Swinehurst High Street beyond the darkness . . . the pearl button coming off her blouse, rattling into the tin plate; the feel of her under me, against the earth; her laugh vibrating through both our bodies; her thighs holding me; my fingers in the cool grass and the cinders, and her hand drawing my head down . . . and the flames of the fire in blue eyes; the lace and the lick of powdered shoulders. Kissing lips that opened with mine, tasting the life of the lizard of her tongue . . . as she bent to kiss my cheek, hair spun gold in the firelight, diamonds blazing, a pink nipple for my mouth. Behind her the hams against the blackened ceiling . . . Once I opened my eyes and saw the hard-working hairdresser, a squat black figure against the window, the light around her making fuzz on her cheeks. Her eyes were flecked with yellow, like her fucking kittens. The bedclothes heaved as she pulled on the grip of a cricket bat.

'Jeffrey?' she said, as I turned away, staring at the shadowed panels of the door, the hook on which Uncle Frank's overcoat had hung. She had let go, there being little to hold onto now, and I pulled the covers over me, trying to breathe as if I were asleep.

'I'll have to wash it,' she said, after a silence; meaning her nightie I suppose, but I didn't answer. For some reason the lines of an army song ran through my mind: 'First he fucked the parlour maid, then the cook against the wall.

Cor Blimey said the butler, he has come to fuck us all!'

'Jeffrey!' she said, shaking my shoulder. 'Don't go to sleep!'

Being unable to think of anything else I could do, I got quietly out of bed, starting to gather up my clothes.

'Are you all right?' she asked, sounding genuinely concerned, as if she had opened a main artery.

'Yes, thank you,' I said, opening the door.

'Give me a kiss then.'

I went back to the bed and kissed her hot forehead. She held me by the arm. 'Did you like it?' she whispered, with eager pride, as if it were something she'd invented.

'Yes,' I said, but she held onto me.

'It's better we're both virgins when we're married,' she said. 'Don't you think so?'

'Yes,' I said, taking her hand off my arm, finger by finger.

'We'll save ourselves for each other.' She repeated that. 'Save ourselves for each other.' She was holding my vest. 'Just think what it'll be like when we're married!'

'Yes,' I said, freeing myself, doing just that as I left the room.

Outside De Kuyper's door were two rounds of sandwiches on a plate. She hadn't bothered to cover them, guessing that I wouldn't be long. Cheese with Branston pickle, and, for old times' sake, lemon cheese oozing between buttered Hovis. Plus a crust, thickly spread; my favourite.

In my room, the same moonlight fell on the false moustached face of the sleeping Ron. His sensual lips, as he called them, were softly burbling. The only role I could see for him in films was as an already dead corpse, in long shot. Sitting on my bed I unscrewed a bottle of dandelion and burdock, taking a mouthful as the body awoke, lying motionless, ceasing to burble, its eyes open.

'Give us a drink,' it said.

'It's flat,' I told him, handing him the bottle.

He sat up in his vest, touching the hair under his disc to see if it had grown in the past hour. The moon was refracted through the glass of the bottle as he drank, a deceptive froth sinking towards his sensual mouth.

'All right?' he asked, looking at me, eyebrows raised.

'Yes,' I said. 'Fine.' I pushed the plate of cheese and pickle within his reach.

'It's tiring, isn't it?' he said, looking into a sandwich and then beginning to eat.

'Yes,' I said. 'That's probably why the film stars need all that sleep.'

Not much of a joke, but we laughed quietly. I lay back into a stripe of moonlight, crust in hand, imagining Elspeth writing home already; if her wrist was up to it. Grinning exultantly at the blue-eyed pair as she covered page after page to her mother, and to the girls at the salon.

'Ron,' I said. 'I think I'm going to get married.'

Silence. Just a gurgle as he finished the last of the dandelion and burdock.

'Did you hear me?'

'Yes,' he said. 'Pardon.' He screwed the top on, putting the bottle on the floor. 'To her?'

'Yes,' I said, waiting, staring across the room at my shelves. It was light enough to see the green and silver spine of *Coral Island*, and the fat bulk of *101 Things a Boy Can Do*. I thought he had drifted off again, that in a moment I would hear him burble, but: 'Jeff?'

'Yes?' I turned towards him, to listen. Bernard had a cousin who could move his ears.

'I think I've eaten my moustache!'

I started to laugh again, and then he joined in, though denying it was funny. I was still smiling as I finished the Hovis and turned over, pulling the blanket over me. The moonlight fell on the puffing red shunting engines. 'Good night,' I said. 'Or morning.'

'Good night, Jeff,' he said, still feeling for it in his bed.

I slept, not wanting to think about anything, as dawn began to show, pale, along the crest of the blueish hills.

Part Three

Chapter One

De Kuyper defected, which is not a word that Elspeth likes me to use, ten days after Burgess and Maclean. Whether she followed the same route – a friendly phone call, then the night boat from Southampton to St Malo – was never made clear. Understandably, she was reticent about such details. When I asked, as we talked in her flat in Gorky Street, while she coaxed me to another dumpling and showed me her new boots, if it had been 'Kim' as she called him – or a fourth or fifth man or woman, or perhaps the man who washed out Pomfrets' churns – she just smiled, opening a bottle of the apricot brandy from which she had taken her name.

It was a week after we had moved into the new house when my brother-in-law, George, who shouted that he was thinking of changing his name, phoned me with the news. We knew she'd gone of course, being telephoned by a distraught Miss Parkinson who had been left with the washing up; but not where to. I told George I was sorry; but like the sepoys laying waste his city even as we spoke – whom he claimed I had known were on their way, if I had not actually invited – there was really nothing I could do about it. Not wishing to be rude, but out of loyalty to De Kuyper, I then went on to say that I was unaware of the need to be positively vetted, in order to sell boiled sweets in Wibsey, Odsal, Idle, or Cleckheaton.

But it was of course a blow, which could have come at a better time. Elspeth was expecting Desmond, brother for Sonia, who was already swinging her buttoned shoes on Mrs Dooley's toilets. It was also, had we known it, a bare six months before my father slipped beneath the waves at Bognor.

But I go too fast. I left the reader at the end of my first leave, about to join my regiment at Dover Castle. You will of course wish to know what happened.

I had spent two months in the Garden of England, marching up and down, and living in a hut on the famous White Cliffs. Swallowing my disappointment at not being allowed to carry a stick, to wear brown gloves and run up bills, I had worked hard at showing what I was made of. In the foremost of the folding chairs at every lecture, I had filled several exercise books with the tradition and expertise of the Royal Regiment of Artillery. In fact my new Colonel (a rather more distant and reticent man) had commended me, both for my zeal and for the gloss on my boots.

Trained to the proverbial hair's breadth, I was then posted to Plymouth. To the School of Coastal Artillery, an élite establishment where we trained officers to defend our shores; and one hopes that the lesson of Singapore had been learned. That those sitting around on shooting sticks were now taught how to turn their weapons round, should the enemy be swine enough to approach from behind.

I was promoted to non-commissioned officer, in charge of three men in the mould of Kitchener. These I was with, though not of course of; keeping them on their toes and maintaining a standard of spit and polish in the ablutions that was often commented on. I had my own whitewashed office, and was responsible for toilet rolls and chamber pots for the married families. If you wanted one, you had to see me.

In due course, regrettably not being posted overseas to taste action, or to play with the monkeys, I was demobbed. My Colonel (who I heard had written to my previous CO about me), had signed a paper saying that I was medically A1, of Good Conduct, and of Average Intelligence.

Home again, I had hung up my stiffened hat and the white string for the last time. Beside them on my bedroom wall was a pink silk handkerchief, framed in passe-partout, embroidered with the badge of my regiment. (Motto: 'Ubique'.) The following Monday morning I resumed my career at the factory.

A week before my return (it could have been excitement, we shall never know,) Grandidge had fallen down the fire escape, on his way to the Empire Cafe. He had broken his hip, and badly scratched Queen Mary's brass box. A youth named Norman, grade B4 but strong enough for what we required, had been taken on to replace him. So I was just in time, not wishing to see the old customs die out, to join the girls in wheeling him into the toilet.

The vulgar Doreen had moved on, and the militant Maude Skinner was now a District Organiser in Nottingham, from where she threatened my father by telephone. Mrs Farrer, having as she put it seen us through the war, had retired to Mablethorpe, taking with her the lock of my hair. But the attractive Janet, the leader of the mob at my initiation, was still there. Now shop steward, wielding the shears at Mrs Skinner's bench, she was obviously very pleased to see me.

Elspeth and I had been married in Swinehurst, a small motorcade making its way down from Ilkley. Romantically, we had explored the possibility of holding the reception at The Pilgrim Fisheries. But though they were more than willing to push tables together, and to bring the fish in on a gadrooned salver – going so far as to promise a large silver doily, with the chips in the middle and everything scattered with parsley – they had no private facilities, and were not licensed for singing and dancing. So of course it was the old Co-op Café; though with a different band, who were instructed to be firm with Miss Parkinson.

The girls at the factory had given me what I always knew they would – an electro-plated tea set. Which, as I knew how much they earned, was very good of them. De Kuyper, predictably, had given us several books, which stood out among the cut glass and chrome toast racks.

Quite a few of the guests had commented on them, saying one would surely have been enough; though no one went so far as to open them. The card was inscribed 'To Jeffrey and Elspeth; For Their Tomorrow', and Elspeth, at first maintaining that it meant that the real present was arriving the following day, refused to have them in the front room. They were kept, for Desmond to look at when he was old enough, with *Coral Island* under the stairs.

Blissfully ignorant of what was due to happen to my father there, we left by train for Bognor. Elspeth throwing her fresias to Yasmin, who passed them on with a cynical laugh to the aunt from Doncaster. That night, she (Elspeth that is) more or less freely gave her all; lying flat with her eyes closed, after I had agreed to buy her some white shoes and a matching handbag that she'd seen.

Having sacrificed a career in hair styling (something she was never to forget), Elspeth settled down to make a home for me and the furry kittens. They hung in the dining room, still rolling their balls of wool about, watching while we ate Sunday lunch, served to coincide with 'Forces' Favourites'. Mrs Cork predicting, every week, that Cliff Michelmore and Jean Metcalfe would get married. She could hear it in their voices, she said.

Once, for some reason, before she went off with the man in the RAF blazer, my sister and her family came down from Bradford to spend the day with us. I had shown Yasmin round the property, then into the back garden to point out the parsley I had planted. But for some reason she had shaken her head, muttered 'Jesus Christ!' and gone into the house, pulling Victoria off the toilet and shouting for George.

Miss Parkinson was a regular visitor, having a shampoo and set while she chatted to Elspeth, and sometimes bringing my father. Once, my mother had called, passing through on the way to Harrogate with the man in the short fawn overcoat; who had of course waited in the car.

*

It was like the last act of an Agatha Christie play.

There we all were, in the living room of Jasmine Villa, waiting to be cross-examined by a Detective Chief Superintendent of the Special Branch, whom we called Harold, and the man with the tic from MI5. Outside in the London Road were reporters, while photographers held cameras high to snap what they could through the rhododendrons. A policeman was at the front door, in case help was needed, and Harold – an overcoated man in the style of J. B. Priestley – had taken Yasmin's chair, the one from which she had held out a rigid finger to me so many years ago. The man with the tic sat on the pouffe, folded trench coat across his knees, writing everything down.

My father sat opposite Harold, a new packet of mints protruding from his cardigan pocket. In a semi-circle sat all the other members of the family, those (with the exception of Elspeth, on whose behalf I had brought a doctor's note) who had been close to De Kuyper, in the years when she had been engaged in bringing this country to its knees. The children, Victoria and Rupert, and little Sonia in her sun bonnet, were being amused in the back garden by a policewoman with a wart. Bernard's mother had been warned that she could well be called; and Bernard himself had been told to come straight home from the post office.

'I'm only involved because I married her,' said George, starting the ball rolling, while Harold was lighting his pipe. He handed his business card to the Chief Superintendent; who read it, looked at the back of it, then nodded to the man with the tic to write that down. Looking over his shoulder, I saw him write 'Only involved because I married her'. Then he decorated the capital 'O' with a flower in a pot and added a flock of swallows.

'Now then,' said Harold, waving the smoke away with a tweed sleeve. 'What I want to do, is to start at the beginning.' He looked at each of us in turn, and I nodded back to him in agreement. Seeing that De Kuyper was in

Moscow, sending us picture postcards of the Anti-Religious Museum, I didn't mind giving him all the help I could.

'You, I take it, sir,' said Harold to my father, using the old form of address favoured by Lord Trenchard, 'were responsible for engaging her?'

George sat back, a sneer on his face, replacing the references from his employers and the Wibsey Conservative Club in his inside pocket; expecting my father to be exposed in a moment as master spy and Comintern agent.

'Yes,' said my father, shreds of green and silver paper falling unheeded to the floor as he tore open his mints. Harold nodded to the man with the tic to write that down.

'And you are Alfred Simeon Cork?' he asked. 'Of this address; a Northern Manufacturer?' My father said 'Yes' again, the mint then appearing on the tip of his tongue.

'Thank you,' said Harold. 'Can you now tell us, in your own words, how you came to meet the lady? This De Kuyper?'

My father sucked, starting to twiddle his thumbs. 'It was nineteen thirty,' he said, setting the scene; then cleared his throat and pointed at me. 'He was one,' he said.

Everyone, even the man with the tic, looked at me and I blushed, nodding to Harold that it was true.

'I was three,' said Yasmin, giving her husband as good as she got with her elbow.

'One at a time, madam, if you don't mind,' said Harold, holding up a warning pipe. 'Where would this be, sir?' he went on to my father. 'Cambridge, I suppose?' My father looked surprised.

'Cambridge?' he repeated cautiously.

'That's where they mostly were, sir, around that time; though nineteen thirty's a bit early.' Harold exchanged a professional nod with the man from MI5. 'Student, was she? An Apostle perhaps?'

'No,' said my father, worried now that they were talking

about different people. 'Not so far as I know. Huddersfield.'

'Ah, yes,' said Harold smoothly, 'Huddersfield.'

'We advertised for a girl, and my wife said the other one
who came was shifty – or dirty, I forget now – and she got
the job.' My father crunched his mint as quietly as he could
while he unwrapped another, in case there were more
questions to come.

'Not too fast, sir,' said Harold, nodding at the man on
the pouffe, who was writing 'Shifty and dirty and she got
the job'.

'You were saying, sir,' prompted the sleuth after a short
silence, during which the scribe put a new point on his
pencil, with a sharpener in the form of a Red Indian's
head. My father stared back at him, his mouth working,
waiting to be reminded of what he had been saying.

'When she came,' asked Harold, 'did she bring things
with her?'

'Things?' queried my father.

'Things,' repeated the Chief Superintendent, heavily,
and I had the feeling that he could be terrible if provoked.
'Things you would not expect a maid to have.'

My father looked hopefully at his next of kin; but Yasmin
and I, being as we had just said one and three respectively
at the time, were unable to come to his assistance. George
and Miss Parkinson, not due to come in for years, were
amusing themselves as best they could.

'Such as?' asked my father.

'Well,' said Harold, shifting about inside his overcoat,
'if she'd had a wireless transmitter, let's say; you would
have noticed it, wouldn't you?' He smiled, this being a
joke, but my father kept his head very still, careful not to
nod.

'She had a trunk,' he said. 'I remember that.'

'A trunk!' said Harold, approvingly. 'Now we're getting
somewhere. I knew you were going to be what we call "an
observant witness", sir.' He leaned forward, and the man

on the pouffe licked his pencil in anticipation. 'What was in the trunk?'

'I haven't the faintest idea,' said my father.

I raised my hand, feeling I was able to help at this point.

'Yes?' said Harold. (Uncle Harold he had wanted us to call him when he first arrived, but I did not care for his tone now.)

'Books,' I said.

'Books?' The two police officers exchanged sharp meaningful looks. I lowered my hand as he turned back to my father. 'Are you telling us, sir, that you took this woman into your house, from Huddersfield, with a trunk full of books?'

My father's mouth was open, the mint a thin white circle on his tongue. I was about to add that as well as the books, De Kuyper also kept in her trunk the Seebackroscope, which until that moment I had always understood she had sent away for to Ellisdons. I realised now that along with the rubber fried egg, and the nail-through finger, it had almost certainly come from Moscow. Prudently I kept quiet. Though I could have recited the titles of her library from memory, slowly for the man with the tic and the pencil. For of course the attic had been emptied, right down to light bulb and aerial, by Pickfords. But the thought of my own copy of Little Lenin, now supporting the leg of my bedside cabinet, made me hold my tongue.

'I think you are going to say,' went on Harold, pointing his pipe at my father, 'that your wife was responsible for household management. Is that right, sir?' My father said yes, that was exactly what he was about to say, and his interrogator left the books for the moment (though they had gone down in the notebook, in capital letters, heavily underlined), changing his line of attack.

'Would you say that she gave satisfaction, sir? This De Kuyper?'

This caused the scribbler's eyebrows to rise, and a deep flush to creep up my father's neck, rather faster than the cardboard thermometer outside the wool shop during the war. The Superintendent silenced the tutting of George, and the suppressed giggles of Miss Parkinson, with a large and hairy upraised hand. He waited, as did we all, for my father to answer.

'She was very good,' he muttered at length, looking at his watch and shaking it to see if it had stopped.

'Oh, yes, they are,' said Harold, who obviously knew his stuff. 'They've been specially trained.' He looked at us all in turn, to make certain we knew this. 'Looking for our weakest link,' he said, turning back to my father.

'As I understand it, sir,' he said, 'the wife you mention – the one who took in this maid from Huddersfield, with all her books – she's not this lady here?' He pointed to Miss Parkinson.

'No,' said my father. 'His mother.' He nodded at me.

'And she's no longer with us, I take it?' said Harold, spreading the *Radio Times* (nowadays sans its tooled-leather cover) across his knees and starting to clean out his pipe. 'Did she go far?' I think most of us knew what he was leading up to.

'Number 17,' said my father.

'What does that mean, sir?' asked the Superintendent, pleasantly, making a woolly lamb out of a pipe cleaner. 'Is that like they call a you-know-what a Number 9, in surgical goods shops?'

'No,' said my father, not sure what a you-know-what was. 'That's where she went. With him.'

'Did she?' said Harold, mildly. He knew he had a bite and he played the fish carefully. 'Who was he, sir?'

'A Colonel,' said my father, and it was the first time that the homebreaker had sullied his lips. 'He had gnomes in his garden.'

'Is that true?' asked Harold, turning to me, handing the woolly lamb, which was quite good, to Yasmin.

'Yes,' I said. 'At least three of them. Two fishing, and one wearing glasses, reading a book.'

369

'No,' he said, leaning forward to take the pencil away from the man with the tic. 'Is it true that your mother, the first Mrs Cork as it were, went to live at Number 17 with a Colonel?'

'Yes,' I said, not wanting to confuse him by adding that I had met him down The Drain. 'I saw them dancing,' I said, 'and I spoke to him.'

'What did he say?' The Super replaced the pencil in the secret agent's waiting hand.

'As I remember it,' I said, 'he told me to fuck off.'

There was a short silence, during which I looked to see if he had written it down; but he had just put a capital 'F' and a dash. I suppose they would know what it meant back at the office.

Miss Parkinson and Yasmin made a pot of tea then, at Harold's request. While it was mashing, as George called it, the two Intelligence Officers walked on the front lawn, the one with the tic reading aloud from his notebook, until Harold told him to shut up. We had biscuits as well, it being something of an occasion, with orangeade for the policewoman and her charges. Pomfrets, who were now into outside catering, were doing well with the reporters on the London Road.

'Now then,' said Harold, when we reassembled, refreshed and looking forward to more revelations. 'Where were we?'

I was tempted, but George was too quick for me. 'The Colonel,' he said. 'The one with the foul mouth.'

'Ah, yes,' said Harold, watching the man with the tic, biscuit crumbs in his sandy moustache, write 'The Colonel with the foul mouth' as a chapter heading. He turned to me.

'The time you saw him,' he said, and he raised his hand. 'No, I don't want you to say it again. Did you notice what he was wearing?' He drew the edge of his hand across his knee. 'Leather boots up to here? Fur hat on?' He touched his head, to show where people wore fur hats. 'You said he was dancing – did he have his arse on his heels? Kicking his legs out? Begging your pardon, ladies,' he said to Yasmin and Miss Parkinson.

'No,' I said. 'He was just dressed like a Colonel; with a stick.'

'One of ours?'

One of yours, I should have said. Only Miss Parkinson could have claimed that Trewin was with, if not of, her. But I nodded.

The Chief Superintendent stared hard at me, evaluating whether I was telling the truth. Deciding, I think, that I was, he began to fill his pipe and to think up some more questions.

'He sat on it,' I remembered, wanting of course to help in any way I could.

'Did he?' he said, emptying the last of the packet of Babies Bottom into his pouch. 'Sat on what?'

'On his stick,' I said. Then, feeling that we weren't really getting anywhere, I told him that the Colonel had been dropped into the Dordogne. The man with the tic handed me his notebook and pencil, to write it down.

'It's beginning to take a certain shape,' said Harold, the tips of his thick fingers together and his pipe going nicely. 'She arrives here from Huddersfield.' There was a slight nod to my father. 'With a lot of books, and shortly afterwards Mrs Cork – the first Mrs Cork – goes off with this Colonel.'

'Twelve years,' said my father.

'Is it really?' said Harold. 'And then you come on the scene.' He turned in his chair, looking directly at Miss Parkinson. 'I have a feeling,' he said, 'that I've seen you before.'

'A lot of men say that,' said Miss Parkinson, colouring, starting to twiddle her thumbs, something my father had taught her to do. 'I don't think so,' she went on, 'unless it was singing with a band.'

'I've never sung with a band,' said Harold.

'No,' said Miss Parkinson. 'Me. I have. You could have heard me at the Co-op Café at Swinehurst.'

'I doubt it,' said Harold. There was a silence. A bee buzzed, and I looked out of the window for traces of Bile Beans in the sky, for such is the way the mind works.

'Where did you come from?' he suddenly asked Miss Parkinson.

'I don't understand.' Her thumbs bumped together in her confusion.

'When all this was going on – how did you come onto the scene?'

'I was employed by him,' she said, separating her hands to point one at my father.

'Singing with his band?'

'No.' She watched the detective's face, for a clue as to whether she should smile at this. 'I was his secretary,' she said, deciding it was better to be safe than sorry.

'Eating at the Queen's Head.' He smiled down at his boots.

We all sat up straight at this. The man knew more than we had bargained for. He knocked his pipe out into the fireplace, indicating that the kid gloves were off, the verbal fencing was over.

'All right,' he said, addressing us en famille. 'Let me tell you what I think.' We waited, and the man with the tic, speaking for the first time, asked if he should write it down. The Chief Superintendent shook his head.

'It's more than obvious,' he began, 'that this person, this De Kuyper, over a period of more than twenty years, turned this – ' and his hand swung out to indicate the house and grounds, the London Road, the town and probably as far afield as the Soke of Peterborough, ' – into what we call a hotbed of intrigue and subversion.'

George cleared his throat and leaned forward. 'If I may, Chief Superintendent – '

'No,' said Harold, 'you may not.' He went on: 'If we had been on the scene earlier, I've no doubt that we would have found a lot of evidence. Unfortunately – ' and he looked along the semi-circle of Corks, ' – it has all been removed.' He said this in a tone which boded ill for Messrs Pickfords. 'Now,' he said, taking out and fingering his Babies Bottom, 'I'm not an unreasonable man.' We all nodded, to show that we realised that. 'Not that I can make promises, mind you – but you all know the saying: "You scratch mine, I'll scratch yours." ' We all nodded again, to show that we did indeed.

'What,' said my father, raising his hand to show that he was about to speak, 'what do you mean, when you say this house was a hotbed of intrigue – and whatever it was?'

'Subversion, sir,' said Harold.

'Yes,' said my father. 'That. What do you mean?'

'I mean, sir, that having infiltrated – to use the correct word – the household, the ménage as it were, this woman then set about filling the place with her accomplices, bringing in various specialists.'

'Specialists?' said my father, leaning forward, manfully trying to keep up, but thinking now of the Ear, Nose and Throat Hospital.

'People trained to a hair's breadth,' explained Harold, 'in mixing invisible ink, say, or taking snaps with little cameras. Some of them no bigger than matchboxes.' He held up thumb and forefinger, but it made things no clearer to my father. 'Skilled,' continued Harold, 'in the composition of inflammatory pamphlets, the making of bombs.' His hands made the shape of a melon. 'And the disaffecting of working-class people.'

'Disinfecting working-class people?' said my father, the strain showing on his face, a mint unwrapped in his fingers.

'Dis-ah-fecting. Upsetting,' explained Harold. He spoke quite kindly to my father (indeed, who could not?). 'I don't mean that everyone in the house would be – ipso facto – in league with her. It's more likely that if she found someone who was, shall we say, a little weak-minded, she would keep him here to put people off. A "Front" as we call it.' He dragged his eyes away from my father.

'Whereas,' he went on, 'those with backbone, those respecting and paying allegiance to God and HM the King, would be got rid of!' The man with the tic, with nothing to do, was staring at him from the pouffe, utterly fascinated.

'When I say "got rid of",' said Harold, raising his pipe, 'I do not necessarily mean "bumped off", as our American cousins would say. But let us look at the facts.' He spread his fingers to tick them off, his pipe now between his teeth.

'One,' he said. 'Uncle Frank dies.' He was looking at me, so I nodded. I had actually seen him buried.

'He respected the King,'said Yasmin.

'Agreed,' said Harold, forefinger on thumb. 'He used to write to him.' With a small smile, dropping his official manner for a moment, talking off the record as it were, he explained that they had all his letters on file, with a memo from the Gentleman in Waiting.

'Two,' he said, again the man determined to get at the truth. 'Mrs Cork, your mother,' he reminded me, 'a lady whose devotion and loyalty, at least to God and HM the King, cannot be doubted for a moment, is replaced by this lady here.' He turned to Miss Parkinson, who modestly lowered her eyes.

'Three,' he said, turning to face Yasmin. 'The daughter of the house is seen, often, with members of the armed forces.'

'There's no need to emphasise "members" like that,' said Yasmin, a little waspishly I thought.

'This is my wife you're talking to,' said George, but without enthusiasm, pointing to her as if proper introductions had not been made.

'Were you not in the King's uniform yourself, when you met the lady?' The Superintendent was warming up now. Then, as George was waiting, he added: 'Sir.'

'Yes,' said George, nodding his thanks, feeling in his inside pocket for his references. 'I was. *And* with leather gloves and a cane.'

'Something to do with beds,' said the Special Branch man, evenly.

'Well, yes,' said George. He licked his lips, but his moment was past. Harold had turned to me.

'How's Red Fred these days?' he asked.

'Red Fred?' I repeated, shaking my head, feeling all eyes upon me. 'I don't know any Red Fred.'

'Don't you?' he asked, heavily. 'Or Aunt Ada? And their daughter, The Rose of Swinehurst as I believe she's called?' The man with the tic was scribbling again with a vengeance.

'I didn't know she was called that,' I said, my stomach tightening, expecting him now to produce infra-red photographs taken in the chicken run.

'I dare say,' said Harold, and I did not care for his tone. He stood up, stretching himself, then began to put his things into his carrier bag. 'Thank you very much for the tea,' he said. 'And the biscuit.' He took the notebook from the MI5 man's hand and crossed out the last line, the one that said 'Thank you very much for the tea.'

'You'll be hearing from us,' he said, while the man with the tic put on his raincoat. 'I shouldn't go too far.' My father asked if Carlisle was all right, and Harold said that it was. Then they left by the front door, the policeman who had been posted there falling into step behind. Out on the lawn to give them a wave, as you would to anyone, I saw Harold handing out a press release to the reporters; one each except to the *Daily Worker*, telling them all how to spell his name. Then, after a quick peep at his handcuffs for the man from the Associated Press, the police car moved away from the kerb, its siren clearing the London Road. It had been some time since we had seen anything like it.

The press (known I believe as The Fourth Estate), hung

around for a little while, shouting up through the rhododendrons things like 'Are you guilty?' and 'Say something
in Russian!' But it was nearly half past five, and soon peace
had returned to Jasmine Villa. I went into the house and
rejoined the family. More tea had been made, and Miss
Parkinson sent to play with the children. As I sat in
Harold's chair, George returned from the telephone, on
which he had been talking to his solicitor.

'You can be hung,' he said grimly, and then to reassure
my father, 'but not drawn and quartered. At least that's
what he says.'

'Shut up!' said Yasmin, who had at this time already met
the man in the RAF blazer. 'Don't go making a fool of
yourself. Nobody's going to be hung.'

I agreed. I said that at the most it would be a stiffish
fine, and we would be bound over to keep the peace.

'You and your Red Fred!' said George, and venomous
is the only word. 'What do you mean, "A stiffish fine?" '
He tapped his tie pin, the Cleckheaton coat of arms, 'I'm
not bloody guilty!'

'He means we're not guilty,' said his wife, but mildly,
her mind on better things to come.

'And neither is she,' said my father, with touching
loyalty, pointing at the door through which we could hear
'Patta cake patta cake, baker's man'.

'And I'm certainly not,' I said. I had the uneasy feeling
that a scapegoat was being selected. We all looked at my
father, but I felt bound to say, 'And he's not either.'

'So we've got nothing to worry about,' said Yasmin.

'No,' said George, already regretting the three minutes
of his solicitor's time. 'You might be right.'

'On the other hand,' I said, my lively imagination coming
into play, 'they could make a case.' I put my feet on the
pouffe, still warm from the man with the tic. 'Let us
consider,' and I began to tick off the points on my fingers,
like the Chief Superintendent. 'One,' I said. 'De Kuyper
was a spy.' I looked at them in turn, as Harold had done.

'And she's in Moscow,' said Yasmin.

'Agreed,' I said. 'They can summons her, but she probably won't come.'

'So we're all right,' said George.

'No,' I said, 'we're not. Two,' having nearly forgotten to say that. 'The facts, as the police have them, are substantially correct.' I went on tapping my second finger, daring them to contradict me. 'My mother *did* leave. My Uncle Frank *did* die. I *was* evacuated to the Deliuses, where I *could* have been influenced by Uncle Fred. And *you*,' I said, pointing a toe at my brother-in-law, *'were* in the armed forces when you married into the family.' I spread my arms, forgetting what number three was. 'It all fits,' I said.

'Bloody rubbish!' said George, standing up. 'Get your coat on.' This was to Yasmin.

When they had gone we sat for a little while, my father and I.

'Jeffrey,' he said suddenly, while I was silently rehearsing my Goodbye, Dad, 'What was she doing?'

'Miss Parkinson?' I said. 'She was playing "Patta cake patta cake, baker's man" with them.'

'No,' he said. 'De Kuyper. What was she doing here all that time?'

'I don't know,' I said. There was long pause as we both sorted back through the years. 'Spying, I suppose,' I said finally. You couldn't really call it anything else.

'On me?' he asked, his mouth still working, though he had finished his mints.

'No,' I said. 'Not just on you. On Great Britain.'

He thought about this, nodding slowly as it began to make sense to him. 'And telling Moscow all about it,' he said.

I nodded, remembering how often I had met her in the post office.

Chapter Two

Although we were not arrested, things went from bad to worse over the next few weeks; and not only at Jasmine Villa. In Bradford, George was summoned to the town hall, to make a statement and to look at photographs. (All of which he identified, stabbing his finger into the album and shouting, 'That's another of the bastards!') Becoming increasingly bitter about the whole affair, he had taken to wearing his medal at work, telling Yasmin there was a definite atmosphere in Wibsey whenever he arrived with his jars.

'Jeffrey,' said my father one day, 'I want you to go an errand for me.'

'Of course,' I said, adjusting my homburg in front of the office mirror. I did wonder why Norman, Mr Grandidge's successor (whose mother had sent a note, complaining about the state of his underpants), was not going, but assumed it to be an errand of some delicacy. How right I was.

'No,' said my father, drawing the cretonne curtains he had fitted along the glass partition. 'Not the bank. I want you to go to Moscow.'

Of course I just stared at him, then at my watch, my mind reeling, trying to understand what he meant.

'I don't mean this afternoon,' he said, obviously thinking me about to hurry down the stairs and onto a tram. 'Tomorrow will be all right.'

'Yes, of course,' I said, sitting down. What was he talking about? Go to Moscow? He was well aware that Harold, the

Detective Chief Superintendent, had given us permission to travel no further than Carlisle.

'You'll need some money,' he said, swinging open the heavy door of the safe.

'Thank you,' I said. Was this the way they worked? First the ringleader, Mata Hari herself, then all the minions and dupes disappearing one by one? And the spy master, the brain at the centre of the web, what of him? Would he follow on the night boat from Southampton, once he had safely dispatched me, Miss Parkinson and Rupert, George and Yasmin and little Victoria? I saw problems right away with Elspeth.

'I think I'll have problems with Elspeth,' I said.

'Why?' asked my father, keeping his back to me as he counted out ten-shilling notes. 'You can tell her you're going on a sales trip.' This was post-war business jargon which he had picked up and was rather proud of.

'She's not going with me?' He must have heard the surprise in my voice for he turned round, closing the safe before I could see what was inside.

'Why?' he said. 'You're old enough to go to Moscow on your own.'

'Yes, of course I am,' I said, signing a petty cash slip for the money.

'That should be enough for a return ticket,' he said, 'and a bit of spending money.'

'A return?' I was swept by mixed feelings. Relief that I was coming back, and the knowledge that I hadn't the faintest idea what was going on. Then I saw that he had two envelopes in his hand.

'This is your passport. With a visa,' he said. There was a short silence, during which we were both impressed, neither of us having had either before. 'And this – ' It was a foolscap envelope, heavily sealed with two utility labels. ' – I want you to give her this.'

I stared at the envelope, at his writing in capital letters, to make it easier for the Russians to read. It was addressed

– or rather it had no address; it said simply 'Comrade De Kuyper. Personal.'

'I'm going on a sales trip tomorrow,' I told Elspeth that evening. I had already been to the travel agents, having been let out of work early. 'Moscow, return,' I had said, behind my hand, after waiting till the shop was empty. But no trouble. The girl had written out the ticket, which I had now in my inside pocket with the letter. She had been on the telephone as I left, no doubt dialling Whitehall 1212. I would not have been surprised to hear the siren of Harold's car, blue light flashing as it bounced through the unmade roads of the estate, causing the neighbours to draw aside their curtains. Then he would be on the door-step, the man with the tic close behind.

'Hello, hello, hello!' he'd say. 'What's this then? Taking liberties are we?'

'Carlisle?' asked Elspeth, knowing the close association between the firm and that town. She took the strawberry jam tart from the box, leaving the lemon cheese for me, a thought that I appreciated, though it was a pale imitation. Stirring my tea, I decided to confide in her.

'I'm going to Moscow,' I said.

'In Russia?' she said, her eyes widening, the jam tart halfway to her mouth. I nodded that that was the one.

'Are you coming back?' was her next question, the jam tart remaining where it was.

'Yes,' I said, showing her the return ticket, and telling her of the errand I was doing for my father. I said I drew the line at steaming open the letter. Then she said she didn't want to know what was in it, because that would make her an accomplice; and I would look a right fool at the airport when they opened it.

'They don't open letters,' I explained. 'Just your case. Then they put a secret chalk mark on it.' She wanted to know why they didn't open letters, and I told her they were shrewd enough to know that if it was a confidential letter you would have put it in the post. I think she understood that.

'What is it then?' she asked, holding the envelope up to the light. 'If it's not plans?'

'I don't know,' I said, telling her that it could be anything, but was probably a curt note about De Kuyper's superannuation, seeing that she had left without giving notice.

'Just think,' she said later, when we were in bed and I had nearly finished. 'This time tomorrow you'll be in Russia!' Elspeth was being more reasonable than I expected, allowing me to bring forward 'My Night' from Friday, because I wouldn't be there. It would give me something to remember, she said.

Early the next morning I was driving south towards London, speeding down the Great North Road. I threw Elspeth's sandwiches off the bridge into the River Ivel, where they make the famous soft cheese. Chief Superintendent Harold had not of course appeared on the doorstep; but as what is known I think as 'cover', I had on the seat beside me a case of samples; the larger sizes.

It was my first time on an aeroplane, and I did not realise that they gave you drinks. So I slept most of the way from Berlin; missing, I am afraid, most of Central Europe. When I woke up we were approaching Moscow, and I looked eagerly out of the window for onion domes, for Cossacks in long overcoats skating on the frozen Volga. But saw only a building that looked strikingly like the Nabisco factory.

The customs men, in uniforms reminiscent of the Lincolnshire Road Car Company, were interested in my samples, feeling the liberty bodices with their thick Slav fingers. But they soon waved me through. I had brought along my Little Lenin, laying it down with my passport, with a smile (which transcends all language barriers), and this must have done the trick. As my taxi left the airport it was snowing, the cold air filled with white flakes against the dark buildings, like one of those scenes under glass that you shake to make a snowstorm.

'Rosebud,' I said softly to myself in the back seat, my luggage on my lap, glad that I had remembered to bring my scarf.

'Da,' said the driver, the flash of his gold tooth in the mirror.

The next morning I drew the heavy curtains, looked out at an alien sky heavy with snow, and realised where I was. Looking down I saw people in boots, women in headscarves, single-decker trolley buses with funny writing on the sides; and a man in the doorway of a building opposite the hotel looking up at my room.

Instantly I stepped behind the curtain. I had expected something like this to happen, of course. The mere waving of a somewhat tatty copy of Little Lenin was hardly enough to clear me of suspicion of being a 'plant', an agent provocateur. The reader must remember that the Cold War was then on. Only made worse by all the people catching the night boat from Southampton. I whirled around in my dressing gown as there came a heavy knock at the door.

'Come in!' I cried, in English; and the door opened to reveal a 'babushka', one of those women shaped like Mrs Moss. She was carrying a breakfast tray and I smiled at her, reaching for the glass of tea, putting the lump of sugar between my teeth and pouring through it the scalding amber liquid. She seemed reassured to find that I was au fait with their customs, and even laughed as the slice of lemon slid down my chin. Then she went to the window and waved good morning to the man in the doorway; pointing at me and then into her mouth, indicating that I was having my breakfast and that now was a good time for him to go and buy a paper, or spend a kopek. It was only when she had gone, after making loud clucking noises over the sample liberty bodices, that I saw the note tucked beneath the red rose.

'Dear Jeffrey,' it said, in the handwriting I knew so well. 'What a lovely surprise. Meet me in Red Square at ten o'clock. Natasha.'

Natasha, eh? I thought, wondering if that was her real name. Was she to be like one of those wooden Russian dolls?

I thought that was pretty good. An hour later, outside St Basil's, I put it to her; if she was Natasha beneath De Kuyper, was there yet another identity concealed, and then another, right down to a tiny swaddled baby that I did not know? She smiled appreciatively as she brushed the snow from my overcoat, tutting over my sodden knees, for I had slipped and fallen in running towards her across the cobbles – arms held wide, shouting the only name I knew her by; the man from the doorway being kind enough to help me up.

'Don't ask too many questions,' she said as we walked towards the Kremlin. Its red flag (what else?) streamed against a patch of blue sky, and there was a long queue of people waiting to go in. I was in two minds about wanting to see Little Lenin, not knowing how much it would cost, but when De Kuyper (as I insisted on calling her) said she had seen him twice already, we walked on and sat on a cannon.

'What do you think of it?' she asked, exchanging waves with the man from the doorway, who had found a cannon of his own not far away.

'It's very big,' I said, staring out across the river towards Poland. Then, after a pause: 'Why did you do it?'

She looked at me, the familiar creases forming as she smiled. I see her now in her sage-green uniform, against the painted black of the huge cannon. The Sergeant's chevrons on the sleeves of her loose tunic, her trousers tucked into soft leather boots. Grey hair neatly inside her cap, the sun glinting on the red enamelled star, bright as the one behind us on the Kremlin spire.

'You know what I mean,' I said. 'Taking the night boat

from Southampton, without telling anybody. All that in the papers.'

'How did he take it?' she asked, and I knew that she meant my father. I told her that he had come home to find her gone, and that though Miss Parkinson had stepped into the breech, doing the best she could with an egg on toast, he had been inconsolable.

'I tried to warn him,' she said. 'Just after your mother left.'

'What?' I said, surprised, knowing that they weren't allowed to tell. 'That you were a spy?'

'No,' she said, smiling, 'that she couldn't cook.'

'De Kuyper,' I said, a few minutes later, after I had taken her photograph, then given the camera to the man from the doorway to take one of us together. Having said the word 'spy' I wanted to follow it up. 'I know I can't ask too many questions, but – did you tell them everything?'

'All I knew,' she said, simply. 'There wasn't a lot to tell.' She jumped off the gun carriage and took my arm, and we walked to a favourite cafe of hers, to eat apricot dumplings and drink what she teased me into believing was fermented mare's milk. On the way she promised to tell me the whole story.

Out of the wind which blew from Brest Litovsk it was warm, almost like England. Trees and shrubs were in leaf, and a crowd of youngsters passed us chattering away in Russian, looking like Junior Rechabites with their red scarves and shining earnest faces. Who would think, I thought, that I was on my way to a cafe in Moscow, arm in arm with a KGB Sergeant, who was about to tell me the story of her twenty-two-year mission in a foreign land. I could write a book about it.

'I can't very well begin at the beginning,' she said, when we had been served and she was sucking her mare's milk through a straw.

'You mean who recruited you?' I had, as you will notice,

384

the terminology off pat. I bit into my first dumpling and found that I was enjoying it.

De Kuyper nodded, far away both in time and place, staring past me at a large mural of black stallions chasing white horses to get at their milk. No doubt she saw the back room of some hump-backed tutor's lodgings; shabby young men in stained flannels, waitresses in lisle stockings, averting their faces from each other on the dimly lit stairs; making light and innocuous conversation before they were called in, one by one, to raise their hand and say a few words, collecting their kit on the way out.

'Let's just say,' she said, 'that I joined in the late nineteen twenties.' I nodded, spearing another dumpling, waiting for her to go on.

'My orders were,' she said, 'to establish myself, and to wait.'

'You were a mole!' I exclaimed, and she patted me on the back to clear the apricot that had gone down the wrong way. A Russian family at the next table smiled sympathetically, as we would if we saw some Russians eating faggots for the first time.

'Yes,' she said. 'Though we didn't use the term then.'

'A sleeper!' I said, another dumpling on my fork, dipping it in the jam; and she nodded.

'So I went to Jasmine Villa.' She said the name, I thought, as if she were saying Pentonville, or Wormwood Scrubs. 'And then you came along, and then Hitlerism, and the war in Spain, and then The Great Patriotic War.' She toyed with a plastic radish on the table, containing some kind of Russian sauce, thinking of important events that had happened.

'Then your Uncle Frank died, and your mother went off. And then Elsie [Miss Parkinson] came along. And then I heard on the wireless that they'd both gone, on the night boat from Southampton.'

'Guy and Donald,' I filled in, absolutely enthralled.

'I didn't know them personally,' she said, nodding, 'so

I sent a message, saying if we were all starting to move, didn't they think I might as well come too?' She sucked up the last of her mare's milk as I stared at her, open mouthed as I had finished my dumplings.

'What about the spying?' I said. 'All the subversion?'

She smiled wanly, fingering her badge for outdoor cooking, then shook her head. 'Let me put it this way,' she said. 'When I filled in the debriefing forms, it was twenty-five minutes of "Nil, nil – or nyet, nyet – wasn't there, didn't know him, didn't know it was going on"; instead of ten days pouring out stirring tales to be serialised in *Komsomolskaya Pravda*.' She fingered the top button of her tunic, no doubt making sure that it was fastened. 'I had nothing to report,' she said quietly, then biting her lip, her eyes sad.

'Nothing?' I said. 'Surely you must have done something in all that time?'

'Nothing,' she repeated, then forced a bright smile. 'But they told me I might have to wait years before I was activated. I just kept hoping the call would come – that I'd hear my call sign on the wireless – or there'd be some message on the Biro calendar.'

'The Biro calendar!' I exclaimed, then lowered my voice, realising this was top secret stuff. 'The Biro calendar!' I hung forward over the table, pushing aside the plastic radish.

'It was one of our ways of getting in touch,' she said. 'The way the girl held the wooden spoon. Like the dots on the milk bottle tops.'

The milk bottle tops. 'Pomfrets!' I hissed, funnelling my mouth with my hands, excited now that the story was unfolding. 'The man who washed out the churns!'

'No.' She smiled. 'Not him.' I waited, but it was obvious, and understandable of course, that she was not going to tell me. My mind whizzed around the town, the faces of those I had grown up with passing before me, as on a film when the loose pages of a calendar whirl like blown leaves while a train thunders across America. Was it a Pomfret?

The one on the railway? The old sea dog? Old man Pomfret himself? Or a Pomfret by marriage perhaps? I thought back to the bungalow with the bricked-in grandfather clock, to the powerful wireless in the bedroom; and, for some reason, to the veal, ham and egg pie.

Across the tables, between the happy Muscovite families sucking up their mare's milk, the man from the doorway nodded affably to me. He was eating the Soviet version of a Kunzle cake.

'I never saw any dots on the milk bottle tops,' I said.

'No,' said De Kuyper. 'They never came, did they.'

We went for a ride on the Underground train, then walked along Gorky Street. (Which wasn't his real name, she told me, like Lenin and Stalin; and herself of course. They seem to have a thing about that.)

De Kuyper treated me now as an adult businessman – which I appreciated – and when we got to her third-floor flat asked if I would like a drink. After ascertaining that she did not mean horse's milk, I accepted a small vodka, and with a plate of cheese straws we settled down on the settee.

Pickfords, whatever the Special Branch had against them, had done a good job in transporting her room intact from Lincolnshire to Moscow. The old books on the shelves were familiar friends, though I noted that those on the top shelf now had their brown paper jackets removed. The full-length portrait of Jean de Reszke was now reversed, showing Uncle Joe, with a pipe like Harold; and on a small table – and I found this touching – was a framed remembrance of an afternoon tea on the lawn of Jasmine Villa. My mother in the height of fashion, a plucked eyebrow raised at De Kuyper's effrontery; Yasmin with shingled hair, and me at the front. No sign of my father, who was probably at the Queen's Head, but the blueish hills were quite clear in the background. I realised that there was no sign of the Duke of Windsor (in the flat I mean, not in the photograph). It seemed that De Kuyper's strong feelings at the time, unlike those of the Bishop of Bradford, had almost certainly been a 'Front'.

'I've brought you something,' I said, taking the letter from my inside pocket. She hesitated for a moment before taking it from me, obviously worried that it might be from the Inland Revenue, or of course a summons.

'From him?' she asked, looking at the liberty bodice motif we had just started to use, and the Gothic lettering: 'Prop A. Cork & Son'. I nodded and went to stand at the window, raising my glass in salute to the man in the doorway as she read the letter. Several pigeons, and Little Lenin himself, painted large on the wall across the road, stared in at me.

Hearing her refold the single page I turned, as she turned away to brush what can only have been a tear from her cheek. Clearing my throat loudly, to let her know that she was being observed, I sat down again. The letter was on the embroidered cushion, the warmth of the room making the paper – cramped so long under my arm – unfold against the white broderie anglaise of the antimacassar. I could read, could not help reading, the last line.

'And that loneliness, from the time it became unendurable to the heart of man, has scattered and sown stars.'

And then the signature, in the black ink of his Waterman pen: 'Alfred'. And a very small cross, one to fit in the box that says you want no publicity should you win the pools. A kiss?

Chapter Three

'I'm back,' I called, opening the door, a fancy bottle of mare's milk tied with a scarlet ribbon under my arm. But there was no answer. Then I heard Elspeth crying in the kitchen.

'Your father!' she cried out when she saw me. Red eyed, she sat at the kitchen table.

'My father?' I gasped. Fear clutched at my heart, as it does when we hear of a loved one slipping beneath the waves.

'And your sister, and George!' she said in a quavering voice, pointing a shaky finger at me, 'and you in a minute!'

What with her face, and the half-set home perm, I was glad of the excuse to turn away to put down the mare's milk.

'Me in a minute?' I repeated, not really understanding what was going on.

'Yes, you,' said the man with the tic from MI5, in the doorway, having emerged from under the stairs, holding out a summons.

Could it be true? Did this kind of thing happen in this country? Could a Northern Manufacturer and his son, who had served both God and King, be accused – on the evidence of Harold's notebook – of treason? Yes. Seemingly they could. Such was the climate of the time.

The next morning we met, in Mr Rim's office over the building society, anxious to learn our fate. My father and I, and my sister and her husband. They had not been charged, but were present in case their summonses were in the post.

'It's not a divorce, is it?' asked our legal adviser, fiddling among the papers on his desk. He had polished his glasses to look at Yasmin's knees, it now being common knowledge about the man in the RAF blazer.

'No,' I told him. 'Treason. I telephoned you about it.'

'So you did,' said Mr Rim, finding his Toc H diary, in which I saw 'Cork. Treason. 10.30.' He unbuttoned his cardigan and sat back, looking at Yasmin's chest and then the rest of us. 'What's it all about?' he enquired in his kindly manner.

I looked at my father, hat in his lap, staring at Mr Rim's qualifications. 'Those whom the gods intend to destroy . . . ' as they say. I really think it had all become too much for him. On the next chair, George too was in a state of shock, having been peremptorily removed from Odsal, Wibsey, Idle and Cleckheaton, and posted to Keighley, part-time, where nobody knew him. 'It's the Brontë Country,' he told people, but they just cleared their throats nervously and looked away.

'We're a spy ring,' I explained to Mr Rim, heavily ironic. 'We've all got to go to the Old Bailey.'

'The Old Bailey, eh?' said Mr Rim, pushing back his chair so that he could see more of my sister. He raised his well-known warning finger: 'The Central Criminal Court,' he said, giving it its proper name.

'Is that it?' said George, who had behaved well so far. 'Is that what you call legal advice?' But Mr Rim raised ten pale fingers, indicating that there was more to come, that we would get our money's worth.

'Tell me first,' he said, 'in the strictest confidence of course, whether or not you are guilty.'

'No, I'm bloody not!' said George, forgetting himself somewhat I thought.

'And you, my dear?'

'No,' said Yasmin, then, the slightest of flushes rising under her pancake, 'not of treason.'

'Nor me,' I said, and pointed to my father: 'Nor him

either.' My father nodded, pleased I think that I had begun to take some of the weight from his shoulders.

'Not guilty, eh?' said Mr Rim, making a note of this. 'And you're a spy ring, you say?' He put down his pen on the blotter and brought the tips of his fingers together, the way they do. 'I think you'd better tell me all about it, Jeffrey,' he said, feeling free to address me thus because he had handled my grandmother's business.

'It's quite simple,' I told him. 'It's because of De Kuyper.'

'Ah!' he said. The white bust of Sir Hartley Shawcross, the kind of thing that had been popular in many households a few years before, was reflected in his spectacles.

'She *was* a spy,' I said. 'She's in Russia now.'

'Is she?' he said, mildly surprised. There was a pause, just the sound of a mint against my father's teeth. Then Mr Rim said: 'I think I remember reading something about this.'

'Well,' I went on, 'we're being accused of being her minions, her accomplices; helping her in her spying.'

'I see,' he said. 'That's quite a serious charge.' He smiled reassuringly at Yasmin. 'Can I see your summonses?'

We handed them over, explaining that Yasmin's and George's were probably in the post, and after glancing through them and tutting, he got up and selected a fat tome from his bookcase. As they never tire of telling you, solicitors have to spend a lot of money on books.

'You realise that you could be hung?' he asked, turning to us, spectacles on his forehead and finger on the relevant passage.

'Yes,' I said, 'we know that. But not drawn and quartered.'

'No, that's true,' said Mr Rim, after reading a footnote. He closed the book. 'Well, who would you like to defend you?' He took a mint from my father's offered bag as he sat down and they both sucked and twiddled, waiting for us to decide between Spencer Tracey and Sir Hartley Shawcross, the only barristers who came to mind.

After some moments Mr Rim, who although not being in London was well up in legal matters, took out his mint in a fold of his handkerchief and explained that Spencer Tracey was quite out of the question. He was good, he said, make no mistake about that; modelling his act on Clarence Darrow: who specialised in defending those who would insist that we were descended from monkeys. But attorneys, said Mr Rim, savouring the word, unaccustomed as they were to wearing wigs – and, in the case of Mr Darrow, often appearing before the bench in braces – were not allowed to practise in this country. He could not agree with George that Clarence was 'a poof's name'; and added that Sir Hartley would be more likely to be leading for the prosecution.

'There is, however,' and his fingertips were touching again, 'the Honourable Jarvis Harpe. The Right Honourable, I should say.'

I was of course impressed, and Yasmin said that his mother's house had been in *Woman's Weekly* quite recently. So we all said yes, we would like him; though George added the proviso that he wore a wig, and was reasonable. He also said that if he didn't get a summons, he was changing his name by deed poll, and it was no good sending him a bill. This last of course to Mr Rim, who showed us out, managing at last to pat Mrs Cheeseman on the bottom.

Only ten days later we were climbing the narrow stairs to Jarvis Harpe's chambers, being shown at once into his office. Through the Quality Street window, outside in the cobbled yard, a man lit a gaslamp with a pole. Looking around, my first impression was that he (Jarvis Harpe that is) was certainly wigged, and indeed gowned, over a herringbone suit and gold watch chain; but by the amount of books he had bought was unlikely to be reasonable.

'My dear Cork!' he said, in that loud voice they have, coming forward hand outstretched as we were ushered in by his clerk. A small man, wigless, with what I believe are called rheumy eyes. My father, quickly pulling off one of the pigskin gloves he wore when in London, shook the barrister by the hand. Then it was my turn for a firm squeeze, and we were both led by the clerk to the rear of the room, into a dock, a three-quarter size reproduction of the one at The Old Bailey. Wearing a policeman's helmet, the clerk stood behind us to enhance the desired effect. A magic lantern, switched on by a sallow youth in an alcove – as Jarvis Harpe himself flicked off the lights – provided ushers and gentlemen of the press, incisive counsel bobbing and weaving, even a benign judge laughing at his own jokes. In sepia; a silent film. Even the sparrows in the slanting beams of sunshine. The Northern Manufacturer, one gloved and one bare hand gripping the spiked rail before him, blinked bravely as the light flickered on his face, trying to understand what was going on.

'Very good,' said Jarvis Harpe, bending at the waist to get a jury's eye-view of the defendants, as the sallow youth, blindfolded and holding sword and scales, appeared in a sheet to impress upon clients the solemnity of the law. The barrister (after waving him away, telling him not to fall down the stairs again) then put us through a short but intensive course on shoulder drooping, the tilt of the head to show a profile, the lowering and rolling heavenwards of eyes. Not forgetting the nervous laugh and the loud positive defiant tone when you were telling what he called 'a pork pie'. He warned my father, possibly having been instructed in this by Mr Rim, against thumb twiddling, and showed us how to unobtrusively clean out our ears. He was, when all was said and done, a master of his craft, worth every one of the gold sovereigns we had been told to bring with us.

'Now then,' he said, when the lights were on again, 'let us see, shall we?' and we smiled and nodded as he unfastened a bow of red ribbon and unrolled the documents of our case.

'The Crown versus Cork and Cork,' he said, smiling and making a slight grimace. (We later discovered that he was a well-known wag, doing impersonations of Arthur Balfour at country houses at the weekends.) 'Has your solicitor told you of what may happen, if you are found guilty? That you could be hung?'

'But not drawn and quartered,' I said.

'Exactly!' boomed Jarvis Harpe, jutting forward. 'Just the point I was about to make.' He had quite obviously summed me up as the most alert and intelligent, the spokesman as it were of the spy ring; and as no summonses had arrived in Bradford – Yasmin and George deciding to draw the curtains and stay right out of it – he did not have my sister's knees to distract him.

'Now then,' he went on, 'the way I have decided to handle this case, is to proceed as if you were not guilty. As if, in effect, you were innocent.'

'That sounds fine,' I said, turning to my father. 'Is that all right with you?'

'Yes,' said my father, cautiously.

'And we *are* innocent,' I thought it best to add.

'Indeed,' said Jarvis Harpe, drawing out his gold watch and raising his eyebrows at the time. 'But that is not something that you should tell me.' He stood up, after whistling down a tube, first ascertaining that the sovereigns were already invested on 'change', as he called it, then making an appointment for us on the following day.

The next morning, remembering us with a friendly nod, Jarvis Harpe outlined to us the prosecution's probable line of attack. He would, he said, 'he' being Sir Hartley or whoever led for the Crown, almost certainly start with the case against my father. This would cover the recruitment, induction and training of the young De Kuyper; the establishing of spy headquarters in the quiet fastness of Lincolnshire; the setting up of the factory as a 'cover'. 'We should avoid, if possible,' said the wag, his eyes twinkling, 'the use of the word "Front" in conjunction with liberty bodices.' And we should expect much to be made of the frequent trips to Carlisle and St James's. This was to say nothing – and he hoped no one would – of what my father got up to in the garden shed.

Then it would be my turn, he said, moving his Oxo mug out of the way and ticking off the points on his fingers. 'He'll try to show the jury that you have a thing about uniforms.' He smiled so that I would not take offence, as he went on to say that I was either 'a coxcomb or a prat', as he put it, or part and parcel of a search for military intelligence. He began to itemise: 'Rechabite, Royal Artillery, best friend a sailor boy.' He paused on the fourth finger: 'To say nothing of you being found in the London Road playing the part of a dwarf clergyman.'

I blushed. Was there nothing that the Establishment was not prepared to use against us?

'Is there nothing the Establishment is not prepared to use against us?' I asked.

'Certainly not,' said Jarvis Harpe, surprised that I should ask. 'You can't have people spying, can you?'

'I suppose not,' I said. But I must say that I expected better from Sir Hartley.

When my father asked what he was likely to get, the barrister said that those below, at the sharp end of the speaking tube, were laying five to two that he would be detained during His Majesty's Pleasure.

Chapter Four

The Old Bailey. The Central Criminal Court as Mr Rim called it. Big Ben, above the roar of London's traffic, told us we were on in an hour, after some people who had been making half crowns. (Interestingly, using an improved version of my Germolene tin.)

'Good luck, Guv!' cried the cabbie through his scarf as he rumbled away, forgetting in his emotion to give me the change.

'Hold it like that, sir!' cried a bevy of journalists, trilbys pushed back, some of them down on one knee, as I paused on the steps to wave. 'Chin up, sir! Give us a nice clenched fist! Who's the geezer under the blanket?'

It was of course my father, and as the policewoman with the wart took his other arm and we moved towards the entrance, the camera of Movietone News panned with us from the roof of a car. With a final wave to Leslie Mitchell, who raised his free hand to his homburg in reply, we passed beneath the grim portals of 'The Bailey'.

My father, who had had no appetite that morning, had been reluctant to leave behind his hat. I had understood how he felt, but told him that apart from the problem of keeping it on under a blanket, unless we were Jews – which we were not – we would hardly be allowed to wear them in court. After some discussion we had chosen hairy sports jackets and flannels, giving us the look I thought of modern-day yeomen, with subdued ties and clean handkerchiefs. Jarvis Harpe, after the rheumy-eyed clerk had inspected us and reported back, said it was exactly right.

'Now,' said our barrister, when we were in his little room. 'Are we all here?'

Lifting the edge of the blanket to show my father, I was reassured to see that our counsel wore a new – or at least clean – wig for the occasion. Rheumy Eyes, standing on an antique stool, sprinkled powder on it from a silver sifter as the Great Defender paced his Oriental mat; the tension showing in the way he practised his gestures, silently mouthed his interjections. The two clerks (the sallow youth carried our references and things, along with a bag of mints sent to my father by 'A Wellwisher'), murmured: 'Very good, sir! Oh, yes indeed, sir!' as Jarvis Harpe turned on the heel of his kid boot, flaring the hem of his gown.

'Call Cork and Cork!' came the cry, loud outside in the tiled passage. We heard it passed from flunkey to flunkey, in the ripe accent of those who had, within living memory, pulled their wives' underwear onto donkeys' front legs.

'We're on!' exclaimed Jarvis Harpe, nodding to his clerk to take the mint from my father's mouth and then, between them, tearing the blanket from his grasp.

I think it fair to say that we entered the courtroom in some style. Applause was not allowed of course, but everyone was looking at us. Even the judge, an old man with eyes like the clerk, stared at us as we entered the dock. He gave a little nod, by way of 'Hello' or 'Good morning', which I thought was civil of him in the circumstances.

'Good morning, m'lud,' I said, bowing of course, nudging my father to bend from the waist. I nodded approvingly to Yasmin, on the first row of the public benches in her shortest skirt. On her bosom she wore the pillbox-hatted plaster of Paris brooch, the half-crown model in gold paint, which Mr Rim said was all I had going for me.

The preliminaries over we were allowed to sit, while counsel who was leading for the Crown rose to outline the case for the prosecution.

It was not, of course, Sir Hartley. No doubt he was busy

lifting the burden from the working people of St Helens. But I did not particularly care for Sir Vincent Goneham. I found it hard to forgive the sheer nastiness – there is no other word – with which he began. Venom, spite, bigotry – quite frankly I was shocked at the way he attacked my father and myself. To say nothing of De Kuyper, who was not there, and like the Queen unable to answer back. My father's thumbs bumped, then came to a halt, as he heard himself described – not as a Northern Manufacturer; no mention of our yeoman stock, of our being The Backbone of England – but as a cold, calculating recruiter of maidens from Huddersfield. A renegade who for years had used the liberty bodice as nothing but a front. (As Sir Vincent said this, Jarvis Harpe's eyes met mine, before rolling upwards to the ceiling.)

'Mr Cork,' said Sir Vincent, after my father had given his name and address and opened his mouth wide, to show the judge that he had swallowed his mint. 'Alfred Simeon Cork?'

My father turned to the judge again for guidance.

'You must answer the question,' said his lordship. 'Just say "Yes".'

My father did so, and Sir Vincent began to move about, his polished boots squeaking faintly. 'Can I begin by taking you back to a certain day in the year nineteen forty-five?' he asked, his tone softening, becoming almost chatty. 'When your son – the defendant Jeffrey Cork – came to your study wearing a lapel badge, depicting a shovel?'

My father said that he could, and that he remembered it well. 'It was next to his Nignog,' he said, touching the carnation in the Britannia Metal vase which had been Miss Parkinson's idea. 'He said "Good afternoon" and sat down facing me. "What do you want?" I said to him.'

'And what did he want?'

' "Do you think it fair," he asked me, "the factory?" '

'Did he indeed. And what was your reaction?'

'I buttoned up my waistcoat and tightened my tie, jerking my Adam's apple free of the knot. "What do you mean?" I parried. "The factory?" ' Sir Vincent and the judge exchanged approving nods at having opened the proceedings with such a model witness, while I stared at my father open mouthed. I had known him all my life and now, suddenly, and in this of all places: verbal diarrhoea!

'He was selecting a quote from *The Theory of Surplus Value*' my father went on, his voice strengthening so that you could almost hear him. 'He had his Little Lenin in his hand.' He held up his left hand to show them, and I suddenly recalled him filing his nails carefully that morning at breakfast.

'Please go on.'

' "I want to tell you," he said, "about the ethics of owning the means of production." ' Never exactly booming (you will recall that he was known in the trade as 'The Mutterer'), my father's voice now carried to the four corners of the court. Turning to the judge with a courteous bow, he said: 'I slipped a mint into my mouth and drummed the Lone Ranger's tune on the leather arm of my chair, my lord. "Go on then," I said to him.'

'Did you?' said the judge.

'And did he?' Sir Vincent, arms akimbo, was fascinated.

' "Take your raw materials," he said,' my father declaimed, beginning to tick them off on his manicured fingers, as indeed I had done at the time. ' "Your cotton and your rubber buttons, and your broderie anglaise." ' He paused, leaning again towards the judge, in danger of impaling his Adam's apple on the spike: '*If* you can get it, I said to him.'

'Indeed,' said Sir Vincent, who really knew nothing of the paucity of broderie anglaise in the mid-nineteen forties.

' "Let's say that each item costs sixpence," he said' my father continued, still quoting – but not looking at – me.

'All right,' said Sir Vincent, a sport, game for anything: 'Let's do that.'

' "That's one and six," he said, "For the cost of a garment." ' My father held up a neat index and little finger to illustrate this. 'Then he said: "Shall we say a shilling for the cost of labour?" '

'That makes a total of half a crown for a liberty bodice,' said the judge, putting down his pen. 'Did he mention overheads?'

'I'm obliged to your lordship,' muttered Sir Vincent, who had been trying to work it out but had not been quick enough.

'Precisely what I said to him, sir,' said my father, realising that the judge was no fool. 'Rent and rates and string, I told him, and depreciation on the machines.'

'How much did he allow for that?' asked Sir Vincent.

'Threepence.' My father looked at me, then, endeavouring to be fair, lowered his eyes. 'Fourpence, eventually.'

'Two and ten,' pronounced the judge, who had done arithmetic at Oxford.

'I'm obliged, m'lud,' said Sir Vincent, taking the opportunity to blow his nose. 'Tell me, Mr Cork,' he went on, putting his handkerchief away in his sleeve, like the girls did up their knickers at Guinevere's. 'What did your son say then?'

'He wanted to know how much he would have to pay for one,' said my father.

'He wore them, did he?' This was the judge, and I stared at him hard, trying to work out if he was being funny.

'He wanted to know how much they sold for, retail,' explained the Northern Manufacturer. 'He was, I think,' and here he made a gesture which he must have rehearsed while pushing down his half moons that morning, 'attempting to discover the profit margin.'

There was a rustle throughout the courtroom as people shuffled uneasily, looking down to see if their laces were fastened. My father then added the gratuitous information that I had sucked in my cheeks and had pretended to study my fingernails.

'I thought for a moment,' he said, 'that he meant that we ought to put our prices up.' There was a warm murmur of approbation in the court as he went on to say that while under that impression, and quite frankly interested, he had pushed his mints across his desk towards me.

'But that was not so?' said Sir Vincent, his boots squeaking as he rose and fell, showing a little of his silk socks.

'No, sir,' said my father. Then, in a low voice: 'He began to talk about The Theory of Surplus Value, and shares for the women. And *wages as well!*' The judge, having to take a sip of water, silenced the tutting and allowed the star witness to write down on a slip of paper my phrase about 'A spectre haunting Europe'.

' "What about a co-op?" he said.' My father's voice was raised again and people could take their cupped hands from their ears.

'A co-op what?' asked Sir Vincent, as the jury passed the slip of paper from hand to hand. 'Are we talking about milk tokens?'

My father said they were not. Or about funerals. But about the women all owning equal shares and meeting every Monday in the boardroom, deciding what to do. He explained that the idea had been to use his office, with him sitting at his own desk, and that chairs would be no problem as the co-op members would not be in there all that long.

'Indeed,' said Sir Vincent. He breathed. 'When your son spoke of "equal shares" – did he elaborate on this?'

My father told him I had talked about a cake; and had indeed drawn one on his blotter.

'I see,' said Sir Vincent, for a change. 'And what did you say to that?'

My father said that he hadn't really minded, as the blotting paper was due to be changed; but on the matter of equal shares he was quite unequivocal. 'There were none!' he almost thundered. 'It was all mine!'

I noted that the judge, albeit discreetly below his desk,

joined in the tumultuous applause; my father bowing to the four corners of the courtroom.

'Thank you, Mr Cork,' said Sir Vincent, who seemingly was not averse to that kind of thing. He revolved, giving a squeak and a twirl, and changed his line of attack.

'Where was your younger son at the time?' he asked, meaning of course Rupert, the one destined for the Church. My father told him that he had at that moment run down the hall, shouting that he was 'Going wee wees', and waited for the next question.

'Would it be true to say,' asked Sir Vincent, losing interest at once in the incontinent young Curate, 'that you were angered by your eldest son's suggestion that the women be given equal shares?'

My father said that 'distraught' was probably the better word. He told the court how he had debated with himself as to whether he should phone for the people with the wet sheets. It had been then that I had said to him that the whole country would be run like that soon. When Uncle Fred was in.

Sir Vincent was rising as this was said, and his eyebrows rose along with his pin-striped turn-ups. 'Run like what?' he enquired. 'When Uncle Fred's in where?' Then, coming down: 'Who's Uncle Fred?'

'Run like our factory,' explained my father, quite the orator now, making fly-wheel motions with a manicured hand. 'When Uncle Fred was in Parliament. Uncle Fred Delius,' he added, to make everything clear. 'Him with the cucumbers.'

'I asked him,' he continued smoothly, as Sir Vincent's mouth opened and closed, 'where he had heard this kind of talk.'

'And what did he say?' asked Sir Vincent, not prepared to keep his mouth closed for long.

' "Mainly from books," he said.' My father exchanged slow meaningful nods with m'lud. 'Karl Marx, and Lenin; Little Lenin as they called him. And Sir Hartley Shawcross.'

'And,' suggested Sir Vincent, delicately ignoring the reference to his learned if wayward colleague, 'from the man who washed out Pomfrets' churns?' But my father shook his head.

' "Are you smoking opium?" I asked him,' he said.

'And?' prompted Sir Vincent.

'Player's Weights,' replied my father, with understandable distaste, being of course a smoker of Wills Whiffs. ' "Are you drinking?" I then asked. I knew that he had left the Rechabites.' He paused for dramatic effect, attempting to mimic my voice. ' "Not yet," he said.'

'Did he?' said Sir Vincent.

'He did,' said my father. 'I had thought of pouring him a large sherry, following it with a large cigar, in order to make him sick; but I decided against it. "What about women?" I asked him.'

'Indeed,' said Sir Vincent, clearly interested. 'What about them?'

'I told him that I had been meaning to speak to him, but he said that he had a pamphlet.'

'From the Board of Trade?'

'From the Reverend Eli Wannamaker.' My father took a deep breath. ' "Are you – have you – you know – " I asked him. "Are you sleeping with them?" ' He grasped the spikes, made smooth by the hands of countless villains. ' "Not *sleeping* with them, no," he said.' I thought I caught a flicker of the judge's right eyelid; though I could not be certain.

Suddenly my father looked me straight in the face. ' "Do you believe in God, Jeffrey?" I said,' he said.

Without thinking, though it was a question that deserved a moment's thought – and quite forgetting that I had not yet sworn to tell the whole truth, etc – I replied: 'No,' I said. 'But I do believe in keeping clean.'

'And the Church of England?' asked the judge, when the ripple of applause had died away; and there was no flicker of the eyelid now. 'What were your views on that?'

'I was not sure, m'lud,' I answered. One could only go so far; and as the reader knows, I was never an extremist.

'Thank you, Mr Cork,' said the judge. 'And you, Mr Cork,' getting some amusement from that. 'Sir Vincent?'

'I'm obliged, m'lud,' said counsel, giving a perfunctory squeak and a bow. 'No more questions.'

My father was still looking at me, as the bald man prodded him to indicate that his big moment was over. Averting his eyes he sighed, his tide audibly receding, then his thumbs began to revolve again.

'Call Jeffrey Cork,' cried Sir Vincent, and I detected renewed appetite, a metaphorical licking of the lips.

'You are Jeffrey Cork?' he asked as I rose in the dock, murmuring to the policewoman with a wart to stand back a little. I said that I was indeed, and smiled across at the gentlemen of the press as they wrote this down.

'And you were born in Jasmine Villa, London Road, on March 29th, nineteen twenty-nine?'

That was correct I said, rising and falling a little on the balls of my feet, ready for the fray.

'Your father is your co-defendant, Alfred Simeon Cork?'

'Yes,' I said, receiving from my father, albeit a little late in the day, a weak smile and a mouthed 'Thank you'.

'And your mother was Gloria Theda Cork?'

'She was,' I said.

'And still is,' said Sir Vincent, a smile flickering around his violet lips. The judge thought this was pretty good and smiled back at him, enquiring if that was Theda-Cork, hyphenated. All those in uniform, propped against the panelled walls, smiled at this; and several of the reporters held up their notebooks, indicating that they had written it down. But I realised that all this badinage was but a facade; that the incisive questioning was about to begin. Being an old hand at the game, Sir Vincent was polite, almost amiable, as he led me into well-prepared traps.

'Would you tell us, Mr Cork,' he asked, 'something of your early life?'

'Of course,' I said, inclining my head, and he gave a slight bow by way of appreciation. The judge smiled encouragingly, and I inclined my head again to him. Looking around the court I waited for the last sniff and footfall to die away. A sense of timing is something I have always prided myself on. Sir Vincent waited; breathing heavily, his little wig rising and falling. Addressing myself to the jury opposite, noting the reporters poised to tiptoe out to the telephone, I cleared my throat.

'I was born,' I began, watching Jarvis Harpe and raising my voice as he moved upwards a flat hand, 'just four years before this country came off the Gold Standard.' I paused for effect, looking round the court, every face of course raised to mine. 'At Number 10 Downing Street,' I continued, 'Mr Ramsay MacDonald, Prime Minister, a Scottish illegitimate crofter's son with a moustache . . . ' but Sir Vincent had raised a pale hand from his gown to stop me.

'Thank you,' he said. 'Can we move on a little? I think the court would prefer to hear about political influences; the early scenes of spy activity you saw around you.' Hands on his bottom, he flipped up his gown and began to walk about. 'Tell us, please, something about your father.'

I looked at the judge, who smiled and nodded to me to go ahead, and started again. But the pale hand was raised.

'Tell the court, for example,' said Sir Vincent, 'what career your father had in mind for you when you were young.'

'A Christian scholar,' I said simply.

Sir Vincent, who had been walking away from me, stopped, his hand-made boot inches from the floor; and with a movement that would have drawn applause from Kitchener turned round on the other foot.

'A Christian scholar?' he echoed, squinting to see if the judge had heard.

'Yes,' I said, about to say that it might have been a Muscular Christian, but deciding to leave it as it was. 'He,' and I exchanged nods with my father, 'sent away for a book of instruction. From an advertisement illustrated with a pointing hand.'

'A pointing hand?'

'Yes,' I said, 'cut off at the cuff.' Demonstrating – for the King's Counsel appeared a little slow to take things in – I sawed at my wrist, pulling off one of the buttons that prevented you wiping your nose on your sleeve. There was an almost tangible silence in the courtroom, except for the breathing of the policewoman with the wart, who had bent down to pick up the button. Sir Vincent slipped a finger inside his wing collar to ease out more of his neck, his eyes never leaving mine. Though it was unlikely to have been him, a remembrance came to me of the time I had waited for a half crown from a visiting adult, in my velvet suit, and had been kicked between the legs.

'Perhaps you would care to tell the court,' he said. 'What form this instruction, indicated to you by the pointing hand, cut off at the cuff, took?' There was a pause while I bowed to the judge, to acknowledge his encouraging nod.

'What exactly did you do?' demanded Sir Vincent.

'I worshipped God in the morning,' I told him, 'praising Him and asking Him to look after the King. In the afternoon I traced maps of Africa. The red parts.'

'I see,' he said.

'Avoiding the Belgian Congo,' I added.

'Of course,' said Sir Vincent. 'And when did this come to an end?'

Jarvis Harpe rose to his feet, and not before time I thought. Adjusting his waistcoat, he bowed.

'M'lud,' he began, 'I must protest at my learned friend's assumption that my client no longer worships God in the morning, or traces maps of Africa in the afternoon.'

'The red parts,' said the judge.

'Indeed, m'lud,' said Jarvis Harpe. 'I am obliged to your lordship.' And hitching his striped trousers he sat down.

'Are you,' continued Sir Vincent smoothly, 'still worshipping in the morning and tracing in the afternoon?'

'No,' I admitted. I told him that I had given it up after my father had found me in the London Road, with collar reversed, wearing a mask of Rudolph Valentino on the back of my head, and trying to walk backwards to Bernard's. Then of course I had to explain that Bernard was the erstwhile friend, Riff and sailor boy who lived next door. 'Over the hedge,' I told him, using my hands, in case he thought we lived in a terraced house.

'The one in fact,' said Sir Vincent (who, it turned out had a map of the London Road, Exhibit 6) 'who impaled his scrotum on the iron spikes of your gate?' I agreed that that was so.

'Tell me,' he said, both hands on the lapels of his gown – and if you had not known him, you would have thought he was being friendly – 'tell me something about your early heroes. All boys have heroes, do they not?'

They certainly did in those days I said, in the way that most boys had mice. General Gordon, I told him, was probably my first.

'General Gordon?' he queried. 'You mean "Chinese" Gordon?'

I apologised and said that I did, adding that I also greatly admired Lord North.

'The Christian soldier who the Mad Mahdi got halfway up the stairs at Khartoum?' he went on, ignoring Lord North.

'Yes,' I said. 'Him.'

'I see,' he said, and you could hear all the Waterman pens writing it down. 'Thank you for the moment.'

'Not at all,' I replied, not to be outdone when it came to the civilities. We both sat down, while they shouted for the Reverend Eli Wannamaker outside in the corridor.

'Reverend Wannamaker,' began Sir Vincent (the oath had been waived of course, because of the status of my old mentor), 'we are trying to establish precisely what kind of atmosphere and influence surrounded the defendant during his formative years.'

I smiled at the Rev Eli Wannamaker, tapping my chest to show that Sir Vincent was referring to me.

'I was, I think I can say,' said the clergyman, returning my smile and exchanging respectful nods with the judge, 'one of a group of Christians, charged with protecting and formulating his moral character.' He continued to smile at me, while careful not to give the impression of being in any way pleased with the way I had turned out. He was in his best black, with snowy collar and white gloves for the occasion, his silk hat gleaming on a spike of the witness box. The last words I remembered him saying to me, not counting his 'Hello, Jeffrey' at Yasmin's wedding, were 'I'll give you titties!'

'This group,' asked Sir Vincent, twirling and flaring his gown, 'comprised yourself – and who else?'

'Myself,' said the Rev Eli Wannamaker, counting on his cotton fingers, 'the boy's grandmother who came on Fridays, for a short time, and De Kuyper.'

There was a frisson through the court. People sat up, scratching themselves, turning their heads; expecting to hear her name ring through the corridors, to see her march unrepentant into the dock.

'The grandmother,' said Sir Vincent, ignoring De Kuyper for the moment, as he had Lord North. 'She was close to the boy?'

'For a short time. Not after the essay.'

'Ah!' said Sir Vincent, and it was the first real moment of drama. There was a murmur in the court; several reporters, co-respondent shoes off and fingers to their lips, tiptoeing out in stockinged feet to warn their editors to hold the front page.

'The Crown offers this in evidence, m'lud,' said Sir Vincent, 'Exhibit Number One.' (No one can say 'Numbah Wun' like a wigged, titled, violet-lipped barrister.) I watched as my exercise book, obviously obtained somehow by the man with the tic from MI5, was borne past the jury on a tray and handed to the Rev Eli Wannamaker.

'Page three, I think,' said Sir Vincent, 'after the childish drawing of a house, with smoke emerging from the chimney.' There was something close to a smirk on his face – directed of course at Jarvis Harpe – as, hands on his broad bottom again, he flipped up his gown. The witness, spectacles on and throat noisily cleared, had found the place and now began to read.

'Across the road . . . ' Eli made an acting gesture with his free hand, as if sowing corn, ' . . . you could see the blueish hills.' The pale hand of Sir Vincent stopped him there.

'Thank you,' he said, and now his eyes were on me. 'Can you tell us, Reverend Wannamaker, the effect this had on the grandmother? I refer of course to "the blueish hills".'

'She remonstrated with him of course,' said the Rev Eli, disappointed as the exercise book was taken from him by the bald man. He had obviously thought it his turn for a tide in the affairs of men. Making the most of what he had left, he raised his voice and used both arms. ' "You can't say blueish hills," she told him. "Hills are covered with grass, which is green!" '

'Indeed,' said Sir Vincent in the silence that followed. 'And what did the defendant reply to that?'

'He said that they looked blueish to him.'

A nudge ran along the ranks of the jury, and the judge nodded pleasantly for the treacherous clergyman to continue. Far from shame, he stared me right in the face.

' "Write down the essing greenish hills!" she said to him,' he thundered; suddenly striking a pose as he realised that he was being drawn for the *Illustrated London News*. 'Then . . . ' he paused to tuck in a wisp of hair, ' . . . she applied to him, in his own interest, a crochet needle.'

'And?' prompted Sir Vincent.

'The boy lay on his back, knees pale in the light from

the window, looking up his grandmother's nose.' The clerical chin was lowered to the waistcoat, the right emphasis of sorrow rather than anger as he finished.

'And the relationship between them?' pressed Sir Vincent, 'After he had maintained that the hills were blueish, and she had stabbed him, understandably, with the crochet needle?'

'Were never the same again.' Eli raised his head slowly. 'On all future visits, before the Silver Ghost had come to a halt – Jurgens the chauffeur liveried and goggled at the wheel – she would wave her stick out of the window and shout this.'

'Shout what? Oh, this,' said Sir Vincent, as he read the slip of paper carried to him by the bald man. As he passed the jury, twelve hands stretched out with interest.

'It was no surprise,' continued Eli, 'when Jurgens inherited the money and married Mrs Gorman.'

'The cook?' enquired the judge.

'Indeed, m'lud. The family cut them dead when they came to the bring and buy sale.'

'I'm not at all surprised,' said the judge. He nodded to Sir Vincent, who bowed and fiddled with his papers.

'Can I take you forward a number of years?'

The Reverend Eli Wannamaker said that he could, nodding and smiling at the judge, who nodded back, but for some reason had stopped smiling.

'Thank you,' said Sir Vincent. 'Do you recall an evening during the war when you called at Jasmine Villa?'

'I do,' said Eli, as if he were about to take the barrister in holy matrimony.

'Could you tell the court what happened?'

'Yes,' said the clergyman. As he marshalled his thoughts, Sir Vincent walked away for a twirl and a turn round, grinning mischievously at Jarvis Harpe as he flared his gown. 'Would you please do that?' he asked politely.

'Gladly,' said the man of the cloth, unfastening a button.

He gave a light 'Ahem' and began to address the court. 'It was in the summer, I think, of nineteen forty-three. I was of course a fighting Padre, doing what we then called "my bit" to defeat the Hun.' He paused, eyes lowered, in case there was a burst of applause.

'Imagine,' said the Rev Eli, pausing again with raised finger, 'imagine my surprise when I called at the home of one of my parishioners, to find that the boy – this boy!' The finger was directed at me. 'Was about to be told "the facts of life"!'

The nudge ran again through the jury.

'You had I believe told him "what was what" yourself some time before?' said Sir Vincent.

'I had,' agreed Eli.

'In a pamphlet, with disgusting diagrams in red and black?'

'Indeed,' said the reverend gentleman, and the bald man picked up his gadrooned tray, hopefully expecting a copy to be produced in evidence.

'And who,' asked Sir Vincent, as if he didn't know, 'was about to inform the boy as to "what was what?" '

Every head in the court swung with the clergyman's accusing finger, but Yasmin had already lowered her veil and was searching for something in her handbag. George, rather ostentatiously I thought, shuffled as far as he could away from her on the bench.

'I see,' said Sir Vincent, looking at Yasmin's knees. 'Why was the boy's father not called upon?'

Eli explained that my father had been in Carlisle. I breathed a sigh of relief that he had made no mention of abortion or incest.

'Abortion and incest,' he then went on, 'were the two words I heard on entering the house.'

Sir Vincent was smiling at Jarvis Harpe, bending at the waist to catch his learned opponent's eye.

'Abortion and incest, you say?' said the barrister. 'And the father away in Carlisle?'

'Yes,' agreed Eli, a tremor in his voice. 'And the mother gone.'

'One is bound to say that one is not in the least surprised,' said Sir Vincent. 'Please continue, Reverend sir. Tell us please about the abortion and incest.'

I think it fair to say that one could have heard a pin drop.

'Well,' said Eli, doing his best, and being of course trained to a hair's breadth in the art of letting people down. 'I must say that I did not actually *see* any abortion or incest . . .'

'Come, come,' said Sir Vincent, making a beckoning motion and waiting with a smile.

'Well,' said Eli again, 'we went into the parlour. "The front room" I believe they called it. And the young lady made Ovaltine; and he . . .' Again the finger was levelled at me, 'He poked the fire!'

'Did he indeed!' said Sir Vincent. 'Because his father was in Carlisle?'

It was the witness's turn to say, 'Indeed.'

'Please go on,' said Sir Vincent.

'Well,' said the clergyman, 'there was some talk of a rigid finger, but then the young lady suggested that the boy ask questions. I thought it rather apt to call it a Brains' Trust.'

'Indeed,' said Sir Vincent, inclining his wig in admiration. 'In which you played the part of Commander Campbell, to Miss Cork's Violet Bonham-Carter?'

The Rev Eli Wannamaker indicated modestly that that was so.

'Perhaps you can recall the first question?'

'Yes, indeed. "What is the difference," the boy asked, "between a cock and a dick, and a thing and a tool, and a hampton and a willie?"'

'I don't know,' said Sir Vincent, intrigued. 'What *is* the difference between a cock and a dick, and a thing . . .'

'I have not finished,' said the witness, reprovingly.

'What is the difference between a cock and a dick, and a thing and a tool, and a hampton and a willie – *and*, as I believe they say in and around Swinehurst – a pork dagger?'

'A pork dagger!' repeated Sir Vincent with open admiration. He shook his head. 'I give up. What *is* the difference between a cock and a dick, and a thing and a tool . . .' but it was the turn of the witness to halt the barrister by means of a pale raised hand.

'They are all the same,' he said. 'Or at least that was Lady Violet Bonham-Carter's opinion.'

There was the release of pent-up breath, then the murmur and the nudge ran round the courtroom again.

'I must say,' said Sir Vincent, 'the court is much obliged to you. Do you by any chance recall the next question?'

'I do,' said Eli. He took a deep breath, holding it – his black shirt inflating – while deciding whom to address. Then, to his lordship: 'Why . . . two . . .'

'Titties,' finished the judge, as if saying 'Snap!'

The effect can be imagined.

'I'm obliged to your lordship,' said Eli, bowing and releasing the rest of his wind, but Sir Vincent – rather testily – told him not to do things like that.

'Then,' said the eloquent witness as he straightened up, remembering the next question from a young listener in Lincolnshire: 'Why can't they wear trousers?' This he addressed to the judge, inviting his answer with a smile.

'I don't know,' said Sir Vincent, raising his voice, determined to get back into the act. 'Why can't they wear trousers?'

'Because,' said the parson, still to his lordship, his finger up again, stiff as the one in the firelight, 'they are an abomination unto the Lord!'

After hesitating, in case his lordship intended a riposte, Sir Vincent snapped: 'I don't wish to know that! Kindly leave the witness box!'

'Indeed!' said his lordship gravely, and indeed icily: 'I

take your point Sir Vincent. It is becoming very like the Holborn Empire, with Spit and Cough the Phlegmish comedians on stage.' His wise eyes rolled upwards, as if he already saw the marks of fly buttons on the ornate ceiling. 'I think we will adjourn now for luncheon.'

'As your lordship pleases,' said a subdued Cough, bowing and wiping his face with a handkerchief.

Chapter Five

'How are we doing?' I asked Jarvis Harpe, when we were gathered in his little room. It was elevenses of course, not luncheon, with tea in crested cups and biscuits on a Law Society doily.

'Quite well,' said our man, whose clerk had brought him a bun. 'But it's early days yet.' He ate like the prep-school boy he had undoubtedly been, nibbling round the edges of the bun, a handkerchief spread on his lap to receive currants and crumbs.

'I thought you were very good,' I felt bound to say, even though his morning's labours had been restricted to showing me up for having ceased to trace the red bits. 'Especially the way you turn round, with your cape all flowing round you.'

'Very kind,' said Jarvis Harpe, standing to be brushed down by the clerk, who received the crumbs from the handkerchief with murmured thanks. Then the sallow youth came in, his eyes widening as he noticed the remains of the bun, and whispered into the barrister's ear.

'Thank you,' said the barrister, civility costing nothing, and atoning for his favouritism. Then he turned to me. 'His lordship wishes to see us in his chambers,' he said, sotto voce, then nodded to the blanketed shape in the corner. 'I think we can leave your pater here.'

I agreed, and followed him along a narrow carpeted passage to an oak door. A discreet knock in a code they have and we were admitted, to find his lordship finishing an egg. Beside him, cutting and lining up the fingers of toast, sat Sir Vincent.

'Sit down, Jarvis,' said the judge, taking off his bib. I took it that he meant me as well, and we both drew up chairs. Sir Vincent poured out an extra cup, but Jarvis Harpe while thanking him ('Ta, Vinnie') and asking for two lumps, declined the crusts, saying that he had just had a bun. I confirmed this, saying I had had a digestive biscuit, which tended to make one thirsty, but it did me no good.

'I called you in,' said the judge, 'to put a stop to this nonsense. Is that quite clear?' Slurping their tea, both barristers bowed in their chairs. Wiping his mouth he turned to Sir Vincent. 'I take it,' he said, 'if I had not intervened, that the next line – after "Women in trousers are an abomination unto the Lord" – would have been "Unless you are a tram conductress?" ' Sir Vincent's big head nodded sheepishly. 'And then we would have gone on to Spanish Fly; culminating in why don't they lift the lavatory seat?'

There was an embarrassed silence, while the judge reversed the shell of his egg in its silver cup and drew a face on it.

'And then, to round off the chapter, we would have had that religious fellow shouting "I'll give you titties!"; and no doubt a reprise of the brawl, and this chap's sister [he nodded towards me] being asked to stand aside because of the prostrate clergyman?'

'Indeed,' the two barristers muttered shamefacedly.

'It will not do,' said the judge, unrolling his notes, his eyebrows rising as read them. 'I am prepared to allow your next witness; and of course,' his voice softening as he said the name, 'it will be a pleasure for the court to have the Hon Wendy. But I warn you!' He addressed the red-faced Sir Vincent. 'After that there will have to be a change of tactics!'

Bowing, saying that we were much obliged to his lordship, we then withdrew, hearing him crush the skull of the Reverend Eli Wannamaker with a rat-tail spoon.

'What did he mean?' I said, aghast, as I followed Jarvis Harpe into the toilet 'for a quick one'. 'What was that about the Hon Wendy?'

But he shushed me with his free hand.

'Call Rufus Real!'

I stared open mouthed as I heard the uniformed salts of the earth shouting outside in the corridor. Rufus Real! Friend of my youth! Was it possible? I had not seen nor heard from him since the night he had posed halfway up the stairs for the box Brownies, with a teddy in his hand, like Chinese Gordon awaiting his end.

For an awful moment I failed to recognise him as he entered the court and crossed to the witness box. He had aged, like someone in a ghost story. Then I realised that his white hair was a wig; and his black gown and the way he clasped his hands across his striped bottom meant that he was one of them.

'If I may,' said Sir Vincent with a small bow (though I missed the sign they give when they meet), 'I shall address you as the learned witness.'

Rufus inclined his head gracefully, and the two lawyers did a twirl and a twitch together, clearing their throats in unison.

Rufus a barrister! I had never imagined such a thing! Though I had often wondered how he had got on with the lady in the Rue Mazarin. Being uncertain as to whether a defendant could speak without being spoken to, I held up the palm of my hand, moving it from side to side like Al Jolson.

'I see you are acquainted with the defendant,' said Sir Vincent. 'He's giving you an Al Jolson wave.'

'Yes,' said Rufus, waving back, giving me a smile in which I detected not the slightest embarrassment. 'We were at school together.'

Rising on my toes I could see the *Daily Express* writing

this down. Nudging the policewoman with the wart, I exchanged nods with my father.

'And this school was . . . ?' asked Sir Vincent.

'Traggets. On the Isle of Avalon.'

'Once the site of Camelot,' I said, being unable to contain myself, but more for the benefit of the *Daily Express* than Sir Vincent.

'Thank you,' he said, but of course insincerely, holding his black lapels as he stared at me, then turning back to Rufus. 'It is in fact,' he went on, showing off now, 'where King Arthur pulled a sword called Excalibur out of a stone. The King's death was written about in French. You probably know the story?'

'I do indeed,' said Rufus, and they bowed to each other.

'Perhaps you would tell us a little about the school?'

'Indeed,' said Rufus. 'It was divided into five houses; Lancelot's, Gawain's, Merlin's and Arthur's; which was of course the main house and had a flag.'

'And I understand, a round table in the hall?'

'Yes,' said Rufus, giving 'Indeed' a rest; but his legal training compelling him to add, 'But not, I think, the original.'

Sir Vincent accepted that with an incline of the head. 'Please go on.'

'Then there was Guinevere's,' continued Rufus, 'for girls.'

'Girls, eh?' said Sir Vincent, somewhat coarsely for a barrister, and it was Rufus's turn to incline his wig.

'Boys wore grey,' he said, 'with a badge of a red-silk embroidered table top.' He touched the clip of his Waterman pen. 'Girls wore grey, but without trousers, and with a blue-embroidered table top.' He added that this was to ensure they did not get mixed up, and received a nod of a wig.

'Quite so,' said Sir Vincent. 'And the name of the headmaster?'

'Dr Hazlit.'

'And his wife?'

'Mrs Hazlit,' said Rufus. He hesitated: 'They have, I'm afraid, since slipped beneath the waves.'

There was a very short pause, then Sir Vincent continued, apparently unmoved. 'You were in which house?'

'Gawain's.'

'The same house in fact as the defendant's father?'

'Yes,' agreed Rufus, nodding at my father, though they had never been introduced. 'He,' and he gave me a nod as well, and another rather awkward Al Jolson wave, 'he was in a corner bed, under a barred window, next to Tonto.'

'Tonto?'

'Broomhead,' said the judge, before Rufus could answer. 'He wore a homburg hat.' He crooked and wagged a finger, and when Sir Vincent approached said to him, in a voice so awful that all eyes went to his curls, to see if he had put on the black cap. 'Do not try the patience of the court too far!'

'I won't, m'lud,' promised Sir Vincent, bowing and making a face. He turned back to the court. 'As our lordship has pointed out – and we are obliged – ' he bowed again, 'master Broomhead wore a homburg hat. This was in the Hebrew fashion, I take it?'

'No,' said Rufus, seemingly still fairminded, 'more in the style of Sir Alec Douglas-Home. And because of his father.'

'Broomhead's father? Who was in fact a Big Button Maker?'

Rufus agreed that he was. Then, memory flooding back, and Sir Vincent waiting for him to go on: 'On Open Day – his mother and sister wore crimson felt, recognisably descended from the homburg. It was the first time we heard the old English proverb.'

'Old English proverb?'

'Red hat, no drawers,' said Rufus; adding earnestly: 'I have found there is a great deal of truth in that.'

'Indeed,' said Sir Vincent, slipping something into his mouth. I saw my father sit up, watching intently, thinking of course that it was a mint.

'Can I take you,' said the prosecuting counsel, after he had washed down his pill, 'back to the dormitory? The defendant is in his corner bed; next to him is the Button Maker's son in a homburg hat. Who would have been in the bed opposite?'

'Wheelan,' said Rufus. 'And then me.'

'Thank you.'

'He was from Bury St Edmunds.'

'Really?'

'Yes. Nobody spoke to him. He had found a dried elephant's penis at home – in the attic I believe – and brought it to school in his cricket bag. He had to bend it a little.'

'Did he.' Sir Vincent was careful not to add a question mark.

A bee buzzed. Sparrows flew up the shafts of sunlight slanting through the tall windows. I smiled across at a man in the jury who had been staring at me all morning. The policewoman with a wart was sucking a sherbet lemon, though my father had not yet noticed this.

'Did he say where it came from?' asked Sir Vincent, still talking about the elephant's penis. 'Or what his parents used it for?'

'No,' said Rufus, shaking his head. 'It was slung by wire underneath his bed. He manipulated it by means of a string and a system of pulleys. Something like the arrangement Jeffrey had for raising Agatha Jennings in a banana crate.'

'By Jeffrey, you mean the defendant?'

'Indeed,' said Rufus.

'And by Agatha Jennings, you are referring to the person who threw a cow pat at him?'

'I didn't know that,' said Rufus softly, looking at his fingernails. There was another pause, and I took the opportunity to touch my father, to see if he was still warm.

'When he pulled the string,' enquired Sir Vincent, obviously intrigued, 'when he began to manipulate it – '

'He used to swing it out across the lino,' explained Rufus, using an arm. 'He would tap the grizzled foreskin on the end of one's bed.'

'Did he?' said Sir Vincent, then brightened: 'Which was I believe more than the defendant could do at the time for Miss Jennings?'

'Indeed,' said Rufus with a grin; rather gratuitously I thought. Sir Vincent hitched his gown and began to move about.

'That could have been a frightening thing, could it not, for boys of your age?' he suggested.

Rufus agreed, but said that in my case he remembered my saying that De Kuyper had prepared me for worse.

That name again. The buzz and the nudge. But Sir Vincent ignored the stir in the court, just as he had ignored my mention of Lord North. 'I ask you to consider,' he said, 'as a young man who has, if I may say so, already gained some success in a most distinguished profession – why do you suppose that the boy did that? Thumped that great swinging thing on a string on the black enamel of your bed end?'

'I don't know,' said Rufus. 'Possibly a cry for help.'

'Thank you,' said Sir Vincent, as did the judge, sensing that the prosecution had run out of steam and ideas. Deflated, Sir Vincent sat down, tucking in his gown. 'Your witness,' he said; and 'gracious' was not the word.

'I am much obliged,' said Jarvis Harpe. He stood up slowly, stretching, nodding to the jury and smiling at Rufus. 'Mr Real,' he began, pronouncing it perfectly. 'You were aged twelve were you not, when you first attended Traggets?'

'I was.'

'Did your family have a house in London?'

'We did. And one in the country. Not far from the Nabisco factory.'

'Indeed.' Jarvis Harpe inclined his head, as if pleased to hear that. 'You were in fact something rather special as far as the school was concerned?' A raised hand said that there was more to come. 'A young person of breeding, something new to the academy?'

'I suppose so. Yes.' Rufus went modestly pink, which went well with his wig.

'Someone who would make an undoubted impact on an impressionable boy?'

'Possibly.' Rufus touched the curls on the nape of his neck.

'Possibly?' My barrister was being waggish now, over-acting incredulity. 'As you will learn, Mr Real, the court-room is no place for modesty! How were you dressed when you arrived at the school?'

'Dressed?' Rufus blinked, remembering. 'In striped trousers, I think.'

'Tight?' Jarvis Harpe smoothed his hips, eliciting an intake of female breath somewhere in the courtroom. 'Like Lord Snooty? And wearing a top hat?'

'No,' said Rufus. 'I believe Dr Hazlit said that one homburg was enough.'

'Indeed,' said Jarvis Harpe, agreeing with the departed reader of the *Sunday Dispatch*. 'You wore in fact a cap with concentric rings, in puce and yellow?'

'I did. Like William Brown.'

'And this went well with your swallow-tailed coat?'

'I think so. Yes. Though some people thought it gave me a faintly Jewish appearance.'

'Quite so,' said Jarvis Harpe (who was himself, so I was later told, circumcised. For aesthetic reasons of course). He leaned forwards, both hands patting his own bottom, a slight smile as the unknown woman began to whimper quietly. 'I take you back now to Traggets – it is evening and you are bathed and in your jarmies. Opposite you is the son of a Big Button Maker, and my client.' His finger waved vaguely in my direction. 'Next to you, from the bed of the young man from Bury St Edmunds, what my learned friend so eloquently called "the great swinging thing on a string" begins to thump its grizzled pizzle. What did you do?'

'I leaned over and . . . ' Rufus made a snipping motion with his fingers. There was some applause, which was instantly quelled, in a shadowy corner of the court. 'It lay on the linoleum, quite dead,' said Rufus.

'Did it shrink?' asked the judge, in a hoarse voice and on behalf of every man in the room.

'No, m'lud. But we heard Wheelan blubbing in the dark.'

Jarvis Harpe examined his fingernails for a slow count of three.

'You had, I would imagine, Mr Real, quite clear-cut ideas at the time as to what you intended to do later in life?'

'I had,' agreed Rufus.

'Please,' said Jarvis Harpe, with a grand gesture towards the jury, like Mandrake the Magician drawing attention to his assistant's legs. 'The court would, I am sure, be interested.'

'Well,' said Rufus, with an introductory bow to the jury: 'On my sixteenth birthday I was to be taken to Paris, to be deflowered by a friend of my father's on the Rue Mazarin.'

'And if you were good?'

'I was to have my first bicycle. At seventeen I was to join my father's regiment. At twenty-one, if my father had slipped beneath the waves by then, I would enter into my inheritance. Become monarch of all I surveyed.'

'Thank you,' said Jarvis Harpe. 'Can I take you now to your relationship with the defendant.' He pointed at me. 'You were friends?'

'Yes, I think one could say that. Though I was never as close as Bernard.'

'Bernard?'

'The sailor boy who lived next door. The one who impaled his scrotum on the spikes of their gate.'

'Oh, yes. Him.' Jarvis Harpe dismissed the Chief of the Riffs. 'Could you tell the court something of the extra-mural activities you shared with the defendant?'

'Masturbating, and urinating on fireflies you mean?' asked Rufus. 'Of course that was a practice unknown to us – masturbating that is, not urinating on fireflies – until Mr Beeston told us about it.'

'Mr Beeston? Your housemaster at Traggets?'

'Yes. He introduced it one Monday morning, with coloured charts and a working model.'

'He warned you about going blind? Of hair growing in the palms of your hands?'

'He did.'

'I'm glad to hear it. Have any more of his teachings stayed with you?'

'Well,' Rufus's eyes met mine, 'he used to say never disregard the old and the ugly. They may not smell nice, but they will be grateful.'

Jarvis Harpe repeated that, slowly, word for word. 'Was it not he, Mr Beeston, tutor in Social Responsibility, who said: "Red hat, no drawers," when the wife and daughter of the Big Button Maker came to Open Day?'

'It was,' agreed Rufus. 'He also said that they were all the same size lying down. And he strongly recommended leaving it in for five minutes after one had finished. He used to say that they would be your slaves for ever.'

'Quite,' conceded Jarvis Harpe. 'Though the ladies do tend to forget what one does for them.'

'Indeed,' murmured Rufus, who I assumed knew as much as I did by now.

'In the churchyard at Shepton Mallet,' said Jarvis Harpe, 'while pulling your plonker – if I may so put it – do you recall meeting someone there?'

'Yes,' said Rufus cautiously, alarm now in his blue eyes. 'But I didn't touch her!' He turned to the judge, who was writing down 'Pulling your plonker'. 'I only used to watch, m'lud.'

424

Jarvis Harpe smiled, shaking his head. 'Not Miss Heath, Mr Real. Mr Pickles.'

'Mr Pickles?' repeated Rufus blankly.

'On the wing of a sleeping angel, chewing a straw. No work, no school, no home, no responsibilities – '

'No fuck all!' said Rufus loudly, remembering, looking suddenly proud and pleased.

' – slept on the ground,' went on Jarvis Harpe. 'Did not bathe in the mornings or wash behind his ears, and for a bog he went behind a tree.'

'A dirty bastard!' Rufus summed up concisely.

'You were in favour of kicking him? Of seeing what was in his handkerchief?'

'Yes. Quite frankly, I was.' Rufus was defensive but stood his ground.

'No further questions,' said Jarvis Harpe, motioning his learned opponent to get up.

Sir Vincent rose slowly, but refreshed after his sit-down. 'Did you in fact kick him and see what was in his handkerchief?'

'No,' said Rufus, with regret, 'I'm afraid not.'

'Thank you,' said Sir Vincent. He nodded to say that was all and turned to face the door. 'Call the Hon Wendy!' he cried.

It was no thrill to Rufus of course, who wandered off to join his rather smart lady friend, but I gripped the spikes before me as the cry went up in the corridors: 'Call the Hon Wendy!'

And there she was, as the hatless uniformed buffoons fought to open the door for her. Framed in the entrance she paused for effect. There was the sound of breath being sharply drawn in, the buzz again and heavy nudging; the sharp crack of fly buttons chipping plaster from the cornices, as she walked unaided down the aisle. Behind her, with two clerks and a barrister who held a watching brief, came the small solicitor I had last met in the garret; and behind them the French maid and a chauffeur, with rug and vanity case.

425

Several people tore out their buttonholes and tossed them in her direction; and one man, standing on a bench, oblivious to the crash of the mallet and the glare of the flashbulbs, shouted: 'God bless you, ma'am!'

She wore a dark costume, to show that she understood the seriousness of the occasion; a large flower in the wide brim of her hat. Her smile now was for the judge, who had stood up in order to see better. When she bowed, it was like the cameo at the start of a Gainsborough film. As she took the oath, the bald man holding the book for her, there was utter silence in court – then a collective sigh at the sound of her voice.

'I swear to tell the whole truth, and *nothing* but the truth,' she said, quite beautifully.

'So help you God,' prompted the judge, who of course knew it by heart.

'So help me God,' she agreed, smiling her thanks as he sat down, his right hand disappearing at once inside his robe.

As her eyes and her smile turned towards me, I took deep breaths to regain control, as we were taught to do at Traggets when wearing bathing trunks. Realising that an Al Jolson wave was hardly appropriate, I lowered my head, very nearly getting a spike up my nostril.

The Hon Wendy! I could hardly believe it! As you know, I still had the new penny and the portrait she had given me. (Though Bernard and I had eaten the orange while watching the Japanese paper flowers open in a glass of water.) Since then I had only seen her once, at Royal Ascot kissing a horse. But, the quality of the *Daily Telegraph* being what it is, it had long since disintegrated in my wallet. Now I shyly lifted my eyes to take in her ravishing beauty.

'That's the woman who fed her cat on sprouts!' muttered my father, pulling my sleeve.

The preliminaries over, Sir Vincent having played the gallant – asking her if she wanted to sit down and have a glass of water, and was the window open enough for her

426

– he leaned on the witness box, very close to her, and, after breathing in, pointed to me.

'Do you know the defendant, madam?'

'Yes, of course!' The Hon Wendy beamed me a radiant smile, and gave me what was almost an Al Jolson wave, her rings flashing in the sunlight and frightening the sparrows. 'Hello, darling!' she called. 'How are you? How's the leg?'

I smiled and bowed, moving back against the police-woman with a wart to avoid the spike, lifting my leg to show that it was all right now and that I was wearing long trousers.

'Perhaps you would be kind enough to tell the court how it was that you happened to meet?' Sir Vincent's tone and his face implied a tale of a lady tossing a smile and a farthing through a carriage window, to an urchin who had just wiped mud off her wheels.

'He came to stay with us,' said the Hon Wendy. 'He was a friend of Rufus's.'

'Indeed,' said Sir Vincent, in the voice of Ripley. 'Was this at your town house?'

'No,' said the Hon Wendy, 'at the one we have near the Nabisco factory.'

'I see. Was he invited?'

'Not by me.' She was smiling at my father, having just placed him as Dr Fu Manchu, walking backwards out of her kitchen. 'I believe he just dropped in.'

Which was true enough, I suppose. I composed myself, still taking deep breaths, remembering that the Hon Wendy was a witness for the prosecution.

'This was in the early morning, I believe,' said Sir Vincent. 'Not normally a time, even for a friend of your son – to drop in?'

The Hon Wendy, dimpling, admitted that they did not have many people dropping in in the morning. This, I reflected, while watching her mouth, was yet another difference between the Reals' house and Victory Cottage, where men with books or cucumbers under their arms started arriving at eight o'clock.

'Was he – did he appear somewhat out of place in your establishment?' Sir Vincent was looking right at me as he spoke.

'No,' she said. 'I don't think so.' She frowned, and the Official Court Artist reached for his rubber. 'You can always tell by the way they take their breakfast. I noticed he laid a good base of kedgeree and kippers on his plate, then the haddock and the bacon and egg, leaning sausages against it all around.' As she spoke she demonstrated with her pretty fingers.

'Filling in the spaces with scrambled egg?' Sir Vincent, as I had never doubted, had been around.

'Yes.' The Hon Wendy nodded. 'The ones that are not – ' there was the slightest of pauses, ' – used to our way of life, always take too many sauté potatoes, and lay their sausages flat. Then, of course, by the time they reach the end of the sideboard . . . ' She shrugged her slender shoulders.

'There is no room to get their kidneys on the plate,' said Sir Vincent, helping her out.

'Indeed,' she said, probably having heard Rufus practising. She smiled at me and I smiled back, starting to purse my lips to blow her a discreet kiss, but was dissuaded by the shaking head of Jarvis Harpe.

'And then what happened?'

'Well, Honore,' she pointed to the French maid, who dropped the court a neat curtsey, showing a black silk knee with a smudge of chalk, 'Honore carried it to the table for him . . . ' she paused, taking a slow deep breath, while Sir Vincent – and everyone else of course – watched her bosom swell. 'And then he asked for Daddies Sauce.'

There it was again, the buzz and the nudge running round the room; though quelled instantly by Sir Vincent's upraised hand.

'He asked,' he said, slowly and distinctly, 'for Daddies Sauce?'

'Well,' said the Hon Wendy, flushing becomingly, realising that she had perhaps gone too far. 'He sat down and tucked in what my son later told me he called "a serviette" – and said "Could I have the sauce, please?" '

Sir Vincent kept his hand up, in case the buzz and the nudge should start again.

'He did not actually say the word – "Daddies"?'

'No,' admitted the Hon Wendy. 'But Gartree told me that when he selected the HP from the cruet, he overheard him murmur, "No one can seriously pretend it is the same." '

'And by that you took him to be referring to Daddies?'

'Well,' said the beautiful Member's wife, 'it's either one or the other, isn't it?'

'You don't consider A1 to be a serious contender?'

'No,' said the Hon Wendy, firmly. 'I do not.'

'I see.' Sir Vincent thought it safe now to bring his hand down and walk about. 'What happened then?'

'Well, Honore wound me up, and I spoke to him, to put him at his ease. I said to him, "Tell me all about yourself. Who are your people?" '

'And who were they?'

'He said, "Yeomen." '

'Did he?'

'And of course I said, "The backbone of England." And then he told me his father was a Northern Manufacturer.'

'Did he mention liberty bodices?'

'No,' said the Hon Wendy. 'He most certainly did not. I said that if his father was a Northern Manufacturer, then he probably knew J. B. Priestley; and he said no, he didn't, but they had the same taste in peas.'

For a moment I thought that Sir Vincent was trying to 'get off' with the policewoman with the wart; then realised that he was smiling at me. But by the time I had responded, thinking that perhaps I had been hasty in my first impression of him, he had turned back to the Hon Wendy.

'The court is obliged to you, madam,' he said, inclining his head. 'If I can move on to later that same day. Did a police constable call at the house?'

'Yes,' said the Hon Wendy. 'Gartree came out with his card when I was in the garden.'

'By Gartree, you mean "Four For Your Friends"? "the Kensitas Man"? "The Lemon Barley Water Kid"?'

'The butler, yes.'

'Please go on. What was the purpose of the constable's call?'

'He said they had received a communication, from somewhere called Swinehurst I believe, that a boy had run away.'

'Did he have a name?'

'No, I don't think so.' The Hon Wendy looked surprised at the question. 'We call them all "Officers" anyway. They like that.' She smiled at the hatless ones leaning against the walls of the courtroom, and they blushed and grinned awkwardly.

'Did the boy who had escaped from Swinehurst have a name?' asked Sir Vincent patiently.

'Yes.' She caught my eye, then looked away. 'Jeffrey Cork.'

'Thank you,' said Sir Vincent. 'And what did you say to this?'

'I asked him to sit down of course, the officer that is, but he said that he was on duty. Then I told him that we did have a young person staying with us, a friend of my son's, but I didn't know his surname. I said that he could go up the back stairs and interview him, if he so wished.'

'Which he did?'

'Yes. Gartree told me he found him dancing.'

'Dancing?'

'In his top hat, if you know what I mean. He was doing "Putting on the Ritz" according to Gartree, and he shot Gartree with his bannister.'

'Did he.' Sir Vincent sniffed. 'Did you see the police constable – the officer – again before he left?'

'Yes. He came out to say goodbye.'

'And what had he discovered?'

'He said the boy's name was Frank Lynne. He showed it me written in his notebook; just after the page that tells them what to do.'

'And did you believe him?'

'I didn't like to argue with him.' The Hon Wendy hesitated, remembering: 'He had a purple tongue.'

'But you did send C. Aubrey Smith to make certain telephone enquiries?'

'Gartree? Yes, I did. We found that the boy's story was true. He was from a reasonably good home, and his father – though a tradesman – was well respected. The boy's uncle, I believe, had once applied to be High Sheriff of Lincoln.'

'But it was this "reasonably good home", as you put it, that the boy had run away from?'

'No.' The Hon Wendy hesitated again, biting the pink cushion of her lower lip. 'He – the boy – had been placed in a . . . ' She closed her eyes, and for a moment I thought they were going to allow her to write it down, but then she made the effort. ' . . . A working-class home.'

Sir Vincent, who had no doubt heard worse in his time, merely moved his eyebrows. 'In Swinehurst?'

She nodded. 'Yes. That's where he had brought the bannister from.'

Sir Vincent nodded, as if he understood. 'And you – as an act of Christian charity – arranged for his family, these relatives of the High Sheriff of Lincoln, to come down and collect him?'

The Hon Wendy hesitated yet again. 'I don't think the uncle ever *became* the High Sheriff of Lincoln. I believe they took his trousers away and sent for the doctor. But yes, I did send for the boy's father, to collect him.'

'Thank you,' said Sir Vincent. 'No further questions.'

As Jarvis Harpe rose, moistening his sensuous lips and checking his flies, I looked at my father. He had, sometime before this – probably on the line, 'the boy was sent to a working-class home' – seized and pulled on the Horne Bros label in the collar of his sports jacket, so that he looked now like The Headless Coachman.

'Madam,' began Jarvis Harpe, bowing and allowing a count of five. With a quizzical look to ascertain that she was both impressed and dominated – or as much as she was likely to be, seeing who she was – he continued. 'My learned friend mentioned "Christian charity" a moment or two ago. Did that enter your mind – or indeed your heart – when you chose to give the boy away?' The Hon Wendy lowered her pretty head, her face in shadow, a small handkerchief – a complete contrast to that of Mr Pickles – dabbing at her perfect nose.

'I did what I thought was best,' she said softly. So quietly that no one heard.

'She did what she thought was best!' cried the bald man, who doubled as the court interpreter, and Jarvis Harpe thanked him with a curt nod.

'It did not cross your mind that he would be taken back to this . . . this working-class home?'

The Hon Wendy shook her head, handkerchief on nose going with it.

'You did not pause to consider what he might become? Stunted by a lack of fresh air and green vegetables?' There was a count of two. 'Possibly he was already too old to develop rickets.' Jarvis Harpe let her off that one with a nod. Then the barrister's voice rose in the wrath we were paying for; lips curling and nostrils beginning to dilate: 'But the strain on his young eyes in the guttering candle-light? The shame of the earth privy? The appalling perform-ance in the zinc bath? The broth?' He declaimed that almost as well as he did 'the earth privy'. Taking a deep breath, his voice actually trembling, he finished on, 'Not to speak of the pease pudding!' He was good.

'I didn't know,' she murmured inaudibly.

'She didn't . . . '

But Jarvis Harpe silenced the bald man. 'A sorry specimen, madam.' His head began to move, slowly from shoulder to shoulder. 'And it never crossed your mind? You never saw him as wire bespectacled, pale and rough skinned, rotten toothed and round shouldered – his vocabulary restricted to "Oh Cor! Fuck me!" in the obscure dialect of Swinehurst?'

'I did!' she cried, loud enough to keep the bald man on his buffet. 'My husband thought he might have made a boot boy, but I said that he was totally unsuitable.'

'You did?'

'Yes. I remember my exact words. I said he would be certain to be passed over in any contest for a position as a telegram boy.'

'Thank you,' said Jarvis Harpe. His wrath having subsided, he beamed at the witness and then mouthed at the judge – so that it would not be written down – 'What about lunch?'

In a state of shock at what I had just heard, I was being restrained by the policewoman with a wart, using the regulation whore's grip as introduced to the force by Lord Trenchard. Everyone began to leave the court, chattering and laughing, recalling the high spots of the morning. I heard several people say that we were better than the people who made half crowns. The judge of course had gone first, with a wink to the Hon Wendy; who left now, with her entourage, without looking at me.

Then we were alone, The Headless Coachman and I, and were led down the steep stairs in the footsteps of Crippen.

Chapter Six

'Cor! Fuck me!' I said bitterly to Jarvis Harpe. Quite out of character, coming from the mouth of a young business-man, but I was understandably distraught. I had been repeating it, outraged, ever since lunch had started. Even to the man from Simpson's, in his long apron and dickie bow, when he wheeled in the trolley with its domed and gadrooned silver lid.

'A slice for you, sir?' he had said, taking me for one of them, ready with a bib and a mustard pot; but I had stood up, opening and pointing to my knees.

'Rickets!' I almost spat into his face. 'Cor! Fuck me!'

'Yes, and me, sir,' said the man, who had probably heard worse in his time, steering out the beef on silent wheels.

'They grease 'em with lard,' said Jarvis Harpe, interested – though no one else was – as he dabbed on horseradish and forked the pink meat into his mouth.

Yasmin, who had finished, her veil still turned up, and white beneath her pancake with shame and fury, was feeding The Headless Coachman. While George, sucking a Rennies, drafted a letter on my behalf to the Law Society on the back of a Bassett's price list.

'Have you any idea,' I demanded of our man, tapping on the pink newspaper he was reading, 'how I would have turned out if life had been fair to me?'

'I think so,' he said, lowering the paper. 'Top hatted; cane spinning through your fingers; pink faced and bright eyed. And, of course, tall, to make up for your chin.'

'Precisely!' said Yasmin, and waspish wasn't the word.

'The taste of champagne and frogs' legs on your lips.'
Jarvis Harpe smiled at me. 'The world your oyster,' he
rounded off, toasting me, the Worthington E foaming in
his mug.

There was a silence, except for him drinking, and a rustle
as George turned over to the fancy boxes of liquorice
allsorts. Then our man unfastened a button and leaned
back in his chair. 'I have something to tell you,' he said,
then lowered his voice as Yasmin indicated that The Headless Coachman had mercifully dropped off.

Cleverly, Jarvis Harpe had allowed us to express our
indignation at the shameful revelations, while eating and
keeping quiet about what had passed between himself and
his lordship when we were having our soup. In the Judges'
Robing Room, while his butler had first pickings from
Simpson's trolley (a precaution against Fenians), he and
Sir Vincent had been told in no uncertain manner that it
had to stop.

'I can see it now,' the old boy had said, wigless, making
a sandwich of his smoked salmon. 'Your first question,
Jarvis, will be something like "When the police constable
left, with his purple tongue, how did you feel?" And then
that dolt,' (our man spared us nothing) 'will take up the
rest of the afternoon with rubbish about a Memorial Meeting, held for him at the Swinehurst Tabernacle. How he
would be remembered as "a cautionary tale, told to children who rode alone on trams". You, no doubt,' (the
plastic lemon pointing at Jarvis Harpe) 'would have
suggested the possibility of the townsfolk putting up a
statue, in the Bradford style – either that of Snowden, or
the black woman dressed as the old Queen.'

The judge had then dipped into his Brown Windsor,
saying again, wagging his spoon at them, that he was not
going to put up with it.

'He has a point, of course,' said Jarvis Harpe as he told
the tale. 'Obviously we would have moved on to the
episode at the Reals' place. We've already had you dancing

in your top hat, shooting Fluff Ears with your bannister; and the breakfast business. The vignette of young Master Rufus in his jarmies, with his clean teddy, would certainly have come up again.' He paused, eyeing me: 'You're rather fond of that one.'

I agreed that I was, and Jarvis Harpe took a sip from his mug and continued.

'There would have been a reprise of course of Wheelan's thing, when you discussed the length of it with the Hon Wendy on the chaise longue.' He paused again, smiling at Yasmin. 'A frisson,' he explained, 'like "Cor! Fuck me!" ' His mimicry was so good that we – with the exception of George – were forced to return his smile; and encouraged by this, and of course by the Worthington E, he said it again, visibly upsetting the clerk who had just entered with the treacle pudding.

'That is to say nothing,' said Jarvis Harpe, motioning for much more custard, 'of what my learned friend would have made of the snooker.' We watched him eat, interested in his use of fork and spoon; then he smiled into his bowl. ' "The pink ball beside her ear!" ' he mimicked, wickedly, if a little cloying because of the syrup.

'He was fourteen!' protested Yasmin. 'He wouldn't know what it meant. Did you, Jeffrey?'

'Yes, I did,' I said. 'Six. Five for the blue and seven for the black.'

'I rest my case,' said Jarvis Harpe, patting my cheek and grinning impishly at my sister. He then rolled up his serviette and pushed it through a silver ring: a filthy habit they have.

'So he doesn't – his lordship doesn't – want to hear any more about what happened?' asked Yasmin. 'Not even the end of Part One?'

'As the bag of chicken shit inflated and they moved off into the shrubbery?' murmured Jarvis Harpe; then sang, softly in a pleasant tenor: 'Little man you're tired, I know why you're blue, someone took your kiddie car away . . . '

436

The clerk hummed Jack Payne's arrangement, moving the custard jug slowly from side to side, and Yasmin sat back in her chair.

'I see what you mean,' she said. The waspishness had gone. She was looking at the barrister in a different way, as if seeing him suddenly in an RAF blazer.

George, who was not blind, told his wife to cover up her legs and demanded to know what was going on.

'The nonsense has got to stop,' said Yasmin. 'that's right, isn't it, Jarvis?' and he smiled and said that it was, but she was not to call him that during office hours.

'Never mind office hours!' said George, demanding that the pre-war tea be re-staged, on a chalked rectangle to represent the pre-fab. 'Like they do with a stiff.'

Jarvis Harpe, his mind on cheese and biscuits, said that he didn't think so. It could well be, he said, that Mr Cheeseman was a far-sighted patriot, deserving of commendation. But in another place. The court was hardly likely to be interested in his warnings about 'them' arriving, with their mangoes, in their sheets, down the Great Horton Road. 'In their bullock carts,' he said to the clerk, asking George to stand out of the light so that he could choose an apple.

'Ballock carts!' said George, standing his ground.

It could have been nasty. Yasmin told him to shut up, and I was about to say that they both ought to keep quiet, seeing that they hadn't even been summonsed – when the sallow youth opened the door and asked if he could have me. Jarvis Harpe, looking at the clock and saying that we had ten minutes, said that he could.

Outside the door the sallow youth took my arm, drawing me into the shadows; but I had already seen them. Filling the corridor with a murmur of voices and the rattle of cups, the witnesses assembled for the afternoon session stretched away into tiled infinity, under a haze of smoke in the half light, like the endless queue in 'The March of Time'.

437

All in their best, with almost everyone wearing a hat, the dress uniforms of the Second Foot making a bold splash of colour. The walking-out livery of the Lincolnshire Road Car Company was drab in comparison, though the inspectors – in a tight knot apart – wore decorations on their black raincoats. But it was the 'Number Ones' of the Meat Market Police that had attracted the girls, including of course the vulgar Doreen. On a shooting stick sat my old CO, taking a pie from a carton; while at a respectful distance the Padre and the Cook Sergeant leaned against the wall. Still further away, ramrod stiff, was the Provost Sergeant, alone but for the vegetarian beside him on a light chain. Beyond them was Kitchener, in new gym shoes, watching Albert Croxley carve his name with pride. Then more of The Daredevils: the lewd Scot and Rockfist Rogan. Ron sat with Miss Parkinson – blushing at the whispers of the sea-going Pomfret beside her – his cavalry twill emerging from beneath the pages of *Picturegoer*. Then Maude Skinner and Janet, and for some reason Norman, the Head Packer; and in a space cleared by Gartree, officious in a bowler hat, the Member walked up and down, watched over by Uncle Harold and the man with the tic. The landlord of The Boy on the Barrel, and Mrs Moss – and then I saw my mother, with the man in the short fawn overcoat.

'Can they testify against their own?' I whispered to the sallow youth, who replied succinctly that they both can and do.

There was then a commotion at the far end of the corridor, as yet another witness arrived. For a moment I thought it was the Queen, come to tell of the loyal wave I had given her on Ludgate Hill – but then recognised the banana-yellow hair of the lady from the Haymarket. Alone of all those there, she saw me and smiled, twiddling her fingers. Before all eyes could follow hers, giving a vague Al Jolson wave, I pushed the sallow youth before me into the lavatory.

'There's more,' he said, as I closed the door. 'Round the corner. Old schoolteachers, and a big lady wiv a chain round her, and snotty-nosed kids grown up . . . '

I told him I did not wish to hear any more.

Then he told me, jerking his sallow head, that he had one for me next door. No, not in the ladies', in the stationery room. 'She asked to see you private,' he said, keeping his voice down, below the rushing of the waters.

Could this be the Queen? Sportingly appearing as a character witness? Sitting now on a parcel of forms, flanked for propriety's sake by ladies-in-waiting, ready to laugh and reminisce about the soldier's horse doing its business, and the state of Ron's handkerchief?

'She said she was a Pomfret,' said the sallow youth.

So it was not the Queen.

It was of course Agnes, whom I had not met since she had bitten through my hand. Unlike the Queen she had moved the forms to sit on a chair, and was dressed in black, with matching accessories. Quite frankly I thought that a black band, as she had worn in the Victory Parade, would have been enough. One couldn't go on mourning what had happened at the French seaside for ever; especially when you carried your knickers around in your handbag.

'Jeffrey,' she said, standing up, 'thank you for seeing me.'

'Not at all,' I said, noting the bulge in her patent handbag as I cautiously closed the door. The sallow youth, for a swiftly grasped florin, had agreed to remain within earshot. 'What can I do for you?'

'You can get me out of it,' she said, simply. 'I don't think you want it any more than I do.'

'What do you mean?' I countered, blowing my nose to give myself time to think. She couldn't be talking about abortion! I hadn't been to bed with her since 1945, and that had hardly been anything to write home about.

439

'Giving evidence,' she said. 'It'll be embarrassing for both of us.'

Her dark eyes were wide and glistening, and I thought back to that first post-war morning – the erotic beat of the ass's jaw bone in the darkness of her bedroom. (Only a week before, in *Tit Bits*, I had read how they made the long eggs for the veal and ham pie. A British invention.)

'I don't know what I can do,' I said. 'They're all out there!' I waved my hand at a big cupboard. 'Soldiers, and The Member, and Ron and Miss Parkinson; and that big woman wiv a chain round her . . . ' She was nodding, probably having said hello to her sea-going relative on the way in; with I suppose an incline of the head to Ron, for old times' sake.

'I know,' she said. 'So why don't you stop it? Don't you think it's a chapter best forgotten?'

I was beginning to think she was right, though there were memories I was reluctant to let go. Remembering her without her vest on, I gave her the fourth of the Five Boys' Faces, suggesting that there was no need for her to tell the *whole* truth.

'It's up to you,' she said. 'But the man from the Provident Clothing Club's out there.'

'Oh,' I said. That was different.

'You don't want all that about us making fruitgum faces; and you coming round to dip your wick.'

'I came round to water your garden,' I pointed out. 'And to tie up your peas. You were a widow woman, whose husband had run amok on the sands and been shot.' I could have added that she was also known as a slice off a cut loaf.

She opened her handbag, and for a moment I thought she was going to take them out, to flaunt them at me; but she was looking for a Zube. Watching her put away the tin, without offering me one, I realised that whatever there had been between us had gone.

'Who was it said "Get your trousers off"?' I asked,

440

lowering my voice, my hand behind me against the key-hole.

'Me,' she said, cool as any of Uncle Fred's. 'You were the one trying to get them off over your shoulders!'

I stared at her. When I left her, in a moment, I would say 'Excuse me', heavily exaggerated, while pretending to pick a blade of grass off her back.

'I've nothing against De Kuyper,' she said. 'She paid her bill. If she prefers fermented mare's milk . . . ' she made a gesture, as if to say that it took all kinds. 'It's something that Pomfrets don't do.'

I nodded, to say that I knew that.

'But I don't want you going on about my husband,' she said, 'running amok on the sands and having to be shot.'

'Well, he did,' I said. 'And he was.' I smiled at her and shrugged.

'He cried,' she said, in a voice I hadn't heard before. 'And he wet himself. And they had to shoot him.' She touched the powdered skin of her temple with a pink fingernail, where the bullet had smashed his head.

It was hot in that little room, and I stared at the brass initials on the flap of her handbag, while she went on about her bricked-up clock, and about me saying that bungalows were suggestive.

'Agnes . . . ' I said, looking at my watch.

'There is a line,' she went on, as if she hadn't heard me, 'Where Sir Vincent – after he asks you if you kept your socks on, and you say that you had no assurance that the bed was aired – where he refers to me as "A Slice Off A Cut Loaf", without so much as a question mark.'

I nodded, noting a film of dust already on my polished brown shoes, listening hard for the bell.

'Like the second edition of the Webbs' *Soviet Communism: A New Civilisation*,' she finished, starting to pull on her gloves.

I didn't know what to say.

'Cheap jokes,' she went on, 'as a build-up to that ridiculous scene.'

'Which one?' she forced me to say, unrecognisable now as the manageress of a dairy. I twiddled the doorknob behind me, in the hope of attracting the sallow youth's attention.

Opening her handbag she took out the bulge and laid it on the pile of official forms. It was the chapter. The utility label, not quite straight on the brown paper cover, read 'Part Three. Chapter Six'.

'Agnes,' I said, holding up my wrist again and tapping my watch. But she had glasses on now, with transparent pinkish frames, something else I didn't know about her. Licking her finger – with the same tongue that had once sought mine – she turned the pages, which I saw were heavily marked in red.

' "The rheumy-eyed clerk," ' she read out, finding the place, ' "lowered the pick-up of a portable gramophone, that was wound and ready to go, under the very nose of Sir Vincent".'

'Please!' I protested, but there was no stopping her.

' "Olé, I am the bandit," ' she read on, or sang on, ' "the bandit of Brazil. The familiar light-brown voice sang out, maracas and bones and asses' jaws all going." ' She read coldly, sang with the minimum of rhythm, and stared at me through her National Health specs as she paused to turn the page, the lapels of her costume rising as she took breath. I felt a fool. In a turmoil as to whether to show her my watch again, or just to leave the room – giving up the idea of picking imaginary grass off her shoulders – I was relieved to hear a knock at the door. Of course I opened it at once.

'Two o'clock. We're on!' said Jarvis Harpe brightly, smiling and nodding past me at Agnes. 'Good afternoon, Mrs Pomfret.'

'She's not giving evidence,' I said, stepping out and closing the door quickly, in case she started to sing again.

442

'Very wise,' said the barrister, rearranging his papers as we walked together along the corridor. Without comment he showed me each affidavit before passing it over his silken shoulder to the sallow youth. I glanced at them but said nothing, being relieved to find the corridor almost deserted. Only Gartree, hat on his lap, reading Ron's *Picturegoer*.

' 'E pissed 'isself,' said the first one, faintly typed on a primrose form, 'wet 'is trousers. Kneeling in a corner 'e was, upsetting everybody. Crying like a girl.' It was signed 'H. Pender. (Sgt)'.

'In order to maintain order and discipline, I had no alternative,' I saw on the second form. 'Had it been possible, I would of course have allowed him his privacy and left him my service revolver; but on being informed by his platoon Sergeant that he had been a milkman in civilian life, I realised that he would not have known what to do.'

I said I did not wish to see the third one, which dealt with ballistics, with the impact of a .45 bullet from a Browning revolver in the back of a milkman's head.

'Thank you,' whispered Jarvis Harpe, to a man in a white coat holding a specimen jar. 'But we won't require you after all.'

The sallow youth opened the door, giving me a sly wink, and we entered the court.

All eyes were upon us of course as we quickly took our places. The judge returned an almost imperceptible nod as I bowed to him on entering the dock. My father, having unwrapped and lined up the mints A Well-Wisher had sent him, had gone back to sleep. Sir Vincent coughed gently into his fist, 'If I may proceed, m'lud?'

The judge indicated that he could, and at a snap of Sir Vincent's large white fingers, a pimply youth wheeled forward a mahogany lectern. On silent wheels, like Simpson's beef, it came to a halt with a tiny squeak. It held the book behind slim brass bars, bright as stair rods. One part to a polished shelf, each chapter bound in calf and numbered bold and black. Sir Vincent drew out Part Three, Chapter Six, the one from Agnes Pomfret's handbag, and held it up towards the judge. Then, with a dramatic gesture, he dropped the volume into the rosewood tray beneath the lectern, designed originally to hold the Vicar's things. 'If your lordship pleases,' he said, dusting his hands.

'The court is obliged to you,' said the judge, very close to a smile.

'Marimbas and maracas,' said Sir Vincent, addressing me, 'would not have been a good idea.'

'Indeed,' I said, looking contrite.

'Gramophones playing, his lordship tapping his carafe with his nail file, simulating the jaw bone of an ass – it would not have done a great deal for the dignity of the court.'

I agreed, hanging my head.

'My learned friend and myself shouting "Olé", clapping our hands and stamping our feet, dancing the flamenco with a Mrs Pomfret, while the members of the jury la-la'd the chorus of "The Bandit From Brazil". You would agree that it is hardly the direction in which justice is served?'

I said that I did, a little curtly, not knowing why he was going on about it.

'Thank you,' said Sir Vincent, running a finger along Part One and selecting a volume. Opening it, seemingly at random, he smiled; first at the page, then at me.

'Can we deal now with the sub-plot?' he asked.

'By all means,' I said, though not sure what he meant. Fortunately the judge was no wiser.

'No, m'lud,' explained Sir Vincent, 'not the pigeon. The matter of who stabbed the defendant with a dessert fork.'

'Really! M'lud,' said Jarvis Harpe, half standing up; probably finding it difficult because of the pudding.

'Not relevant, no, Mr Harpe,' conceded the judge. 'But interesting.' He motioned him down again and nodded to Sir Vincent to proceed.

'I am obliged to your lordship,' he said, then asked that the Hon Wendy be recalled.

'Hon Wendy,' began Sir Vincent, after complimenting her on her choice of outfit for the afternoon, 'perhaps you could set the scene for us. Who was at table that evening?'

'Me,' said the Hon Wendy, lightly touching the left one, and all eyes lingered before moving to her adorable face, contorted now in thought. 'And him.' She smiled at me, and I recalled reading somewhere about drowning in such eyes.

'And your husband,' prompted Sir Vincent, mindful of course of the proprieties.

'Yes,' she agreed. 'To the right of Stanley Baldwin.'

'Perhaps we should make clear exactly who your husband is,' said Sir Vincent, taking it that most people knew about Stanley Baldwin. He exchanged bows with The Member, who had risen in the public benches at a nudge from his man. 'He is a Conservative Member of Parliament, is he not?'

The Hon Wendy agreed that he was.

'Winner of a tournament, so I believe. At Le Touquet?'

'Yes,' said the Hon Wendy. 'And a runner-up.'

'A runner-up?'

'Yes.'

'Thank you. So that is the scene at table that fateful evening, in your most gracious home. There is present yourself, the defendant, and your husband. Was there anyone else?'

The Hon Wendy pouted prettily in thought, then: 'On his – ' she pointed at me, 'on his left was the wife of one of the men in porridge-coloured suits.'

'I see. The men in porridge-coloured suits were also present?'

The Hon Wendy admitted that they were, and that the sexes were seated alternatively; agreeing with Sir Vincent that some people might consider this to be suggestive, in the way that one hesitated to open a door in a strange bungalow. Not, she added, that she had ever been inside one.

'Thank you,' said Sir Vincent, pleased with himself. Jarvis Harpe, who had almost got to his feet in order to object, changed his mind and sat down, giving me an apologetic shrug.

'Now then,' said Sir Vincent, 'dinner was served. Or "sarved".' (Jarvis Harpe was not the only wag and mimic.) 'The doors were thrown back and in came the scullions; white-haired retainers, with platters and dishes, pigs' heads and things; the hot gadrooned edges of hall-marked dishes appearing beside one's right ear. Tiaras bobbed at the crested china; cutlery flashing in the correct order. Corks popped to laughter. Faces distorted in crystal. Carmined lips paused while food was swallowed, to pass on a barbed jest, a wicked aside.' Sir Vincent paused himself, his voice dropping an octave: 'A gentleman's hand disappeared benath the double damask, to scratch himself or to feel his next-door neighbour.'

There was silence in the court as Sir Vincent patted his mouth with a folded hanky, receiving appreciative nods from his learned friends.

'Something like that. Yes,' said the Hon Wendy.

'And was it not then that Gartree – "Fluff Ears" as I believe he is known – coming up *behind* the defendant, like the Japanese or the Mad Mahdi, poured hot soup between his legs?'

'Yes,' she admitted, blushing; as of course would any hostess in the circumstances. 'I told him about it.'

'He knew!' thundered Sir Vincent, terrible when he was like this. 'He could feel it!' For a moment he held his bespoke crutch, before remembering where he was.

The Hon Wendy murmured that she meant that she had told Gartree, but Sir Vincent was now going strong, and seemingly on my behalf.

'Was it not but a moment later that he,' – and to save

446

any misunderstanding he pointed at me – 'became aware that his flies were being undone?'

'I wouldn't know,' said the Hon Wendy, modestly lowering her eyes. 'But if that was the case, it could have been the hot mulligatawny, rotting the thread.'

'The mulligatawny rotting the thread,' repeated Sir Vincent, then again to himself. With an effort he continued: 'Is it usual for mulligatawny – at whatever temperature – to pick off fly buttons and to tweak out one's shirt?'

The Hon Wendy was forced to agree that it was not; at least not in her experience.

'So,' continued Sir Vincent, 'you do not believe that it was the cold fingers of the hot mulligatawny – if I may so phrase it – that "*gripped him*"?'

'No,' agreed the Hon Wendy, after her pink cat's tongue had gone right round her lovely lips. 'But it could have been the Chaplain.'

A buzz and a murmur of course, and the nudge again let loose. Sir Vincent waited, eyebrows raised.

'The Chaplain?'

'Yes. He was opposite.' The Hon Wendy pointed in front of her, adding 'He had his own marrow spoon.'

'Did he?' said Sir Vincent, not impressed, probably having one himself. He took a deep breath. 'So now we have yourself, the defendant, The Member, two men in porridge-coloured suits and their wives, and the Chaplain. With his marrow spoon. Is that correct?'

The Hon Wendy nodded that it was.

'And what did people do?' He held the moment. 'What was the reaction around the table when the dessert fork entered the young flesh?'

'I remember my husband saying, "The boot boy's stabbed himself." I said, "Give him air!" '

'Did you?' said Sir Vincent.

'Yes,' said the Hon Wendy, defiantly. 'I did. They were all round him with their hanging pearls and décolletage, masticating. "Give him air!" I said.'

447

The St Johns Ambulance men either side of the door exchanged professional nods.

'Then what happened? Did you cradle him in you arms?'

'Yes. His head against my bib. I remember someone saying "Are they pierced? If they are he's ruined." But they were not.' The Hon Wendy gave me both a smile and a nod; and of course a frisson.

'I'm sure we are all pleased to hear that,' said Sir Vincent. 'What happened then?'

'The footmen came in with a five-barred gate and carried him into an ante-room. He was crying and attempting to cover himself.'

'And you withdrew? You left him there?'

'Yes. With the French maid. Some people gave him sixpence as they went out; and one man left two pennies for his eyes.'

'Really,' said Sir Vincent.

'Yes.' The witness was a little flustered. 'She – the French maid – had put on her bib, with the big red cross.' We all watched as the Hon Wendy's finger went down between them, then across from one to the other.

Sir Vincent, hesitating, as if about to ask her to do it again, decided to press on. 'And then you all returned to the table, leaving the boy – as it were – in French hands? Did you see him again?'

'I believe he joined us for the Cabinet Pudding.'

'He was fully recovered?'

'He was walking rather funny. Because of the Germolene, I suppose.'

'Did people speak to him?'

'I heard someone say "Look out, the young forker's back!"; and my husband asked if he wouldn't feel happier with a spoon and pusher.'

'And then?'

'The ladies withdrew. I don't know what happened then, though I did see them wheeling in the machine.'

'The machine?'

'The baby dolls in a glass case. You turn the handle and they drink. The first one to empty the bottle gets his penny back.' Surprised that she had needed to explain the sport, the Hon Wendy had made winding motions, pursing her lips; even bending at the waist and uttering encouraging cries. I think we all enjoyed that.

'I believe your husband is rather good?' said Sir Vincent, no tyro at the game himself.

'Not as good as he was,' said the Hon Wendy, and Sir Vincent inclined his head in sympathy.

'And then?' he asked. 'When they – the gentlemen – rejoined you in the music room?'

'One of the ladies was singing as they came in, and Jeffery,' she pointed to me, 'he said that he recognised the song from his prep school.'

'Did he?' Sir Vincent turned to look at me.

'Yes. He began to beat time with his hands; shaking a leg to free his underpants from the ointment.'

'Indeed,' said Sir Vincent. 'Perhaps you would like to sing it for us now?'

It was with a shock that I realised he was addressing me. Of course I turned to his lordship for guidance – not sure whether they were licensed for singing and dancing as it were – and after a pause the judge gave the slightest of nods; then struck a note on his carafe with his nail file. As the court fell silent I cleared my throat hurriedly, smiling at the bald man who stood ready to accompany me, fingers on the holes and eyebrows raised.

'Riding down to Bangor . . . ' I began, still clear as a bell, though of course my voice had long since broken, ' . . . on an eastbound train. After weeks of hunting, in the woods of Maine.' My father, who the judge had ruled must at least be visible to the jury, stirred uneasily in his sleep.

'Rode a student fellow, tall and slim and swell.' Jarvis Harpe was erect, on cue, one suede boot on a deed box; his voice and the sight of his suspenders causing Yasmin to fan herself rapidly with a programme.

'Great big bushy eyebrows, beard moustache as well.' Sir Vincent, a pleasing baritone, was as befitted senior counsel the louder of the two. Both barristers turned in unison, white cuffs extended to bring in the jury; who were conducted by their foreman, extempore, with his Waterman pen.

'Rumpa pa de dah di, didi dah di dah di dah,' they sang, all of them pleased to stand up, the ladies taking the opportunity to pat their hair.

'Thank you,' said the judge, in a tone of voice that made them sit down at once, and me decide not to bother with the second verse.

'Much obliged, m'lud,' said Sir Vincent, who had obviously enjoyed it, on behalf of himself and his learned friend, who had resumed his seat to the whispered plaudits of his clerks.

'Hon Wendy,' said Sir Vincent, smoothly resuming his cross-examination. 'After the soirée – what happened then?'

'The usual after-dinner things,' she replied. 'He' – again the finger, and the frisson – 'sat by me on the chaise longue, while my husband showed people his trophy. I asked him – ' again the finger, meaning me – 'how he was, as one does, and he said that he was tired, and would I mind if he retired.'

'And what was your reply?'

'I said that he wasn't to outgrow his strength. I told him to run along, and that I would have something sent up to his room.'

'By which you meant Scott's Emulsion?'

'Certainly not.'

'Did you reassure him?'

'I think so. The Chaplain was about to produce an egg from the back of my husband's neck.'

'I see,' said Sir Vincent. Then, 'Thank you.' Closing the chapter he replaced it on the lectern, raising a finger for the pimply youth to wheel it away. 'Your witness,' he said, and sat down.

There was a pause before a somewhat startled Jarvis Harpe rose to his feet. Closing his own copy of the chapter he fiddled with notes for a moment, before giving up and stuffing them into the pocket of his gown. 'Thank you,' he said to his learned friend, with some irony I thought.

'Hon Wendy,' he began, walking about, thinking on his feet, as of course they are trained to do. 'Should fortune some day smile on me – so much so that I was invited to stay at your house – the one near to the Nabisco factory. What would I be likely to find laid on my bed?' He held her answer with a raised hand and a smile. 'Let me put it this way. Would it be the usual form for a guest to find on his bed a face flannel, a cake of soap in the shape of a pig – and be expected to sleep in a tea towel?'

All eyes were on the young hostess as the court waited for an answer. I noted that Jarvis Harpe had omitted the individual pot of Vaseline, but said nothing.

'A pig?' queried the Hon Wendy, genuinely surprised.

'With a string tail,' said Jarvis Harpe, making a descriptive movement behind him which my sister never forgot.

'I don't know anything about it,' said the Hon Wendy firmly, taking two small pads soaked in witch hazel from the French maid. Jarvis Harpe hesitated, watching her, and I thought, 'Hello! Here comes the individual pot of Vaseline!' But no.

'The boy then went to the WC, I believe?'

The Hon Wendy stared at him with thick, white expressionless eyes, like Little Orphan Annie. 'Did he,' she said, without a question mark, in the style of the Webbs.

Jarvis Harpe was now addressing the jury. 'Actually he quite liked it in there. It was the first time he had experienced toilet paper of quality, and he kept a piece – a single leaf – ' the barrister's long fingers made a small square, as he lowered and softened his voice, 'to take away with him as a useful souvenir.'

He had them. All eyes (except those of the witness of course) were riveted on the invisible sheet of toilet paper. 'Would you like to tell the court about your toilet paper?' he asked.

'No,' said the Hon Wendy, fingers pressing in the cotton wool, making a 'moue' as the witch hazel ran into her mouth. 'I don't think I would.'

Jarvis Harpe's face suggested that the jury read into that whatever they could. He stared at the blind and beautiful witness. 'Is it not printed, in Izal green, beside each perfor-ation: "What I Have I Hold!"?'

The Hon Wendy, though her adorable mouth moved, said nothing.

Jarvis Harpe revolved, foiled, waiting for his gown to settle. 'Some time later,' he asked, 'did you hear a com-motion?'

'A commotion?' Removing the pads from her eyes, the Hon Wendy blinked wetly at the barrister.

'The sound of someone falling headlong over a butler's tray?'

'Possibly,' said the Hon Wendy, carefully.

'Possibly?' This of course was the kind of thing beloved by all barristers; deep incredulity and heavy inflection. 'A pot of chocolate; assorted biscuits by Huntley & Palmers; a champagne glass and six Balkan Sobranie cigarettes, all racketing and crashing about in the cor-ridor?'

'All right then. Yes, I did.' The Hon Wendy was visibly annoyed. Pleased by this, ('Get 'em going' was how he described his technique in the *Law Society Journal*), Jarvis Harpe inclined his head gracefully.

'What did you do?'

'I opened the door, of course. And there he was, lying there.'

'In shirt tail and garters?'

The Hon Wendy's eyes, reinvigorated, met his and held them. '*He* was in shirt tail and garters,' she said carefully.

'I wore a white and puce off-the-shoulder gown. Made by a little woman.'

It was of course sauce for the gander, and Sir Vincent, who had been examining his handkerchief, smiled; it being common knowledge in society that the Hon Wendy gave as good as she got.

'The man behind you,' asked Jarvis Harpe, inclining his head to acknowledge how well she was doing. 'The one in your bedroom with his mouth open. He was wearing shirt tail and garters?'

The Hon Wendy, unable to catch the judge's eye, replaced the cotton wool, saying nothing.

Jarvis Harpe smiled, though of course she couldn't see him. 'Did you then say to the boy "We are playing hide and seek? You won't give us away, will you?" '

Silence; just the tip of a pink tongue appearing.

'Very well. Let me set the scene. Outside in the corridor The Member is approaching, in shirt tail and garters. Perhaps you could tell the court if it was the practice, at houses in the vicinity of the Nabisco factory, for everyone's trousers to be collected for sponging and pressing after dinner?'

The Hon Wendy's perfect mouth was still, but the cotton wool fell out of her eyes. Jarvis Harpe pressed on.

'When the boy pushed you inside the room and closed the door, what did you hear?'

'Not a great deal,' said the Hon Wendy, starting on her fingernails, with the manicure set the French maid had given her when she ran forward to pick up the cotton wool. 'Because of the snakeskin-covered gramophone. I believe he asked my husband if he was "It".'

'And what did your husband reply?'

'He said, "You're the boot boy, aren't you?" Or something like that. "Feller with his trousers open".' She busily buffed up her nails with a little pad.

'What did the boy say?'

'He said, "You are getting warm." ' She breathed on her

453

clean fingernails, giving us all a frisson. 'My husband told me later that he then did a little dance, in some sand from the fire bucket. Like Wilson, Keppel and Betty.'

'Indeed,' said Jarvis Harpe, as if they were a firm he dealt with. 'And then?'

'Then the door opened and he fell in. One hand under his chin, and the other turned outwards on his kidneys. You know. Doing snake charmer's music down his nose.'

'So you were – not to put too fine a point on it – caught? In flagrante delicto!' Jarvis Harpe looked for, and received, an appreciative nod from the judge.

'Not at all,' said the Hon Wendy, on her own ground now. 'I was doing my petit point.' (She pronounced this carefully, to avoid any misunderstanding.) 'Until he – ' no finger, just a flash of the blue eyes, ' – started shouting, "Come out, come out, wherever you are!" '

'And how did The Member react?'

'He said did I know him. And I said that his father was a Northern Manufacturer. And then Gartree came in and threw him out. I said, "Good night," ' she ended, looking at me, but without a smile.

'Do you know what the boy did then?'

The Hon Wendy hesitated. 'I heard him do a little shuffle in the sand. And then I heard Gartree.'

' "Four For Your Friends"?'

'Yes. "You're not the usual clarss of guest we get here," he said. "You're more like a boot boy." '

'Did you hear the boy's reply?'

' "Good night, lackey," he said, quite distinctly. "After the war, when we nationalise the means of production, distribution and exchange, what are you going to do then?" '

Jarvis Harpe took the opportunity to blow his nose, while the Hon Wendy was allowed to rinse out her mouth.

'That was a quotation, was it not, from a talk given to the Young Men's Movement, at the Swinehurst Tabernacle?'

'I didn't know that at the time,' said the Hon Wendy.

'Did you hear any more?'

' "Fuck off," ' said the Hon Wendy, articulating well.

'You're quite certain of that?' asked Jarvis Harpe, as delighted as the rest of us. But the Hon Wendy disappointed him, and us, by declining to repeat it. 'Absolutely positive,' she said.

'And that was the final line? The curtain as it were?'

'No,' said the Hon Wendy, writing something on a slip of paper which she handed to the bald man, who shuddered and handed it to the judge. 'He said that, before he stepped over the custard creams and into his room.'

'Thank you,' said Jarvis Harpe, as the note was held up in front of the jury. The St Johns Ambulance men, ready for something like this, hurriedly unbuttoned their soft black bags. 'Hon Wendy,' he continued, as an elderly gentleman's head was forced between his legs. 'You did not of course hear the knocking on the boy's door, or the tapping at his window?'

'I did not.'

'Or him speaking into a cocoa tin?'

'Certainly not.'

'Perhaps you can tell the court just when you first set eyes on the spy?'

'The spy?' queried the Hon Wendy, uncertainly. 'You mean the air-raid warden?'

Jarvis Harpe nodded, which is really not allowed, being difficult for the Pitman people to write down.

'Well,' she said, 'I went down to the kitchen.'

'Would you like to describe this to the court?'

'I'm sure we all know what a kitchen looks like, Mr Harpe,' said the judge, in the tone of voice he had used to stop us singing.

'I thought perhaps, m'lud, that the jury – '

'Did not have kitchens?'

This was a joke. The judge did not go so far as to laugh, but the bald man's shoulders heaved convulsively.

'A kitchen is cavernous,' explained the judge, while the

jury listened intently. 'At the time in question it would be at rest, until the calls came for bouillon and kippers and suchlike to take away. There would be hams on hooks in the ceiling,' (he was using his arms now) 'the great fly-wheel of the mincer would cast a shadow like that of a mighty beam engine across the white tiles. Gadrooned pies would be cooling on window sills, and there would be a large cat eating from a tureen. A fat cook, her shoes off, would be dozing in her chair by the fire.' Pleased with himself, he turned back to the witness box. 'Is that substantially correct, madam?'

'I am obliged to your lordship,' said the Hon Wendy; which is something better left to one's barrister.

'Indeed, m'lud,' said Jarvis Harpe. 'Hon Wendy, you were in the kitchen when the spy – the air-raid warden – entered?'

'Yes. On a Windsor chair. On a square of red carpet.'

'The boy's father was with you?'

'The Northern Manufacturer? Yes. He was in a hairy sports jacket, with slits for the hilt of his sword, and buttons here – to stop him wiping his nose on his sleeve.' The Hon Wendy's white arm was like that which rose from the lake.

'When the air-raid warden and the defendant entered the kitchen, was anything said?'

'Gartree said, "That's 'im!" ' The white arm pointed and she mimed the shooting of samite cuffs.

'That's 'im,' repeated Jarvis Harpe, storing material for his next house party.

'Yes. "Fuck off! I said to him," he said,' she said.

' "Fuck off, I said to him, he said," you said?' repeated Jarvis Harpe, like the rest of us hardly daring to believe his luck, so soon after the earlier frisson.

'Yes,' said the Hon Wendy, quite carried away. ' "Fuck off out of here, I said," he said. "I don't want your clarss here, I said," he said. Then he repeated what he said to him when he was jumping over the biscuits.' She was flushed now, and the French maid came forward spraying cologne. 'That's what I wrote down on the paper, m'lud,' she explained. The judge, opened mouthed, right hand again beneath his robe, nodded that he understood.

'And then they left?' asked Jarvis Harpe. 'By the trades-man's entrance of course.'

'Yes. As soon as their manure inflated.'

'Which seems a good point for us, also, to leave,' said the judge, sighing, taking off his spectacles and blinking. 'Thank you, madam, for a most entertaining afternoon.'

The Hon Wendy was helped back to her seat by the French maid, the chauffeur plumping up the cushion, leaving Jarvis Harpe with his mouth open.

'M'lud! I really must object!'

'Bear with me, Mr Harpe. I wish to address the jury on a matter of some importance.' He waved down Sir Vincent, who was also getting to his feet. Spectacles wiped and on again he looked around the court. 'I have considered making my comments, members of the jury, into an appen-dix. Or even a separate chapter: "The Judge Speaks".' The judge smiled, liking the sound of that. 'But no. I will make my views known now.'

We were all quiet, for this was obviously a serious matter.

'A young man and his father, Northern Manufacturers both, are on trial for spying,' began the judge. 'You will agree with me that we have heard precious little evidence on that aspect so far.' He sucked in his cheeks, and the silence was so profound that we could distinctly hear the pop. 'Despite my warning to learned counsel during the luncheon interval, we have been presented with noth-ing but a farrago of irrelevant rubbish.' He pressed in his teeth with a finger. 'A blatant attempt – which, as I say, I foresaw and warned against – to repeat certain "Jokes", and so-called "Good lines". The jury will note the inverted commas.' He was looking now at the learned friends, both of them engrossed in pushing back their cuticles.

'Good, bad, mostly indifferent; I think I can say that I have been tolerant to a fault,' said the judge. 'The afternoon began, you will remember, with the court being misled by learned counsel for the Crown.' He stayed the rise of Sir Vincent. 'I do not infer any impropriety – but you will recall Part Three, Chapter Six, being dropped with a most satisfying thud into the tray beneath the mobile lectern. The one originally intended to hold the Vicar's things.' He paused again, and I stared at him with admiration; thinking how pleasant it must be for people to wait, while you thought of what to say next.

'One was led to believe,' said the judge, and there was heavy irony, 'that we were about to deal with the sub-plot. Not, as one would suppose, with the unfortunate death of the parrot – a matter in which you may share my concern – but with the matter of precisely who stabbed the defendant with a dessert fork. Eh?' The judge bent forward, listening intently as the bald man lifted his wig and whispered into his ear. 'Very well,' he said. 'A pigeon, then.' He settled himself comfortably again. 'You have heard who was at table that fateful evening, at the Reals' house, in the vicinity of the Nabisco factory.' He began to tick them off on his fingers. 'The charming hostess; the defendant; two men in porridge-coloured suits and their wives; The Member, and the Chaplain. With his marrow spoon. The Hon Wendy has described – very well I thought – how dinner was "sarved" ' (all those who worked there smiled broadly and appreciatively at this), 'and how the man Gartree came up *behind* the defendant, like the Japanese or the Mad Mahdi, and poured hot soup between his legs.'

There was an interruption then as a woman stood up in the public benches and screamed 'STOP IT!' She was led out sobbing by the policewoman with the wart, along with – in the whore's grip – the Lewd Scot who had been sitting next to her. The judge waited impassively for silence. 'I come now,' he continued, 'to the sing song. Having been spared "The Bandit of Brazil" – with court officials tapping things and learned counsel stamping and clapping their hands – what did we get?' He reminded us by tapping his carafe with his nail file. 'Riding Down To Bangor.' I could feel him looking at me.

'After the incident itself,' he went on, 'after The Member had said "The boot boy has stabbed himself. More peas anyone?" the footmen entered with the five-barred gate. Perhaps you felt with me that this was merely in order to reprise the line "One man gave him two pennies for his eyes." ' The judge turned over the page of his exercise book. 'Personally I would have preferred – from Part One, Chapter Nine, where the defendant first meets the Hon Wendy, alluding to Mr J. B. Priestley – "We had the same taste in peas." I thought that was good.' He moved his mouth about for a moment. 'Then we had "The Game",' he said, winding his hand in the air to remind us. 'And then the cake of soap in the shape of a pig, with a string tail. I must say that I fully expected the individual pot of Vaseline; and would not have been surprised had we had the "Something for the weekend" that had sailed at the Battle of Actium. However – ' The judge was on the last page of his exercise book now, though I could see that he had notes written in the margin around the multiplication tables. 'The WC incident was dealt with tastefully, as was the matter of the shirt tail and garters. This of course was "a bridge", to the line: "He gave a little shuffle in the sand"; and the introduction of Gartree, old "Four For Your Friends". That I thought amusing. Though it was perhaps gratuitous to quote from the talk given to the Young Men's Movement.' His lordship closed the book, reading from his blotter from now on. 'Here we have the second or third use of the word "Eff You Cee Kay".' He looked at us all, and we all looked around as if we had dropped something. 'And the punch line, as I believe it is called – "He jumped across the custard creams." ' The judge sighed. 'And then some more eff you cee kaying. After I had described a kitchen for you, we had lines like – ' There was a pause while he focused, ' – ''Eff you cee kay off, I said to him, he said, you said?'' that's what Mr Harpe said.' He shook his head sadly. 'And then, their manure having inflated, they left. End of Part One.' The judge then stood up – striking terror into my father, who had just woken up and thought he was about to put on the black hat – but, after freeing something, sat down again.

Chapter Seven

'He meant it, didn't he?' I asked, as Jarvis Harpe speared the last lobster ball, wiping up the jam sauce. 'It's going to be different tomorrow, isn't it?'

'He did, and it is,' said the barrister, looking around for something else to eat. ' "No more", he said; and no more he meant. "An end to self-indulgence." ' He smiled, wag that he was, playing with his balls with his free hand so that I would know he was quoting his lordship. 'Never had Chinky food before, eh?' he asked, a stray bean shoot being drawn up into his mouth, and I agreed, uneasy because I had just pocketed a pot spoon. I was also not sure as to who was paying.

'Mr Harpe,' I said, deciding against 'Jarvis' – and assuming, rightly as it turned out, that it would all be itemised on Mr Rim's account – 'what's going to happen next?'

'I don't know,' he said, dabbing his lips with his serviette. 'This and the remaining chapters were wheeled away, if you remember, on the lectern with the shelf for the Vicar's things.' Lifting the teapot, which matched the pot spoon, he called loudly, in what he said was Chinese, for more hot water.

It was an informal conference with our legal adviser, intended to discuss tactics for the following day. The Headless Coachman, with Yasmin and George, after buying something for Miss Parkinson, had gone to see Ivy Benson and her All Girls' Orchestra. Jarvis Harpe had said it was a pity, seeing we were here, not to make the most of London. He sat now in his frilly shirt, under the coloured

461

lantern, the fair-haired ladies either side of him toying with their prawns, while he outlined Sir Vincent's probable line of attack.

'He will,' he said, 'make clear to the jury first of all that you are a pillock.'

I waited for him to go on, to come to the point.

'He will not do this,' he went on, 'by repeating jokes, or by reprising so-called humorous scenes.' He then lit a cigar, because one of the fair-haired ladies said that she liked the smell. The other, who had 'Doris' in brass on her handbag, asked him how Sir Vincent would prove that I was a pillock. Anyway, she said, looking at me in the way Miss Parkinson had done that time outside the bathroom, I was on trial for spying; not for being what he said. The relaxed barrister smiled through the smoke.

'Indeed,' he said. 'If I were in Vinnie's shoes, I would set out to cast him as a *political* pillock.' He looked appraisingly at the size of Doris's handbag, then at me. 'Tomorrow morning,' he said, 'I think you are due for a surprise.'

'Really?' I said, prepared for anything. Then he told me that the prosecution intended to 'put up', as he put it, Miss Rosemary Delius that was. I stared at him, being unprepared for that.

'That was what?' asked the girl who was on my side, but I ignored her.

'Rosemary?' I exclaimed. 'They wouldn't!'

'They would,' said Jarvis Harpe, nodding seriously, and of course he knew them better than I did. Taking his hands from the girls' knees he spread them in a gesture: 'The Deliuses are in town,' he informed me.

Actually they were in a boarding house in King's Cross, very like the one Alec Guinness booked into in 'The Lady-killers', with the same railway cutting at the back into which he dumped Herbert Lom and all the others. Having watched from a doorway a frail Uncle Fred and Aunt Ada, going out for a walk with a banner – and brushing away a tear, I am not ashamed to admit – I was now in the front parlour, waiting, having sent up my card.

'Are you going to nobble her?' my father had asked that morning in the Regent Palace Hotel. I had stared at him as he brushed his hat, wondering how much he really knew.

'Just talk to her,' Jarvis Harpe had said, before taking the girls home, leaving me in Holborn to watch the trams go down a hole in the ground. 'You can't of course offer her money,' he had added, smiling at me as he winked good night.

Cut-glass lustres shimmered, chimed as they touched; dried bullrushes rustled in the draught as the door was opened. I heard no Boccherini from the first floor. In the doorway, rather than a déclassé Cecil Parker, who had drawn the short match, stood Rosemary.

She had matured it seemed to me, mainly in those areas in which she had always been ahead of Elspeth. I stood up to shake hands; then, remembering what Jarvis Harpe had said on the telephone that morning, I raised and kissed her wrist. That was the spot, the lawyer and man of the world had maintained, a little-known erogenous zone on which they tested free dabs of Phul Nana in Woolies.

'Hello, Jeffrey,' she said.

'Rosemary,' I said, 'it's good to see you'; having got that from Jarvis Harpe as well.

We walked in the back yard, in the pale sun and the soot, then stood looking over the wall. 'Is there much talk?' I asked, 'in Swinehurst?' She shook her head.

'I don't see much of the old crowd,' she said. 'We've got a semi. Pebble dashed with a bay window. Mam and Dad come out every Sunday.'

'For a pre-war tea?'

She nodded, looking down at the signal gantry.

'Rosemary,' I said, 'have you got a summons?'

She nodded, tight lipped, not looking at me; as if she saw big Danny Green in a heap on the lines below.

Turning away I touched the soft heart of a sunflower,

463

regretting not having poster paints with me, for then I could have sketched in a face. To make her smile.

'How's your husband?' I asked.

'Very well,' she said; 'thank you.'

'You know what they'll ask tomorrow?' I said.

'Yes,' she said, her back to me, lighting a cigarette and watching the match fall away to land on Peter Sellers's velvet collar.

'Are you going to tell them?'

She turned to face me, eyes wide and blue-grey. I don't think anyone ever looked at me like that. 'Do you want me to?' she asked.

'Well,' I said, 'you'll have to take the oath, and tell the truth. I wouldn't want you to get into trouble.'

'I know,' she said, nodding.

'But,' I continued, 'to leave things out is not the same as lying.' She was silent, so I carried on. 'I mean – you can mention Doris Allerdyce if you want. I don't know how you feel about that?'

'I haven't seen her in years,' she said; then was silent, probably, like me, remembering the scene. 'What about the Guinness?' she asked.

And I suddenly recalled not giving her back the change, that night in The Boy on the Barrel. I went all red and hot and had to turn away, going behind a shirt that was hanging there.

'They know about that,' I said. 'That I left the Rechabites.' How much was it? I tried to remember.

'And about your smoking?'

'Yes,' I said. 'String and Player's Weights.' I decided to send her a postal order when it was all over. Anonymously.

'What is it then?' she asked, lifting up the shirt tail with a practised hand, (she was of course a married woman now). 'What is it you don't want me to say? About us?'

Excusing myself I stepped into the lavatory. The sun made a wide stripe under the door, in which I read a square of the *Evening News*, while I decided just how to phrase it.

'Rosemary,' I began as I emerged, replacing the twig through the hasp to secure the door and checking to make sure my dress was adjusted. 'About Chester . . . '

'What about him?' she said. She had moved along the wall so as not to hear anything. 'He went to start a new life, with the groundnuts.'

'Did he?' I said. I hadn't known there was any demand for tram drivers in Africa; but I suppose that it was a job reserved for white men, like the Brotherhood of Railroad Engineers.

'I meant young Chester,' I said, sitting beside her on the wall, an easy target for a maniacal thief with a long scarf. 'You're not going to bring all that up, are you?'

'About you running away in the night, with the Panda and Sunny Jim?' She raised one of her rather nice eyebrows.

'Yes,' I said. 'And what we talked about. You know . . . about giving it a name.'

'I don't know,' she said. 'What if they ask me?'

'You could tell them it was an African tram driver,' I suggested. 'They'll never find him now.'

'What about the truth?' she asked, and I could see myself in her eyes.

'That *is* the truth!' I said. I might have been young and innocent I told her – naive even – but I knew what he was doing, after he had knocked out his pipe and taken off his hat, grunting and bouncing on the bed.

'It used to amuse you,' she said, smiling.

'Not as much as it did you,' I said, which I thought was rather neat.

A train went underneath us then, and neither of us spoke until we could see each other again.

'I don't know why you're so fussy about your reputation,' she said. 'There's pages about you in the *Daily Express*.'

I was shocked, not having seen a newspaper in days.

'And pictures,' she said. 'We all recognised your dad's hat under the blanket.'

That finished me with Lord Beaverbrook.

'Why do they have two titties?' she quoted, having the grace to look away. 'Why don't they lift up the lavatory seat?'

I felt myself going red. 'I know it's not very nice,' I said.

'Agnes Pomfret. *Mrs* Agnes Pomfret, with her veal, ham and egg pie!'

'She was a widow,' I told her. 'He was shot out of hand.'

'And the Hon Wendy, and the French maid, and Lillian Braithwaite. And her!'

I didn't know how she had heard about Lillian Braithwaite. 'Who's her?' I queried.

'Her from Ilkley,' she said.

'Oh, *her*,' I said.

There was another short silence.

'Are you happy?' she asked, her back still towards me. I was about to answer, and to ask if she was, when the train came back beneath us and the signal fell with a great clang, as it did when it hit Sir Alec. When the smoke had cleared she had, like him, gone.

I looked quickly over the wall, down into the trucks rattling past below; then heard the lavatory door close. After a few moments I tapped softly on the weathered wood, considering whether to pick the sunflower and push it underneath the door; or perhaps put it in my lapel for a laugh. But it was hardly the place.

'I have to go,' I said through the keyhole.

Silence. Just the rustle of the *Evening News*. I shrugged; there was no more that I could do. 'See you in court,' I said.

There was no answer.

'I'm not at all surprised,' said Jarvis Harpe into the mirror. 'But you shouldn't tell me about it.' Rubbing a little rouge into his pouched cheeks he turned for approval to his clerk, who threw up both hands and rolled his rheumy eyes. 'You know my views on ethics.'

'I do indeed,' I said, handing him his spray.

We were, as you will have guessed, in the barristers' changing room; and I had been reporting back on my sortie to King's Cross. So far neither Uncle Fred nor Aunt Ada had been seen in the corridors, but word was out in The Bailey that a surprise witness was to be called.

Then in came the bald man to summon us, and leaving behind the wigged men in jock straps telling jokes, waving aside autograph hunters and sensation seekers, eyes narrowed against the flashbulbs, we marched into court. Jarvis Harpe at the head, then me leading my father.

I looked around the court, at the now familiar faces, inclining my head to the judge and smiling at the jury. The witness box was empty. Who was it going to be? Agatha Jennings? I glanced quickly at the windows, to see if the hatless policemen, in the small hours, had rigged up a rope and pulley mechanism so as to recreate the events of long ago.

'Call Rosemary Miles, née Delius,' cried the bald man.

'Call Rosemary Miles, née Delius,' they cried outside in the corridors. So it was to be her. Had my journey to King's Cross been in vain?

She was of course the focus for all eyes as she entered, and I lip-read the soft pink lips of the Hon Wendy, who obviously couldn't stay away, saying 'common' to the chauffeur, who didn't know where to put himself.

'Are you Rosemary Miles, née Delius, of The Semi, Hobbeycock Hall Estate, Swinehurst?' asked the bald man, and Rosemary said that she was. She then promised to tell the whole truth and nothing but the truth, but would have nothing to do with God. This produced a murmur, and an audible tut from the judge; then Sir Vincent rose to his feet.

'You are, so I believe, also known as The Rose of Swine-hurst, are you not?'

'I am,' said Rosemary, who had quite pointedly not been offered a drink of water or asked to sit down.

'You were born and brought up' – and Lord Trenchard would have lifted his braided hat to the way Sir Vincent said 'Brought up' – 'at Victory Cottage, Swinehurst, were you not?'

'I was,' said Rosemary, as cool as her father's finest.

'Your father being Frederick Gerard Winstanley Delius; better known as Uncle Fred, indeed as Red Fred; and your mother as Aunt Ada?'

That was so, agreed Rosemary.

'You were at one time, so I believe,' and Sir Vincent cleared his throat lightly before he said it, 'a tram conductress?'

'I was,' said Rosemary.

Sir Vincent did a little twirl to see if his clean gown billowed nicely. The judge, suppressing a smile, raised a finger to him, a warning not to go too far.

'Do you know the defendant?' Sir Vincent put out hand, as if introducing us.

'You mean in the Biblical sense?'

I closed my eyes tight. With an effort of will I transported myself to Farmer Giles's Snack Bar, in a corner with a bowl of Cream of Tomato Soup. But not for long.

'The Biblical sense?' And, believe me, Edith Evans wasn't in it. 'Can you explain that?' Sir Vincent stood, arms and indeed legs akimbo, his wig moving as if it were alive. Opening my eyes I saw that the courtroom was half empty; the press having left en masse for the telephone. Several ladies had slumped down out of sight. The Hon Wendy, made as I knew of sterner stuff, was fanning herself vigorously.

'Certainly,' said Rosemary, perfectly calm; her clear voice pitched as taught at the Tabernacle: 'We were lovers.'

Well, of course there had to be an adjournment, which created havoc with the smooth running of the court, there being no buns or tea ready at that time in the morning.

'Good grief!' said Jarvis Harpe, when we had fought our way through the hysterical crowd into his room and he had closed and locked the door. My father, shrouded, was slumped in a corner.

'I should have pushed it under the lavatory door,' I said, meaning of course the sunflower.

'I quite agree,' said my barrister, almost savagely, removing his wig and undoing his waistcoat. 'Well,' he uttered from behind his desk, after moistening his lips with what he said was Gee's Linctus. 'A pretty kettle of fish!'

'I suppose so,' I said. Though not invited to do so I sat down, hardly realising that I had begun to twiddle my thumbs.

'Do tell me,' Jarvis Harpe said, heavily ironic and averting his eyes. 'What I am to say when I go back in there?'

'I don't know,' I said. 'What do you think?' He gave a short laugh.

'We were lovers!' he said,; and there was a twitch and a moan from under the blanket.

'We were,' I admitted. 'Once.'

'I do not wish to know,' said Jarvis Harpe, unlike the Sergeant of the Meat Market Police, 'how many times.'

We sat there in silence, he doing a crossword puzzle which I refused to help him with; until the bald man came for us.

'Mrs Miles,' said Sir Vincent when the packed court had reassembled, the judge having brought in several colleagues to sit with him. By the discreet movement of their chins it was obvious that buns had somehow been found for *them*.

'Or may I call you The Rose of Swinehurst?'

469

'I don't think so, Sir Vincent,' said the judge. 'No, I don't think you can. Ask her that question again.'

'As your lordship pleases,' said Squeaky Boots, enjoying himself no end. He turned away to put on a straight face, then pointed to me: 'Do you know the defendant?'

'I do. In the Biblical sense. We were lovers,' said Rosemary, quietly, but everyone heard.

'Thank you,' said Sir Vincent. He walked away, then of course returned. 'May I ask when this was?'

'Nineteen forty-five,' said Rosemary, and I was moved, despite my discomfiture, that she remembered the year.

'When the war had finished,' mused Sir Vincent, as if you had not been allowed to do it during a State of Hostility. Rosemary nodded.

'Was this . . . ' Sir Vincent paused delicately ' . . . a long liaison?'

'About five minutes,' said Rosemary. 'A good five minutes'; and I was grateful to her for that.

'Indeed,' said Sir Vincent. He hitched up his gown. 'Was this in a hotel?'

'No,' said Rosemary, while I looked at the ceiling, realising now what Jarvis Harpe saw in it.

'Not in a hotel?' said Sir Vincent, taking his time, making the most of it. 'In your own house perhaps?'

'No, it had been taken down.' Rosemary explained that the Doric portico had become unsafe, and Sir Vincent said that he quite understood.

'Not in a hotel, not in your own house?' Although I did not look, I was aware of him ticking off the possible sites on his fingers.

'Are you telling the court that it took place in the open air? Alfresco as it were?' There was silence, just a murmur of 'Oooh!' and a few tuts and I assumed that Rosemary had nodded.

'In your garden? In the summer house? On a mossy bank of the ha-ha perhaps?'

'M'lud,' said Jarvis Harpe, and I was pleased to know

that he was still with us. I lowered my eyes to have a look at him standing up. 'Do we have to know precisely where it took place?'

'Yes,' said the judge, decidedly, wiping his mouth. 'It helps us get the picture.'

'As your lordship pleases,' sighed Jarvis Harpe, having I suppose done what he could.

'Come along, Sir Vincent,' said the judge. 'Ask her where it took place.'

'Where did it take place?' asked Sir Vincent, instantly and point blank.

'In a chicken run,' said Rosemary.

'Thank you,' said Sir Vincent.

'Yes, thank you,' said the judge.

Sir Vincent walked slowly to the mahogany table, lifting up his learned friend's suede feet to riffle through some documents. 'A chicken run, you say?'

'Yes,' said Rosemary.

'Come along, Sir Vincent,' said the judge. 'Ask the witness to explain to the jury what a chicken's run is.'

'I am obliged to your lordship,' said Sir Vincent, with more than the usual sincerity.

'A chicken run,' explained Rosemary, without waiting for the question, 'is a wired enclosure in which you keep chickens.'

'A poultry farm, in fact,' suggested counsel.

No, Rosemary said, not a poultry farm. More an allotment, dozens of them on a scruffy piece of waste ground. All wired off, with huts, and tin plates for the chickens' dinners. There were paths between them, and sometimes – and I felt her eyes on me, though I had gone back to the ceiling – you fell over people on these.

'I see,' said Sir Vincent. 'And this is where . . . on the path as it were . . . you?'

Yes, Rosemary said, but not on the path.

'Thank you,' said Sir Vincent; then: 'Very much.' He appeared somewhat at a loss as to how to follow this up.

'Where had you been?' asked the judge, always willing to help, 'before you had the idea of going into the chicken's run?'

Rosemary told of the Victory Meeting at the Tabernacle, and the walk to The Boy on the Barrel. While I gripped the spikes, waiting for Doris Allerdyce and her mauve court shoes. But no.

'This, I take it, was a public house?' asked Sir Vincent.

'Get on!' snapped the judge, who was not really interested in public houses. 'Ask her when they decided to go into the chicken's run.' Then, since he had the floor as it were, he put the question himself. 'When,' he asked Rosemary, not unkindly, 'did you decide to go into the chicken's run? Did you . . . or perhaps the defendant, say, "Shall we go into the chicken's run?" '

Rosemary told him that I had wanted to walk her home, which was true; and that I had said, quoting Clark Gable: 'Give us a kiss then.'

'Give us a kiss then,' repeated the judge, sonorously, as if it were an imperishable line. He wrote this down, slowly, his still masticating colleagues watching him; Sir Vincent taking his silence to mean that he could get back to work.

'Have you ever,' he asked, 'thought of the defendant as a father?'

'Never,' said Rosemary.

I looked at Uncle Frank's watch, but it was nowhere near lunch time.

'Did you not,' pursued Sir Vincent, 'on a previous occasion, when the defendant was camping in the grounds of your house, say to him, and I quote: "I am in trouble"?'

'Yes,' said Rosemary.

'What did you mean by that?'

'That I had fallen.' At last Rosemary had taken hold of the spikes.

'Fallen?' repeated Sir Vincent, doing his best with rather a good word. 'Can you be more explicit?'

'I was in the club,' said Rosemary, doing the best she

could, and I think everyone approved the way her eyes went down to her plain black court shoes.

'Indeed,' said Sir Vincent, not having said that for some time. He allowed a pause, a silence, in the style of his learned friend. 'In other words you were enceinte? In, shall we say, a delicate condition?'

Rosemary agreed that she was.

'And you were, very properly of course, asking the putative father to do, as they say, "The right thing" by you?' he waited for her nod, though it was almost imperceptible. 'What was his reply?'

'He said that he was fourteen. He showed me his identity card, in a celluloid wallet.'

'*Fourteen?*' queried the judge, his colleagues leaning forward with him.

'According to *The Doctors' Book* it is quite possible, m'lud.'

'Indeed!' said the judge, and the bun chewers nudged each other, one of them proudly taking out his diary and pointing to an entry with a gold pencil.

'Did you tell him,' went on Sir Vincent, 'that you were a young woman of property? That your mam would give you some sheets?'

'Your mam?' queried his lordship, but Sir Vincent, feeling he was doing rather well, merely smiled and continued.

'Did you say, and again I quote: "You'll get many a nudge of admiration?" Did you not quote an aphorism, taken I believe from the wall of the Swinehurst Tabernacle, to the effect that you cannot do it on bread and jam?' There was a little violet froth on Sir Vincent's lips.

' "*Your mam would give you some sheets?*" Have I taken that down correctly, Sir Vincent?'

'You have, m'lud.' Licking off the froth he turned back to Rosemary. 'What did he say to all this?' A finger in my direction, in case there was anyone left who didn't know.

'He said that he had not yet reached puberty.'

'M'lud,' said Jarvis Harpe.

'Sit down,' said the judge. 'Had not yet reached puberty?'

'No,' said Rosemary, and we all noticed that as well as doing without God, she dispensed with m'lud. 'So I started to tell him the facts of life.'

Unable to get down the steps I attempted to vault the spikes, heedless of what had happened to Bernard, but was restrained by the policewoman with a wart.

'The facts of life, eh?' said Sir Vincent, smiling at me. 'Please go on.'

'I told him that the woman always pays.'

'Indeed,' said Sir Vincent, but without conviction.

'I told him, in short, that it takes two to tango.'

'That is true,' said the judge, who was now following every word.

'And then I told him that Mam would start feeding him up. It was then that I said that you can't do it on bread and jam.'

'I see,' said Sir Vincent. 'And what did he say to that?'

'He said he hadn't done it.'

There was then, as you will have guessed, a pause.

'Hadn't done it?' asked the judge.

'What do you mean, he hadn't done it?' asked Sir Vincent.

'M'lud!' It was a cry from Jarvis Harpe, making a final effort to earn his fee. 'My client was a virgin!' He stood tall, arms akimbo, and the word had a fine ring to it.

'A virgin?' repeated the judge, and it was obviously a word he liked.

'He just lay there with his Panda and Sunny Jim,' said Rosemary, 'with his little leg twisted under him. I went into my house and waited, but I knew he wouldn't come. I heard him take the tea towel and the bannister and run away.'

There was a long silence. Even the policewoman with the wart declined to look at me.

'So what you are saying,' said Sir Vincent, who had not

been knighted for nothing, 'is that the defendant was not the father of your child?'

'Exactly,' said The Rose of Swinehurst, sounding rather tired, looking at her watch and not saying a word about the African tram driver.

'I don't know,' said Jarvis Harpe over lunch. 'If Vinnie's finished, then we can trot out the character witnesses, I suppose.' He sucked up his soup, the long bib tucked into his cravat. 'I'd like to make my closing speech tomorrow morning, if that's all right; then get off to Goodwood. Monday, I suppose the old boy will sum up. Then you'll know all about it, won't you? Pass the bread, please.'

'Thank you,' I said, turning away as he wiped his plate. 'And that's it, is it?'

'It's all been a blur,' said my father, to his fish, and I was inclined to agree with him.

On the steps of The Bailey a few minutes earlier, en route to the restaurant, while waving to Leslie Mitchell and carefully guiding my father's feet, I had met my mother. It had of course, after the events of the morning, taken considerable courage on my part to face the public; but there had only been the one blanket.

'I'll go on,' Jarvis Harpe had said, raising his hat and nodding to the man in the fawn overcoat.

'Hello, Jeffrey,' said my mother.

'Hello,' I said. There was a movement under the blanket, as if my father were trying unsuccessfully to raise his hat.

'I didn't like to come in,' said my mother. 'But I've been following it in the *Express*.'

'Have you?' I said.

'Did you really see De Kuyper in you-know-where?' she asked, her hand cupping her mouth because of the gawping crowd around us.

'Yes,' I said. 'She wished to be remembered to you.'

I couldn't help wondering, as I helped my father into a taxi – the mufflered cabbie winking and saying 'Good morning, Guv' – whether *she* had been the one! They had after all, or so I had been told, women as captains of ships.

'You don't think,' I said now, putting down my knife and fork, 'that it could have been my mother?'

Jarvis Harpe raised a finger for me to wait, until the waiter had removed his bones.

'As the recruiter and spymaster, you mean?' He squeezed a lemon and set to with his personal fish eaters. 'It's possible, I suppose.'

'After all,' I said, having gone straight on to the chop, 'they have women as captains of ships.'

'So I've heard,' he said, reaching for the peas.

We ate in silence, listening to a selection from 'Naughty Marietta', to which he knew the words. 'You don't think,' I said, just about to start on my pudding, 'that she ought to be in court? In The Bailey?'

'Your mother, you mean?' He sipped his Vimto, savouring each mouthful before swallowing. 'As a character witness? Not allowed, old boy.' He jerked his head sideways at my father, meaning what would she say about him.

'What do you think we'll get,' I then ventured, floating a spoon on my tea, trying to appear unconcerned.

'Well,' he said, 'you could be hung of course.'

'I know that,' I told him.

'But not drawn and quartered,' said my father, still keeping up with us.

'Hard to say, really,' said Jarvis Harpe, smoothing my father's hair. 'I shall of course, if you can afford it, take your appeal as far as the House of Lords.'

'Thank you very much,' I said, speaking for both of us.

Because I had gone straight on to the chop, I finished first and, wanting some time alone before the afternoon session, excused myself. Jarvis Harpe said that he would see that my father got back.

Purely by chance, a few moments later, I found myself in a leafy square, outside the town house of the Reals.

Under a chestnut tree, against railings which were surprisingly still there, I surveyed the handsome facade. A police constable, not unlike the one with the purple tongue who had interrogated me – but of course with all the added sophistication of the Metropolitan force – emerged from the area steps and, checking to see that his dress was adjusted, walked away in the direction of the Haymarket. As he passed, I looked for traces of pie around his mouth.

By the kerb, with a snakeskin-encased gramophone, a hamper and a punt pole on the back seat, was a car with a leather strap around the engine and the brake on the outside. As I watched, Rufus in blazer and flannels, without his wig, ran lightly down the steps with a girl who bore a striking resemblance to Lillian Braithwaite. They roared away, not having seen me, a footman in the dickey with his eyes closed.

I looked up at the windows, at the flag that flew to show they were in, hoping perhaps for a glimpse of the French maid, or the cheery sweep waving from the roof. My eyes coming slowly down the white stucco until they met those of the Hon Wendy.

Quickly, as you can imagine, I took my hand out of my trouser pocket, but she could not see me. She was staring out between the pink silk of the boudoir curtains, in the direction of Oxford Street.

Hesitating, I thought about a wave, but just then a taxi drew up and out got a bowler-hatted Real Senior, The Hon Member, who seemed to have grown since I last saw him. I watched him enter the house, and then the Hon Wendy disappear from the window. Then I heard a bell ringing and the door opened, and out he came again. The bell continued to ring, loudly through the still-open door as he hurried off down the street, and I wondered if perhaps he was now a part-time fireman. As he turned the corner I crossed the road, speculating whether the Lemon Barley Water man had accompanied them into town, in the dickey with the footman, the wind ruffling the hair in his ears.

Climbing the steps, I coughed lightly into my hand as I entered the marble foyer.

'Jeffrey!'

It was the Hon Wendy, from the top of a curving stair-case, posed like Olivia de Havilland beside the chandelier, against oil paintings of herself, and wearing what I can only describe as a negligee.

'Hello,' I said, waving and starting to cross the red carpet. I knew that they often had drawing rooms and salons on the first floor, so that it was perfectly in order to go up; if of course she wasn't coming down.

'How lovely of you to call,' she said as I reached the landing, holding out a hand to me which, on the spur of the moment, I raised to my lips. No Phul Nana of course, but did not Kipling say something about them all being sisters under the skin? Hers was soft as little Sonia's, and the taste brought back memories of the string-tailed pig; not to speak of the Battle of Actium.

'Jeffrey,' she said again, and she smiled over her shoulder, jerking her lovely head for me to follow as we made our way towards what she called her 'sanctum'.

'You've just missed The Member,' she said, patting the silk of the chaise longue beside her, as she had done the night I had missed the indoor fireworks.

'I know,' I said, sitting down, my raincoat folded on my knees. 'I really came to see you.'

'Oh?' She smiled, then before I could speak, 'Would you like something?'

'Yes,' I said, 'I would.'

It had come to me as I crossed the road towards the house, as if triggered off by the alarm bell.

I was on trial at the Central Criminal Court you say? Charged with assisting people to catch the night boat from Southampton; with the shadow of the noose over me – even if I could no longer be drawn and quartered. But was I different from any other successful businessman, down for the Fat Stock Show or The Ideal Home Exhibition? I was, you must remember, in the prime of life, and had been recently under considerable strain. George and Yasmin had at least seen Ivy Benson; but all I had to show for my time in London was the pot spoon from the restaurant.

I well knew that this was the time of day that married men called on women, with flowers and scent and a box of Milk Tray. In Vienna, for example, it had long been de rigueur for a man of substance – certainly for a manufacturer like myself – to have a mistress in a first-floor flat. Blonde, in housecoat and slippers, she would await him eagerly every day, with cake and schnapps and the bed turned down.

I make no bones about it, if the reader has not gathered as much already; that I had long nurtured a passion for the Hon Wendy. I do not ask for the reader's approval. I only say let he who is without sin – and stuff like that. Anyway, I had determined to set my cap at the young Mrs Real, the Hon Wendy; or, failing that, and if she were on the premises, the French maid.

'I would like,' I said, choosing my words carefully, 'you.'

Straight out like that. And I looked at her as I said it, having read that you can make their knees turn to water.

'Actually, I meant tea,' she said, but she got up and closed the sanctum door. Quite obviously her knees were as yet unaffected. 'Perhaps it is a little early,' she said, sitting down again and smiling at me, having a go at *my* knees as it were.

'It is dusk in Vienna,' I reminded her, in the appropriate voice; going on to tell her about the time difference and giving a brief outline of what the Viennese did in the afternoon.

She wasn't in the least surprised. In fact, quite possibly she already knew; for with a light laugh she jumped up to draw the curtains and switch on the dim pink lamps. As she delicately lowered the pick-up of a record player I stood up, my raincoat falling to the white carpet. Adultery, yes; I quite knew what I was doing. But not Edmundo Ros!

It was Strauss of course. A string orchestra playing 'The Blue Danube', and the Hon Wendy held out a slim hand towards me. We waltzed, kicking the raincoat aside, my arm around her slender waist and her hand in mine; whirling to the music, nearer and nearer to the enormous white bed.

'Imagine that we are in Vienna,' she breathed into my ear. 'And you have just arrived in a hansom cab.'

I could see it. Top hat, cloak and cane, spinning a schilling to the cabbie and hurrying up the steps in my spats. 'It's five o'clock,' I whispered. 'The same time every day.' Then I saw by the ormolu alarm at the bedside that it was a quarter past one. I stopped, though still holding her, my hand where Elspeth would never allow in public. 'I've only got half an hour,' I said.

She made a face, a moue I think it is called, like when the witch hazel ran into her mouth, and switched off the music.

'I'm sorry,' I said, 'but I have to be at The Bailey at two. The Old Bailey,' I added, to make it quite clear.

She nodded, moving slowly back towards me.

'I'm sorry,' I said again. 'I should have come round before, with the scent and the Milk Tray.' I thought it best not to mention the evening wasted watching trams go down a hole in High Holborn. Then I pulled the velvet ribbon on the Hon Wendy's bosom and the negligee opened, like the ruched curtains at the Pavilion De Luxe.

She had not a stitch on. Her body was white in the shadows, like asses' milk. I touched her gingerly, and she touched me – and I must admit that it was I who said 'Oooh!'

'I've always wanted to,' I said, having trouble with my tie pin.

'I know,' she said, in that husky voice they all adopt at this point.

I do not really know how to conclude this chapter. I have no wish to be smutty, or to give offence; but by God it was nice! Socks off, my toes gripped the silk sheets in what can only be described as a paroxysm of pleasure.

'Just like Vienna,' she said, the sewer music now playing, blowing a smoke ring and poking a jewelled finger through it.

'Or, indeed, the Rue Mazarin,' I said, seeing us both together in the wardrobe mirror, pink and sweaty and puffing on our Balkan Sobranies. The ormolu clock was under the pillow; The Bailey was the last thing on my mind. Even had I been found guilty in my absence and sentenced to be hung; and, my legal advisers being wrong, drawn and quartered as well.

Epilogue

The Lincolnshire Penny Bank's heavy door, with its bronzed and gilded potato (which De Kuyper always reminded me I had paid for) was locked and barred. Even the money-box in the window had been withdrawn a moment before by a pale hand in a clean cuff. In the granite entrance, with picnickers already below me on the rose marble steps, I noted that it was not yet three o'clock.

Opposite in the yard of The Bull hotel, for which (with The Boy on the Barrel and all other hostelries) the Licensed Victuallers had applied and got an extension as soon as he had taken to his bed, I could see the dark silent ranks of policemen, their capes wet with the fine rain. I must have pressed my lips together on seeing the spikes of the Clwyd Constabulary, brought in overnight with a Territorial detachment from the Soke of Peterborough. The twenty-five pounder guns of the soldiers, as used at El Alamein, were shrouded with tarpaulins. The story carried in the souvenir edition of the *Lincolnshire Standard* that they were there to fire a salute had raised a thin ironic cheer along the pavements.

Officers conversed quietly, tapping leather-covered sticks into gloved hands. From the rear of a dark Farmer Giles's Milk Bar came the nervous sound of horses, of leather and steel 'Tack', as there would have been at Omdurman in that hour before the dawn.

I had thought of trying to reach The Pilgrim Fisheries, but realised it was hopeless. The marble range would be a floe of lard, the overalled elbows of the staff together at an upstairs window.

All movement along the pavements had ceased. The crowd stood in families, staring from beneath umbrellas at the empty road. A school photograph the length of the town, the gaberdined halt and the lame on chairs in front.

From the steps of the bank I could see the Home and Colonial. Dark sawdust, the butter pats and cheese wire locked away; despite the deputation from the Chamber of Commerce. Policemen, their boots dry on the mosaic, were trapped in the doorway by the silent crowd. Only the sound of the rain. On the slate roofs, on the plywood of the triumphal arch; soaking the bunting and banners across the street; the words beginning to run and drip. The clean water ran from the cobblestones, coursing along the grooves of the tramlines. I remembered a penny I had once had that a boy had flattened under the wheels. He had said that one could hear, if one knelt in the road, on a dry day, a tram approaching from as far away as Glasgow.

To my right was the town's premier outfitters, the Bon Marché, the Doric iron pillars swathed in wet black crepe. November's wreath, with 'Sincere Condolences' in Indian ink, leaned against a display of the new string vest. The staff, dressed ready to open, to let in the crowd under the glass canopy, filled the stockroom window, in sepia, as if about to sing.

Suddenly I became aware of a face in the crowd. Bernard. I knew that when it was over, when the people had slowly moved off to the Memorial Meeting and the sing song, he would want to know what happened. I would have to fill in what had been left unsaid by the *Daily Express*; flesh out as it were the sketches of the *Illustrated London News*.

Not that our name crossed the The Beaver's lips now. From the front page, to a paragraph inside with Rupert and Adam the Gardener, we had now been dropped. *Tit Bits* had declined to take up an option on my father's memoirs (ghosted of course by George), but Yasmin had managed to place a short piece in *The Red Letter* under the pseudonym of Nimsay Kroc. To say, as Leslie Mitchell did in his 'Voice over' when we went to see ourselves at the Pavilion De Luxe, that it was 'a farce' was, I think, uncalled for. The judge, at the side door of The Bailey in a suit and a homburg like everyone else, had played shamelessly to the camera. I flushed with anger in the darkness, waving away Captain Drew's proffered choc ice, remembering how he (the judge that is) had scorned the affidavit from Mrs Dooley, OBE, retired now and digging in Westphalia; telling the jury not to give undue weight to the bean bags.

' "Bound over to keep the peace" has a certain ring to it, don't you think?' Jarvis Harpe had said, when I went to return the blanket. 'Quite frankly, I thought you might be topped.' He smiled. 'Though I did tell you that you couldn't be drawn and quartered, didn't I?'

I had left him there, breathing through his nose before entering the swing doors. I had also met and nodded to Sir Vincent, who had been quite affable, and had shaken hands with the policewoman with the wart. The bald man had smiled at me in passing.

My father spent most of his time now on the lawn, attempting to read *The Friendship Book of Francis Day*, while Miss Parkinson did what she could in the kitchen. In spite of a stiff letter from Mr Rim, 'Uncle' Harold had hung on to the Biro calendar, saying that the Black Museum was interested.

And now this.

The factory was closed of course for the day, as was the brush works below, but not Woolworths. Nor, I was surprised to learn, Macfisheries. Norman, successor to Mr Grandidge, who now called himself a Head Packer – whose mother had turned out to be a florist, and who had forgiven, if not forgotten, the state of his underclothes – had taken a collection the previous afternoon. The girls, while not neglecting to complete the final order for Messrs Marshall and Snelgrove, had played suitable music in place of the Big Ben Banjo Band.

Staying at Jasmine Villa (Elspeth and little Sonia remaining at Ilkley until things had died down), I had left before breakfast, hearing my father and Miss Parkinson moving upstairs. The Pomfrets' mobile canteen, en route to Swinehurst, had passed me at speed in the London Road. Mrs Moss, who wore pearls and had opened early, said that it was a big day for private enterprise. Pocketing the bag of mints, I left the shop without a word. Outside in the market place the special buses were drawn up, the drivers talking quietly, each with a black band on his arm. Already people were assembling, with sandwiches, knitting and periscopes.

Under the immense sky the countryside was more empty, more flat than usual. Smokeless chimneys, no children or churns awaiting collection at the crossroads; a tractor silent on a farm headland. What I thought could have been vultures on the struts of a pylon. Flags flew from an isolated manor house, the curtains drawn as the family slept off the celebration of the previous two nights.

There was little traffic at first. Bicycles of course, then farm waggons, the horses decked as if it were the First of May; drivers and their families huddled under sacking against the rain. A labourer in a clean collar, book in his hand, a flower in its metal vase in his lapel. Then families on foot, some pushing prams; a wheelchair with an old man reading aloud; an old woman singing.

Near to Swinehurst, where the Meat Market Police were building a sandbagged bunker facing north, carbines stacked, helmets laid along a dry stone wall that had fallen down, the stream thickened. People almost marching now, three and four abreast. I had to sound my horn, to wind down the window and shout for them to give way. Then a squadron of the Hertfordshire Dragoons (TA), bright scarlet and pipeclay making a brave show, the plumes of their helmets groomed like the manes of the shire horses, forced their way through. Men, who only the day before had been making Shredded Wheat, clearing the way with the flat of their swords. The officer, befrogged and shakoed like George the First, tall in the saddle with a trumpeter a pace behind, called out 'Good morning' and 'Get out of the way!' It was, and I knew this, the last I was to see of Rufus Real.

Now, as I gravely nodded to Bernard, his mother smiling wanly at me as he nudged her, the town hall clock struck the hour. A clash of baskets and a clicking of clocks as fantail pigeons beat the air, bearing messages to Chester le Street, and the bells of the Tabernacle began to toll. Hens, bantams that were free, rose from their tin plates to circle the chicken runs, to settle on the roofs of the hand laundry and the estate agents. Looking down I saw the mauve court shoes of Doris Allerdyce on the far pavement. The years had not been kind. Far off, from Victory Cottage, where they had taken down what was left of the bannisters to get him out of the front bedroom, there came the first strains of the music.

The Guard of Honour, boots together and heads bowed, every ten yards on both sides of the road. The wet gold of their watch-chains, bare arms below the rolled shirtsleeves glistening with the rain. Without raincoats or caps their sodden waistcoats were black as those of the railwaymen in the crowd.

The High Sheriff's mounted bodyguard, an 'elite corps' as they were referred to in the *Lincolnshire Echo*, in dress uniform to show respect for the dead, wheeled around the corner in line abreast, like horses on a roundabout. The pennanted lances, the tight chinstrapped faces and blank eyes, let us know that the streets had not been abandoned to anarchy. The horses, groomed that morning by Lillian Braithwaite and her cadres, trained and used to the noise of crowds, expecting to feel blood alleys beneath their hooves, razors slashing at their girths, pawed and slipped nervously on the wet cobbles.

They passed in silence, one light brown horse leaving what people put on their rhubarb in front of the Bon Marché. I found myself looking at the Sergeant who held the horse straight, white gauntlet patting its neck as if to say that today it didn't matter. Ramrod straight, as that 'right marker' I had been that afternoon in the market place, Pickersgill dressed his troop with his eyes, a pathetic attempt at a moustache on his white face, as they passed at the trot.

The music came louder now, surging in slow waves as the rain, almost imperceptibly, quietly ceased. The sun, in the east despite the time of day, lit and warmed the town as the clouds opened, so that the wet clothes began to dry, to steam like the heap outside the Bon Marché. (Which was being shovelled up by the steward who had won the toss.)

The sun flashed from the gleaming instruments of The Temperance Band as it slow-marched towards us, the polished boots pointing each pace, the drum major, black-draped mace reversed, his eyes down and hand away from his hip. We knew, even those of us who had seen nothing like this before, that on their return the mace would be hurled, wheeling and flashing against the sky, to be caught and whipped between his legs by white-gloved hands. While the band played the Tabernacle version of Colonel Bogey; the man in the leopardskin crossing his arms to thump both sides of the drum. But now it was 'The Dead March from Saul', as people whispered to those who did not know. As they passed me, turning the wet pages in the lyre-shaped clips, I saw between the euphoniums, on the far side of the road, the face of Agnes Pomfret. This time our eyes met, and this time we smiled, as the man with the triangle went by, embarrassed as always to be by himself. I could see that she wore again the black armband she had sewn herself in our darkest hour.

Now, alone in the centre of the road, boots sliding forward each slow pace, as Yellowbellies had crossed the Fens in their pattens, the man who had been excused that day, without pay, from washing Messrs Pomfrets' churns. No pouch between the legs for him, as was mandatory for the Junior Rechabites. He carried the flag, fist over fist, the tassel on the golden rope winding round the varnished staff, as the standard snapped then streamed in a sudden breeze. There was scattered applause from the crowd and, to be fair, quite a few tuts.

And now a child, alone. I felt the eyes of Bernard's mother on me as I took out my handkerchief. Sturdy Chester J. Delius – who as you know could well have been mine – walked between the tramlines. Appropriately he wore his tram conductor's set, his ticket punch and leatherette money bag, the cardboard coins done up at the end of his shift in pale-blue paper bags. The tin badge flashed on his peaked hat, piped with scarlet like the jug of Alfredo the pigeon; and tags of Lincoln green, his cub's garters, held up his grey stockings. On a cushion he carried the cucumber that had swept all before it at Spalding the previous week.

Behind him came other children, wearing wellingtons, dressed as clowns or snowmen. One as an Oxo cube and having to be helped. No tramps, though I noticed a halfcaste. Indeed, several people called out to him and someone threw him a sweet. I thought back to those urchins who had arrived here with me as evacuees, wetting themselves on meeting a tree. All, except for the Oxo cube, who was in a bit of a state, carried cushions before them. On one lay his book, on another his reading glasses, the bridge mended with pink sticking plaster. On a third his map of the world with the red bits marked in.

Then – and this brought sobs from all around me, handkerchiefs being stuffed into mouths – a bigger boy wheeled past his bicycle. Black, sit up and beg, a brown-legginged Robin Hood below the lamp; the muffled bell, the chainguard painted with acanthus leaves. Panniers heavy with pamphlets, the pulpit and the pot of whitewash rattled by in the pram-wheeled trailer. His boots, upside down, turned slowly with the pedals; and a black cloth I had seen Aunt Ada use hung from the saddle.

Then creaking, a crunching of the granite earth itself. The breathing of men straining and heaving to swing the weight around the corner. The shadow first, blotting out the sun, making the Clwyd Constabulary draw together in The Bull yard and finger their batons.

Shunters lay on their staves, jammed in above the wheels, forcing down with oaths the iron leaf-springs. The chain, from Brunel's photograph, held now by a hundred volunteers. Two to a link, black steel across their shoulders tearing and staining red the flannel shirts. You could hear the cries of their wives, and of the Licensed Victuallers, as they leaned backwards taking the strain, steel-tipped heels against the cobbles as they slipped. Last was the anchor man, chain around his waist, eyes closed; the fat son of Mrs Moss, for whom the open-air school had worked wonders.

They slowed the weight, the speed, on the incline by the Maypole Dairy, the shadow darkening the green and gold of the facade. Though a delivery bike foolishly left outside was crushed. Now the earth shook. We could feel it through the paving stones and the marble steps as it rumbled, slithered slowly past us, the iron-bound wheels screaming on the cobblestones. Beneath the green foliage, from the gun-barrel axles, loose chains clanked like a platoon of ghosts.

I saw people put out a hand to touch it, moving past, wet
Nothing but black iron . . . Olive fronds and quotations,
with the . . . composers, ladies in evening dress played
and violins behind an iron balustrade, moving themselves to tears. (Though you could not hear them, because
of the Temperance Band.) In a niche beside an iron
Spartacus, who stared at the Bon Marché from his cross,
a child held a white dove; keeping its plumpness still, the
bird's bright eye watching the passing faces. I did not

recognise the child, but he had most likely come with the ladies in evening dress, who were certainly not Swineherdians.

The iron rings, for the harness of a hundred horses, were filled now with the flowers of his garden. Wreaths and posies hung in cellophane, tissue, silver paper, from the iron finials and ornaments; and everywhere the single roses, taken from lapel vases and thrown from the crowd.

'We will take up the sword' said our card, suggested I think by Mrs Skinner on the telephone, and signed 'From the girls at A. Cork & Son'. The wreath was in the form of an open book, though half a page of Ruskin, whoever he was, had been beyond the skill of the Head Packer's mother.

'Catafalque,' said a man beside me, and I nodded. I was looking for my own tribute, left that morning at the Tabernacle.

The crowd in front of us pressed back, bunching their toes as the first of the enormous wheels passed in the gutter, the iron biting and splitting the stone. Already, rumour had it, two boys and a dog had been mangled and were being seen to by the St Johns Ambulance Brigade.

As if drawn by Gustave Doré, the story moved past us in pictures, in panels framed with black iron garlands. 'Acanthus leaves,' said the man beside me, pointing, almost touching, and I agreed.

On pulpits, and firing squads, barricades; before flags, tribunals doors; marching, picke ing pursued and thumpe tinying and knocking on Trenchard; those that had gone b ing, praying; be-looked away as a particularly explicit paing. lady, towing a coal truck through a mine by Lord chain between her legs.

Heads back, the sun on our faces, we could see h on his horsehair sofa as he rumbled past the stockroom window of the Bon Marché. Stiff on the scrolled mahogany,

490

recognise the child, but he had most likely come with the ladies in evening dress, who were certainly not Swineher-dians.

The iron rings, for the harness of a hundred horses, were filled now with the flowers of his garden. Wreaths and posies hung in cellophane, tissue, silver paper, from the iron finials and ornaments; and everywhere the single roses, taken from lapel vases and thrown from the crowd.

'We will take up the sword' said our card, suggested I think by Mrs Skinner on the telephone, and signed 'From the girls at A. Cork & Son'. The wreath was in the form of an open book, though half a page of Ruskin, whoever he was, had been beyond the skill of the Head Packer's mother.

'Catafalque,' said a man beside me, and I nodded. I was looking for my own tribute, left that morning at the Tabernacle.

The crowd in front of us pressed back, bunching their toes as the first of the enormous wheels passed in the gutter, the iron biting and splitting the stone. Already, rumour had it, two boys and a dog had been mangled and were being seen to by the St Johns Ambulance Brigade.

As if drawn by Gustave Doré, the story moved past us in pictures, in panels framed with black iron garlands. 'Acanthus leaves,' said the man beside me, pointing, almost touching, and I agreed.

On pulpits, gibbets, barricades; before flags, tribunals and firing squads; rioting, mutinying and knocking on doors; marching, picketing, reading, waiting, praying; be-ing pursued and thumped by the forebears of Lord Trenchard; those that had gone before went past again. I looked away as a particularly explicit panel showed a naked lady, towing a coal truck through a mine by means of a chain between her legs.

Heads back, the sun on our faces, we could see him on his horsehair sofa as he rumbled past the stockroom window of the Bon Marché. Stiff on the scrolled mahogany,

Then creaking, a crunching of the granite earth itself. The breathing of men straining and heaving to swing the weight around the corner. The shadow first, blotting out the sun, making the Clwyd Constabulary draw together in The Bull yard and finger their batons.

Shunters lay on their staves, jammed in above the wheels, forcing down with oaths the iron leaf-springs. The chain, from Brunel's photograph, held now by a hundred volunteers. Two to a link, black steel across their shoulders tearing and staining red the flannel shirts. You could hear the cries of their wives, and of the Licensed Victuallers, as they leaned backwards taking the strain, steel-tipped heels against the cobbles as they slipped. Last was the anchor man, chain around his waist, eyes closed; the fat son of Mrs Moss, for whom the open-air school had worked wonders.

They slowed the weight, the speed, on the incline by the Maypole Dairy, the shadow darkening the green and gold of the facade. Though a delivery bike foolishly left outside was crushed. Now the earth shook. We could feel it through the paving stones and the marble steps as it rumbled, slithered slowly past us, the iron-bound wheels screaming on the cobblestones. Beneath the green foliage, from the gun-barrel axles, loose chains clanked like a platoon of ghosts.

I saw people put out a hand to touch it; a tentative finger. Nothing but black iron before us now, moving past, wet with the rain, as if polished with Zebo. Black iron faces, closed eyes with tears of rain. Olive fronds and quotations, each in its iron cartouche. Halfway along, beneath heads of the great composers, ladies in evening dress played cellos and violins behind an iron balustrade, moving themselves to tears. (Though you could not hear them, because of the Temperance Band.) In a niche beside an iron Spartacus, who stared at the Bon Marché from his cross, a child held a white dove; keeping its plumpness still, the bird's bright eye watching the passing faces. I did not to take home the crowds; the sirens and hooters of the factories, blending with the wailing of the 'All Clear' from the siren on the roof of the town hall. Feet in the cockerel's stirrups, an arm around the brass pole, I could see the dredger 'Britannicus' on The Drain, bucket raised high, dripping, while the crew took off their hats. Rockets soared and exploded far to the south, and barges on the canal gave up puffs of white smoke, the bargee's families beating painted buckets on the narrow decks. Then the horns and bells, the clangour and the roar from the rows of trams and buses, joining with the bells of the Tabernacle that were pealing joyfully now.

Suddenly, startling me as the only rider with a tap of his baton and a nod of his bandmaster's hat; a roll on the snare drum and a clash of cymbals; the great carved and gilded Gavioli in the centre of the roundabout began to play. I knew the tune of course, but not the words, and began to wave my toffee apple in time between the cockerel's ears. As Swinehurst became a blur of slate and red brick, of trees and immense sky, as we rose higher, faster, and I tightened the reins, gripping the cockerel's flanks with my knees, the man collecting from all classes swung easily between the empty saddled pigs and horses. He was singing, as was the lady at the heart of the roundabout, hair under a blue cloth, grey eyes smiling at me as she clashed coins from one hand to the other to counterpoint the music. 'Out of your age-long dream of toil and sorrow' sang the man as he held out a hand for the money, wondering I suppose what I was doing there.

Not THE END

493

Acknowledgements

I would like to thank Eddie, archivist of the Lincolnshire Road Car Company; the manager of the Lincolnshire Penny Bank, (Swinehurst Branch); Mrs Gladys Easton, historian and trustee of the Swinehurst Tabernacle and Delius Memorial Fund; Mr and Mrs Sandler (Johannesburg) for details of Gerald Bright's real silk bolero jacket; Mrs Alice Grandidge, for allowing me to see the brass box sent by Queen Mary, full of chocolate, to her late husband; the adjutant of the Duke of Lincoln's Second Foot; the Right Hon Rufus Real, QC, MP; The Law Society; the manufacturers of Daddies Sauce; the Vimto Preservation Society; the makers of Robinsons Lemon Barley Water; the Publicity Director of Nabisco Foods (Shredded Wheat Division); Accrington Stanley FC; Mrs Vera Rawstron, for the recipe for 'cinder tea' and help with the black lady dressed as Queen Victoria; the *South Wales Echo*, for an objective account of strife in the Welsh coalfields; Sgt Pickersgill, late of the Clwyd Constabulary; the late Arthur Mee; the Grandmaster of the Order of Junior Rechabites (UK); the High Sheriff of Lincoln; Mr H. Moore OM; the Council for Christians and Jews; the makers and patentees of 'Joan the Wad'; the Hendon Police College and the family of the late Lord Trenchard; D.C. Thomson & Son, the City of Jam; the late (Miss) Richmal Crompton; the Thomas Henry Gallery; 'Mr Lobby Lud'; Hovis Ltd; the False Rabbi of Pomerania, and Mr Harrison; Old Tragettians; the Broomhead family; the Watchett family, Somerset; the Dooley Research Foundation (Westphalia);

the Independent Order of Oddfellows; the late Maurice Richardson; the late King George VI (Chief Boy Scout); Mrs Ada Delius; the Pan Africa Tramcar Co; Miss Parkinson; The Very Reverend Eli Wannamaker; The Warden, Hobbeycock Hall; Mr Havelock Ellis; the makers of the Jowett Javelin; Kensitas Ltd; The Police Federation; The *Daily Telegraph* (Map Department); Mr S. Pomfret, chairman of Pomfrets PLC; South Lincolnshire Co-operative Society (Funerals and Milk); management and staff of the Co-op Café, Swinehurst; Alice and Dot of The Pilgrim Fisheries; Osrams (Funland), Swinehurst; Meat Market Police Old Pals Association; the editor of the *Lincolnshire Standard*; the descendants and many admirers of Edmundo Ros; Guinness PLC; The Nignog Club, Bradford, (Defunct); Mrs Gloria Cork, Maida Vale; Society of Socialist Clergy; the Swinehurst Temperance Band; the Woodcraft Folk; Percy Bysshe Shelley; the late Little Lenin; the makers of Trebor Mints; Sir Hartley Shawcross (on behalf of the people of St Helens); the (new) landlord of The Boy on the Barrel, Swinehurst; the Big Ben Banjo Band Appreciation Society; Troise and his Mandoliers Waxwork Museum; the Tailors' and Garment Workers' Union, for news of Mrs Skinner; the management of the Queen's Head; the lady in the Empire Cafe who saw Mr Grandidge fall; J. Dunne, the Hatters; Messrs Macfisheries; Messrs Woolworth Ltd; Bassett's Confectionery Ltd; Messrs Biro Ltd (flour, not pens); the makers of the Waterman Pen, for the use of their dignified slogan; Mr Bernard Ramsden, Marbella; the Commanding Officer, The Army Film Unit, for permission to view the film 'The Lavatory Seat'; the Commanding Officer, The Army School of Hygiene, Aldershot; Aeroflot (especially Olga); Miss Doris Allerdyce; the Friends of Olivia de Havilland (UK); the late *Reynolds News*; the late *News Chronicle*; Dame Anna Neagle; Mr Clark Gable; The Three Stooges; the late Lord Beaverbrook (Max Aitken, 'The Beaver'); Davenport's Magic Shop; Ellisdons Joke Shop; the Holborn Empire; The Haymarket Association;

The Vegetarian Society; the Senior Jewish Chaplain to the forces; Miss Anne Shelton; the Army School of Catering, for the recipe and offered sample of braised liver; Mr Kim Philby; the Harrogate Wartime Historical Society; John West (Salmon) Ltd; MI5, London; Wibsey Conservative Club; Colonel Trewin, the Dordogne; Miss Lillian Braithwaite, for memories of the Tramps' Supper; Messrs Cadbury, for the use of their tins; the curator of the Raleigh Cycle Museum; all the staff at the Central Criminal Court (especially Charlie); the archivist, Bourneville, for news of the Ovaltinies; the Commandant of the Swinehurst Sea Cadets; Forsters Spice Ltd, Bradford; Sir Vincent Goneham QC, for his note to Mr Rim; the Right Hon Jarvis Harpe QC; Jurgans Motors Ltd; Messrs Gilbey, makers of 'Green Goddess'; the London Rubber Co, for their kind letter; A. Gartree, for information on his natural son; The Danziger Brothers Society, for permission to see their undeservedly forgotten 'The Headless Coachman'; the lady on the Rue Mazarin (and Celeste); the trustees of the Wilson, Keppel and Betty Memorial Fund; Messrs Gabbitas Thring; the Provident Clothing Club; the Musical Director, Potato Marketing Board; the Workers' Music Association; trustees of the Horse Trough Maintenance Fund; members of the committee of The Pie and Pea Supper; the Labour Party; Marx Memorial Library; Ms Rosemary Miles; the girls at Farmer Giles's Snack Bar; the editors of *Tit Bits*, *The Red Letter* and *Sunny Stories*; the trustees of the British Library, for permission to examine early editions of *The Friendship Book of Francis Day*; the curator of The Black Museum; the Commanding Officer of The Hertfordshire Dragoons (TA); the 'Show Biz' editor of the *Lincolnshire Echo*; management and staff of the Bon Marché, Swinehurst; Isambard Kingdom Brunel; National Union of Railwaymen; the Maypole Dairy; St Johns Ambulance Brigade; Swinehurst Allotment Society; Edward Carpenter; Johnny Mercer; and the makers of Zebo, Scott's Emulsion, Germolene, Vironita, Cherry Blossom, Carnation milk, Jeyes

Fluid, Gee's Linctus, Victory Vs, Tizer the Appetizer, Babies Bottom, Oxo, Palm Toffee and Zubes.

Cigarettes by Abdullah, Passing Cloud, Player's Weights and Balkan Sobranie.

Viros
Corfu
June 25th, 1989

Vermin Blond
Richard Davis

'A brooding story of evil and infatuation . . . *Vermin Blond* heralds a
very promising new talent'
CARLO GÉBLER

*'Everyone called him Gaby. To have known him meant to be uneasy
ever after . . .'*

Why should a middle-aged solicitor abandon his wife, his home and
his job, to dispose of a dead friend's estate? To find the answer Mark
Palfreyman must delve into his past and confront its demons.

He looks back to 1968 and his last year at St Clement's, a boys' public
boarding school, and the people who dominated his adolescence: his
family, well-meaning but an embarrassment; Ambrose, the crushingly
rude senior tutor; Judy, the history master's girlfriend and Mark's
'Ideal Woman'. But looming over them all is Martin Gabriel – Gaby –
the rebel angel who dazzles man and woman, master and pupil alike.
Mark, too, is captivated, but as he is drawn into Gaby's select circle,
he glimpses a darker, grimmer side to the 'vermin blond' charmer.

Vermin Blond brilliantly captures the claustrophobic atmosphere of
an all-male society. Its savage denouement is at once believable and
shocking.

'I was impressed by the assured authorial voice, and completely
gripped by the characters throughout'
ROBERT CARVER, OBSERVER

'Davis knows his patch well and acutely observes the tribal alliances,
cold-shower ethics and repressed sexuality of this warping
environment'
NICHOLAS MARSTON, GQ

0 552 99948 7   **Published May 1992**

BLACK SWAN

Stripping Penguins Bare
Michael Carson

'As gay, lapsed Catholic, comic writers go, Carson is difficult to beat.
In *Stripping Penguins Bare* he fires a resounding answer to Lodge's *How
Far Can You Go?*
BERNARD O'KEAFFE, LITERARY REVIEW

MARTIN BENSON, THE 'FAT HOMO' HERO OF MICHAEL CARSON'S WIDELY
PRAISED *Sucking Sherbet Lemons*, is now at university, devouring the
lyrics of Dylan and paying homage to Plato, his catechism and prayers
to St Maria Goretti forgotten. But Benson is easily influenced by those
around him and soon he is beset by the same worries and anxieties he
thought he'd left behind at St Finbar's seminary.

Ruminating on life's imponderables, Benson is swept up by his role as
Vice-President of the Overseas Students' Society, and he battles
through social injustices, hot on the heels of the prejudiced landladies
of Aberystwyth. But as he strives to carve out a philosophy for
himself, Catholic doctrines return to pester him, and dark fantasies of
seduction by the world in general and Enoch Mohammed in particular
serve to thicken the cloud of unknowing that surounds him.

'Martin Benson, an anti-hero in the tradition of Kingsley Amis . . .
Stripping Penguins Bare has moments in which the ridiculous
successfully ambushes you'
SABINE DURRANT, THE TIMES

'MICHAEL CARSON IS WONDERFUL ON WINCE-MAKING UNDERGRADUATE HABITS
. . . I fIND MYSELF LOOKING FORWARD VERY MUCH TO THE THIRD BENSON
NOVEL'
JENNIFER SELWAY, THE OBSERVER

0552 99465 0

BLACK SWAN

A Prayer for Owen Meany
John Irving

'His books have done for young people now
what *Catcher in the Rye* did for young people
in the fifties'
SUNDAY TIMES

In the summer of 1953, two eleven-year-old
boys are playing in a Little League baseball
game in Gravesend, New Hampshire; one of
the boys, Owen Meany, hits a foul ball and
kills his best friend's mother. Owen doesn't
believe in accidents, he believes he is God's
instrument. What happens to Owen after
that 1953 foul is extraordinary and terrifying.
At moments a comic, self-deluded victim,
but in the end the principal, tragic actor in a
divine plan, Owen Meany is the most
heartbreaking hero John Irving has yet
created.

0 552 99369 7

BLACK SWAN

A SELECTION OF FINE WRITING
FROM BLACK SWAN

THE PRICES SHOWN BELOW WERE CORRECT AT THE TIME OF GOING TO PRESS. HOWEVER TRANSWORLD PUBLISHERS RESERVE THE RIGHT TO SHOW NEW RETAIL PRICES ON COVERS WHICH MAY DIFFER FROM THOSE PREVIOUSLY ADVERTISED IN THE TEXT OR ELSEWHERE.

☐	99421 9	**COMING UP ROSES**	*Michael Carson* £4.99
☐	99380 8	**FRIENDS AND INFIDELS**	*Michael Carson* £3.99
☐	99465 0	**STRIPPING PENGUINS BARE**	*Michael Carson* £5.99
☐	99348 4	**SUCKING SHERBET LEMONS**	*Michael Carson* £4.99
☐	99455 3	**KINGDOM SWANN**	*Miles Gibson* £4.99
☐	99208 9	**THE 158LB MARRIAGE**	*John Irving* £4.99
☐	99204 6	**THE CIDER HOUSE RULES**	*John Irving* £6.99
☐	99209 7	**THE HOTEL NEW HAMPSHIRE**	*John Irving* £5.99
☐	99369 7	**A PRAYER FOR OWEN MEANY**	*John Irving* £5.99
☐	99206 2	**SETTING FREE THE BEARS**	*John Irving* £4.99
☐	99207 0	**THE WATER-METHOD MAN**	*John Irving* £4.99
☐	99205 4	**THE WORLD ACCORDING TO GARP**	*John Irving* £6.99
☐	99141 4	**PEEPING TOM**	*Howard Jacobson* £4.99
☐	99063 9	**COMING FROM BEHIND**	*Howard Jacobson* £4.99
☐	99252 6	**REDBACK**	*Howard Jacobson* £5.99
☐	99399 9	**MIDNIGHT EXAMINER**	*William Kotzwinkle* £4.99
☐	99440 5	**THE HOT JAZZ TRIO**	*William Kotzwinkle* £4.99
☐	99408 1	**THE COVER ARTIST**	*Paul Micou* £4.99
☐	99461 8	**THE DEATH OF DAVID DEBRIZZI**	*Paul Micou* £4.99
☐	99381 6	**THE MUSIC PROGRAMME**	*Paul Micou* £4.99
☐	99403 0	**DIARY OF A MISPLACED PHILOSOPHER**	*Joseph North* £3.99
☐	99389 1	**THE PARTY AGENT**	*Nigel Pickford* £4.99
☐	99419 7	**THE REDNECK BRIDE**	*John Fergus Ryan* £4.99
☐	99360 3	**UNNATURAL SELECTION**	*Daniel Evan Weiss* £4.99
☐	99437 5	**HELL ON WHEELS**	*Daniel Evan Weiss* £4.99

All Black Swan books are available at your bookshop or newsagent, or can be ordered from the following address:

Black Swan Books, Cash Sales Department, P.O. Box 11, Falmouth, Cornwall TR10 9EN

UK AND B.F.P.O. customers please send a cheque or postal order (no currency) and allow £1.00 for postage and packing for the first book plus 50p for the second book and 30p for each additional book to a maximum charge of £3.00 (7 books plus).

Overseas customers, including Eire, please allow £2.00 for postage and packing for the first book plus £1.00 for the second book and 50p for each subsequent title ordered.

NAME (Block Letters) ....

ADDRESS ....

....